"Absolutely everything I want from a story. Love. Laughs. Crafting sessions and fiercely loyal ferrets. Van is daring and driven, Will is sweet and sexy as hell, and together, they are perfection. This is definitely one I will read again and again."

~Kristen Simmons, author of the *Article 5* series and *The Glass Arrow*

Praise for *A Little Too Familiar*

"A romp of a paranormal romance in the best possible way! Solid world building, a family you'd love to belong to, and a couple you root for the first page. I need the sequel, STAT!"

~Jeanette Battista, best-selling author of the *Moon* Series & *Books of Aerie* series

"Intricate world building, sexy and smart leads who can't live without each other, a diabolical villain you will delight in hating, vengeance pigeons, murder ferrets—all while sneaking in beautiful messages about the family of the heart. What more could you ask of a story?"

~Molly Harper, author of the *Half-Moon Hollow* & *Mystic Bayou* series

"Wildly inventive, thoroughly romantic, and cozily delightful, Lish McBride will leave you head over heels for this world and her characters."

~Gwenda Bond, *New York Times* bestselling author of *The Date from Hell*

"Full of charm, found family, adorable animals and the sweetest alpha ever, *A Little Too Familiar* is a wonderfully cozy delight. Here's to many more books in this series!"

~Stephanie Burgis, author of *Snowspelled* and *Scales and Sensibility*

ROUGH AROUND THE HEDGES

AN
UNCANNY ROMANCE
NOVEL

by

LISH McBRIDE

Rough Around the Hedges © 2023 Lish McBride

Cover design & illustration: Jenny Zemanek
Book design: Vladimir Verano

print: 978-0-9984032-4-3

e-book: 978-0-9984032-5-0

Published in the United States by

DEVO-LISH

Contact email: lishmcbride@gmail.com
lishmcbride.com

Please contact the publisher for Library of Congress Catalog Data

To everyone who kept the world spinning over the last few years—especially medical workers, teachers, scientists, delivery people, and food industry folks. You made it possible for me to stay safe and none of you got the respect or support you deserve. Thank you.

CHAPTER ONE

Will

This bookclub was fast becoming a confrontation, and a stealthy one at that. No one else was aware except me and my Nana.

Mel was hosting, so we were in her living room, which always made me think of that TV show I'd watched once about nature reclaiming human spaces. Everywhere you looked, there were either plants or piles of books or both.

I loved it. It was like a plant library.

Angel, unaware of the verbal bomb she'd just tossed, tried to answer her own question. "Least favorite trope…" Her knitting needles paused as she considered.

While she pondered, Nana ran in full tilt, spearing me with a look.

Oh no. I knew what her answer was going to be.

"Friends to lovers." She kept her gimlet eye on me, like I wouldn't have guessed exactly where that the comment was aimed—my heart, all four chambers simultaneously. "That's my least favorite trope. Sometimes people are just friends. Let them be friends."

It was a verbal knife, lovingly buried into the front of my chest. The fact that it was done in kindness took away some of the sting, but not much.

My grandmother's bookclub was romance focused and met with alarming frequency, usually twice a month. In my experience, no one reads with the frequency, speed or veracity as a romance bookclub. You know how in movies they show people or cows wandering into a pool of piranhas, and with a dash of media magic, they're instantly nothing but bones?

That's my Nana and her bookclub friends, and the cow is their TBR pile. No joke. I almost lost a hand once, getting between them and a ghost romance.

The bookclub was a mix of about ten people, all hailing from different backgrounds, brought together by their love of romance novels. I was the only person that identified as male allowed so far, and I'd had to prove myself before I'd been allowed to fully join. Not in a gatekeeping way, but because they wanted to make sure I wasn't going to be a dick about the books they loved. I read the books, showed up, spoke about them respectfully, and brought treats.

I was not above bribery.

At first it was because I was driving my grandma to the meetings anyway, and I thought it would be a good way for us to spend time together. I'd been coming to the meetings for almost two years now, and it was the best decision I'd ever made. I'd learned a lot about women and made some cool friends that I might not have made otherwise. Also, hint to all the dudes out there? If you want to learn more about what women want in bed, or in a relationship, read a romance novel. They're a treasure trove of knowledge. I guess that goes for everyone, even the folks who aren't dudes.

Knowledge is power.

Plus some of them have pirates.

I tried to not roll my eyes at Nana. She was about as subtle as a freight train. "Billionaire CEO."

One of the women, Sajni, slapped her hand down on the table, her brown eyes laughing and telling me she was about to tease me. "How can you hate sexy billionaires? Don't you want a sugar daddy? Sugar mama?" She thought for a second. "Sugar parent?"

I shrugged. "I have a hard time letting go of the reality. It seems to me that once you hit a certain income bracket, you lose contact with the real world. There's no one around to tell you no, and it's hard to not become an asshole. Plus, I have issues with late stage capitalism."

Sajni tented her hands beneath her chin. "But he could whisk you away to a private island for a romantic picnic and maybe you'd swim with dolphins and then have hot beach sex."

"Sand," I said very seriously. "Gets everywhere. And dolphins can be assholes." She laughed and I smiled back. "You can love it, it's just not for me." I took a bite of my cookie, waving it about to illustrate my point. "As a runner up, I'm going to have to say romances set in tattoo shops."

There was a collective groan this time. It was a well discussed topic.

"I'm not saying there aren't brooding, ex-navy seal bikers out there tattooing people to get over their broken hearts, I'm just saying it's not as common as you think." I spoke from experience. I'd been working in tattoo shops for years. "And the covers? It's all tribal and barb wire and *no*."

"I get that." Mel adjusted her glasses. "It's rough when writers don't do their research. It's like when I'm reading one set in a library and it's clear that they didn't talk to a librarian."

Angel nodded but didn't look up from her knitting. "It's hard to let go of the reality sometimes to see the fantasy. I'm not a big fan of the billionaire trope, either, but I love friends to lovers if it's done well."

I smiled at my grandma over the rim of my mug. She scowled and turned away.

I knew why. She was protective. Nana loved all her grandkids, but I'm her favorite. That wasn't me being conceited. It was just that she raised me and we were closer than she was with my half siblings. Her other grandkids lived in Chicago. She video chatted with Owen and Sorsha frequently, but it just wasn't the same.

And my grandma knew something that very few people knew—I'd been in love with my best friend since I'd met her. I never planned to tell her, either, for the very simple reason that she wasn't in love with me. Oh, she loved me. If I ever snapped and killed someone, she would absolutely be there to help me hide the body. I had no doubts about that.

So, help me break several laws? Yes. Look at me like I was a tasty snack? No.

I'd made my peace with it, but Nana worried. It didn't matter how often I'd told her that I wasn't pining away, nor did I harbor any secret hopes that Vanessa would come around. As long as I was the first guy she always turned to, it was enough.

It had to be enough.

That didn't mean it was easy to watch her date. The idea that someday she might meet someone, get married and that I'd have a front row seat as her best man to watch as my heart slowly shriveled and died wasn't something I liked to think about. It made me slightly sick. But I would do it, if that was what Vanessa needed me to do. If that made her happy.

I would probably pay a witch to hex the groom so he had boils on his wedding day.

Painful boils. I mean, I'm not a *saint*. And much like bribery, I'm not above being petty, either.

Once bookclub ended, I helped tidy up Mel's living room, gathering mugs and plates and loading them into the dishwasher. We said our goodbyes and headed out to my old subaru. I counted to myself as I buckled up, because I knew what was coming.

"You know I adore Vanessa—"

I'd made it to five. Nana missed her record by a hair. I rested my head against the steering wheel. "Nana. We've been over this."

She huffed, straightening her own seatbelt. My nana was not a big person—she was barely over five feet tall—but she often *felt* like a big person. Force of personality, I guess. She kept her gray hair short, wore red lipstick every day of her life, and still loved to go hiking every chance she got. Nana was only in her sixties, and had just finally succumbed to wearing glasses when she read. I loved her with all my heart, but I was getting tired of her meddling.

"You lie to yourself, sweetheart."

I dug deep for patience, because she meant well, but I was tired of this conversation. "Yes, I'm sure I do, but not about this."

She crossed her arms over her chest. The scowl she sent me was of the very skeptical variety.

"Nana, I don't know what it was like when you dated—"

"Who says I'm not dating?" She took out her phone. "You think I can't swipe right?"

I held out my hand for her to fist bump as I started the car. "That's great. I'm very happy for you. But I don't like meeting people on apps. I've been busy at work. It's made it difficult." I threw on my blinker and eased on the gas, driving Nana home.

I didn't believe in soul mates, not really. Or if I did, it wasn't a single person, more of a tier, like best friends. I didn't think people only got one shot and if they blew it, they'd die alone. And though I knew Vanessa wasn't interested in me romantically, she'd raised that bar pretty high. I wasn't going to date someone unless I thought there was some potential there.

A lot of people can date casually, and I thought that was great, but I apparently wasn't one of them. Why waste everyone's time? I knew what I wanted, and what I wanted was a partner. Nothing wrong with consenting adults fucking around, but I wasn't into it anymore.

"I just worry." She reached out and pinched my cheek.

"Do you want me to crash this car?" I batted her hand away. "I know you're worried. But I'm not lonely. I have good friends. I love my job. I have a roommate that will keep me from being one of those dead bodies that no one finds for weeks. I might get a cat." When I stopped at the light, I glanced at her. "I have you. I'm pretty lucky."

She sighed. "At least I raised you to think masturbation was normal and healthy, otherwise I'd *really* worry."

And that, gentlefolk, was my Nana. No subject was taboo, and when I'd edged into puberty, my education had been *thorough.* I had no idea what she did for my half-siblings. I guess she assumed their parents would handle it…though I'm sure she sent books. Nana thinks most problems can be solved with books. I'm not sure she's wrong.

"I still think your parents made you gun-shy." She picked a piece of lint off her jeans. "You're staying for dinner?"

I wasn't going to get her going on my parents, so I ignored her comment and answered the easy question. "Of course. What are we making?"

"*We* are tired. How about we swing by Adobo A-Go-Go and pick up dinner?" "Done." I never turned down Adobo A-Go-Go. They served Filipinx fusion food—or

basically whatever Jen and Lara felt like making, though some staples were always available. Like lumpia. My mouth watered at the thought.

I'd initially gone to Adobo A-Go-Go to support the cousins of my best friend, ride or die, and current boss, Bayani Larsen. While the original choice had been out of loyalty to an offshoot of my chosen family, that wasn't what kept me coming back. No, that was the food. Dear gods, the *food*. I would do a lot of unspeakable things for a dinner crafted by Bay's cousins. Luckily, I didn't have to.

Tonight's book club had fallen on a Wednesday evening, which meant the Adobo A-Go- Go would be parked close to Nana's. She opened up the app that would tell us where, exactly, they were tonight, just to be sure.

We got our order to go, deciding to eat outside on Nana's patio. Mercifully our discussion stayed on safer subjects like our various jobs. I worked at Ritual Ink, which was owned by Bay, as an arcane piercer. Nana was a librarian at Seattle Uncanny University. Between the two of us, we had a lot of good stories. I was tossing our takeaway boxes into Nana's compost when my phone buzzed. I fished it out of my pocket, opening it automatically when Nessa's name flashed across the screen.

Loch Nessa: I can't get Savvy to stop crying.

I opened up the message, tapping out a reply. *What's going on?* Nessa babysat her niece all the time. She was perfectly capable of doing it by herself—Nessa was usually a confident person. But every once in awhile there was a pocket of inexplicable doubt that would leave her wobbly. Small children was one of them. Despite having basically raised her sister Juliet, sometimes she panicked with Savvy. That was one reason she usually babysat with another one of us in tow. She didn't need us, but she liked having the support.

Loch Nessa: She's chewing and drooling a lot? Like when she was teething?

I might be more comfortable with kids than Nessa, but I didn't have childhood development books memorized, so I did a quick internet search. *The internet tells me it's probably molars. What did Jules say?*

Loch Nessa: I didn't ask her. If I call her, she'll come home. She felt bad enough about going out to for fun.

I grimaced at that, knowing full well she was right. Jules suffered under the delusion that asking for us to watch Savvy when it wasn't for work or school was asking too much. Any bump in the road would make her come home. Because somehow single parents were supposed to be fucking magic and do everything themselves. I'm a firm believer in "it takes a village" and Nessa, Jules and Savvy were part of mine.

Jules knew she needed a break, time to herself, but asking for it still filled her with parental guilt. *Tell your sister to stop being selfish with our baby. I'm coming over. Hold fast.* Dots appeared, and I knew what was coming and so I typed fast. *If you tell me that I don't need to come over and start making polite texty noises, I will personally tell everyone that you didn't cry when we watched the first ten minutes of UP. Like an unfeeling monster.*

Loch Nessa: I cried!

Will: Barely. The rest of us were ugly sobbing. Loch Nessa: You. You were ugly sobbing.

Will: It's just so sad. They loved each other so much. It wasn't lost on me that the movie about childhood friends loving each other and sharing their lives was particularly revealing of my issues.

Loch Nessa: Then again, you cry during Lilo & Stitch.

It was true. Every time that little alien walked into the forest with his duckling book and said, "I'm lost" I proceeded to lose my shit. *I'll be there in twenty.*

I stashed my phone, and went in to grab my keys. "You're leaving?" Nana's eyebrows winged up.

I usually stayed longer after dinner. I knew exactly what telling her would do, but I also tried hard not to lie to my Nana. "Nessa texted. Savvy is teething."

Nana shook her head before hugging me and kissing my cheek. "Of course you should go. Just … be careful, my heart."

I kissed her cheek. "I will, Nana. I promise."

I tried to ignore the fact that my step quickened as I went to the car, my heart feeling light that when Nessa needed help, she texted me first. She may not want me, but she needed me, and that was enough.

It had to be.

CHAPTER TWO

Van

Everyone has that voice in their head—the critical one, that corrects them if they're doing something wrong. It can be a helpful voice. A guiding voice. It can also be the voice of despair, of self flagellation.

I had two. One was the voice of my mother. It was spectacularly unhelpful, but easy to ignore. More of an annoyance than anything actually painful.

The other voice was my father's, and I'd spent most of my life learning to gag that voice. I knew it was cruel and cutting. It didn't do me any favors. But still it whispered pure poison in my ear in my weakest moments. It was the voice of bad decisions and poor choices.

You know that cartoon staple where the character has a devil on one shoulder and an angel on the other? My angel was bored, had no interest in a moral compass, and had left for a tour of sun-drenched islands with a man named Sergio when I was still in elementary school. She rarely blew into town, and when she did, it was on the arm of a guy with a spectacular tan and pockets of cash. She seemed happy, at least.

The devil, however, was sneering, rigid, critical and I couldn't stop listening to him. I'd done my best to avoid my father for years. When I did see him, we acted like strangers and didn't acknowledge each other. It was a solution that suited us both.

Which was why I hated so much that his was the voice I heard most as I walked back and forth, rocking Savvy and humming. The voice was telling me that I was crap at this, I was a bad aunt. A bad sister. A shit human. And somehow my niece could sense it on a cellular level and that was why she cried.

I knew—*knew*—that was nonsense. That was the worst thing about internal voices. Even when they lied, you still listened.

The front door opened and I almost collapsed in relief. It was a bit of a running joke in our friend group that Will gives off a calming pheromone, but it must be true. He had an incredibly soothing presence, and right now to me and my clanging nerves, he looked like a big, tattooed angel.

He set a bag down on the table, stripped off his hoodie, tossing it onto the back of the couch while he toed off his shoes. My roommate, Declan, strictly enforced the "no shoes in the house" policy in our home.

Without a word, Will came over and held out his arms. Savvy threw herself into them with a hiccup. Now that she'd stopped crying, my ferret familiars, Kodo and Podo, peeked out from their hiding place under the couch.

Some help you two were, I mentally grumbled at them.

She's loud! Kodo squeaked.

Podo chittered a lengthy lecture about healthy kits having good lungs at Kodo that I mostly tuned out, returning my attention to Will and Savvy.

Will cradled her to him, rocking her exactly like I'd been doing, rubbing a big hand over her back. "Bag."

I dug into the bag he'd set down, pulling out a variety of things. A teether for the freezer. Frozen waffles. Generic baby acetaminophin. Apples and a six pack of cider. I lifted up the cider, my eyebrow raised.

"The cider is for you," Will said, using one hand to rub Savvy's feet as he rocked her. "I hit the internet hard at the store—it said chilled food like apple slices, or frozen waffles could help. You could also give her chilled purees or a cold wash cloth to chew on. The acetaminophin is safe—I double checked with the pharmacist, and I know Juliet gave it to her before."

Inexplicably my eyes teared up and I was suddenly overwhelmed with feelings. I hated feelings. They were the opposite of helpful.

Will stopped rubbing Savvy's feet so he could sling an arm around me and pull me close. "Hey, hey, it's okay."

I shamelessly buried my face into his chest. "It's just her crying makes me so jangly and I—." I growled in frustration.

Will started gently rocking both of us. "It's supposed to make you jangly. She's upset and that makes you upset, because you're not a robot."

"I want to be a robot."

"I know," he said. "But where would we put the oil?"

I snorted. "That doesn't even make any sense." I didn't pull away, because it felt good to be soothed. To know that someone, for a second, had me. Would take care of me.

That was the worst thing about becoming an adult. Everything was on you. But for a second I could pretend that I wasn't in charge, and also admit that I didn't know what I was doing, and it was okay. Will wouldn't judge me.

So I closed my eyes and accepted that he would make things better. He even smelled good. Will's job involved burning incense, sage and other things, so sometimes his scent was a mixed bag, but sniffing him always made me feel better. See what I'm saying about calming pheromones?

And yes, I recognize that smelling my best friend was probably weird. I just didn't care, because it always made me feel better.

I opened my eyes and my niece was staring contentedly back at me. He hadn't even used the teething shit yet. Just himself. "I both love that I have you as a secret weapon, while being simultaneously resentful that you have that ability."

He laughed into my hair. "If I wasn't here, you'd handle it. But I am here, so let me help out."

#

I would have loved to say that Savvy was magically happy after that, but that would have been a filthy lie. Despite the balm of Will's presence, she was still uncomfortable and grumbly. We had to dose her with acetaminophen and use some of the frozen stuff he brought. Eventually she fell asleep and we deposited her on my bed, tucked in carefully with Kodo and Podo on watch. They curled up around my niece, happily snuggling in. If she so much as twitched, they'd let me know.

Familiars beat baby monitors hands down.

Before I could tip toe out of the room, I found Will frowning at papers on my desk.

Papers that I'd meant to hide away. It wasn't that I was ashamed about them it was … well, I just wasn't sure how I was feeling about the whole thing.

He looked up, searching my face. "You didn't tell me you were trying to get your hedge witchery license."

There was no accusation in his tone, no hurt, but I still bristled. "Doesn't matter. I'm not getting it."

His eyebrows scrunched down in an adorable scowl. I know some people find Will intimidating. He's huge—built on sturdy lines, the kind of person who has to duck under things on a frequent basis. I wasn't short, but I rarely needed to duck. Will had visible tattoos on his neck, his arms, and when he reached up to grab something, a bright flash of the wildflowers on his belly. The way he was standing now, dressed all in black, shoulders squared, scowling, would probably make a lot of people nervous.

People who didn't know his blond hair had been spiked up by Savvy's hands. Who'd never seen him giggling on the floor with two bouncy ferrets. People who didn't know that when he hugged you, he gave all of himself.

He held up the papers. "This filled out application suggests otherwise."

I snatched them out of his hands. "I was thinking about it, okay?" I pulled open a drawer and shoved the papers inside. "I changed my mind." Will examined my face carefully, the hard lines of his mouth softening as he blew out a sigh. "That so?"

I crossed my arms. "Yeah."

"Any chance this has something to do with your father?" Will said the words gently, but that didn't keep them from scalding me.

Mostly because he was right.

When I didn't answer, he rubbed a hand over his face. "Nessa, you usually tell me this stuff. Why hide it?" His eyes were so gentle it actually hurt to look at him. "I'm safe."

Oh no. He'd pulled out the "Nessa." Everyone else—Will included—called me Van.

Except when we were alone. Then Will called me Nessa. No idea why. I just knew that I liked it. A secret name, just for us. I didn't have a good answer for his question. Embarrassment, maybe? Like this was the final thing to make Will see me for the awful fucking mess I really was.

I shrugged.

"Okay." He put his hands on my arms, rubbing them with his thumbs. "Tell me now?" "None of your business, Willhardt."

He winced. That's right, buddy. If you're going to pull out the Nessa, then I'm going to pull out the Willhardt. Which was Will's *actual name.* Like on his birth certificate. It was, apparently, the last name of some distant ancestor and his dad had liked it. Made him sound like a knight. You can bet it went over *real* well in school.

"Don't be mean." He kept rubbing my arms, waiting. Patient. Will could wait forever, which meant I might as well tell him now.

"Fine," I said, more than a little petulant. "I wanted to take a bigger hand in business at Wicked Brews. See about becoming a partner." Wicked Brews was a coffee shop, potionary, bar and my home away from home. I slung coffee there now, did some assistant manager stuff, but I wanted to do more. I wanted to help make the potions and magical edibles that my bosses sold to the public. But for that, you needed a training, a license.

Will smiled and at it was like the sun coming out. A cliche, I know, and boring, but it wasn't just because the world got brighter when Will smiled. The sun came up every day—it was expected, routine. But it was also a tiny daily miracle, one that we counted on. Will's smiles were like that—a tiny, daily miracle that I needed to live.

Even when he was annoying the shit out of me.

"That's great. I had no idea you were considering it." That stupid sunshine smile grew brighter, then suddenly eclipsed. "What crushed your dream?"

"My father."

He sighed. "I should have expected that."

To get a hedge witch certification, you needed a degree. Which was no problem. But to get into the degree program, you needed copies of your training certification in magical studies. Because my father didn't trust anyone to teach us that stuff "properly" he'd done the training himself. Well, him and a selection of graduate assistants.

Okay, basically just the grad students.

He'd assumed we'd follow in his footsteps as arcanists. We didn't. Cue my father's massive disappointment in us.

Juliet was almost done getting her license to work as a transitional therapist otherwise known as a General Uncanny Counselor, which had the unfortunate acronym of GUNC. Still, I was so, so proud of her.

My dad was mortified.

If he was dismissive of that, you can sure as hell guess how he'd feel about my choices.

To him, hedgewitchery was the magical studies equivalent of a fast food job. Which was ridiculous, but what can I say, what my dad lacks in warmth and redeeming features, he makes up for in classist, mysoginist fuckery.

I explained all this to Will, who understood the problem immediately.

"Your dad will never sign off on your forms, will he? Not if you're not using them to become an arcanist."

"Got it in one," I said, hugging myself tighter.

Will looked thoughtful for a moment, his hands still on my shoulders. "Can you recertify? Get someone else to sign off on them? Retake the courses?"

I laughed and it sounded terrible, even to me. "To recertify, I'd have to explain why. They'll contact my dad." Who would do everything in his power to block the process. "His former grad students could *maybe* sign off, but they're all too in awe or afraid of him. Retaking the courses would take three years and more money than I could scrape up."

As it was, I was going to have to get scholarships and things to take my hedgewitch classes. It was doable, as long as I never did anything, went anywhere, or ate actual food. But beyond the money, time was an issue. If I took summer classes and doubled up in classwork, I could get my hedgewitch certification in three years. If I had to retake all the training certification I'd already done? I was looking *at least* six years.

I couldn't reasonably ask my bosses to wait that long to start training me as a partner. I was fucked. My dad had once again taken something I wanted and smashed it to pieces and he hadn't even known he was doing it. He was truly gifted at being an asshat.

Will grabbed my chin with one hand and tipped it up so I was looking at him. "So I guess we go ask your dad."

I laughed again, even though it wasn't really funny. "So he can tell me no to my face?" "Your dad must want something. Surely we can figure out what we can leverage to get his signature?"

I let out a shuddery breath. I could, but it was never that straight forward. My dad liked to use the stick and the carrot simultaneously and just for fun he sometimes threw out the carrot right when you were about to grab it. I wouldn't be able to trust anything he said, and said so.

Will shrugged. "We'll try. If he offers something, I'll be there to witness. You won't be alone, Nessa." He wrapped me into a hug and I snuggled into it.

"What if he says no?"

"Then he says no and we move on to the next step."

I hiccuped and realized I'd started crying. "What if he says yes?"

He squeezed tighter. "Then we get it in writing and notarize the fuck out of it." "What does that even mean?" I said, laughing for real this time.

He smiled down at me, a sly revealing of teeth. "I don't know. But it sounded good, didn't it?"

CHAPTER THREE

Van

I waffled on how to approach my dad. Make an appointment? How embarrassing would it be if I tried to make an appointment with my own father and couldn't get one? No, that option was right out. Show up at the house? Show up at his office? If I showed up at the house, he might not let me in. Same with his office, but he'd at least have to be polite-ish there, so as not to cause a scene.

My father hated nothing more than being embarrassed. Office it was, then.

Of course, getting politely booted from my own father's office would be more than a little humiliating. The one upside of my childhood was that my pride had it's teeth throughly kicked in before I'd even reached my teen years, so I had little to lose.

Or so I told myself as I stared up at the brick edifice of the magical theory wing of Seattle Uncanny University. The building faced an ornamental lake, which I'm pretty sure was elementist made. The magical theory building was nothing short of magnificent, three stories, capped by an ornate copper dome which seemed to be a cross between a cupola and a small lookout station. I'm pretty sure most students snuck up there to smoke.

The rest of the building was full of large, white framed windows, though most people only really noticed the huge stained glass window that started at the top, running down the center. The colored glass took up two stories and had a spell attached to it, letting it change with the weather, season, and important school events. Right now it mimicked the lake—blue and green rippling waters, with sunlight carving golden paths along the surface. As I watched, a fish surface on the image, leaping up and landing with a splash.

The building was meant to intimidate and it did its job exceptionally well. I was certainly ready to bolt.

Courgage. I had it, right? I just needed to *find* it. Not a lot—I only needed enough to climb the steps and enter the building. From there, I'd let momentum do its job. I assumed my dad still had his coveted corner office. Just some steps and an elevator and I'd be there.

My folder of paperwork slipped in my hand. Anxiety made me sweat.

"Worst he can do is say no," Will said. He squeezed my other equally sweaty hand, not seeming to notice that my palm was actually disgusting.

"Worst he can do is call security and have us escorted off." I squeezed back. "I used to know the security officers by name. One of them retired. We still exchange holiday cards."

"Your dad is such an asshole." Will didn't move—didn't try to pull me along, or take me back to the car. He simply waited to see what I wanted to do.

What I wanted to do was stand there and stare at the building for several long, quiet minutes. Students walked by, those that had stayed on for summer courses, their flipflops echoing across the quad.

Maybe I didn't have to go in.

Maybe I could just get a new dream. Something that didn't involve my father whatsoever. Like one of those people that hugged baby pandas or maybe a puppeteer. I didn't know anything about pandas and puppets creeped me out, but right now that didn't seem like such a big obstacle.

Will side-eyed me. "Do you need a shove?" "Please."

He dropped my hand, grabbed my shoulders and pushed me along the sidewalk. "That didn't mean I actually wanted to play tugboat." I slapped at his hands.

"If I'd tried to pull you, you'd dig in your heels. This way, resistance is futile." I tried to dig in my heels. He was right. It was harder this way, damn it.

"Toot-toot." He pushed me up to the doors, wrapping an arm around my shoulders so he could grab the handle of the door. In a second he had me through, the door whooshing shut behind us.

The magical theory building was mostly classrooms on the first and second floors, with labs interspersed. You had to go up to the third floor to find the offices. They had a perfectly nice elevator off to the side of the lobby that would whisk to the top in a blink.

I took the stairs.

"You're really dragging this out." Will stepped closely behind me, no longer pushing, but definitely herding.

"We both need more cardio." "I get plenty of cardio."

Will worked out, so he probably did. I haven't stepped foot into a gym since high school.

With each step of the stair, I put up my mental armor. The trick with my dad was to approach him on an intellectual level. No emotions, no reactions. He fed off those things, and I refused to make him stronger.

I refused to show him where he could hurt me.

All too soon, we were at the top of the stairs, and I was so locked down, I probably looked like a robot. Will kept sneaking looks at me, concern molding his features, but I barely registered it. The upside was, I no longer needed him to play tugboat with me.

The secretary sat at an old desk—he'd started guiltily when we'd walked in, and I'd bet he'd been playing a game on his laptop or something. A few plants failed to liven up the off- white walls, and the carpet had seen better days. I wondered whose bright idea it was to use carpet. The things that had been spilled up here. I shuddered to think.

While the general area needed an update, I knew the offices would be the exact opposite, each arcanist trying to outdo the other to look important.

"Can I help you?" The secretary had recovered, now wearing a faintly officious expression.

I considered smiling at him, but I knew, when I was like this, that my smile was scary, so I didn't bother. "I was just coming up to see when Professor Woodbridge's offices hours were."

The secretary sorted through some papers, trying to find the one he needed. He squinted at the paper. "It says two to four, Mondays, Wednesdays, and Thursdays."

Today was Tuesday. Oh, well, I tried. Before I could turn, the secretary continued. "But he's often back there right now. He's got a class in half an hour." He frowned up at me. "Doesn't like to be interrupted, though."

'That's okay," I said, heading in the direction of my father's office. "I have a feeling he's not going to be happy, even if I wait until office hours."

Will ambled after me, tossing a "thanks" over his shoulder at the secretary. "Sure," the secretary said. "Your funeral."

He said the words low, but I heard them all the same.

#

My dad's door was shut, and either someone was in there, or he was on the phone. I couldn't really make out what he was saying, but I knew the tone he was using. My dad used that tone to efficiently and coldly eviscerate people using only his words. I paused in front of the door, my hand frozen and ready to knock.

Now would…not be a good time. But I also wasn't sure I could work up the courage to do this again. And it wasn't like Will and I had endless days off, either.

I didn't consider myself a coward, but if Will hadn't been standing there with me, I would have sprinted away from my dad's office right then. I still thought I might.

Will's hand slipped into mine and squeezed.

I sucked in a shaky breath, held it, and then knocked as I let it out.

"Come in." The words were issued with a snap of command and I heard underneath it the unspoken followup—*this better be worth it.*

I opened the door and came face to face with my father for the first time in months as he ended the call on his phone.

My father was a tidy man of medium height with the kind of papery white skin that made you wonder if he ever went outside, or if the sun was so cowed by his presence that it refused to give him so much as a freckle. His silver hair was thick, but expensively cut and styled. Though I couldn't see much of it past his arcanist robes, I knew his white button up shirt was crisp.

Everything about my father had a bite to it, even his clothing.

His office hadn't changed much. One wall held a whiteboard—he'd scribbled notes for whatever spell he was currently working on. No cheap carpet visible here—my feet sank into a hand-knotted Persian rug full of deep blues, vibrant reds, and regal yellows. The walls were painted a warm sand color, offsetting the darker wood furniture.

A bookcase stacked full of books covered the back wall. A heavy wooden desk with a inbox, the papers neatly stacked. Pristine desk blotter, a cup of tea off to the side. Two leather chairs faced the desk, the seats low on purpose. My dad liked the psychological advantage of sitting higher. The air smelled like tobacco and something acrid, probably leftovers from spellwork. My father didn't smoke—smoking was a vice and vices made you weak.

I almost crossed the room to throw open one of the windows.

"Vanessa." My father's sharp gaze moved to Will, and for a moment, I thought he might ignore him. He surprised me by adding, "And the piercer."

As a barista, I'd developed the ability to pull out notes of flavor in the espresso I poured.

It was a lot like wine in that way—floral tones, earthy finish, and so on. But long before I got into coffee, I'd developed the same ability with my father's voice. This one held a note of a sneer —subtle but there— with a customary snide aftertaste. Arsenic with a sour lemon finish.

With Elliot Woodbridge it was best to ignore any and all slights and just move right along if you wanted to get anything done ever. It didn't really matter—no matter what you replied, it would have a poor mouth feel.

"We haven't been formally introduced," Will said dryly, holding out his hand. "Will." My father ignored the hand. "Arcanist Woodbridge." And with that, Will was dismissed.

"To what do I owe the pleasure, Vanessa?" His eyes shifted to the clock on the wall.

Right. His time was precious and I was already wasting it.

"I need you to sign off on my training certification in magical studies." I blurted the words with zero finesse. With a shaking hand, I pulled the already filled out paperwork from my folder, setting it onto his desk. "I highlighted the parts you need to sign."

He folded his hands, setting them down on top of the papers. "What do you need them for?"

Lying was useless, but I was tempted to do it anyway. So tempted. I knew my father, though. He'd unearth my lie as soon as I turned in the paperwork. I tilted my chin up. "I'm applying for the hedge witchery course."

He guffawed. Actually *guffawed*. "Cute, Vanessa."

I pulled up the chair he hadn't offered and took a seat. My knees felt watery, and I wasn't sure I could stand up on my own much longer. Will took the other seat, not saying a word, but even the sight of my friend there, sturdy and unmoving, felt like a lifeline. "I'm not kidding."

A muscle by his eye ticked. "I forbid it."

I set my folder in my lap, taking a second to rebuild my walls. I couldn't let him see how difficult this was for me. Will slung his arm out onto the back of my chair, his hand settling between my shoulder blades, and I found my equilibrium.

"You can't forbid it," I said evenly. "I'm an adult. All you can do is delay it." He smiled at that, and I thought furiously—how could I twist this? How could I make him do what I wanted? My mind blanked, offering me only an unhelpful white noise.

"Of course," Will's tone was thoughtful, like something was just occurring to him. "People might talk, you showing up in the novice classes." He slung his legs out, crossing them at the ankle. Will turned a guileless expression toward me. "You should hear some of the gossip Nana tells me." He leaned close to me, stage whispering. "The things she hears in the library." He widened his eyes, playing at looking scandalized.

Will, you brilliant bastard. I tapped a finger to my lower lip. "You know, you're right. And it's not like our last name is really common." I turned to my father, faux concern on my face. "An arcanist's daughter, in magical theory 101, at my age? Bound to draw some curiosity."

Will tsked. "It would reflect poorly, wouldn't it?"

Beyond poorly. I showed up in a beginner's class? People would either think I was a fuck up that couldn't master the basics, or my dad had neglected my education. In his mind, both would make him look bad.

The twitch by my father's eye grew worse. His gaze narrowed, but the muscles in his face smoothed, relaxing. "If you want to throw what little talent you have away, so be it. I'll sign your papers."

I'd been ready to argue, the words already on the tip of my tongue. "I—what?"

Elliot Woodbridge smiled, and I had the sense his expression was as false as the ones Will and I had been using. "Not now, of course. I would be remiss if I didn't run any sort of diagnostic."

He spread his hands out, like he was offering something, which I guess he was. He was offering me another roadblock. "After all, it's been years, and you weren't exactly an exemplary student. You can't expect me to sign *my* name without doing my due diligence. My name means something, Vanessa."

This was okay. I'd expected stipulations. My dad always made us jump through hoops like we were circus ponies. "Okaaaaay."

There had to be more.

I was right. He sighed. "You know, Vanessa, I'm not the villain here. This estrangement between us—you and Juliet—it pains me." He placed a hand over where his heart should be. I had no evidence that an actual organ resided there. "I haven't even met my only granddaughter."

Unease trickled through me. He'd shown no desire to reconnect—or connect at all in Savannah's case—with us. "What do you want?"

He steepled his fingers, a wounded expression on his face. "I want my family back. Is that too much to ask?" He looked at the ceiling, sighing heavily. "If only we could start again, before your mother poisoned you both against me."

My father forever labored under the delusion that any and all ill will we harbored towards him was built on things my mother said and not things we'd witnessed or dealt with. "Mom doesn't talk about you much." It was out before I could stop it. I was baiting him out of habit, though mom really didn't talk about him much. Our last conversation had been about her current boyfriend Terrance's bitchin' yacht.

The wounded expression chilled, his eyes calculating. "Three tests to make certain you have the basic material down—tests of my devising. And I want to meet my granddaughter. I want time to get to know her."

"I can't guarantee that," I said, gritting my teeth. "That is—rightfully—under her mother's purview." Juliet would do it for me—because she'd know if I asked, it was important to me, and because deep down there was part of her that hoped our father would step up. Be a real parent. Be an actual grandparent. It didn't matter how much you learned, how much therapy you had, there was part of you that always hoped.

My father waved this away. "Of course. I expect you to talk to her, put in a good word.

You two were always…close."

And he's never understood it, our bond. He did everything he could to sever it, but we'd stayed stubbornly connected. "I can do that." I held up a finger. "As for the tests, I want them all verified by an outside source. Another arcanist, signing off that the tests fall under what would normally be found on the magical studies finals."

"Done." Once again, his neatly folded hands sat on his desk blotter over my paperwork. "Then we have a deal," I said.

My father smiled and it chilled me down to the marrow in my bones.

CHAPTER FOUR

Vanessa

I set the uneasy feeling aside as I stepped into Wicked Brews after the meeting with my dad. Wicked Brews had two parts—the coffee shop/potionary, where I worked, and the bar where my sister, Juliet, worked. The two were connected by swinging saloon doors, though both had their own door to the outside world. I bounded into the bar half, a wide smile on my face.

Later, after I celebrated my victory, I would temper my expectations. My father wasn't known for handing over things easily or for sticking to his word, at least not with us. He would string me along if he could. But still—I'd stood up to him and demanded what I wanted. I'd taken a step toward my dream and it felt *good*.

My cheeks hurt from grinning as I looked around for my crew. I'd texted all of them as soon as we'd left my father's office that I had news. Miraculously, my roommates Lou, Trick and Declan were all able to meet up. Our schedules didn't often overlap like that.

The bar was long and romantically lit—the walls the same earth tones as next door. The tall chairs around the sprinkling of tables as well as the booths lining the walls popped with a lilac and silver faux leather covering. A half wall separated the booths along the wall closest to the cafe side, where families could bring their food and sit and eat while their parents ordered from he bar. Silver metal stars full of light hung from the ceiling along with chandeliers that looked like they had candles. The atmosphere was warm and cozy—pure magic.

A long wooden bar top separated my sister from everyone else as she mixed drinks. She saw me and waved, pointing toward the large round booth in the corner on the other side of the half wall in the family area. All my roommates and a few extras had piled in. From the animated look on her face, Louise was telling a story as she piled her hair up into a messy bun. Her boyfriend, Declan, watched her adoringly, his bearded chin resting in his palm.

Next to them sat Trick, decked out in signature black, except for the leather pad on his shoulder where his familiar, Dammit, perched. Dammit was a fledgling pheonix, though he wouldn't be a fledgling for much longer. His adult feathers were coming in, purple and blue hues to go with his firey reds and oranges. Bay, Lou's brother, bounced Savannah on his knee as he listened, expertly moving his beer out of her reach. Will's roommate Jim sat on the edge, taking up the rest of the booth.

Jim was a minotaur, looking a bit like a mix between a brawny lumberjack and one of those long haired steers they had in Scotland. He took up a lot of booth.

I bounced over to the table, waving my hands in hello and accidentally interrupting Lou's story. "Sorry," I said, after they'd all greeted me. "I didn't mean to barge in and cut you off, Lou."

Lou shrugged. "It's cool. I was just talking about work." She lit up as she smiled at me. "And we're not here for that. We're here for your news." She clasped her hands, her eyes wide, waiting.

I pulled up a chair, snagging another one for Will who was parking the car. "I should wait for Will. It's kind of his news, too." After all, there was no way I would have made it through that meeting without him. I wanted to give credit where it was due.

"News?" Juliet said as she approached the table, her eyebrows tilting up. "About you and Will?"

"Yes," I said absently, straightening the chairs. One of the legs was catching on a lip on the floor.

Trick put his beer bottle down with a thunk. "Is it time?" He looked at all of them. "Is it finally time?"

"Fucking finally," Bay said, covering Savannah's ears belatedly. "I was starting to get tired of all the longing, the moping looks, the endless scribbles of both their names in little hearts

—and that was just Will. Jules, bring out the champagne." He clapped Savannah's hands for her, making her giggle. "I've had a few bottles set aside for over a year."

Juliet clapped her hands in glee, unconsciously mimicking her daughter. "Got it!"

Declan slid out of the booth. "I'm getting the presentation. Even if we didn't have to have the intervention, we put a lot of work in."

I…had no idea what they were talking about. Had they somehow known about my plan? That didn't seem likely. But what else could it be? I just stood there, a perplexed look on my face as Juliet pulled out several bottles of chilled champagne and glasses.

Declan dug around in the storage closet next to the bar, dragging out several poster boards. He brought them over, handing one off to Lou, the other to Jim.

"I've been preparing a speech, but we won't need it now. Still, I'm really proud of these." Declan pointed at the one Lou was holding, which showed a graph with two lines. One shot directly up, while the other nosedived down past the lower axis and off the board.

Jim handed over his keychain. "Use my laser pointer."

"Thanks," Declan said, clicking on the laser and pointing at the lines. "You'll notice that one line, the one going up, represents you continuing to be oblivious to the obvious connection between you and Will." He traced the laser along the other line. "As you can see, as the top line continues, the other one, representing our group's harmony and your overall happiness in romance plummets."

He pivoted the laser onto the next poster board which, frankly, had what can only be referred to as a fuck-ton of glitter. The title in bubble font at the top said, "As the Prophecy Has Foretold" for some reason.

"Did I miss a craft night?" I asked, my voice choked.

"Yes," Trick said. "Please pay attention. We worked hard on these."

"Now we were pretty drunk by the time we got to this one," Declan said, scratching his beard with one hand. "But if I read the chart correctly, our compiled data suggested that if you and Will got married, you'd have ten thousand babies."

Bay nodded sagely. "And they would be adorable."

"I am not birthing ten thousand of anything," I squeaked.

"You can adopt," Jim said. "Or foster dogs if you don't want children. We support your life choices." Jim heaved a sigh. "I'm losing a roommate, but gaining a daughter." Savannah patted his arm, babbling.

Declan had moved the laser to the last poster board. "I can't even read this one."

Lou snatched the laser pointer from him. "The red circle represents you, the blue circle represents Will." She used the pointer to highlight where the two circles overlapped, which was quite an overlap, taking up two thirds of each circle. That part was almost entirely glitter, with faint hints of purple peeking out in places.

"The overlap represents how you will be sitting in a tree, K-i-s-s-i-n-g." She pointed the laser on me. "It's science."

"You made a venn diagram of me and Will?" I asked, confused. What was going on here? "I'll admit, it got a little out of hand," Lou said, handing her pointer back to Jim. "But we

were getting desperate, and we'd split a bottle of whisky Jim had brought over…"

A loud popping sound made me jump, Juliet cracking open the first champagne bottle. "I'm so glad we finally get to bust these out." She handed me a glass. "Though we should wait to toast until Will gets in here." Her smile was wide, her eyes bright. "Such tremendous news."

"Toast?" What the fuck was going *on*? I glanced back and forth between their excited faces and the pasteboards. What did it all mean?

"I see Vanessa told you," Will's voice rumbled behind me and I turned to him instinctually. Finally. I relaxed, relieved. Will was here and he would fix whatever the fuck madness was happening. I could always count on him to make sense of things.

"Yes," Lou said. "And we're so happy for both of you." Lou sighed, her eyes starry. "So tell us all about it. How did you finally get together? What finally changed?"

Declan slid an arm around her. "Slow down. We haven't even toasted yet. And if they don't want to tell us, they don't have to."

"Oh, right," Lou said, chagrined. "Sorry. I'm just excited."

Juliet shoved a glass into Will's hands before raising her own. "To Will and Vanessa!"

Everyone sipped their glasses, while mine stayed frozen in my hand. My attention fully on my best friend. He looked bewildered, reading the poster boards. As he read, all the blood left his face, his knuckles white on the stem of his glass. Eyes wide, he tipped his glass back, sucking down an entire glass of champagne like it was a shot of tequila.

Will looked…unmoored.

The group's joy dimmed, going quiet. Will slammed his glass down on the table, cutting the awkward silence. Then he turned on his heel and walked out of the bar, the door closing noiselessly behind him.

We all stared.

"What the fuck just happened?" I asked, still holding my champagne. My brain was blank except for that question as it whirled ceaselessly around in the empty space, so I repeated it. "What the *fuck* just happened?"

Declan's words came slowly, his tone measured. "I think we just fucked up really badly and I'm sorry."

I whipped around to them, spilling some of my champagne. "What the hell? What is this?" I waved at the whole, glittery mess. I was never missing a craft night again. Clearly my loved ones couldn't be trusted with glitter.

"We thought," Lou slumped, her eyes wet. "I'm so sorry, Van. We were just so happy for you. We thought you'd finally figured it out."

"Figured what out?" They all looked back at me with what could only be called pity.

Even Savannah appeared concerned as she babbled at me.

35

I say again, *what the fuck?*

Juliet nudged my glass at me, her voice gentle. "Your feelings for Will. We thought you'd finally figured out how you feel about him."

I glared at me sister. "He's my best friend. What is there to figure out?" I tossed back the champagne much like Will had.

Juliet refilled my glass. "Oh, honey. Maybe look at the poster boards again."

"That's not…" My hand shook, the champagne spilling onto my hand. "Will's not. We're not. Like that." I tried again. "We're not like that."

Juliet sighed, and I felt like I'd maybe failed her somehow. Like I just wasn't getting what she was saying. But she was wrong. Will and I were friends. Best friends, but that was it.

"Okay," she said, her tone still gentle, aggravating me for some reason.

"And even if *I* did, that isn't how Will sees me." Of this I was absolutely certain. Juliet glanced at the group, her free hand splayed out, imploring.

"Maybe," Trick said thoughtfully, "We should have used more glitter."

"I told you we should have made a powerpoint," Declan grumbled. "No one can argue with a powerpoint."

Bay handed Savannah over to Jim before sliding out under the booth. He popped out on the open side right in front of me. "Whatever. I'm going after Will."

I put down my glass, wiping my sticky hand on my jeans. "No, I'll go—"

Bay held a hand out, stopping me. "No offense, but you're the last person he's going to want to see right now."

I opened my mouth to object, but Bay's expression was mulish. "No, Van. Later. Right now, he needs a buddy."

"I am a buddy," I said weakly.

"No," Bay said, giving my arm a squeeze. "You're a lot of things to Will, but a buddy isn't one of them.

Will

I was pretty sure I was going to puke.

My hands were jammed in my pockets as I fast-walked down the street. I wasn't running, but I was close.

My breath sawed in and out of my lungs as I plunged forward heading…where the fuck was I heading? I didn't know. I didn't care. As long as it was *away*.

Fuck. Just fuck. "Will!"

Bay. I ignored him. Fucker could jog if he wanted to talk to me.

Which of course he did. I heard his shoes slapping the pavement before he came alongside me. I couldn't get mad because I would have done the exact same thing.

"Are you okay?"

"I don't want to talk about it." I shouldn't have slammed that champagne. It had been a panic move, and now that sweet, bubbly liquid was sloshing around in my stomach.

"It's going to be okay," Bay said. "We can fix this."

I skidded to a halt. "Can we? Because I'm not sure we can." Vanessa's expression— shock and horror. Like someone had *died*. I scrubbed a hand over my eyes. "Did you see her face?"

"Yeah," Bay said reluctantly. "I saw her face." He grabbed my shoulder where it met my neck and squeezed. "Are you going to be okay?"

I planted my hands on my hips, trying to keep my world from spinning. "No. I think I'm going to be sick."

And then I was, puking up my glass of champagne into someone's sidewalk pea patch. I gagged, my body shaking.

Bay kept his hand between my shoulder blades, letting me know he was here for me. Like I'd ever doubted that fact.

"Now what?" Bay asked.

I spat onto the ground. I was feeling a little better now, at least. "Now that everyone told Vanessa that I loved her and she made this face?" I twisted my face into an expression of extreme horror, making Bay smile, even if it was a small one.

"No, we can spin this, if we want," Bay said. "Play it off that we were wrong." He squinted at me. "If that's what you want."

I didn't like that look on his face. "What does that mean? Why wouldn't it be what I want? She's my best friend." I scrubbed the back of my head. "I just want everything back to normal." The idea of losing Nessa—not having her in my life—made my vision dim and my throat tighten. No fucking way.

Bay crossed his arms, examining me. "How long are you going to do this? Put aside what you want?"

"If it keeps her in my life?" I asked. "Forever."

"That's no way to live, brother." He slapped a hand on my shoulder.

"Tell me about it." But I'd do it. If it made her happy, if it kept her around, I'd do it in a heartbeat.

As I sat there, panting from adrenaline and my walk, sun on the back of my neck, the taste of regurgitated champagne in my mouth, I had a thought. *I can't keep on like this.*

Maybe…maybe Bay and Nana had a point. Maybe I needed to move on in some way. Not away from Vanessa—she would always be part of my life. That was non-negotiable. I could step back out into the dating world. Try to meet someone I to share my days with. There was nothing wrong with being single, but I was tired of it. I wanted a partner. I wanted to be someone's favorite person. Their dinner date, cuddle buddy, and plus one.

And as much as I wanted to keep Vanessa by my side, they were right. The way I'd been chugging along was no way to live. Not for me.

And I now had three different poster boards covered in glitter spelling that out, loud and clear. "We're going to need to burn those poster boards."

"Okay," Bay said. "We can do that."

I straightened to my full height, the world spinning a little less quickly as things righted themselves. Bay was spot on. Somehow, we'd fix this. And while we did that, in the time honored fashion of good choices everywhere, I was going to get absolutely, positively, drunk off my face.

Bay, proving once again his place as my best friend, whipped out his phone. "I'm supposed to watch Savannah, but I'm going to see if one of my baby sisters can do it—or my parents. Then you and I will hit the town my friend."

#

With Juliet's okay, Bay handed off Savannah to his family, who were overjoyed to babysit. After that, we went to a hole in the wall bar a couple of blocks from my house called the Skipper's Lament, which was somehow seedy as hell, full of netting, plastic fish, and shells, but was also chock full of hipsters and bespoke cocktails. I didn't give a fuck as long as they had liquor. I would have laid down in the alley if that had been the only option.

Bay found us a booth, and we started ordering shots.

Somewhere around the fourth shot, Bay talked me into joining dating websites.

"A respectable one," Bay said, squinting at me. "Nothing against the hookup apps, but you aren't going to be into that."

"No, he would not," Jim said, sliding into a booth.

I hugged him tight. "Jim!" I leaned heavily into my roommate. "I love Jim." I handed him one of the three full shot glasses lined up in front of me. "How did you find us, Jim?"

"Bay texted me," Jim said, trading me the shot for a glass of water. "And while I'm down for the current plan, I don't want to roll either of you into the hospital. Please hydrate and pace yourselves."

"No offense, Jim," I said, taking another shot. "But pacing myself seems like a terrible plan." I wasn't sure if the alcohol would make me numb, or make me hurt. Either was welcome. I just needed outside my head for the night. Jim glared at me until I drank half of my glass of water.

"Okay, but which ones are respectable?" I dug out my phone, ready to download some apps as Jim and Bay argued. I had several text alerts on my phone. A few were from Lou, Declan, Juliet and Trick—all apologizing for this evening.

Most of them were from Vanessa.

Loch Nessa: We need to talk. I want to make sure we're okay.

Loch Nessa: Are you okay?

Loch Nessa: Will? Just tell me you're okay.

Loch Nessa: Please.

I didn't know what to say. Lie and say I was fine? Tell her I felt like my insides had been cut out with a jagged blade? I spent several seconds staring at my phone, frozen in indecision.

For the first time since I'd met her, I didn't want to think about Vanessa. I didn't even want to look at her.

Not forever. Just until I could get my game face back on.

I ignored her texts, pulling open the app store. Determined now. "You each pick one. I'll put a profile on both."

CHAPTER FIVE

Vanessa

It took me hours to go to sleep. I kept checking my phone, arguing with myself that I should give my friend space, but that I also wanted to be there for him. Upset, worried, and angry at the whole stupid thing. I loved my roommates dearly, but I would have cheerfully strangled every single one of them tonight.

I mean, not really, but they were all getting decaf until they were back in my good graces.

Kodo and Podo finally had to take away my phone and chitter at me until I went to bed. I thought for sure I'd toss and turn, but I fell asleep the second my head hit the pillow.

In the dream, Will and I were at the beach. Somewhere warm and tropical, both of us walking barefoot in the sand. Lights from nearby buildings winking in the night, playing peekaboo between the occasional clump of palm trees. Will wore swim trunks and a *Lilo & Stitch* shirt that said, "I'm lost" in adorable cartoon font. It made me uneasy—an off note in an otherwise idyllic scene.

Water lapping at the shore, a warm breeze caressing my skin, the scent of summer flowers on the breeze. I felt at peace, happy in a way I hadn't felt in a long time. I realized we were holding hands, fingers intertwined, and it should have been strange, but it wasn't. In the dream, it felt right.

Music drifted out from somewhere, an old song, slow and lovely. Will laughed, pulling me to him, arms going around me, like we were going to slow dance.

"People don't actually do this?" I asked, grinning at him.

"What, dance?" He guided my arms around his neck, his going around my waist. "Pretty sure people dance all the time." Our bodies lined up to slow dance, the warmth of him was both a comfort and a catalyst, sparking heat along my own skin.

I waved a hand in the air. "No, this. Dance on the beach. It's like something from a movie."

A smile tugged at his lips. "Art imitating life, life imitating art—does it matter?"

One of my hands slid down, resting over his heart, the beat steady. I relied on that beat.

For a few minutes we danced, movements slow and languid, our bodies getting closer with each step, like two sand castles toppling into eachother.

I looked up into his face, expecting a laugh or a smile—because when wasn't Will happy? When wasn't Will joy? Whatever joke I'd been about to make died. Will wasn't smiling. Instead he was looking at me like I was the beat he relied on, too.

Like I was everything.

It was the kind of look you either walk away from, or respond to in kind. I didn't walk away.

It seemed like the most natural thing, going up on my toes, brushing my lips against his.

Soft. A question kind of kiss.

And Will answered. Holy shit, did Will answer.

One hand slid up to the back of my head, cradling me like I was precious, his lips hot and hungry. His tongue slid against mine and I shivered. Desire flooded me, and suddenly I was just wearing way too many clothes. Why the fuck did people wear clothes, anyway? I couldn't think of one good reason right now.

Will's hand slid under the back of my shirt, blazing against my skin, and I wanted that. More of *that*. He hefted me up, my legs going around his waist, his arm a buffer between my back and the palm tree he pressed me again. I rubbed up against, trying to get friction and oh. *Oh.* I wanted more of him—his weight, his heat, his skin.

I yanked the hem of his shirt over his head, throwing it down into the sand. He laughed into my mouth. "That was my shirt."

"I hate that shirt," I said, nipping along his jaw. "That shirt is dead to me. Gone forever." And not just because it had been in my way, but because I hated the idea of happy Will in a sad shirt. Of happy Will alone.

He slowed then, eyes on mine, fingers drifting over my brow, my cheek. "Then come find me." He sighed against my lips. "If you find me, then I won't be lost."

I tightened my arms around him. "You're not lost. You're right here."

He smiled then, but it was the kind of smile that breaks your heart. "I'm not here. I'm not here at all."

And that's when I woke up, sitting up so fast in bed that I dislodged Kodo, who fell with an indignant squeak. My breath sawed in and out of me, sweat slicking my skin. I was a weird cocktail of horribly sad and incredibly turned on.

I'd never had a sexy dream about Will and *holy shit* had that been a sexy dream until the end.

That was it. I would murder my roommates slowly.

#

I stomped out of my bedroom, not caring if I woke up anyone in the house. I was pissed. Horny and pissed. I didn't want to think about the first one, but I could do something about the second.

I had a short opening shift at Wicked Brews, meaning it was six in the morning and my roommates were all still asleep. Or they should have been. As I stomped into the kitchen, I was greeted by Declan making omelets, Trick making coffee, and Lou making big eyes at me.

Dammit chirruped sleepily from his perch on Trick's shoulder.

"What is this?" I growled at them, waving a hand at the scene.

"We felt really bad," Lou said, scooping up my ferrets from the floor. "Not only did we hurt you and Will, but after you left the bar last night, we realized you never got to tell us your real news."

"We were there to support a big moment," Trick said, digging the creamer out of the fridge. "And we borked it."

"Is 'bork' even a word?" Declan grabbed a handful of chopped bacon and cheddar cheese, sprinkling it onto the egg.

"I don't know." Trick slapped the creamer down. "It's really early."

"Why are you even up?" I slid into one of the chairs surrounding the dining room table.

Trick poured me a cup of coffee and set it in front of me. "We knew you had to open. This is penance."

Lou pointed a finger at the whiteboard cork board combo that Declan had hung on the kitchen wall. A copy of our various schedules had been pinned to it. Declan was a freakishly efficient house mom.

"We thought if we were very nice…," Lou said, wrapping her hands around her own coffee.

"And if I made you omelets," Declan added.

"You might forgive us enough to tell us your actual news," Trick finished, collapsing into the chair next to Lou. "We were dicks and we're sorry."

As I sipped my coffee, I felt the majority of my anger drift away. "It's not a big deal. I— I'm going to go get my hedge witch license. See about maybe talking Thea and Emma to make me a partner or something." I mumbled the last bit into my drink.

Lou straightened, her eyes bright. "Really? That's awesome!" She wrinkled her nose. "And we shit on it."

"You didn't shit on it." I sighed. "Just sort of… glitter bombed it."

"In our defense," Trick said, scratching Dammit's head. "You did say the news involved you and Will, and I don't see how you going back to school has anything to do with him." Dammit nipped his ear gently.

"Though we are very proud of you and excited for this new journey of yours."

I quickly caught them up, which didn't take much since all of them were intimately familiar with how awful my dad was.

Declan slid my omelette in front of me. "Your dad's a tool, but we'll do anything we can to help you get your license."

"You don't…" I fussed with my coffee, suddenly feeling vulnerable. I hated feeling vulnerable, even though I knew no one in this room would ever hurt me on purpose. "Think it's kind of…silly?" I shifted in my seat, hurrying on before they could respond. "I mean, I know it's not a big dream or anything, but—"

Lou set her hand on my arm. "Van, a dream is a dream. It doesn't matter what size it is, as long as it's yours. That's what makes it important."

"It would feel good, you know?" I stared at my coffee mug, which as almost empty. "Not helping people exactly but sort of…easing their way. Making their days a little bit better. A little brighter." Maybe then I could finally drown out my dad's voice, the one that said I was useless.

"Just because people take everyday miracles for granted don't make them any less amazing," Lou said gently. "I don't think twice about taking medicine for a headache, or cramps, but we haven't always had those things, and I would be miserable without them."

I glanced up and caught Lou smiling at me.

"Hedgewitchery is like that," she said. "Everyday, often taken for granted, but we all rely heavily on it. You would make a big difference."

Trick refilled my cup. "We're really proud of you, Van. Now eat your omelette before it gets cold, or Declan is going to mope."

"I'm not going to mope," Declan grumbled, sliding a cheese omelette in front of Lou. He hesitated, spatula in hand. "I would reheat it for you, though." He frowned at my omelette.

I quickly shoved a bite into my mouth. "It's great. Don't touch it." He would obsess over it if I wasn't careful, so I sent Kodo and Podo at him to beg for bacon, smiling as he slipped them each a small piece.

#

My short shift at Wicked Brews was from seven to eleven—I was mostly there to do some quick inventory, place orders, and check in shipments from suppliers. It went by fast, and soon enough, I was slipping into my hoodie and checking my phone. Will still hadn't responded.

Well, fuck this. It wasn't like he'd asked for space—everyone else had told me to back off and I had. But it wasn't like Will to ignore my texts. What if his phone was lost or broken? The last part of my dream came back to me. What if Will needed me and couldn't ask for some reason?

If he wanted me gone, he could tell me to my face.

I packed up a lemon blueberry muffin and a coffee and caught a ride share to Will's house.

Jim greeted me at the door. "Oh, heeeeeyyyy Van." He drew the "hey" out really long. It made me feel awkward.

"Heeeeey, Jim." I held up my wares. "I brought these for Will. Sorry, I didn't think you'd be home."

"I took a personal day," Jim said, waving me in. "He's in a blanket burrito on the couch."

I toed off my shoes and followed Jim into the livingroom. Jim lived in a three bedroom ranch style home, that had high ceilings and a mostly open floor plan. He'd renovated it when he bought it, making it more minotaur friendly. He'd brought in a decorator, and the place had a rugged, outdoorsy feel to it. Lots of natural fibers, plants, things like that.

I found Will curled up on the giant sectional couch, watching a deep sea documentary. He was pale, with dark circles under his eyes. I didn't think Will had slept any better than I had. I sat down by his feet. "I come bearing gifts."

Will glanced at me, his attention going back to the TV. "Thanks." His voice was too soft.

It was like my friend was only half inhabiting his own body.

I set the coffee and the muffin on the table and marveled in the awkwardness. I'd sat on this couch just like this so many times. Why was it suddenly weird?

Jim clapped his hands together. "Well, I'm going to go somewhere else. You two have fun now." Then I heard the rattle of keys as Jim grabbed them from the bowl in the entryway and the click of the door as he left.

I poked Will's foot. "You didn't respond to my texts. I was worried."

Will sighed, then shifted, wiggling in his blanket until he was sitting up. The blanket dropped away, revealing Will's chest as he reached for the coffee I'd brought. "Sorry. I was—we got really drunk. I guess I spaced it."

He wasn't looking at me when he said it, and I was pretty sure at least half of what he was saying were lies. Normally I would have called him out on that but I was suddenly distracted by his half naked state. I've seen Will in his underwear about a billion times. Between the blanket burrito and his pajama pants, he was mostly covered and yet…

And yet.

I couldn't seem to look away as he moved. Watching the bunch and stretch of his muscles. The surety of his movements. Will lived fully in his body.

I'd known in the abstract that my best friend was good looking. But he was also just Will.

Nothing new here. I wasn't sure if it was those ridiculous glitter infested poster boards or the dream from the night before, but it was like my view of Will had abruptly shifted. Like when you see a band live, and you finally make it to the front of the stage—the songs were the same, but now you can feel the vibrations of the stage, smell the sweat of the musicians. The energy so close, the base so loud, it was like a second heart beat. There was a fullness to it that wasn't there before.

That's how it was now. Will was the same person, but I'd pushed beyond the mosh pit, up past the bouncers, so I could lean against the stage. Will's scent was in my nostrils, and I could feel the heat from his skin. I wanted to touch him, like I had in the dream. Stroke my hand down his back. See his eyes go hot, his mouth soften. He was the base beat thrumming through my blood, my second pulse.

I caught myself before I reached for him. I had a new catch phrase and it was, *what the fuck?*

This couldn't be real. It was yesterday, messing with my head. It had to be.

I closed my eyes. I wanted everything back the way it was—my best friend, with none of this extra and unwanted baggage. I could push it back, right? Get us back on track?

When I opened my eyes, Will was frowning at me. "Are you okay?"

"Yeah?" I manufactured a smile. "Busy morning. Guess I'm a little tired."

Normally Will wouldn't buy this for a second. He would gently nudge the truth out of me. This new Will simply nodded, breaking off a piece of muffin in his hands.

Were we just cool with lying to each other now? Was that our new status quo? If so, I hated it.

My hands were sweating now. It was like talking to a stranger. How could I fix this? I licked my lips. "So, with everything yesterday, I didn't get to talk to Juliet about dad. I was thinking of going over there now. Do you…do you want to go?"

Will chewed a bite of muffin carefully as he grabbed his phone off the coffee table, checking the time. His expression became apologetic. "I can't. I have a coffee date at two. I still need to shower and shave." His smile was so faint it was like the ghost of a ghost. He was haunting his own face. "I smell like bar."

"Oh." And as I sat there, I realized that I had fully expected Will to go with me. Not that Will didn't have a life, it was only… it had always been tangled up in mine. Will was always with me. I was always with Will. He was my faithful sidekick. My bad ass backup. He never missed big life stuff, and talking to Juliet about my dad was kind of a big life thing.

It was absolutely reasonable that he had his own stuff. A date. People dated. Totally, completely, normal. *Normal.* I wanted things back to our status quo, and this would get us on the way to that. So, yippie, I guess.

But I was still being haunted by that stupid dream, because thinking about Will going on a date instead of going with me felt like a betrayal. Like I was being left for another woman.

Which was ludicrous.

I smacked my hands on my thighs. "Excellent. Good, good. Yup. Yuppers." Oh, gods, someone please shut me up.

Will stopped chewing and stared at me, his brows pinched.

I didn't blame him. I was acting really weird and couldn't seem to make myself stop.

"Right. Let me know how it goes!" My voice sounded bright and tinny in my ears. I stood up abruptly. "I guess I should get going. Hit the ol' dusty trail." Holy fuck, what, was I a cowboy now?"

Will didn't even make fun of me. He nodded slowly, finishing off the last of his coffee. "You can stay if you want. The place I'm meeting Becca, Juliet's is on the way. I could drop you off."

Becca. *Becca*. What a terrible name. *Becca*. I bet she talked with her mouth full and never tipped.

I pretended to look at my phone as I tried to get a fucking grip on myself. Will was my friend. I wanted him to be happy. I wanted him to meet a nice person who would be a good partner.

Becca was probably an angel who volunteered at a pet shelter and actually made it to craft nights.

"Sure," I said, tucking away my phone. "That would be great." I slapped my hands together. "I can help you pick out your outfit! Gotta look sexy for your date!" That was it. I officially hated myself.

"Okay," Will said slowly, folding up the blanket and draping it across the side of the couch. "Sounds fun."

It did not sound fun. It sounded like being drug naked through blackberry bushes.

We both seemed to know it, but somehow we'd tacitly agreed to not discuss it. Like we obviously weren't going to discuss anything involving the poster boards.

Which was weird, because we usually talked about everything.

But if it got us back to normal, I was willing to give this new not-talking thing a go.

CHAPTER SIX

Will

My friend was possessed. That was the only possible answer. I was trying on my third outfit—I found a grease stain on the first shirt, and Van thought the second one was 'trying too hard.' She sat perched on the edge of my bed, her expression slightly manic, and every few minutes her knee started bouncing. She'd catch it, stop, only to start up again a second later.

"Did you have too much coffee today?" I slipped the third shirt on over my head, Van tracking the movement, her lips parted.

"What?" She seemed slightly dazed—her eyes were glazed, her color high. If she was getting a fever, she'd tell me, right? Guilt stabbed at me. Sure, she'd be honest with me. I'd been honest with her since she walked through my door, hadn't I?

I finished buttoning the shirt, examining myself in the mirror. This one was a nice button up, black with little silver skulls I'd embroidered onto the shirt sleeves. It fit nice, and showed that I was making an effort, but not going overboard, either. I'd have to lose the dress pants— they didn't really go.

I had a darker pair of jeans that would look better, so I shucked the pants I was wearing.

Van made a noise—it sounded like a choked-off squeak. I frowned at her. Her cheeks were flushed. Maybe she *was* getting sick? I fisted my jeans in one hand as I crossed the room, putting the back of my other hand against her brow.

"Are you feeling okay?" Her skin felt cool and clammy against my palm, but I pressed it to her cheeks just in case. "You coming down with something?"

Van swallowed hard. "I'm fine. Overwhelmed, maybe. Lots going on."

She was dodging the question—I knew it, but I also didn't have time to pursue it. I didn't want to be late to meet Becca. That would be rude and not fair to her. That didn't negate the worry in my gut. I reminded myself that Van was perfectly capable of taking care of herself and was going from my place to Juliet's. If she was sick, her sister would take care of her.

"Okay," I said, stepping away so I could pull on the jeans. "If you're sure…"

"Yup!" Van chirped. "I'm sure!" She stumbled over to the window, shoving it up. "Are you hot? It's hot in here, right?"

I shook my head, snapping the button on the jeans. Jim's place had central air. It was cooler in the house than outside, but Van had her head out the window gulping up air like it wasn't eighty five degrees in the shade. Which was making me second guess the jeans. Eh, I'd be fine. Van however…

"That's it," I said, pulling out my phone. "I'm taking you to urgent care or something. I'll get Becca to raincheck."

Van deflated against the window, closing her eyes. "And you would totally do that, too, because you're Will." She huffed, standing up and closing the window. "You're not going to cancel your date. I'm fine, promise. If I start to feel bad, I'll have Juliet take me."

I eyed her, my phone still in my hand.

She have me a reassuring smile. "You go on your date. You deserve it." Van walked over, taking a moment to straighten the collar of my shirt, brushing her hands along my chest and shoulders. Such a simple movement, but I felt it in my bones. "Becca won't know what hit her. You look great."

I looked down, suddenly self conscious. "I do?"

"Yeah," Van said, sounding almost reluctant. "You really do."

#

Dating was awkward as fuck. I'm a generally social guy, but something about meeting a stranger I'd only ever talked to online for coffee made me uncomfortable for some reason. I think it was because no matter how you clicked over chat, it didn't mean you'd click in life. At least, not romantically.

It took me about ten seconds into meeting Becca to know we wouldn't be a match. I mean, don't get me wrong—she was pretty, with a sweet smile. Kindness practically came off her in waves. It was *nice*, and wasn't that damning with faint praise?

We spent most of our time chatting about books—she was intrigued by my nana's bookclub. There were a few stilted moments of conversation, but nothing horrific. Normal first time meeting stuff. We talked long enough that my coffee got cold. At one point, she laughed and reached over, touching my arm. A casual gesture. A friendly tap.

That was how it felt. Like a friend. Zero chemistry whatsoever.

I had a good time chatting with her. I'd definitely get coffee with her again, but it would be as friends. I felt a little deflated when I left the cafe and got into my car. Had I been hoping for an amazing date, or was I slightly relieved that it hadn't gone anywhere? I wasn't sure, which was a problem.

I rubbed my hands over my face. What was I doing?

Getting on with my life, that was what I was doing. Right? But it felt a lot like I was throwing my life away at the same time. I took out my phone. I wanted to talk to someone about it. Get a temperature check on the situation. Normally, I'd call Van. Obviously that wouldn't work here.

If I called Nana…I knew what Nana would say. Nana would line up more dates for me.

She wanted me to move forward.

Bay was working, so that was out. I called Jim. My roommate was as steady as they come.

Jim answered his phone after two rings, his voice chipper. "If it isn't my favorite roommate."

"I'm your only roommate."

"Sure enough." He hesitated a beat. "You don't sound so good. What's up?"

"I went on a date," I said, in the same tones you'd usually use for, "I got a speeding ticket" or "I need a root canal." Heavy notes of dread.

"Ah." Jim packed a lot into that 'ah.' "It didn't go well?" "It went fine. She was very nice."

Jim made a choking sound. "Nice? It was a date, not tea with your Nana. Nice. Dates should either be spectacular or awful—no in-between. Because at least with awful you have a good story."

"No good story." I closed my eyes and rested my head against the headrest. It was getting stuffy in my car already. "We had pleasant conversation over coffee. She had a good sense of humor and she was pretty. I liked her a lot."

"Just not in the sexy way."

"No, not in the sexy way." I let out a frustrated noise. "Am I making a mistake?"

Jim's voice gentled. "Because you're trying to date even though you've been in love with Van since time began?"

"Has it always been that obvious?"

Jim snorted. "To me? Yes. I knew the first time I saw you together. It's in the way you look at her. To Vanessa? Totally oblivious."

I put my phone on speaker and set it in the holder so I could press the heals of my hands against my eyes. They were stinging for some reason. "Because she's not interested." I let out a long breath. "I'm doing the right thing. Moving on."

Jim was quiet long enough that I checked to see if I'd accidentally hung up on him. "Possibly? I don't know. I'm not an expert on dating. But maybe…you and Van should talk about it?"

I guffawed. It was as awkward as it sounded. "Talk? Did you not see her face yesterday? She wanted nothing to do with that conversation." I'd never seen someone so upset from looking at a venn diagram, even a poorly rendered one, and I'd made it through public high school.

"No, I saw it," Jim said slowly. "And what I mostly saw was shock. That doesn't mean she wouldn't be interested. It's possible she just needed to process."

I shook my head, even though Jim couldn't see it. "I'm pretty sure if she'd been interested, she would have figured it out by now."

"I don't know." Jim's tone turned thoughtful. "People are funny. We're really great about putting blinders on, especially if it's something important. I may not know what's going on with Van, but I know you're important to her."

"Yeah," I said. "I guess."

"So what are you going to do?"

I wiped the sweat off my forehead. It was getting really stuffy in the car. "The only thing I can do—move forward. Go home. Change into shorts. Set up another date."

Jim sighed. "Yes, that's definitely easier than having a conversation with Van and getting this out into the open."

He was being sarcastic, which I countered with an overly chipper tone. "It is. I'll just keep shoving my feelings down until they calcify and I become a hollow shell of a man."

"Like the gods intended," Jim's tone was desert dry now. "Be a real man and repress your feelings until they manifest in weird ways. If you buy balls for your trailer hitch, I'm staging an intervention."

"I don't have a trailer hitch and you think those are funny."

"I do, but I wouldn't buy them for my own truck, and they aren't very *Will*. I'm concerned that you're going to let this embitter you to the point that you are no longer my squishy marshmallow of a friend." I heard a voice in the background of the call and Jim's voice grew muffled for a second. "Look, I got to go. But think about what I said. You've managed to get this far in life without loosing your gooey, nougaty center. It's something I appreciate about you."

"Right," I said. "Stay edible. Got it."

"Yes, that's exactly what I said." Jim laughed. "Look, I really do got to go, but I'll be around tonight if you need to talk. Just think about what I said, please? Maybe dating isn't the best way to move forward until you've talked it out with Van."

We said our goodbyes and hung up. I sat for a few minutes in my too-hot car, thinking about my choices, and how staying soft, in some conditions, just meant you melted away until there was nothing of you left.

I turned on my car, went home to change, and take another crack at the dating apps.

CHAPTER SEVEN

Vanessa

Juliet also lived with Trick, but in a daylight basement apartment that had its own entrance. I was currently standing in front of her door, paralyzed by mild panic. It was a nice door, painted white, a bunch of red flowers lining her little stoop.

I didn't have much of a plan in place for talking to my sister. I never had to have one before—Juliet and I had been through a lot, and she was a person in my life that I could just open up my mouth and vomit up whatever messy thing wanted to come out. But this...this felt like a lot to ask. I felt horrible even considering it.

Let Dad back into our lives? Let him meet Savannah? After the shitty way he treated all of us? It didn't feel right. Even with major groveling, which he wouldn't do. Because honestly, I didn't trust that he would mean a single fucking word. The only important person in my father's life was himself. That was something that never wavered.

But even knowing that, there was always a small part of me that thought, "what if this time was different?" I knew it wouldn't be, but I don't think I'd ever completely lose hope that my father would suddenly morph into a caring human being. I should, though. I really should. He would never change.

I knocked, my fist feeling heavy. With all of this spinning in my head, I wasn't at all surprised that I blurted the whole mess out the second Juliet opened her door.

"*Iwanttobeahedgewitchbutdadwillonlysignoffonmymagicalstudiesifhegetstospendtimewit hyouandSavannah.*"

Which would have been an unintelligible mess already but was made worse by Juliet doing the same style of word explosion back at me. "*I'msosorryIscreweduptheothernightwithyouandWill*—" She paused, hand resting on her door frame. "Wait, you're going to be a hedge witch?"

At the same time I said, "You don't have to apologize."

Juliet's expression turned rueful. "You better come in and I'll get us some snacks and then we'll take turns talking like normal people, or this will go on all day."

Juliet lead me into her kitchen, which really only fit one person. While she dug for something to eat, I dropped into one of the chairs at the compact kitchen table in the attached eating nook. My sister put on water for tea and set out a plate of cookies.

"Where's Savvy?"

A small smile appeared on her face. "Bay took her to the Children's Museum. He likes to play on their toys and you need a child to get in."

I thought it was probably closer that Bay wanted to give her a break, but Juliet was more likely to accept it if she thought it was something Bay wanted to do. Otherwise she would feel guilty taking up more of his time because Bay and his family already babysat Savannah regularly. If it wasn't a necessity—like work, or class—Juliet felt like she was taking advantage.

I both understood where she was coming from and didn't. My niece was fun and we loved Juliet. Why wouldn't we pitch in to give her some breathing room? Why wouldn't we fight to hangout with Savvy?

Plus Bay really did enjoy the train set there as well as the dinosaur skeleton in the roof play area. I texted him, asking for pictures. He immediately sent me several of Savvy wearing a pilot's hat, sitting in a cockpit. Followed by Savvy as a farmer, Savvy playing in the water room, and finally a selfie of them getting ice cream. Their smiles were so big, my heart squeezed.

Once the tea was poured, Juliet settled in across from me. "Okay, so do I need to apologize more?"

"No," I said. "I'm over it and you gave me cookies. I appreciate the sentiment, thought." Juliet looked skeptical for a minute, but decided not to press. "Okay then. Spill."

I told her all about my plans, ending with our father's stipulations. By the time I was done, all the cookies were gone. I was using my thumb to methodically crush the remaining crumbs into the plate.

Juliet frowned into her tea, her eyes distant. "It's a terrible idea, right?"

She set her mug down, rolling a hair tie off her wrist and pulling her blond hair back into a ponytail. "You becoming a hedge witch? No. I think that's a splendid idea and I think Emma and Thea would agree. They love you and you're a great fit at Wicked Brews." She collapsed back into her chair. "The part about dad?" She held her hands out in a "who knows" gesture. "It's suspicious, right?"

Juliet toyed with the handle of her mug. "The best rule of dad is to remember that he only does something for himself. You can always count on that. So what do you think his end game is here?"

I stopped crushing the cookie into dust and frowned. "To humiliate me somehow?"

Juliet considered this. "I can see him doing that as a bonus, but he wouldn't think his time was worth it just for that."

I nodded. Sad, but true.

"Maybe..." Juliet tapped her fingers along the table. "Maybe he's trying to save face?

Dad hates to be embarrassed. You know how the arcanists work—small world and all that. Must be pretty embarrassing if they all know that neither of us are talking to him and he hasn't spent time with his granddaughter."

"Yeah, he would hate that."

"I bet one of the other arcanists was bragging on his grandkids or something and Dad couldn't compete, so he's trying to bring us back into the fold. Project the image of the happy family, you know?"

This all sounded sadly plausible. It wouldn't be the first time he'd done it. "The question is, do we let him?" I grabbed Juliet's hand. "I'm not going to lie and say this isn't important to me, but it's not more important than you and Savvy's well being. I won't parade her in front of that monster just to get what I want."

Juliet smiled at me, tight-lipped. "I know you would never ask that. Savvy comes first."

She squeezed my hand. "But I don't think it will hurt. If we control the environment. Give him specific parameters and if he doesn't meet them—if he utters one shitty word to her—we pull the plug." She sighed. "It might be good for both of us? You get your certification signed off, I get some closure, maybe?"

"He'll find some way to make it terrible," I said, my eyes on the table.

"Probably." Juliet reached across the table and took my hand. "And we have to remember that if he does, that's on him. Not us." She squeezed my hand, a tired smile on her face. "Let's try to get what we need out of this. Go in with our eyes open. If it goes horribly, we put the boundary back up and know we tried."

I propped my chin in my free hand, my elbow on the table. "You're doing this mostly for me, aren't you?"

The corners of her mouth twitched, like she was fighting a bigger smile. "Mostly, yes. You deserve your certification. You deserve to go after your chosen career. I want that for you, but I think this will be good for me, too." Juliet slumped back into her chair, her hand sliding out of mine. "Sometimes...even with my training, sometimes I start to wonder if I'm exaggerating. Making too much of the things that he's done. I know that I'm not, logically, but when we don't see him, it can be easy to slip into that mindset."

Juliet gave me that same, tired smile. "So let's do this. Get what you need from dad. I'll get a reminder that it's not all in my head. Then I can honestly say I tried to give him a relationship with Savannah. If he ruins his chances there, well, no surprise, right?"

I snorted. "It he puts one foot wrong with Savvy, we'll gut him."

"Yes," Juliet said. "That. Exactly."

I batted my eyelashes and tented my hands together under my chin, raising my voice until I sounded like a little kid. "You're the bestest sister I could ever have."

Juliet snorted. "Of course I am. I'm giving you what you want."

This time I reached across the table and took her hand. "Just remember, no matter what, I'm here for you and Savvy when dad does his worst." It was never if. Always when. Which made me feel stupid that we were even trying but ... there was that small, minuscule chance he would actually come through.

Juliet couldn't even manage the sad smile now, her face solemn. "Same."

#

I waited to call my dad until I was in my room. I assumed crash position—wrapped myself in a comforter, my ferrets Kodo and Podo crawling all over me, trying to do preemptive comforting. Then on to deep breathing. There are people in this world who don't have to prep themselves to call their parents and I'm massively jealous of them.

Of course he didn't actually answer when I called him. While it was possible that he was too busy, it was more likely that he was screening his calls. I left a message, telling him to call me back.

Then my adrenaline crashed and I must have fallen asleep, because I startled awake to my phone ringing. When had I turned my ringer on? The song *Shout at the Devil*—my dad's ringtone

— came from my blankets from wherever I'd dropped my phone. Kodo fished it out of the blankets, shoving it into my hands. I rubbed a hand over my face, trying to wake up, as I answered.

"Hey, dad."

"Vanessa--I got your call." And didn't he sound pleased as punch about it? My dad happy was both a celebration, because he could be generous when he was in a good mood, and an alert. If he was this happy,

I had to wonder why. Just a false front, pretending to be thrilled that his daughters were caving, or had I missed something?

This was the problem with dealing with my father. A conversation was never just a conversation. I had to filter everything for subtext, tone, motivation. It was exhausting.

I heard paper rustling in the background. "I assume you'll want to move quickly on this.

Regrettably, my schedule is very full. You know how it is."

Reminding me he was a busy man. I rolled my eyes. Someone knocked softly on my door and I covered my phone with my hand. "Come in."

I returned my phone to my ear, listening to my dad flip through his calendar as he made noises about "fitting me in."

Will came through my door, shutting it quietly behind him when he saw I was on the phone. He'd changed since this morning—he now had on shorts and a worn tank top, and for a second I wondered if that was because of the heat or because the date went so well. Like, maybe there was an instant animal attraction and they'd stumbled to a broom closet and he lost his shirt buttons when she tore his shirt open. I shut that thought down immediately because it was none of my business and also because I hated it.

And I hated that I hated it.

I wanted Will to be happy. I just needed to shove him back into the box he'd been living in, the best friend box, and everything would go back to normal. But for some reason I was struggling to make that happen. Why was that so hard?

The awkwardness wasn't just on my end, either. Usually Will would have flopped onto the bed by now, greeting the ferrets and hugging me. Instead her stood leaning against the wall, looking unsure.

I patted the spot next to me on the bed because weirdness aside, I needed my friend right now.

Will eased over, sitting next to me, a questioning expression on his face. "My dad," I mouthed.

He grimaced, scratching Kodo and Podo's heads as they chittered at him in greeting. "I could do your first assessment in a few weeks," my dad said finally, snapping my attention back to the phone. "But I have a spot next monday night for dinner. Let your sister know. I'll set up reservations."

"Or," I said, trying to keep my voice even. "We could have dinner after you assess me on Monday night." I wasn't going to let me dad push off my testing indefinitely.

"I don't take my work home, Vanessa. Evenings are for contemplation, recharging and networking."

I pushed my thumb into the divot forming between my brows, trying to relax the muscles there. Will's hands found my shoulders, massaging the tension away and reminding me to drop them. I always went full hedgehog when on the phone with my dad. Shoulders up and curled in.

Okay, how to play this? Flatter and hope that works, or put us on even footing? I wasn't sure which would work better, so I started with even footing because that was more palatable to me.

"This is a trade, dad. You're assessing me and we're giving you what you asked for. I'm giving up my free time, and while I understand that it's not what you usually do, we're family. Allowances are made for family." He hadn't shut me down yet, so I barreled forward. "I can come over before dinner, and we can do the assessment."

That wasn't a strong enough argument. I could feel it. I needed something more. "The sooner we put this to bed, the better, right? Less chance people would know how behind I was ..." I let my words trail off, letting him imagine how embarrassing it would be. As much as he would hate me learning to be a hedgewitch, it was still better than me being a magical drop out loser.

His sentiments, not mine.

"Fine." His response was so grudging, I'm surprised it made it through his teeth. "Give your sister the details and I'll see you Monday, then." He cleared his throat. "Are you bringing that ... boy ... with you?"

I frowned. "Boy?"

"The one you're dating?" When I didn't answer right away, he made a disgusted sound. "Or are you your mother's daughter and dating more than one?"

I swallowed my angry retort—it wouldn't do any good and my mother didn't care what my father thought of her.

He probably meant Will. I guess from his perspective, my friend looked liked a boyfriend. He'd come to the office with me. Now that I was thinking about it, the time he'd met Will before that certainly painted a very specific picture.

During everything with my roommates Declan and Louise, my dad had showed up in my living room. I'd been completely sidelined, frozen in place. Will had walked out of my room, half-naked, and scooped me up in his arms before saying something saucy and whisking me away. It had been *awesome*.

It didn't seem fair to drag Will into this but the idea of him there as both a support and a buffer was too enticing to resist. I tipped the phone away from my ear and turned to him, keeping my voice a whisper. "You busy Monday night?"

Will pursed his lips in thought. "I work, but I can probably trade shifts," he whispered back. "I'll be there, Nessa."

I nodded at him, suddenly so grateful my throat was tight. It was my turn to clear my throat. "Yeah, dad. I'm bringing *that boy* with me."

And may the gods have mercy on us both.

CHAPTER EIGHT

Will

By the time Vanessa was off the phone with her father, I'd already switched shifts with my coworker. The people I worked with were always really good about that sort of thing—small shop and all that. It helped when they knew why I needed to switch. They all loved Vanessa. It was hard not to, I guess.

It was definitely difficult for me not to.

Monday wasn't going to be easy for her, and I was happy that I was going to be there. It made me uneasy, this whole situation. It was so important to her and I didn't trust her dad not to ruin her happiness. Not to take her shiny, pretty future and shatter it on the ground. Vanessa was tough—she'd had to be tough—but that didn't mean he couldn't make the situation worse. That was his shitty superpower.

Being there for her was good, but maybe not enough. I flopped back onto the bed and let the ferrets crawl all over me, which was what they wanted. I was their favorite playground. They chittered at me nonstop as they climbed onto my stomach.

Vanessa's mouth quirked and she dropped her gaze down to her comforter. "You're being taken firmly to task by the dynamic duo. Apparently you haven't been around as much and they feel neglected."

I *hadn't* been around as much as I usually was, but I couldn't exactly explain why to Kodo and Podo. Oh, they'd understand me if I talked to them, but they would tell Van. They were her familiars, after all. If only those little guys knew I wanted to be here more, not less. I slept over enough as a friend that I actually had a side of the bed.

I just wanted the privilege to be able to pull Van onto my side of it.

But I couldn't have it, so I would focus on what I could do in my current roll as her friend. "I'd like you to come into the shop this weekend. Let me work on you."

Van collapsed onto the bed facing me, scrunching up her pillow until she was happy with it. "Why? You think I need help to pass my dad's tests? That I need a boost?"

I scowled at her. "I think you could run rings around your dad's tests, and even if I didn't, I wouldn't cheapen your victory by cheating." That wasn't how my magic worked anyway, not for the kind of spell she was talking about. That particular ritual worked to align and augment your own magic. I couldn't make Van more powerful. What I could do was make it line up so that her power was working at the best capacity. It would be along the lines of her approaching a test after a full night's sleep, good food, and plenty of studying.

She didn't need that.

"He's not going to play fair." She didn't need the reminder, but I gave it to her anyway.

Van scrunched up her nose. It was so stupidly cute. I clasped my hands together, tucking them under my head to keep from reaching for her.

"He's going to be torn between the embarrassment of me failing, while simultaneously wanting me to fulfill his prophecy of failure. That I'm not as good as him." Her voice went soft. "That I'm more my mother's daughter than his daughter."

I gave up keeping my hands to myself and reached for Van, pulling her tight to my side, her head under my chin. It felt so right, so damned good simply holding her, that I stayed quiet for a moment and just basked. "Every time his words come out of your mouth, I want to punch his smug face."

She burrowed her face into my chest. "I know. Thank you."

I cupped the back of her head, keeping her close, because I knew that if I didn't, I would lean back and see her face. And then I would kiss her. It would be inevitable, like gravity, or like Louise arguing with pigeons.

"He's going to mess with you and play head games," I said, pulling my mind back on track. "We can do a ceremony to help protect you from that. Close to what I did for Declan and Lou when they were dealing with Eva." When Declan's parents had been after Van's roommates, I'd made it so it was easier for them to repel her mental assaults. I would need to look through my books and pick out the right jewels or stones, something to keep Woodbridge's brand of toxic mental shittery from landing on Van and getting under her defenses.

Van was silent for a few moments, before she tipped her head back, staring at me. Her eyes searched my face, her own carefully blank. I wasn't sure what she was looking for, but something happened, some thought or decision that shifted the mood. I couldn't explain it. I was certain though that for at least a moment, a little sliver of time between one breath and the next, that Vanessa saw me. Not as her friend, but *me.*

The moment disappeared as quickly as it had arrived, evaporating before I was even certain it had happened. Van smiled at me and put her hand on my jaw. "Okay. Tomorrow. I'll come in tomorrow. Thanks, Will."

"Of course," I said, my voice abnormally thick. I don't think she noticed.

But I noticed. I might not know what had been going through her mind, but I was almost certain that for a second there, Van had considered kissing me.

I wasn't sure what that meant, but it was *interesting.*

#

I had a coffee date before my shift the next day, choosing Wicked Brews because it was close to the tattoo shop. It felt like such a cliche, the coffee date. It was popular for a reason—coffee dates could be short, or you could linger if they went well. Seattle also excelled at the coffee shop. We were good at building the ones where people could gather, build community. Plus we needed somewhere to get out of the rain.

This coffee date was not going well.

Some people are turned on by tattoos. Nothing wrong with that. No different than liking certain hairstyles or clothes on people. As Lou liked to point out, it's all plumage. You advertise for the kind of mate you want. Not saying you shouldn't look deeper and all of that, but if something can help you narrow the field a little faster, why not use it? If you're into pastel polos and khakis, for example, you're likely into the lifestyle attached to that clothing and have certain life goals in mind.

I...am not pastel polos and khakis. My plumage was all wrong for that set.

My dating profiles had pictures attached, so my plumage was obvious. Can't really hide neck tattoos, nor would I want to. There was a certain percentage of the population, however, that thought tattoos *might* be hot and wanted to date someone with them to see.

Marci, my coffee date, was in that percentage, and while she had obviously thought that tattoos might be a turn on for her in theory, in reality...

In reality my date looked like she was two seconds from bolting from this shop, this neighborhood, and possibly this planet.

I was a pretty big dude. Not as big as my roommate, but I topped six feet and my build wasn't exactly trim. Marci was pocket-sized, like Louise. Unlike Louise, who had a chihuahua like tendency to take on creatures much larger than her, Marci appeared to be freaked out by everything about me.

I was trying to make her more comfortable—my posture was relaxed. I slouched. I smiled. I was using all my pleases, thank yous, and keeping my voice soft.

It wasn't working. I sighed. It had occurred to me that maybe something more was going on here. I was of the mindset that things were best brought into the light, otherwise they fester.

"Marci, I have to ask—are you okay?" She blinked at me. "What?"

I gestured to her and she slid back reflexively. "Sorry, but you seem on edge, and I'm not sure if that's a general condition, as in you've got things in your history that have made you unsure around certain types of men or men in general, or if it's just me."

She flushed.

I gentled my voice further. "Which is fine. I'm not offended or upset, so please don't stress yourself. But if it's the first, then I can help." Nana always carried card-sized handouts that she had with hotlines for depression, assault, or anything she thought might help out some of the students who came into her library. I'd gotten in the habit of carrying them as well.

"Hotlines. Resources." I shrugged. "Or I can just listen. But if it's specifically *me*, as in you thought this was a good idea but it turns out you now have regrets, then we can just call it quits. I'll get a bag for your cookie and we can shake hands as friends and go about our merry way."

Her brows furrowed. "You're not…mad?" I shook my head slowly. "Nope."

She dropped her gaze, looking at her tightly knit hands. Then her whole body softened into her chair. "I feel bad. Like I wasted your time? But I guess I was curious…" She waved a hand at me, though she looked embarrassed. "And you're kinda hot."

I laughed. "Just not your kind of hot. It's cool." I leaned forward. "If you're curious, ask." She tapped her fingers on the table. "Just ask—any question I want?"

I leaned even closer, propping my elbows on the table. She wasn't afraid of me anymore. Fear often comes from not knowing—from things we can't see or understand. Knowledge was the cure. "I am an open book. If you ask something I decide is too personal, or makes me uncomfortable, I'll say so. Promise."

Her eyes lit up.

I grinned. "Go nuts."

She shot questions at me, rapid-fire, everything from 'do tattoos hurt' to 'what did your parents say?' before she finally paused for breath. "Are you…" Red arced across her cheekbones. She dropped her eyes to my lap. "Pierced?"

I threw back my head and laughed. "I'm a body piercer." She flushed harder. "I know, but…"

I put her out of her obvious misery. "I've tried every piercing at least once to see what it felt like and what the healing process was like, so I can better advise people." I dropped my gaze to my lap. "There are a *lot* of different piercings you could be referring to." I moved so close only inches separated us and whispered. "I didn't keep all of them, but I kept a few."

She mimicked me, leaning in. "What are they like?"

I happened to glance up at the counter. Van was pretending to clean the case, but she'd obviously been watching me and Marci.

She had an interesting look on her face. Unhappy, perhaps? She'd been so weirdly enthusiastic about me dating, that I hadn't thought it an issue to meet Marci here. After all, if the date had gone well, she would have had to meet Marci eventually. That look on her face though…I put it together with the one she'd given me yesterday, where I thought for a second she wanted to kiss me.

And again, it was *interesting.*

It made me want to push, just a little, to see what might happen.

I halved the short distance between me and Marci, dropping my voice to a whisper. "Let me get another cup of coffee, and I'll tell you everything." I winked at her.

Marci giggled.

There was a crash behind the counter as Van dropped the paper cups she'd been restocking.

Yes. Very, very interesting.

#

Ritual Ink was my happy place. Cozy, warm, and full of some of the people I loved best. I threw my stuff into my cubby in the back room, snatching a muffin from a plate on the counter. Declan had been baking again.

I sauntered up to the counter, where my favorite werewolf was hunched over the keyboard, scowling at the schedule. I shoved the last of my muffin into my mouth, came up behind him, and wrapped my arms around his chest, snuggling into his back.

He didn't even look up, just patted my arms. "Hi, Will." I sighed. "You smell fantastic. Like vetiver and man."

He laughed. "Did you take that from your book club book?" Declan knew all about Nana's bookclub.

"Sure 'nuff."

Declan leaned back into the cuddle. "What does vetiver smell like, anyway? I've always wondered."

"Like man, I guess." I kissed the top of his head and let go. "Kind of earthy. Grassy." "So I smell dirty?"

I clicked my tongue at him. "I like you dirty."

Bay snorted as he walked through the door shuffling papers. "If you're flirting with Declan, does that mean your date went well or went poorly?"

I pushed his papers down, grabbing his full attention. "Jealous? You know you'll always be my boo."

Bay set the papers down, irritated. "I know that. I'm insulted that you think I'd be so petty as to begrudge my boy here," he waved at Declan, "some affection."

"Sorry, pookie." I patted his shoulder, ignoring Declan as he shook with silent laughter. It was good to see him laugh. "How my date went is a matter of interpretation. As an actual date, it was a non-starter. As a body piercer?" I leaned over Declan's shoulder. "Is my 2:30 slot still open?"

Declan clicked through to today's screen. "Yeah."

"Cool. Block it off. I'm doing a set of nipples." I took out my phone and texted Marci, letting her know we were good to go.

Bay folded his arms. "You keep making friends with them. I can't tell if you're really good at dating, or absolutely terrible."

Declan tossed me his assessing alpha wolf look—the kind where he was making sure his pack was happy and healthy.

I shrugged. Making friends was good. Declan's assessment plus Bay's words had me thinking, though. Was I terrible at dating, or simply not into it? Was this choice one that would lead me somewhere positive, or to an unhappy place? The more I thought about it, the more I thought I might be making a mistake.

Running out and putting up dating profiles might have been a panic response. Yes, something needed to change...but was that the change I really wanted? Until I settled things with Van, resolved the Craft Night Fail, I didn't think I could go forward in either direction.

Jim was right. We needed to clear the air. Talk about difficult and uncomfortable things. It was the only way to get past this. Which was a problem, because Van *hated* talking about difficult and uncomfortable things. That didn't change the fact that it needed to be done.

With that particular epiphany rattling around in my skull, I took out my phone and paused my profile on the apps. It wouldn't be fair for me or anyone else to share forward if I wasn't sure what I wanted.

No, I was going to have to talk to Van. Whether she liked it or not.

And I was honest enough with myself and the situation to know that it was going to be 'not.'

CHAPTER NINE

Vanessa

I tried to study on my breaks at work—My father wasn't going to pull his punches in his assessment Monday. I needed to be ready. Unfortunately, my concentration was shot. I kept rereading sentences, not a single word penetrating and working its way into my mind. It was busy cycling through two recent events like a giddy toddler on one of those spinning toys you find in parks.

The first was me, Will, and my room. How many times had Will held me? Hundreds? Thousands? Why had I never registered how essential it felt? For a moment—a wild, thoughtless moment—I'd almost kissed him. The idea has seemed so natural, I'd barely caught myself in time. I'd seen how horrified he'd been at all that glitter and posterboard. Our friendship wasn't so fragile that a two-second kiss would implode it, but it would make for rough seas when I needed a placid lake.

Every time I thought about that moment, though, I snagged on the fact that Will didn't look weirded out. He'd seemed…receptive.

I wanted to take that apart and make it make sense, but I wasn't getting anywhere because I kept sliding back into the other memory—Will. On a date. In *my* coffee shop. She'd giggled and blushed. She was pretty, and though it hadn't looked good at first, they'd connected on some sort of wavelength. He'd talked to her for a long time. Smiling. *Flirting.*

Which was good, I reminded myself. Perfect, really. But my stomach still hurt. I didn't exactly want complications right now, right?

Right. Placid lake. I wanted a placid lake.

Of course, placid lakes could hide things—like that movie with Betty White and the giant alligator.

I thumped my head against the table top. This wasn't working.

Since studying wasn't happening, I gave up and packed up my books and notes. After I clocked out, I went home for a nap and to check on Kodo and Podo. They needed to be prepped for Monday, too. Familiars were allowed during assessments, even encouraged, because then they could see how well you worked (or didn't work) with your assistant.

Freshly napped, I ate the leftovers Declan had left for me in the fridge. Then I was off to Ritual Ink. Will had put my appointment at the end of his shift, making sure he had enough time for the ritual. The doors were already locked when I got there, and I had to text him to be let in.

Will smiled as he opened the door, making me smile back automatically. There's something about Will's happy nature that calls for that response in you. Not to shove down bad feelings, but to set them aside for a moment and take stock of all of the good around you. No matter what was going on, I always felt better seeing him. Even a few days ago when he'd looked awful, sitting on the couch.

He seemed better now, more like his usual self, as he waved me into the shop. "I have everything ready for you." He locked the door behind me, grabbed my hand, and drew me into the piercing room. The shop was quiet, no music or chatter from other people.

Will dropped my hand and patted the piercing chair, like the kind you get into in dentist offices. "Hop on up." He snapped on his gloves. "I decided to go with amethyst and turquoise for you. Amethyst both protects, psychically, as well as inspires. Turquoise heals. Around your dad?" He shakes his head. "You will need healing on a 24/7 drip, like an IV." He moves to the metal tray that he'd prepped for the appointment.

Will hummed to himself as he lit the incense he'd chosen for the ritual. "Shirt off and hair up, please. We're going to be putting these on the back of your neck, same as I did for Lou and Dec."

Normally I wouldn't have to take of my shirt for the kind of piercing Will was doing—if he was only doing a piercing. We were in his specialty now, which meant it was as much a ritual, as much about magic, as it was a piercing. I put my shirt behind me on the table and put my hair up into a bun. It wouldn't last in there long. My hair was the sort that slides out of confinement quickly.

Will snapped on fresh gloves, pulled out a sharpie, and started drawing symbols on my arms, chest, neck, and a few on my face. He was totally focused until he glanced at me, his usual smile flirting at the corners of his mouth. "You look very serious."

He was so *close*. I was breathing him in along with the incense and I couldn't tell which scent was more heady. "Didn't want to screw up your symbols."

Will stepped back, eyeing his work. "I would just redo it." He capped the pen, moving on to pick up a toothpick dipped in gentian violet so he could mark the placement spots on the back of my neck. "Okay, so you know how this goes—I pierce the skin, the needle hits your blood.

Magic builds, which is what we want. I slide the jewelry in, cap it, and the spell snaps into place. Rinse, repeat. Once you're done with your dad, we can remove the piercings, or you can leave them in."

Will stood right in front of me. I could reach out, right now, and grab his hips. Pull him close. He brandished a hand mirror with a flourish. "Want to check placement?"

Grabbing him like that would be poor form, since he was working, being professional, and was my friend and all. I shook my head. "I trust you."

Will put on fresh gloves before opening the sterilized packs with the piercing needles and jewelry. He frowned at me. "You okay?"

"Yup!" It came out squeaky. Shit.

His eyes narrowed. "Because you're flushed." He grasped my wrist, gloved fingers resting over the pulse point. "You sure you're okay? We don't have to do this. I've pierced you before no problem, so I didn't think to ask, but if this is stressing you out—"

I shook my head quickly. "No, it's fine. Really."

His expression said he wasn't completely buying it. "I don't want you passing out. Slow your breathing and talk to me." Will automatically demonstrated slow, deep breathing.

Great, I was making the situation worse. Why couldn't I be a normal person? Why couldn't I talk about this weird mess and how ever since the Craft Night Incident it was like I couldn't *stop* seeing my friend as... more. Just *more*. And he'd already been a lot.

I couldn't tell which was worse—how much the whole thing was making me panic... or that I didn't see it before.

"I'm fine," I said, breathing deep. "Promise."

Will watched me for a minute, then with a heavy sigh, picked up the needle he wanted. "Okay, then. You change your mind, say something. We can stop this ride whenever you want." He stepped behind me. "I want you to take a deep breath in. Let it out slow..."

Incense teased my nostrils as I did as he asked. I let the breath out slow and steady, even when I felt the needle bite into my skin. The symbols on my body flared purple, bathing the room in lavender light. I felt the heavy buzz of magic along my skin. Before I finished breathing out, Will capped the jewelry, snapping the spell into place. The symbols along my skin were gone as if they'd never been.

I managed to stay focused through the second piercing. As soon as it was done, Will handed me the mirror and began cleaning up from the ritual, going over piercing after care as he did. I angled the mirror so it would reflect the one on the wall. Two sets of stones winked back at me, neatly hovering over each other, two rows of parallel dots.

They looked great and I told him so. Will just grunted, putting out his incense and closing down the room. "Good. Give me a second. I'll give you a ride home."

Ten minutes later we were safely belted into Will's car, pulling away from the shop and heading to my house. It wasn't a long drive. We listened to music the whole time, Will tapping the steering wheel and singing along. We didn't speak until he pulled up in front of my house.

"Want to come in?"

Will kept tapping the steering wheel, his expression thoughtful. He turned the car off.

Sudden silence cocooned us. "What was going on with you earlier? What made you freak out?" He huffed. "I know things have been…"

"Weird?"

"I was going to stay strained, but weird works. Usually I like weird, but I don't like this." Will rested his head against his headrest, his gaze on me. "Are you afraid of me now? Worried that I might freak out again? Did I do something to make you uncomfortable? What?"

My heart contracted, feeling bad for my friend, terrible that I made him feel unsure.

Suddenly I was so tired of all of this. "No, Will. I wasn't afraid. I…" Ye gods, how do people say this kind of stuff? How should I say it, anyway? Telling him I was suddenly distracted by the fact that he was the definition of a thirst trap didn't seem right. I wanted to handle this the right way, but I only seemed to have experience in handling things the wrong way.

Will waited patiently. He knew how hard this kind of shit was for me. I didn't discuss feelings well. Growing up with my dad, you not only didn't discuss feelings, you hid them as best you could. If I expressed my love of something, my dad would know what to take away. If something scared me, upset me, he would know my soft spot.

You didn't want my dad knowing your soft spots.

Will might not be sure what feelings I was having, but he knew I was processing something. So he would be as patient as the sea waiting to kiss the shore.

Fuck it. I wasn't a coward, and I refused to be one about this. "About the other night." His eyebrows went up, the only reaction to the apparent shift in topics.

"At the bar. The glitter madness presentation from the roommates."

"I remember," he said dryly.

"You seemed really upset." My hands felt cold despite the warm summer night, so I folded them together. "Is that…was that…because the idea upset you?" Spit it out, Van. Sheesh. "Were you upset because that's not how you see me?"

Will stared at me so long, his eyes searching my face, that I wasn't sure he was going to answer. Finally he shook his head. Slowly. Barely moving.

I let out another unsteady breath. "Okay. Then were you upset because *I* saw it?"

Another barely there motion, but a nod this time. He swallowed hard, but the rest of him went almost preternaturally still.

"You want me?" There. Now it was out in the world between us. No taking it back, though part of me—one of those soft spots of me—instantly wanted to. His answer was too important—this was too important—and my gut reaction was to tuck those feelings deep. Keep them safe.

But I was starting to understand that "safe" might not be good for either me or Will.

I wasn't sure, but I thought Will had stopped breathing. If he nodded again, I was going to shake him. I needed to hear it.

"Yes." The word was low. Guttural. As if it had crawled out from the bottom of his chest scraping everything along the way.

I hadn't really gone into this with a plan, but I'd thought what would happen was we would air the problem and then discuss. Like two, rational, adult human beings.

Instead, that "yes" acted like a pistol shot. I sprang forward. Or maybe he sprang forward.

I couldn't tell.

It didn't matter. We clashed in the middle, doing our best despite seatbelts and the center console.

Will mouth's was hot on mine. His hands were in my hair, cradling my face. I was nipping at his lips, clawing at his seatbelt, trying to pull him closer. A happy rumble came from Will's chest, as he let go of me long enough to pop the seat belts.

Then we were on each other.

Carnal. Not a word I used, ever. Holy shit, that was the only word that fit. Carnal and *hot*. One hand slipping under my shirt to grab my hip. Will licked into my mouth, before sliding back enough to clasp my lower lip between his and hum. He tasted like cinnamon for some reason.

My elbow hit the horn, startling us both. We jolted back, both of us panting. Will's cheeked were flushed. His lips wet and red. His hair was sticking up in places, his shirt askew. From me. One kiss and I'd completely undone this man.

Been undone by this man. But what a kiss.

I liked it and I didn't like it. It had made me feel so vulnerable, that I think if that kiss had come from anyone other than Will, I would have bolted from this car like a startled rabbit.

The car filled with the sound of our panting breaths, our eyes wide, our backs pushed up against opposing car doors. We stared at each other like we were both something new and possibly unwelcome.

Will huffed a pained laugh, rubbing a hand over his face. "I can't." He shuddered, and turned to stare out the window. "You need to be very careful here, Nessa. Be sure of what you want."

I hated that laugh. The one that told me loud and clear that my friend was hurt, and was afraid I would make it worse. I didn't ever want him to feel that way. I reached out and took his wrist, sliding my hand down until I held his. "Come inside."

He snorted.

I pointed a finger at him. "Do not make the easy joke." My next words were quiet. Soft. "Please. So we can talk?"

The street lamps lit the side of his face, his lips curling at the ends into a small smile. Or maybe it was just shadows moving. "You hate talking."

"About feelings? I absolutely do." I squeezed his hand. "But for you? I'll do it. For you, I'll talk.

A rush of breath left him. "Okay, then. Okay."

CHAPTER TEN

Will

Van held my hand as if I might disappear any minute as she drug me through the house, pausing only to toe off our shoes at the door. It was late, but her roommates were still up. Mine was, too, apparently—Jim taking up a large part of the sectional couch, arms wrapped around a throw pillow, the ferrets perched on his shoulders. Lou sat next to Jim, sandwiched between him and Declan. Trick sprawled on his back, a snoozing Dammit nested on his chest.

"Hey, Van," Trick said, not looking away from he screen. "The new episode of *Mated by Fate* is on and—"

Van kept walking, pulling me straight back to her room. I waved at everyone over my shoulder.

"Okaaaaay," Trick said, drawing out the word. "Good chat."

Two seconds later, we were in her bedroom, and Van dropped my hand. Her cheeks were flushed, her eyes glassy as she stared at the floor. I nudged the door closed with a click, the sound from the living room suddenly so faint I could barely hear it.

We were alone.

Just me and Van in her quiet, empty, room.

The possibilities weighted the air. Any second, that might get awkward. I put my hands on my hips and huffed. Right. Time to talk. "Well, now that we're—"

Van pushed me against the door with a thump. It was like back in the car. A lit match to drought-dry tinder. Instant inferno.

I'm not going to lie—I'd thought about kissing Van.

A lot. Like, *a lot* a lot. It had been many years of unrequited love on my end, after all, and at this point I had some pretty elaborate fantasies built up.

And yet.

My imagination had *failed* me.

Reality was sensory overload. I hadn't captured the exact softness of the skin of her neck under my teeth. The heat of her back under my hands. The weight of her body as it pinned mine to the door like a specimen she wanted to study.

The scent of her—coffee, incense from the ceremony, and something grassy and green. Proof to me that we were intertwined on a basic level, her scent influenced by me. An imprint of our mutual impact.

I wondered if I smelled like coffee.

Van broke away to yank my shirt over my head and I didn't fight her. Goosebumps broke out on my skin where she touched me.

I must have done the same because her shirt hit the floor next.

I have no conscious memory of it. Just suddenly there was skin where before there had been cotton.

It wasn't enough. There was still too much between us. Her knee rode up on my hip and I slid a hand under her, hefting her up until her legs were wrapped around my waist. I spun us, putting her back to the door.

We were both so hungry for each other, so needy, we couldn't get naked fast enough. She was arching to take off her bra while I was leaning back to yank off her socks. I had no idea how we didn't fall down.

So fast, so greedy, yet I was shaking from holding myself back. Drinking in every detail. The soft moan when I bit her shoulder. My answering groan when she bit back. The shuddering sigh the first time I took her nipple in my mouth. The shivery feel when she clawed at my shoulders, lifting herself so that she pushed just right against me.

The lost sound I made when she pulled away, dropping down. Relief as she yanked at my belt buckle.

The smooth silk of her panties and the weight of her ass in my hands as I lifted her again, carrying her to the bed. A thump as we hit the mattress, and the arch of her back to keep us touching. Her sharp intake of breath as I licked the indentation of her navel.

As I went lower, burying my face into the one place I never thought I'd be, but always hoped. She cried out as I nipped along her lips, nosing through the close-cropped hair.

She moaned low as I took a taste of her—salt and musk exploding across my tongue.

Drunk. I felt drunk and underwater, I was so sunk in this moment. My fingers were steady now as I grabbed her to me, holding her in place so I could explore deeper with my tongue. I'd never felt so fucking greedy for another person.

She reached beneath the waves and pulled me up, yanking me away before I'd had enough.

I would never have enough.

Van pushed over onto my back, guiding me to where she wanted me. I didn't fight it, moving any way she nudged me. Wanting to give her what she wanted.

What she needed, glorying in the knowledge that for once, I was both. Her want and her need.

Van's hands slid over my cock as she rolled a condom on, tearing a groan from me, my whole system shuddering from the brief touch. Then she was sliding down, too slow and somehow too fast, and suddenly I was inside her.

Time…stopped.

Stuttered.

Collapsed in on itself.

She was in my arms now, face buried in my neck, hands clutching my hair. The pure pleasure of her, of us, like this, made me shiver.

"Nessa." Her name came out scratchy. Needy. I *liked* it. Liked that she'd torn me down to base elements.

And she hadn't even *moved* yet.

I wrapped my arms around her, holding her tight. "Oh, gods, Nessa." I kissed her hair and she sucked in a breath.

She arched up and I could see her in the moonlight spilling through the curtains. Her head was thrown back. Pale throat exposed. Eyes closed. Bright tattoos muted to blacks and whites in the low light. Nipples beaded.

Perfect. She was perfect, and the sight of her, like this, would stay with me until I decomposed into the earth.

I clasped her hips as she started to move, the pleasure white-hot as it pulsed through my body.

There wasn't a chance in hell I was going to last like this. I gritted my teeth, trying to at the very least outlast her. There was no slowing her down, all I could do was hold her hips, grinding up into her.

Her fingers slid down.

Down.

Feathered over her clit.

I think I whimpered. I *know* I begged. "Please, Nessa. Oh, gods, please…" I have no idea what I was begging for. I was too far gone.

Van cried out, stilling and arching above me. I rolled my hips, trying desperately to drag her orgasm out as long as I could.

But it was too much, and I lost myself to her. Arms wrapped around her hips, face buried between her breasts, gulping in breaths as my body shuddered.

For a tiny eternity, nothing existed but this. A perfect moment, singular in its completeness, its goodness, that I would tuck between the layered muscles of my heart, making it part of myself. Keeping it there with me always. My heart wouldn't beat without touching the memory of us, like this.

I didn't need to put Nessa there. She'd moved into that space so long ago I couldn't remember a time when she wasn't part thudding beat.

The moment ended and I collapsed back, Van in my arms.

I swear I heard a slow clap coming from the living room and I hoped to fuck they were clapping at the show.

Van shook in my arms as I traced her back, stroked her hair, soothed her like she was a feral creature. Which Van kind of was. Her breathing evened out as I stared at the ceiling. The sweat had cooled on my skin and Van was asleep when words finally coalesced into my head with a whiff of doom to them.

What the fuck did we just do?

CHAPTER ELEVEN

Van

Holy shit.

Holy shit.

Those words were on repeat in my head, somehow having a different meaning every time they appeared.

Holt shit, I'd slept with my best friend. Holy shit, I hadn't meant to do that.

Holy shit, it was awesome.

And finally, holy shit, was this going to be a problem?

Will was fast asleep, snoring softly, sprawled over me like a blanket.

Will wasn't a big spoon. Will wasn't even in the cutlery drawer. Will was a tablecloth, constantly covering me no matter how I moved. I should have hated it.

But I didn't.

I fucking loved it.

I also should have been absolutely terrified. We still hadn't talked things out. When we did, I would be as vulnerable as I could be with another person. Normally that would make me shove my partner out of bed and put him into a cab.

With Will I only pulled him closer. Which, again, should have sent me on a rollercoaster of panic and regret.

Instead all I could do was run my fingers through his hair and wonder when we could do it again.

I will say once more, with feeling, *holy shit.*

I needed to pee. I also needed coffee somewhat desperately. Moving seemed like a bad idea, like I might pop the bubble of peace currently surrounding us. It was the last thing I wanted. No, I wanted to stay here, right in this moment when everything was great and reality was stuck in a long commute.

Eventually the situation became too urgent and I had to ease out from under Will. He mumbled and rolled over, cuddling up with a pillow. After I moved my blanket up over him, I realized that at some point the ferrets had come into the room.

Both of them were sleeping on Will's side of the bed.

I threw on some pajamas, taking a minute prepare myself incase any of the roommates were between me and the coffee.

The kitchen was blessedly empty as I got things ready, and I was seated and enjoying my first cup when Lou and Declan sleepily stumbled into the kitchen. Lou's eyes lit up and Declan snorted.

"Go ahead," he growled, which was a bit of a morning thing and not a reflection of how he was feeling. When your roommate was a werewolf, you got used to interpreting their growls. "You begin the interrogation and all get coffee." He gently nudged Lou forward and went for the french press.

Lou practically skipped over to her chair, sitting across from me. She steepled her fingers, eyes shining with glee. I'm not sure what face I made, but she cackled, pointing a finger at me. "Not so fun on the other side of this, is it?"

I glowered into my coffee. "As Trick is fond of saying, I hate taking my own medicine." I had grilled Lou mercilessly when she'd started sleeping with Declan. I sighed. "Go on."

Lou was tender hearted, and for a second, she wavered. Then Declan put a cup of coffee in front of her, leaning down to nuzzle her temple. "Might as well. It will hurt you to keep it in, and Van can take it."

Lou drew in a breath. "Fort vajayjay has been stormed, the white flag raised." She fanned her fingers out. "He laid siege to your battlements. Boiling oil was poured." She frowned. "That analogy got away from me sat the end there."

"You have danced the forbidden dance." Declan's voice was brimming with dry amusement as he settled into his chair, leaning his elbows onto the table.

"The hankiest of pankies." Lou was getting into it now.

"Sheets were shook," Declan added, sipping his coffee. He snorted. "The walls were shook."

Lou snickered. "The entire house was shook. Asses were definitely tapped." "You're a woman now." Declan pretended to throw confetti, his tone dry. "Huzzah."

Will had said those words verbatim when Lou and Declan had gotten together. Declan hadn't been in the room at the time. I narrowed my eyes at him. "Lou told you." I pointed a finger at her. "Not fair. Anyway, Will said that, not me. So words must be thrown in his face, not mine."

"What words are being thrown in my face?" Will asked with a yawn, scratching his stomach as he walked into the kitchen. He was wearing a pair of pajama shorts that he'd left here and nothing else.

I couldn't look away and I felt the heat of my skin as I blushed beet red. Lou snickered and Declan smiled into his coffee.

"I hate you both," I mumbled.

"You love us," Lou whispered. Then louder to Will, "Declan was repeating some of your earlier wisdom to Van."

Will nodded, fetching a mug. "My wisdom is abundant. Nana has taught me well."

He filled his cup, wandering back over to us. It might have been my imagination, but it seemed like Will hesitated before he took the chair next to me. When I glanced at Declan, he was frowning slightly, like he was trying to puzzle something out. Shifters were more attuned to body language than witches were. They were better at paying attention to it, but also interpreting it.

Declan's frown told me I hadn't imagined that hesitation...and I'd probably missed other cues.

Because he was suddenly standing up, grabbing Lou's cup along with his own. "Come on gorgeous."

Lou frowned at him. "What? We were just—" She stopped, frown deepening. I was hazy on the details, because they didn't talk about it much, but from my own observations, the mating bond that they shared functioned on some kind of psychic level.

I wasn't sure what Declan was sharing now, but Lou got up without protest. "Right. Of course. I forgot." She smiled wanly at us both. "Unless Van needs me to stay? To discuss…that thing?"

Bless my roommate for trying in her extremely unsubtle manner to see if I needed her to stay as some sort of buffer for comfort's sake.

"You can go do that thing," I said, my own voice dry now.

"Okay." Lou got up, somewhat surprised when Declan handed off their coffee mugs to her. He moved to our side of the table, putting arms around both me and Will and squeezing us tight. I got a kiss on the top of my head and so did Will. Then he herded Lou out of the room leaving us in awkward silence.

"Did we just get reassurance?" Will asked.

I finished my cup of coffee, taking a moment to get up and refill my cup. "Welcome to life with an alpha werewolf. Do you need a hug? Are you sleeping enough? You need more leafy greens." I settled back into my chair. "I'm actually surprised he hasn't started packing meals for you, too."

Will laughed softly. "He brings snacks to the shop and he makes sure we all take breaks." "Sounds about right."

That conversation exhausted, it grew quiet. I couldn't think of anything to say. Will seemed to be having the same problem. The silence drew out, uncomfortable. I wasn't used to this. Will and I could always talk and our silences were the comfortable kind.

I was considering which panic move to try—pretending I had an appointment and ushering Will out of the house, or faking my death and starting over in another state—when Will set his empty mug down decisively.

"We didn't get a chance to talk yesterday," he said carefully.

I snorted. "You mean because I was too busy climbing you like a damn tree?"

Will relaxed next to me, looking me full in the face for the first time since he sat down.

His grin was a bit bashful and, well, cute as fuck. He just seemed so happily overcome for a moment. My best friend was *adorable*. How had I missed that?

I sucked in a breath, unsure what to do with this information. Unsure what he wanted me to do with it.

"Yeah," he said. "I guess you did." He rubbed a hand through his hair, still looking a little groggy. "And I liked it." His voice got softer. "I really liked it, Van. But…"

Nothing good came after a "but." Panic gripped me and I strangled my mug, blurting a question before I realized I had one. "Are you breaking up with me?"

Will froze, mouth partially open. He closed it. Brows furrowed. "… Are we dating?"

I had a handful of standard speeches I could use here. "Let's be friends" or "I'm not in a good space to date" and so on. Despite my panic, I couldn't force a single one of them out of my mouth.

This was Will.

So I went with the truth. Anything less seemed like a cheat. "Dating you scares the shit out of me."

He dropped his gaze.

I shrugged one shoulder. "Not dating you seems scarier?" His head jerked up. He hadn't been expecting that. "What?"

Might as well go all in. I let out a slow breath, reaching out to take his hand. "Fucking this up terrifies me, but…." Why was finding the words so hard sometimes? "Last night was…." I tried again, because it wasn't just the sex. That was great, but that wasn't the only thing making me want this. "You are…" I threw up my hands in frustration.

Will rested his elbow on the table, his chin in his hand. A slow smile unfurled on his face. "Sexy? Amazing? Expert cuddler? The best you've ever had? A god among men?"

"Please stop." But I was laughing now, which had been his intention.

He shrugged. "What else am I supposed to do, when you serve 'em up like that, Nessa?" I snorted.

He took my hand, loosely weaving his fingers through mine. "Honesty has always served us well. In that vein—I want this. I want you. More than anything. But I don't want to be an experiment or a dabble. Understand?" He rubbed a tired hand over his face. "I couldn't take it."

"I don't think I could take that either," I said, my voice soft. I hardened it. "But I have rules."

Will rubbed a thumb along the soft part of my palm. "Shoot." "No more dates. I don't share."

"Same."

"Never lie to me. Even if the truth is nasty, I want it."

He nodded, expecting that one. My father lied like he was breathing, giving me a low tolerance for it.

"Don't keep things from me," Will countered. "I'm not saying you can't have your secrets, but if it has to do with us, with how you're doing, don't keep them from me to spare my feelings." That thumb traced deepening circles into my palm. "I'd rather talk it out, help you through it, or at least know what's going on so I don't get blindsided."

I nodded.

"Also, we have to wear matching outfits, like, all the time." "That's a deal breaker."

He thought on this as he pulled my hand until it rested against his chest. "What about special occasions. Like, couple photos and holidays?"

"I think," I said slowly, trying to picture being the kind of person who even *got* couples portraits done. "It would depend a lot on the outfits."

#

We had dinner Monday night with my dad. Juliet drove all of us—that way if we needed a convenient excuse to bolt, we'd claim Savannah needed to go home, and hey, we're carpooling so...

I'm told that some people don't have to plan exit strategies for family dinners. I wondered what that was like. My ferrets chittered at me from inside the carrier that sat on my lap. It was a worried chitter. They could feel how tense I was. I reassured them absently, making a *tsktsk* sound.

Juliet and I were both quiet, staring at our dad's house as the car cooled. Neither of us had moved when she turned the car off, both of us deep in our own heads. Will sat in the back, entertaining Savannah. She looked super cute in a summer print dress covered in smiling strawberries.

We'd all dressed up. You didn't show up scruffy to a dinner at my dad's house. Not if you wanted it to go well. Even that wasn't a guarantee, but showing up in tattered jeans and scuffed shoes would definitely start things off on a bad note.

Will had shaved, slicked back his blond hair, and put on a short sleeved button up, the first button undone. He'd put on dressier, slim fitting shorts that looked good on his long legs. Altogether, was rather swoon-worthy, and I couldn't even enjoy it because I was two seconds from stress vomiting in my father's driveway.

My dad lived in this gorgeous stained wood house that sat on a small lake. The yard and landscaping were immaculate. Like something out of a magazine. It was the kind of place where you could imagine elegant, spontaneous, and yet somehow catered garden parties to break out at any moment.

And I wanted to burn it all down. You know, after I stress vomited all over it.

Savannah started fussing and Will took her out of her carseat. "Just keep in mind, you two. It gets to be too much? We leave." He let Savannah stand on his legs, making faces at her so she'd giggle. "We can come up with a secret signal."

"Like what?" Juliet asked. "Like a code word?"

"I'm thinking bird calls," Will said. "If things get dire, just shriek like an eagle. Flap your arms. Ca-caw! Ca-caw! You know, something birdy."

"Something birdy?" I asked.

"You don't think my dad would notice that?" Juliet asked dryly.

Will scoffed. "It will confuse him. By the time he's figured out what's going on, we'll be long gone."

"Caw! Caw!" Savannah clapped her little hands.

"That's right, Savvy," Will, said, tickling her. "Caw-caw."

My hands clenched around the carrier in my lap. "I really need this."

"I know," Will said gently, sitting Savvy onto his knees and bouncing her a little. "But when the cost feels too high and you want to go, just say the word."

Juliet breathed in deep through her nose, letting it out in a gust. Her knuckles were white on the steering wheel. "Okay. Let's do this."

We unloaded ourselves from the car and walked up the path to the front door. Juliet glanced at me. "Chopin?"

"Piano sonata number two," I said with a nod.

Will glanced between us, a bemused expression on his face as he carried Savvy.

"For a short time, dad decided we needed to learn instruments. I was piano, Juliet the flute," I explained.

"We were moderately terrible," Juliet said.

Will grinned at us like the idea of my sister and I sucking at classical music was the cutest thing ever.

"That sonata is a funeral march." I'd forgotten most of what I'd learned from those long ago lessons, but not that particular song. It was simply to apt on too many occasions.

We knocked. Dad's house wasn't the kind of place you simply walked into. I was always a little surprised he didn't have a butler. Or one of those trapdoors under the welcome mat that would drop you into a pit of angry alligators.

The door opened, revealing a man I'd never seen before. He looked to be a little older than me, probably one of my dad's graduate students. He was neatly dressed, hair trimmed and tidy, in khaki pants and a white oxford style shirt. He looked...neat. The kind of guy you'd want as a financial planner or a study buddy, because he'd be well organized and take good notes.

I had no idea why he was answering my father's door.

He brightened when he saw us, a smile lighting up his face. His eyes caught on Will for a second. His smile barely slipped, but I saw it.

The original wattage returned as he held out his hand. "Hi, you must be Juliet and Vanessa." He shook our hands with a firm grip. Polite. He leaned in to greet Savvy, who was still in Will's arms. She shrunk back a little.

"And you must be Savannah!" His voice was that overly-bright one some people used on children because they thought kids liked it. "I've heard so much about you." He turned to Juliet. "She's beautiful."

"Thank you." Juliet sounded polite, but I knew my sister, and her eyes were wary. She wasn't sure about the guy, either. Was he here willingly, or had my dad blackmailed him like he had us? Could go either way, though my dad was usually more subtle when he tried to manipulate people outside the family.

Will shifted Savvy so he could put his hand out. "Will."

The guy shook it. "Nice to meet you, Will." He sounded almost like he meant it. His expression shifted into a rueful smile. "Sorry, I'm always forgetting to introduce myself. "Tanner Adams." Another smile, this one self depreciating. "And here I am, compounding my rudeness by leaving you on your own doorstep. Please, come in." He stepped back and waved us in.

None of us told him we didn't consider it our doorstep.

It had been years since I walked into my dad's house. It hadn't changed too much. Most of the house was as carefully styled inside as it was outside. He'd picked out the art on his walls himself, and then had a professional decorator come in to create the rest of the aesthetic around them.

It reminded me of a museum—nice to look at, but a lot of delicate, breakable things and a white sectional couch we weren't allowed to sit on. With the exception of his office, the house was as immaculate as the landscaping—the product of good house cleaners. I wasn't sure my dad even knew how to clean a toilet. The entire house was a message and that message was, "the owner of this house is an intelligent, educated, well-off man."

Not all arcanists had money. Like any job in academia, my dad's base pay was pretty low, even though he was tenured. He got a stipend for working on the Uncanny Tribunal Committee as well, but the majority of his wealth came from some of the spells he'd pioneered and sold. My father may be a bastard, but there was no arguing that he was a talented bastard.

Tanner led us out onto the back patio where a glass table waited, along with a few plates of hors d'oeuvres. A bar car sat in the shade, a bucket of ice sitting on top, chilling a few bottles of white wines. Tanner continued to play host, clapping his hands together as he got to the bar cart. "Your dad is finishing up a conference call, but should be with us shortly. In the mean time, can I get anyone a drink?"

He examined the bar cart. "We've got some sauvignon blanc, a semi-sweet riesling, a few craft brews, and I believe there's a pitcher of sangria in the fridge if that strikes your fancy." He grinned at us, a wide flashing of teeth.

Juliet had been digging through the small diaper bag she'd brought for Savvy, taking out a water bottle for her. Tanner saw it, and managed an expression of charming chagrin. I was starting to wonder if he practiced his facial expressions in the mirror.

"I guess we don't have a lot to offer Savannah, do we?" He laughed. "Good thing you're prepared." He pulled one of the bottles out of the ice, shaking his head. "Singles guys, I guess. We can't always be counted on to think of these things."

Juliet looked like she was biting her tongue to not point out that, as the father of two children and a man who had been suddenly pushing hard to see his grandchild, her father absolutely should have thought of these things. Will's face was carefully blank, and I suddenly knew that if Will were hosting us, he would have thought of Savvy, even though like Tanner, he was single and childless. Didn't keep him from being thoughtful.

And I guess he wasn't single anymore. He held Savvy protectively, eyes hard on Tanner. I didn't think the poor guy was scoring any more points with Will than he was with us.

"Water is fine for Savvy," Juliet said politely. "But I would love a glass of the Riesling." Tanner nodded, immediately grabbing that bottle and fetching a glass.

"I would love one of the beers," Will said, glancing at me. "Darling?" His mouth twitched like he was trying not to laugh.

Darling, huh? Tanner caught the endearment and perked up a little. Happy that Will wasn't here with Juliet?

"Water, please." I wanted to be clear headed for the assessment. I set the ferret's carrier in the shade for now, offering them a few pieces of cheese and meat from the table as a snack and making sure their water bottle was filled. They would tell me if they got too hot, but right now they were happily snacking.

Tanner finished putting together our drinks and we all took seats around the table except for Will, who put himself on Savvy duty, chasing her around the porch. My father's house wasn't exactly child proof.

A sudden stab of anxiety hit me, and it took a lot of energy to not eagle shriek at Will so he'd sweep me out of here. And my dad hadn't even joined us yet. Ugh. I sipped my drink and tried to breath evenly.

As if feeling my panic, Will looked up and saw me watching him. He winked at me and suddenly I felt better.

We made small talk for a mew minutes, Tanner and Juliet doing most of the talking. Tanner would occasionally make an effort to draw me into the conversation, but I was too nervous to really maintain it. He basically ignored Will.

After about twenty minutes, my father came sweeping out onto the deck, dressed casually in a polo shirt and boating shorts. It looked like he was a few steps away from going out in his yacht. As far as I'm aware, my father doesn't own any sort of seagoing vessels beyond a kayak for the lake.

"Tanner, thank you for handling our guests for me." He smiled, ever the gracious host.

Juliet shot me a look. Our father smiling was never a good sign. He was entirely too happy about something, and it wasn't because he was reconnecting with his children. My tension went up a notch. The thing about being around my father was that even when he wasn't doing anything actively terrible, you were still waiting for him to do so at any minute. Being constantly alert like that was exhausting.

Will swooped up Savvy, bringing her to the table with him, easily juggling his bottle of beer at the same time. He took the chair next to me, taking a moment to hand Savvy a piece of pineapple from the fruit platter to chew on before dropping a hand casually onto my thigh, palm up. I clutched it reflexively.

Will squeezed. *I'm here.*

I took a deep breath and dropped my shoulders.

"Tanner is my TA and mentee at the college." My father poured himself a glass of wine. "He'll be administering your test today, Vanessa, so I can focus fully on my assessment."

Now I was torn. On one hand, it was great to have someone else there that I could appeal to if my dad tried to renege on his deal. But it also meant that there was someone there to witness the whole debacle. Tanner had to be wondering why I hadn't got my certificate ages ago. Why I wasn't already in college.

Or maybe he wasn't wondering at all. My dad often played fast and loose with the truth, altering facts and history until it fit his vision of the world. What had he told Tanner?

I mentally set that aside. Tanner was a stranger and I shouldn't care what he thought. It didn't matter what my dad or his students said about me at the college, what kind of gossip they passed along, as long as I got my certificate and was able to move on from this.

I gritted my teeth into a smile. "Wonderful. Thanks, Tanner."

Tanner beamed at me. "Of course! I'm happy to help." That look of charming chagrin came back to his face. "I've already learned so much from Arcanist Woodbridge. It's nice to feel like I'm giving a little back."

Will made a choking sound, grabbing for his water. "Excuse me."

Apparently he thought Tanner was laying it on a bit thick as well. Kissing ass worked for my father, though, so I didn't blame him too much for that.

Dinner had been left by my father's chef, because my dad couldn't so much as pour a bowl of cereal for himself. There was a gazpacho soup, followed by salmon and crispy fingerling potatoes. Dessert was a cheese plate because my dad doesn't do sugar beyond things like fruit.

I'm sure it was all delicious, but I can't say that I tasted any of it. Tanner and my dad mostly talked to Juliet. Eventually they seemed to realize that Will and I were also there, and turned the conversation on us.

"So, Will," Tanner said, putting a few slices of fruit and cheese onto his plate. "What do you do?"

"I'm an arcane piercer," Will said, taking the crayons and notepad Juliet had dug out of her bag for Savvy. Small children and sitting still for a leisurely dinner aren't a good mix, but Savvy was doing amazing.

Tanner perked up a little. "Oh? That's fascinating. I've actually read some papers on—" "Is that how you met?" My dad interrupted Tanner to ask me, his gaze searching like he

might be able to discern an illicit piercing or something just from looking. "No," I said, not elaborating.

"We met at the university," Will said, either not caring about the undercurrents of the conversation or not catching them. He was helping Savvy draw a bunny. "My Nana works at the library."

Will had already mentioned this to my father the last time we'd seen him, but I don't think he'd been paying to Will at the time. To him, Will wasn't important and therefore most of what came out of his mouth had probably sounded like white noise.

"Oh?" My dad perked up—Will had his attention now. If he was connected to the university, even tangentially, he'd basically just become a real person in my father's eyes. Which was … well, not always great.

"Tell me a little bit about—" My dad started to say, but in my panic to distract his attention away from Will I blurted out the first thing I could think of.

"So, about my test?" I kept my face carefully neutral to hid my wince. My father hated being interrupted.

He scowled, his lips firming.

Tanner blinked, then blushed charmingly. "Of course! How thoughtless of me. I was so caught up in the delicious meal and conversation that I forgot what I'm actually here for." He set his napkin on the table. "You've been very patient, Vanessa. I would have broken down into a panic sweat by now!"

Oh, if only he knew how sweaty my palm was in Will's hand.

I gave him a tight-lipped smile. "I'm sorry if I'm rushing you, but you're right, I am anxious to get the test done."

He stood up, excusing himself from the table. "Alright then. Grab your familiars and let's retire to the dining room."

I gave Will's hand one last squeeze, catching Juliet's encouraging smile from across the table. I could do this. I *would* do this. Letting that thought bolster my confidence, I grabbed the ferrets' carrier and followed Tanner into my father's house.

CHAPTER TWELVE

???

The expansive oak table in my father's dining room was large enough for dinner parties. The closest thing he had to small table for intimate dinners was the one we'd just left. The windows were open, letting in a fresh breeze, tempting me to crawl out a window and leg it to a better place. Like to a pit full of fire ants, or to the DMV on a really busy day. Anywhere but here.

Tanner flicked on the lights, setting the antique chandelier ablaze. The crystals that dangled from it left rainbow prisms on the cream colored walls. A touch of whimsy in a house that wouldn't welcome it.

Last time I'd been in here, there had been a vase of fresh flowers on the table, but that had been removed in favor of papers and various objects Tanner had prepared for my first test. I pulled out one of the chairs, taking a seat.

He slid a few stapled pieces of paper in front of me. "First, a little bureaucracy. Since we're doing these tests in the field, you'll need to sign a waiver."

"A waiver?"

He pulled a few more out of a folder. "It's nothing to worry about—it's standard practice at the university. You and anyone taking part in the tests will be coming in contact with magic created by me and arcanist Woodbridge. The waiver ensures that you won't take legal action against us for anything stemming from that."

I started scanning through the paperwork.

"I've highlighted the spots where you'll need to sign and initial. You'll need volunteers for some of the tests—I assume Will and your sister will be volunteering for that?"

"Probably?" I frowned up at him. "I didn't think to ask."

He smiled at me. "That's okay—I'll take these to them while you look those over." Tanner left, and I spent the next few minutes reading through the waiver.

The paper seemed official—the university logo was at the top—and nothing jumped out at me. Not that I knew a lot about waivers. I could say no, take it to a lawyer…and delay my tests even further. My father was an ass, but I didn't think he'd stoop to forging official university paperwork. I signed and initialed the papers as Tanner came back into the room.

"Perfect timing," he said, scooping up the paperwork. "Ready to get going?" Waiting wasn't going to make me any less nervous, so I nodded.

"Excellent. I thought we'd do basic magic theory first," he said, his voice very different from the one outside. That had been dinner party Tanner. This was future professor Tanner. It wasn't a bad change, just less playful and more business. "So there's the written part where you have to identify basic symbols, terms, and then translating an invocation."

I raised a hand like we were in class, but didn't wait for him to call on me. "Does that mean you want to know what it says, or what the spell does?"

"Both," Tanner said, smiling. "After that, we'll test your familiars. Arcanist Woodbridge placed three minorly hexed objects inside the house. You'll need to use your familiars to both find, retrieve, and deactivate them. I promise there's nothing in the hex that could harm the ferrets, though I will warn that your father made them."

I wrinkled my nose in irritation. "Which means they will bite back at me if I do it wrong."

Tanner nodded. "He finds it to be an effective teaching method." Oh, I'm sure he did. I bet they were nasty little hexes, too.

"Finally, assuming you break those hexes, I'd like you to re-hex the objects with hexes of your choice. I'll be grading them on your use of variety, creativity, as well as your basic construction ability."

So I would be marked down if I used the same hex more than once, if I used the super basic hexes, and if I built them well or poorly. "Got it."

"As per your request, I discussed each test and my approach with another arcanist to make sure it met the testing standards and covered the topics that it should." He said the words easily, giving no indication that me asking for that was strange.

It didn't escape me that it sounded like he was doing a lot of the work here. I wasn't surprised. "Anything else?"

"Yes," Tanner said, clicking through his phone. "The test will of course be timed. You have thirty minutes for each section. If you finish one section early, you can use that time as additional time in other sections. One thing we assess is time management and whether you can prioritize spell work well."

He slid over several sheets of paper stapled together, face down, before passing me two sharpened pencils. "I'll start the timer as soon as you flip over the sheet."

I breathed deep, filling my lungs and then let it out slowly. This made Tanner smile slightly. "Good luck, Vanessa."

He even sounded like he meant it. Maybe I'd been too hard on Tanner. I flipped over the paper and he clicked the timer.

Before I even looked at it, I got up from my seat and went to release Kodo and Podo. I took a second to hold them close, rubbing my nose over their little heads. Familiars weren't robots for us to control, but partners in their own way. They deserved a second of my precious testing time to be acknowledged as such.

Kodo and Podo were linked to me through magic. My roommate Lou had bound them to me with the oversight of her mentor and secondary mother, Ami Larsen. Though we were magically linked at all times, it was in a passive, quiet way. They didn't get my every thought and vice versa. I respected their privacy and they… well, they were shit at respecting mine, so I had a nice mental wall up with a big brass knocker for them to bang when they needed to tell me something.

You know, metaphorically speaking. I threw that door open wide now, letting them know what I wanted them to do while I was taking the written exam. I needed them to sniff out the hexed objects. Tanner had said I could do the test in whatever order I liked, and it would save time if the ferrets were able to look for the objects while I was otherwise occupied with symbols.

Familiars were helpful in lots of ways—one of those was having a sensitivity to magic.

They could sense it much better than I could. Kodo and Podo were great familiars—smart, curious, and able to get just about anywhere. You had to be *really* clear about what you wanted, though, because they could get distracted by cool shiny things. Or food. Or anything that made them curious, which was most of the world.

The familiar bond also made them a lot smarter than regular ferrets though, which is helpful. *Kodo—I want you to go high, okay? You search the upper half of the room.*

Kodo squeaked, excited. *Curtains?*

That was his way of asking me if there was anything I didn't want him to climb or get into. I was tempted to tell him to destroy whatever he wanted, but I figured that would only count against me.

Carefully, I said. *Leave it nice, like you would for Declan, okay?* This was something the ferrets understood. Declan kept things clean and tidy—we couldn't stop him. It was part of his alpha werewolf behavior. We were his pack and he wanted us to be well taken care of, which in his mind translated to making us meals and scrubbing our floors, amongst other things.

Sometimes the ferrets helped.

Got it, boss! This came from both of them. I had no idea where they got the "boss" from.

That was a new thing.

Podo, you stick to the ground. We're looking for three objects. Do not *try to move, touch or deactivate them. Just locate them. Got it?*

They chirruped at me happily and I set them down gently with the warning to be careful. They were more important to me than this stupid test, which made them hop with joy. They knew how significant this test was to me, after all.

Ferrets dispatched, I regained my seat and went back to the to the written test. I scanned the first sheet of identifications. They were all basic symbols, runes, and whatnot—the kind of general knowledge every witch knows by age twelve, usually. I was tempted to zoom through it, but I knew better. I examined each one carefully, looking for any detail that might change the meaning.

I was rewarded two thirds of the way through the page when I saw that the figure for dawn had been inverted, which changed the meaning. It was one of those symbols where the top and bottom were almost identical, except for one squiggly half line at the pinnacle. When I was a kid it was an inversion that tripped me up frequently.

A heavy feeling settled in my gut. This wasn't a general test he'd had lying about in his office. No, I was pretty sure my dad had built this test with me in mind. I'd already known I needed to be careful, but now I knew to look out for anything that had been a weak spot of mine. My dad knew most of them.

For a second, my confidence bolted for the hills. I couldn't do this. The test, every part of it, would specifically poke at my weak spots. I was being set up to fail. I—.

I would not let my father or myself psych myself out.

Freaking out wouldn't help. I closed my eyes for a second and breathed. Through the open windows I caught a snatch of conversation. I couldn't make out the words, more tones, but I recognized Juliet's voice and Will's answering response.

It reminded me that I wasn't alone. I had the support of my sister and Will. If I got up right now, threw the test at my father, and walked out, they would be right behind me. When I got home, Declan would make me cookies and Trick would make me laugh. Lou would hug me and tell me she was proud of me. If Jim was over, he would hug me as soon as Lou was done and offer to beat up anyone who had wronged me.

I opened up my eyes, wrote my answer, and moved on to the next question. Okay, so my father knew my weaknesses and was targeting them. That was fine. Because of the way he taught me, I'd been well versed in what I didn't excel at. My dad wouldn't leave a failing alone.

He'd pick at it incessantly. Which meant I knew what to look for and what stuff to study up on for the next test.

With renewed confidence, I zipped through the written part of the test. After I finished the identifications I moved onto the translation part. It was a variation of a simple spell, the kind a lot of witches would use daily without thought. Which meant I double checked my translation of the invocation to make sure I wasn't missing anything.

It was a tricky bugger that literally translated to trying to contain a typhoon, something no witch in their right mind would try to do, especially on their own. That was a major working that you'd need several covens to even try to attempt, and even then, it would be dicey prospect.

However, that wasn't what this invocation was actually meant to do. What it actually did was stir liquid, like the coffee in your cup or the potion in your cauldron widdershins. It was an overly complicated invocation that I would never use but suited my father's tastes to a T. There were much simpler, less impressive ways to stir liquid. Like using a spoon, for example.

I took a moment to read back over my test, double checking my answers. They looked right to me and I was afraid if I stared at them any longer, I'd start second guessing myself. I slid it away from me and got up. It was time to go after my familiars.

Kodo had found the first object—my father had hexed one of Juliet's awards that was up on display. It was made of blue glass, which held the hex fairly well. In tastefully etched lettering it thanked my sister for her fundraising efforts for the foundation's cause. I frowned at the award, surprised my father had it on display. I knew that when he threw me out, he'd taken down anything of mine. In less than a day, it was like I didn't exist.

Juliet had thought it was really creepy. I'd assumed he'd done the same for her, but here was the award. Well, whatever. I showed it to Tanner to let him know that we'd found the first item.

Tanner examined the object with a smile while I found something to pick it up with. A lot of hexes were activated by touch. I grabbed one of the hand towels from the bathroom and placed it on the table where

I'd taken my test. I'd gather all three objects, then identify and dismantle the hexes.

Podo found the second one—Juliet's high school year book, which was tucked up on a shelf. That was weirder than the award, because it was the only yearbook on the shelf. Both ferrets identified the third— this time a framed certificate hung up on the wall. Juliet had been part of the Young Arcanist's Guild in high school—one of those clubs kids join to help with college acceptance. This one had obviously been for teens hoping to major in Arcane Sciences, my father's field of expertise.

Juliet had joined YAG to make dad happy, or at least to placate him. She'd even started out majoring in Arcane Sciences, but her heart was never in it. You can help people as an arcanist, sure, but it's very hands off. Juliet's current field, as well as my hopeful profession, was more in the trenches kind of work. Hard, but fulfilling. You got to really see how your work helped people.

I used the towel to grasp the frame, taking it off the wall, adding it to the pile on the table.

I scooped up Kodo and Podo, putting them close to the objects and telling them to stay put, though I scratched their heads to let them know how proud I was of them for finding all three.

It was clear that my dad's objects had a theme, and that theme was, "Isn't my daughter Juliet amazing?" I'm sure my dad saw it as both an easy way to shove Juliet's accomplishments into Tanner's face as well as a way to point out my shortcomings. The second part failed, though, because I agreed with my dad on this one point—Juliet was amazing.

Tanner examined the YAG certificate, his eyebrows going up. "Juliet was awarded the Quintessence?"

"Twice." If anything could show you how arcanists thought of themselves, it would be the fact that they named an award the quintessence, which means a perfect embodiment of something. The fact that my sister got the award twice and didn't go into that field, oh it would be the bitterest of fruits to my dad.

At the same time, he must have hated it. He'd only been awarded the Quintessence once when he was a YAG, and while my dad wanted us to achieve, he didn't want us to surpass him.

Tanner gave an appreciative whistle.

I had a sinking feeling about the hexes attached to the objects. If my father had chosen things intended to highlight Juliet's achievements, the hexes would be built to make me look terrible.

This could actually work in my favor. Hexes had a wide range, but they did fall into groups. I could calibrate my diagnostic spell to search for those groups first, which would save me a ton of time. Normally, this was pretty risky because if I guessed wrong, I'd wasted time and magical energy on something that wasn't useful.

I was confident enough in my father's motives to take the risk.

I dropped down into a squat so my eyes were on the same level as the objects. Kodo and Podo climbed onto my shoulders without being asked, preparing themselves for the spell. We closed our eyes and I carefully combined our magics into a ball before I mentally rolled it at the objects, almost like I was bowling.

The ball of magic blew through them and I snapped it back to me like a yoyo before it fell over the edge of the table. It was my own little diagnostic spell and I was pretty proud of it.

I reached out, clasping it in my hands, smiling because my gamble paid off. The yearbook hex was one called Dutiful Daughter. If I triggered that hex, I would feel compelled to be more, you guessed it, *dutiful*. Basically, I would feel inclined to be more like my father wanted me to be—dress a certain way, act a certain way, and so on.

It was a nasty little thing and one that most people avoided because the optics on it weren't great. If people realized you hexed your kid with that, well, like I said, it doesn't look good. And no, there was no specific version for sons. It was the same hex, no matter the gender of your child, or your actual relationship to the person you used it on.

My dad had used it on us when we were little and just seeing it made me feel gross inside. I pointed at the yearbook for Tanner's sake. "Dutiful daughter."

Tanner made a note in his notebook, his expression neutral. I wasted a second wondering what he thought about all of the hexes my father picked, what he thought about me. Then I set that idea very carefully aside. It didn't matter what Tanner thought.

I hovered my hands close to the yearbook, close but not quite touching. I didn't want to accidentally trigger the hex. Hexes don't all look the same to the magical eye. Dutiful Daughter was like a sticky web, covering the object, but also doing its best to stick to you as you unraveled it. The trick was to coat your hands with your own magic first, like gloves, but leave a gap between your skin and the gloves, so that even if the hex attaches, you can just shed the gloves and be okay.

I dismantled the hex pretty quickly and set it aside. Next up was the YAG certificate. "Underachiever's Umbrage."

Again, Tanner nodded and made a notation in his book. I was focused now, not really paying attention to his reactions anymore.

Underachiever's Umbrage was like a gooey sludge, the hex meant to "motivate" underachievers. How? Depended on the concentration of the hex. Sometimes it just made you feel shame whenever you weren't doing something productive. On the more intense end, you might have a feeling of electrical shocks along your skin.

Not painful, per se, more…it's more that you can't relax. Can't settle. Again, a hex I was well versed in. Getting this one off was a bit trickier. Kodo and Podo left my shoulders, bouncing over to the framed certificate.

Are you sure? The hex will affect you until I undo it.

Kodo chirruped at me in irritation. They knew what they were getting into and this was the fastest way.

If you're sure, I said, holding up my hands.

The ferrets sat on their hind legs, lifting one side of the frame until it was at an angle.

That way I could fashion my magic into an edge, sliding the goo off. They didn't make a noise, their usual mischievous faces serious, but their skin twitched occasionally, showing me where the hex was biting at them. A wave of anger swept through me. This whole stupid thing wasn't even necessary. My father could have easily signed off, and now my familiars were getting hurt.

I swept the hex off with too much force, almost hurling it at my father's wall. The ferrets made chiding noises.

We've got this, boss! Kodo reminded me. *We're tough.* I know, I said, *but you shouldn't have too.*

Podo sniffed. *We're a team. We'll deal with bullshit as a team, too.*

I will be shitting into his shoes before we leave, Kodo said, his head held high. *If it makes you feel better, boss.*

I really was the luckiest of witches to have such good familiars.

I'm sure my tone was irritated when I identified the last hex to Tanner. "Recipient's Regret." Arcanist's loved their alliteration. Compared to the other two, this one seemed more mild—you touched the object and it made you aware of your regrets. People loved to bury things that upset them instead of processing those things. Regrets can be a really useful learning tool.

I regretted ever coming here, for example.

Recipient's Regret would make a useful tool in therapy as long as you had the person's consent. The problem with the hex was when the hexer keyed it to specific things that *they* wanted you to regret. If Juliet touched this, she would probably regret changing her major or even having her daughter, depending on what upset our father more.

I had a distinct feeling that if I touched it, I would regret being born. The ferrets grabbed the award easily, nosing along through the hex. Recipient's Regret was a misty thing, with a dull, pulsing heart. The ferrets would dig a hole into the mist so I could stab a stiletto of my magic into the heart of it, dissolving the hex.

I didn't have to worry about them touching this one, at least. Kodo and Podo didn't really regret the way that humans do. To them the past was done and it didn't make sense to fret about it. The only regret they really understood was not convincing Declan to give them a second piece of bacon for breakfast. I envied them a little.

How nice it must be, to not live swimming in regret all the time. Maybe I could take a page from my little friends and live they way they did.

You should, boss. Kodo sneezed, the dissolving hex getting into his nostrils.

Yes, Podo chimed in. *It's okay to be sad about the lost bacon, but only in a way that helps you plan to steal* more *bacon in the future.*

Kodo sneezed again before hopping over to me and away from the hex. *There's really no other way to live.*

Not everything is as simple or as pure as bacon, I told them with affection.

No, Podo said, his voice thoughtful. *Sometimes its as complicated as chicken livers, but still worth it.*

CHAPTER THIRTEEN

??? Will

It was taking all of my energy to not punch Arcanist Woodbridge in his smug face. I didn't consider myself a particularly violent person. I'm more of a "hug it out" or "fuck off, then" kind of person.

But I was ready to make an exception for Vanessa and Juliet's father. What an absolute shit gibbon.

Juliet, at least, seemed to be handling their discussion okay. Woodbridge had essentially dismissed me from the start, which I was grateful for. I was keeping a side eye on Juliet, though, from where I was standing, rocking a sleepy Savannah. Savvy had her arms around my neck, her head resting on my shoulder. Eyes drooping, but not quite out yet. Her mother's eyes, however, were starting to look strained around the edges. Juliet was hitting her limit with her father.

Frankly, I was even more in awe of her and Van now than I'd been before I came over because I'd hit my limit with the man about ten seconds after he opened his mouth.

For someone who had made a lot of fuss about meeting his granddaughter, Woodbridge had barely glanced at Savannah. What was his angle, here? Woodbridge always had an ulterior motive, but I couldn't quite figure out what it was. I didn't think it was reconnecting with his family, though. Oh, he would probably be pleased as punch if Juliet came back into the fold, but that wouldn't be enough for him to go through all of this effort. I mean, I thought his daughters were worth it, obviously, but the sad thing about Elliot Woodbridge was he had no idea what riches he was missing.

It was enough to almost make me pity him. *Almost.*

Van swept out through the sliding doors then, and my heart performed a little lurch. I wasn't sure I would ever move past that feeling, that moment when I saw her and it was like reality took a hitching breath.

And every time it happened, I wanted to go to her and kiss her, just to tell the universe that I understood exactly how wonderful this person was, what a fucking gift she was to existence.

With a small shock, I realized that I could do that. I could step right over and kiss Van.

She was putting her ferrets into their carrier and as she straightened up I leaned in and kissed her cheek. The kiss itself was fast, but I lingered a moment, breathing her in. "Everything okay?" I asked softly.

"Of course." Van smiled brightly, but it didn't reach her eyes. No, those looked as pinched and Juliet's. Time to go, then.

I hummed at her thoughtfully before asking, "Ka-kaw ka-kaw?" A grateful expression flitted across her face. "Ka-kaw Ka-kaw."

She was ready to go, and probably had been since we got to this awful place.

Tanner came out, all smiles. "Passed with first test with flying colors, but what else could I expect from a Woodbridge?"

Vanessa's answering smile was brittle, despite Juliet's delighted hug.

"Naturally," Woodbridge said, though he didn't seem entirely pleased. He didn't really seem anything.

Tanner took out his phone, flipping through a few screens. "While we're all here, we should pick a day for the second test."

Scheduling commenced, everyone deciding on Thursday night, which was three days from now. After that, quick goodbyes were given and we all escaped out to the car. I've never been happier to see a vehicle.

Tanner trotted out after us, calling for Juliet. She frowned. "What does he want?"

I thought it was fairly obvious and said so. "Your number. Want me to tell him to piss off?"

Juliet shook her head. "No, I'll deal with him." She handed her daughter off to Van, who strapped her into her carseat.

Then we climbed into the car and waited, Van watching the interaction between Tanner and Juliet like a hawk.

I gave Savvy my hand to hold as I leaned forward, resting my chin on Van's shoulder. "You're making an unhappy face."

"It's just taking her an awful long time to tell him no."

"Maybe she likes him." I couldn't see it. Tanner was an okay guy, I guess, but didn't really seem to light Juliet's fire.

"My sister wouldn't go near a father approved man with a ten foot pole and bear repellent."

Which made sense, honestly.

After a few minutes, Juliet got into the driver's seat. Tanner was still out front, but for a man who was just turned down, he seemed pretty happy. He waved goodbye to us and went back into the house.

"What did he want?" Van asked. Juliet flushed. "Dinner."

Van's frown deepened. "To which you said…"

Juliet shrugged, clicking her seatbelt. "It's just dinner." She backed up, turning the car around to leave.

"You said *yes*?!?" Van's voice was a screech at the end.

Juliet huffed out a breath. "It's not a big deal, Van. He seems nice, and it didn't seem fair to penalize him just because he's dad's graduate assistant."

The face Van made said she thought it was fair to do exactly that, but didn't argue. "Ooookay," she said, slowly. "If that's what you want."

"It would be nice to have dinner with another adult," Juliet said. "Savvy's great, but…" She sighed.

"It's fine," Van said, her tone softening. "I'm sure we can babysit. Go and enjoy yourself."

"Thanks, Sis." Juliet flashed a smile at her.

Van had sounded completely supportive, but the eyes that met mine in the rearview mirror were troubled.

We didn't talk much on the way home, all of us drained by the evening. As soon as we got to the house, Juliet split off, carry a sleeping Savvy to her bed. Normally, I would follow Van automatically into the house, but suddenly…I wasn't sure. Were the rules still the same? I shoved my hands into my pockets, pausing on the threshold.

Van's brow furrowed. "You're not coming in?"

I shrugged a shoulder. "I wasn't sure what you wanted. Do you…" Fuck, why was this suddenly so awkward? "Do you want me to stay?"

Van searched my face for a moment, her mouth puckered. Then she nodded. Tension poured out of me in a rush. I grinned at her. "Then I stay."

When we got into the house, everything was quiet. Dammit's cage was empty, so I assumed Trick was out. Declan and Lou were either sleeping or out as well. It was weird having the house to ourselves—that rarely happened with so many roommates.

"What do you want to do?" I asked, toeing off my shoes.

"I want to pajama," Van said opening the carrier so the ferrets could bound onto the floor. "Then I want to cocoon into my blankets and watch something fun."

"Sounds like a plan."

We went back to her room. Once inside, Van hesitated for only a second before she stripped out of her clothes and pulled on her pajama tank and shorts. It seemed like I wasn't the only one getting used to the new aspects of our relationship.

I had pajama pants somewhere in Van's room, but I usually slept in my boxers at her place. Though I guess I didn't have to do that anymore if I didn't want to. At home I slept naked. Still, it seemed like she'd hit her limits tonight and I didn't want to shove new things at her to process or think about. Instead I stripped down to my boxers, crawled onto her bed, slid under the comforter, and held it up for her so she could join me.

Van had set up her laptop on the nightstand, angling it so we could both see. I let her pick the movie—she was the one that needed comforting. I snuggled in, thinking of nothing but holding her for the night.

Honestly, wasn't that enough? I'd been dreaming of this—along with other, filthier, versions—for how many years?

And for the first half an hour, cuddling was plenty. Nothing much better than a warm, plaint, Van in my arms.

I wasn't quite sure when the vibe changed—maybe when stretched against me, her arms above her head, or maybe I'd just marinated in her warmth, her scent, for long enough the inevitable happened. Whatever it was, Van turned in my arms, her face tipped up to mine.

I rubbed a thumb along her jaw, tracing the face I knew as well as my own. "You sure?" "Yes."

"Because we can just do this." And I meant it. "Today was difficult for you, I know it was."

"Yeah," she said, brushing her fingers along the back of my neck. It made me shiver. "And I want to stop thinking about it."

Well, that I could help with. I kissed her, a deep, slow, savoring kind of kiss, my hands drifting over her face, her neck, her back. I felt her soft touch blazing along paths down my shoulders, one hand fisting in the short hair at the back of my head.

Like the first time, it seemed like we went from totally fine to *holy shit* between one second and the next.

Our first time had been almost frenzied. We'd fallen on each other like creatures half- starved, which honestly, I think we were. I mean, would I ever not be starved for this woman? I didn't think so. I couldn't imagine a time when I would feel I'd had enough of her.

But tonight was different. The intensity was there, but the pacing different. Slow. Deliberate. Each heady kiss measured, almost drugging. I left her pajamas on, pushing the material aside as I saw fit, stealing momentary brushes against her warm skin with fingers, lips, teeth. I was almost painfully hard, but enjoying the slow torture.

Van didn't agree, letting out a frustrated huff as she rolled me onto my back, straddling me so she could yank off her tank top, revealing perfect breasts. Or at least, perfect to me, because they were Van's.

I'd seen an abundance of breasts in my life—it was literally part of my job—and sometimes a seemingly infinite amount of nipples. It never ceased to amaze me the sheer variety of shape, texture, size, and color breasts could come in.

If you followed Plato's theory of forms, you would know that there was an abstract, unchanging ideal *idea* of breasts. The perfect set that all breasts were trying to be. In general, I thought that was bullshit. The human body was beautiful in its unmitigated variety.

But if push came to shove, in my mind, Van's breasts would be that ideal, that perfect form, no matter how they looked, by simply being hers.

"Are you going to stare, or are you going to touch?" In the low light coming off the laptop screen, Van seemed both annoyed and amused.

"I would like to do both," I said, my voice hoarse, my hands squeezing her hips. I really hoped that at some point the novelty of seeing Van naked would wear off at least to the point that her being half naked didn't make me me feel like I was going to blow my load before she even touched me.

Van huffed, leaning back. "And yet—"

I didn't let her get any further. Instead I sat up, jerked her forward so she was pushing down right where I wanted her, and sucked her nipple into my mouth.

Her breath hitched as she arched into my touch, her fingers digging into my shoulders. I took my time, again savoring, and it wasn't long until Van was fidgeting in my grasp. Rubbing herself against me. Digging at my shoulders.

"Am I not going fast enough for you, gorgeous?" I couldn't keep the laugh out of my voice.

"No, you're not." She buried her face into my neck. "I need you, Will. Now."

My chest tightened at her words and I swear part of me fucking swooned. It was a potent thing, being needed by Vanessa Woodbridge.

I smoothed a hand down her spine. "How do you need me, Nessa?"

I thought maybe she would keep talking into my neck. It can be difficult, telling your partner what you want. But Nessa surprised me by sitting up and locking her eyes on mine.

"I want it hard," she said. "Get me out of my head, okay?"

That I could do. I kissed her, pulling her tight against my body, before rolling us over so she was on her back. I sat up, grabbing her pajama shorts and sliding them off. With one knuckle, I brushed against her folds, trying to gauge how ready she was. I couldn't help teasing her with my fingers. "Fuck, you're wet."

She whimpered, her back bowing off the mattress.

I got up and got rid of my boxers, heaving in calming breaths, trying to steady myself as I tore open the condom package and rolled it on. If I barreled forward as it was, this was going to be over, fast. Vanessa watching me the whole time wasn't helping. Every movement. Every breath, her eyes hot.

I couldn't help stroking myself once or twice, just for her.

When my heartbeat was only a mild thunder again in my veins, I climbed back on the mattress. With careful deliberation, I arranged her on the bed. Hands on the headboard, back to me. I palmed her ass before nudging her legs apart with my knees. Her breath sawed out of her. I slid my arms around her waist, one hand steadying her while the other slid down, brushing over her clit, playing with her.

I kissed her shoulder, brushing my lips up to her ear. "This okay?" Goosebumps broke out over her skin as she nodded frantically.

I couldn't help the lazy grin at her reaction, how keyed up she was. Knowing that I wasn't alone in my desperation. And yet, I still wanted to mess with her, just a little.

"I'm going to need to hear you say it, gorgeous."

"Gods damn it, Will," She growled. "You know what I want."

I hummed, taking my fingers away from her clit so I could run them down her spine. I loved touching every part of this woman. "Minds change. Wants shift. Tell me, Nessa. Tell me what you want."

She growled again, frustrated, but when I palmed her breast, her nipples were hard little points. Nessa *liked* me being a little bossy.

I nosed behind her ear, resting my hands on her hips, my cock resting flush against her. "Do you want me, Nessa? Like this?"

She sucked in a breath.

I kissed her ear, loving that she shuddered when I spoke. Did my Nessa like dirty talk, or just my voice? Both? Only time would tell, but gods *damned* I was enjoying myself. "I need to hear it, love. I want to hear it. Do you want me to fuck you, Nessa, like this?" I nuzzled the back of her neck. "Do you want me to make you scream?"

"*Yes*," she said, the words a hiss pushed through gritted teeth.

I kissed her neck, smiling into her shoulder, one hand smoothing down the curve of her stomach until I could finger her again. "Good girl," I said, rubbing tight, gentle circles over her clit. She shuddered.

With my other hand, I took hold of my cock, lining it up against her entrance, but not pushing in. "Now was that so difficult?" I asked.

"Gods *damn it, Will. I swear to all that is good if you don't—*"

I didn't let her finish that sentence. Instead I slammed into her her, hard like she wanted it, and held myself deep inside her as she panted. "Don't worry, sweetheart. You'll get everything you want." I planted one more kiss on her shoulder and then slammed into her again.

It wasn't pretty. The only thing keeping her headboard from slamming against the wall was her grip on it. The sound of flesh hitting flesh filled the room. The rhythm between us thundering forward as we moved, her arching back, me crashing forward. Both of us moaning at the sheer fucking wonder of it.

I thought my head might explode, it was that fucking good.

It wasn't long until Vanessa froze, her head back, my name on her lips as she came. I kept going, all rhythm, all finesse fucking destroyed, but still trying to draw it out, make it last for her.

A few seconds later I was shuddering after her, moaning her name into her neck, clutching her sweat-slicked body to my own.

Perfect. She was fucking perfect. And in this moment, she was mine.

#

Declan and I both had to open, so we carpooled to Ritual Ink. This was nice because I genuinely liked Declan, and because it would help him get all of his smug out of his system before work.

Instead the asshole had the temerity to just sit there and sip his togo cup of tea while I sipped the coffee that Declan had put into a togo mug for me with a cozy around the base incase it got hot. The temerity of this man, to be so thoughtful.

"Go ahead and get it out," I said. "You'll feel better."

Declan ran a hand through his short beard. "I got my own back already, I think, so what am I supposed to get out, exactly?" He cradled his tea. "I'm happy for you. I know how much you wanted this."

My throat suddenly felt tight. "Yeah."

I could see Declan watching me out of the corner of my eye as I pulled up to Ritual Ink. "But I know you're worried, too."

I turned off the car, but made no move to get out. "Yeah."

One of the things I loved about Declan was—though he could be a pushy bastard when it came to certain things, like keeping us healthy and safe—he was patient, too. He would sit quietly in my car until I was ready to talk to him.

"Van's father—"

Declan snorted. "Woodbridge doesn't deserve that title."

"No, he does not." I sighed. "I've watched Van date for years and… she has issues, you know? Totally understandable issues, but I'm worried she's going to panic and blow this up."

Declan nodded. "She might. Intimacy involves being vulnerable and Van does *not* like being vulnerable." He turned in his seat to face me. "She's never been allowed to be. Can you imagine growing up in Woodbridge's house? I don't know much about their mom, but I don't think she was much of a buffer."

I shook my head. Van's mom was basically a ghost.

"I know what it's like," Declan said softly. "To never let your guard down like that. To be so very careful about connecting with people and even hiding those connections because they could be weaponized against you."

"I guess I hadn't thought about it that way, how similar your upbringing was to Van's." Which was saying something, because Declan's father tried to kill him for the sake of both revenge and a spell not too long ago.

Declan rubbed one hand over the back of his neck. "Yeah, well, Woodbridge is a narcissist, same as my dad. They might be different in lots of ways, but very similar in others." He reached out and clasped my wrist. I realized I was white-knuckling the wheel.

"You're going to have to be patient with Van," Declan said. "Dropping your guard, even to someone you trust, sometimes especially to someone you trust, is hard." "Why especially to someone you trust?"

"Because they have more of a capacity to hurt you than anyone. It's the claw you never see coming, you know? The one wielded by a friend." His voice was soft, even though his eyes were hard now. Unpleasant memories there.

"I would never intentionally hurt Vanessa," I said.

"I know." His smile was a little sad. "Won't make it hurt any less, though." "So what do I do?"

Declan squeezed my wrist and let go. "Be as patient as you can. And if she panics and fucks up, try to be understanding. This is a huge leap for her."

"I know."

"Anything Lou and I can do to help, just holler."

"Thanks," I said. I took my key out of the ignition and opened my door. "We should go in before we're late and Bay fires us."

Declan snorted. "We would have to burn the place down before Bay fired us."

True enough. The flip side of course was that we both worked harder at our job to make sure we weren't a burden on Bay or his business. We all wanted this shop to succeed. It helped that Bay was a talented motherfucker, and for all he grouched about the paper work, he was good at the business end of things. That wasn't always the case. Some really talented tattoo artists had shops that didn't do well because they weren't as good at the other stuff.

But luckily, Bay was. Though Declan was handling more of the daily paperwork and business aspects. He'd recently been promoted to office manager. He'd only been at the shop a short time, but Declan's skill sets were complimentary to Bay's and he could take some of that weight off easily. It also made it so Declan could drop his second job.

Which had caused a fight, since Declan's second job had been doing prep work for Adobo A-Go-Go, the food truck that Bay's cousin's owned. Declan had helped them find a good replacement before he left, so the squabble between the cousins was mostly for show, which was good. I loved Bay's family—so did Declan—and none of us wanted to cause actual rifts there.

We parted ways as soon as we entered the shop. Declan had to open up the shop and I had to make sure I was ready, too. Not only did I have to check that I had enough jewelry and tools sterilized before I went about my day, but I also had to check ritual components like incense, candles, sharpies, different stones, and so on.

I double checked my inventory against my appointments for the day, so that I was sure my spell components were covered. Not every piercing I did was an arcane ritual, but the majority of them were. There were a lot of good body piercers in Seattle, but only a handful that could do what I did.

My first appoint on the books was a septum. I didn't like doing septums as much. There were a lot of angles to worry about with a septum piercing and no room for allowance to be off anywhere if you want it to look even. It was also more difficult to see your piercing marks, and you had anatomy to worry about, whether there were any deviations in the septum. Just fiddly piercings all around.

I must have made a noise because Declan laughed. "Hey, at least it's not dick before noon."

"For which I am grateful." It was a running joke we had—no dick before noon. It wasn't actually true as I wanted to be paid, and didn't have any problem with other people's dicks, or I wouldn't be able to do this job.

It was just sometimes I wanted more coffee first.

The septum was for Marjorie, who was seventy five. She had her two granddaughters with her, both of them probably in their early twenties. Marjorie lived with them and apparently snored like a mack truck was passing the house at eighty miles an hour.

"It's hard for them to sleep through," Marjorie said. "And my akesoite recommended coming to see you, because he thinks I'm not getting good sleep, either."

"Did she give you a prescription?" The akesoite might have had a specific stone in mind, but also, if Marjorie had a prescription, she might be able to be reimbursed for the piercing ritual.

One of her granddaughters, Cassie, fished it out of her pocket, giving it to me. I looked it over carefully. There was a sticky note attached to it for me and I recognized the name on it— Ake. Jensen had referred to me before. He let me know what else he'd prescribed, because he knew I would tailor what gems I picked and the ritual itself to dovetail with what he was doing.

I ended up going with a jade stone, which was a good basic choice for sinus issues and rose quartz, because it worked well for general healing. The ritual went smoothly, and had a nice side effect of distracting me from all the stuff I'd been tossing around in my head this morning. It was good to focus on my work.

After I was done, I took off my gloves, stepping on the trash can pedal so the lid would lift and I could drop them in.

Marjorie was checking out her new piercing in the mirror, doing a little happy shimmy. "I love it. What do you think?"

Cassie and Jess both ooohed and aaahed over it, making Marjorie light up even more.

They were obviously close and she put a lot of stock in their opinions.

"I'm glad you're happy," I said. There was something so gratifying in seeing someone obviously pleased with my work.

"I am," Marjorie said. "Thank you!"

And then, in her giddy glee over the moment, Marjorie leaned forward and flicked my nipple. Repeatedly. Flick might not be the right word, but it wasn't a rub, either. Whatever it was, I froze.

"Is this pierced, too?" Marjorie asked.

Nobody in the room moved for about a half of a second before both Cassie and Jess erupted.

Cassie's eyes were huge. "Grandma! You can't *do* that!"

At the same time Jess hissed, "Consent, grandma! You can't just go flicking people's nipples!"

Sadly, I was used to this. That didn't make it okay, but there was something about tattoos and piercings that made some people think that touching a stranger was totally fine.

In Majorie's defense, she looked horrified. "I'm so sorry! I wasn't thinking!"

"It's okay," I said. "Though I do appreciate the apology. Yes, they're pierced." I had barbells in both, but you couldn't see them unless my shirt was tight. "No, you can't flick them again." I softened the no, because I didn't think Marjorie had meant any harm—she was just giddy from the piercing.

To be honest, I was just glad she hadn't tried to punch me. That happened sometimes.

Still, I liked Marjorie and she was so upset over the whole thing, and I didn't want that. I dipped my head and smiled. "I charge extra for that." Then I waggled my eyebrows at her.

Marjorie cackled. "You! You, I like." She clasped her hands. "Such a cutie-patootie. I want to pinch your cheeks, but I won't." She leaned in. "You know, if you're single, both my granddaughters are currently unattached.

"Grandma!" Cassie still looked horrified, while Jess had her hands over her face while she cracked up laughing.

121

"What?" Marjorie asked. "I didn't touch him."

I smiled at her granddaughters. "My nana is the same way and I wouldn't change a thing about her." I grinned at Marjorie because I also just realized that I actually now had a polite and honest reason to turn the offer down. "As it is, I'm taken."

Because *I had a girlfriend now and she was awesome.* I hadn't felt this goofy over having a girlfriend since I was in middle school.

Marjorie sighed. "All the good ones are."

I opened the door to the piercing room, letting them out. Bay sat at the front desk, an amused expression on his face. "Declan had to step away from the desk for a minute."

Declan was a werewolf, which meant he had exceptional hearing and had likely overheard the exchange in the piercing room. I heard a wheeze of laughter from the backroom. Yup, Declan had overheard the whole thing.

"I can check them out," I said, pulling up the itemized list for Marjorie's payment. I printed out a double for her insurance company, passing the receipt along with Marjorie's aftercare instructions. "You know, Marjorie, Bay here is single." I tipped my head at my friend.

"And he owns the shop."

Marjorie's eyes lasered in on my friend.

Cassie and Jess groaned, both of their faces red now.

I was going to get it from Bay for that one, but it was worth it.

CHAPTER FOURTEEN

Vanessa

I was visiting my boyfriend at work.

I had a *boyfriend* and I liked him enough to *visit him at work.*

Couldn't quite wrap my head around it, so I put that thought aside as I stepped through the doors of Ritual Ink and right into an argument.

"Dude." Bay's arms were crossed, his brows furrowed. I could tell he wasn't actually mad, just kind of mildly irritated.

Will wasn't even that—he was laughing hysterically, one hand gripping the edge of the front counter so he didn't fall down. Declan came out from the back, wiping his eyes, still laughing.

"What happened?" I asked.

Will started laughing even harder.

"He threw me under the bus," Bay grumbled.

Declan came over and gave me a one-armed hug. "A customer was trying to set Will up with her granddaughters. He mentioned to them that Bay was single."

Will's laughter was subsiding and the expression he turned on me was a bit bashful. "I was trying to soften the blow since I'm not single anymore and because Marjorie felt bad for sexually harassing me."

My eyebrows winged up, but Will just shrugged. I couldn't let that go without saying something. "You were sexually harassed by a grandma?"

"It's okay," Will said. "Majorie apologized. I don't think she'd thought things through before she went for my nipple."

Bay scowled at him. "Was this a revenge move?" His eyebrows dropped lower. "Was this because I had sex in the piercing room?"

Nikki, one of the other tattoo artists in the shop came out from the back to peek at the schedule. I'd always been a little jealous of her ability to draw on perfect black eyeliner wings. She snorted. "Who hasn't had sex in the piercing room?"

Will froze, eyebrows slamming down. "Wait, what?"

Suddenly everyone found somewhere else to look, anywhere but Will.

Will rubbed a hand over his face. "Have you *all* had sex in the piercing room?" Absolute *crickets*.

I raised my hand. "I've never had sex in the piercing room."

Will threw me a grateful look before he turned his thunder-face back on everyone else. "Seriously? Do you know how unhygienic that is?"

Bay waved both his hands, like he was shooing Will's arguments away. "Hey, we know how to clean up a station. I'm sure every single one of us wiped the surfaces down afterward."

"Yeah," Nikki said, scrunching up her nose. "We're not dicks."

Will squeaked. "That's not the point—that's…gah!" He put his hands on his hips and tried to collect himself.

Bay shrugged. "Well, if we clean up after ourselves, then it's not a hygiene issue. So what exactly is the problem then?" He dropped his voice to a stage whisper. "Is it because you feel left out?"

"No." Will huffed. "Okay, yes, a little, but mostly it's something I need to know!" Will took a deep breath and let it out. "I don't just do regular piercings in there—I do arcane rituals. Which require a neutral space. If everyone is banging their brains out in said space, then it is *no longer neutral but sexually charged*." He pinched the bridge of his nose. "It changes the ritual."

Everyone seemed to consider this.

"I'll be honest," Bay said. "I hadn't thought of that."

"Sorry, Will," Nikki said. "We were thinking with our bits, not our brains."

He leveled his gaze at her. "Sorry enough to stop hooking up in the piercing room?" Once again, we were greeted by crickets.

Will sighed again. "That's what I thought." He cut a hand through the air. "Just, either do a cleansing ritual or tell me I need to do one. In fact, just tell me. That way I make sure its the right ritual."

"I would say I was sorry," Declan said, a little sheepishly, "But that would be a lie. I *am* sorry that we compromised your space and caused some aggravation."

Bay screwed up his face. "I'm going to try really hard to not think about who you were in the piercing room with, because dude, that's my sister."

"That doesn't keep her from being my girlfriend," Declan said.

"I know, I know, but still." Bay shook himself like a wet dog, making Nikki laugh. "Maybe we can get a little sign," Bay said thoughtfully. "Like the one on your

dishwasher that you flip over to let people know when the dishes are clean or not." "I could make one," Declan said. "No problem."

Will closed his eyes. "I feel like this is a solution to an unnecessary problem. You could, I don't know, just not have sex in there?"

Bay shook his head. "It's the only door here with a lock besides the bathroom." "And you've got that chair," Nikki added.

"The chair is pretty sweet," Declan said. "It swivels—."

"Fine," Will said, throwing up his hands. "Declan, please make a sign." He strode over to me, wrapped his arms around my waist as he tucked his head into my neck. "The other kids are being mean to me."

I laughed, patting his head. "I'm sorry. I brought you a snack, though? Does that help? A cinnamon roll from Wicked Brews…" I crooned the last bit.

"Yes," Will said with a sigh. "And if you wait until after my next appointment, I can hang out with you while I eat it."

#

I hung out with Declan and Bay until Will's appointment was done. As soon as the customer left, I slipped into the piercing room, my bag full of cinnamon roll from work in my hand.

Will was wiping the chair down, a distracted expression on his face. "The things that chair has seen," I said, kicking the door closed.

"One shudders to think." Will threw away the paper towels and stripped off his gloves. I locked the door shut.

His eyebrows winged up as he tossed the gloves in the trash. "Well, well, well, what have we here?" He corralled me to the door, turning his attention on me.

All of his attention.

Will had the gift of caging you in without making you feel trapped. Or maybe that was just me, because Will was on the short list of people I trusted implicitly. This man would never hurt me. So when he leaned in for a kiss, his arms bracketing my face, I could greet him with a smile.

Which he returned after the kiss, his smile a little perplexed. He cradled my face, tracing my chin with his thumbs. "Hey."

"Hey," I said back, feeling a little shy about the goofy grin on my face. "It's still a little weird, isn't it?"

"Yeah," I admitted. "But, like, good weird?"

"Is that a question?" He was grinning at me now.

I looked at him helplessly because I wasn't sure. Had I meant it to be a question?

Will turned serious as he watched me. "I keep thinking I'm going to wake up and realize I've been dreaming. That none of this had happened." He dropped his gaze, his expression troubled. "That tomorrow morning I'll reach for you and you won't be there and for a split second I feel the loss." He tapped his chest.

I wasn't not sure how to respond, how to reassure him, so I kissed him instead. He sighed into my mouth, body moulding into mine, like we'd both hit our melting points at the same time. I tucked this feeling away, this moment, to hold tight next time I was feeling shaky and unsure. That this man cherished me so much that he could hold me like this, be open with me like this.

His hand slid into the back of my shirt, fingers tracing up the small of my back in a heated shiver. We started to go molten, his mouth tracing along my neck.

"Is this an attempt to even the score." My voice was a breathy whisper—I didn't sound like myself to my own ears. He mumbled an incoherent reply and I wasn't sure he understood what I'd asked. "Since you're the only one who hasn't had sex in here, I mean."

Will leaned back, his cheeks flushed. "I would never." He took the bag from my hand— which I had completely forgotten I was holding— and dropped it on the counter. "When we have sex in here, and that is on the table for the future, it's not going to be a revenge move and I'll pick a time when the shop isn't full." He traced my hips with his hands, his eyes hot.

"Pity." Even though I wouldn't want to broadcast what we were doing in here, either.

He hummed in response, his hands still on my waist. He flipped me then, turning my face to the door. Slowly, carefully, Will placed my palms on the wood, his body flush against mine. I felt his voice rumble through me when he spoke, his breath hot on my ear.

"That doesn't mean we can't play a little."

I shivered, but not from the cold as I felt his hands slide around to the front of my jean shorts. He unsnapped the front button. I didn't move, absolutely riveted on what he was doing. His fingers dipped into my panties and my breath caught.

They didn't go where I wanted them. He traced along the outer edges, avoiding my clit entirely. The bastard.

"Tell me what you want, Nessa." I didn't hesitate. "Keep going."

He edged closer, circling, until finally, *finally*, with the softest of touches, he brushed over my clit. Danced away. Brushed it again. Like he was playing hide-n-seek.

I hated it. I loved it.

My breath hissed between my teeth.

"Mmm, not sure what you mean by that." His lips traced my ear, his voice deepening and traveling down my spine.

"Yes you do, you asshole," I pushed the words through gritted teeth. He had the audacity to laugh softly in my ear, causing me to shiver.

He hummed again, dipping one finger into me, sliding back out before I get more than a hint of sensation. I couldn't help arching against him. His other hand skimmed up, brushing against my hard nipple. I stifled a groan as he traced it with his fingers. "Do you want more, Nessa?"

Fuck yes, I wanted more, but it irritated me how easily this man could play me. I was tempted to say no just to regain some control.

But if I said no, he'd stop. I didn't want him to stop.

As if sensing my struggle, he paused, one hot hand on my breast, the other cupping me in a gentle hold, like I was something fragile and worth taking care of.

He planted a kiss behind my ear. "Want me to back off?"

In that second I realized I didn't have to regain control. I'd never lost it. This man was so attuned to my body language that even a hint of me being unsure brought whatever this was to an instant halt. If I said no, he'd button me back up, kiss me and move on with a smile. If I said yes, he'd put his fingers back where I wanted them.

Something inside me that I hadn't realized had been squeezed tight like a fist, relaxed, unfurled. I took one hand off the door and clasped his neck with it. I pulled him in for a kiss. It was sweet, almost chaste compared to where his hands were.

So I nipped his lip. "Don't stop."

He didn't move, his searching gaze locked on me. "Please."

That did it. He grinned, kissing me deep. The hand in my panties left, but only to put my palm back on the door. Then it was back, and this time he wasn't flirting with my clit. We'd moved past the teasing, touching me in sure, steady strokes.

He slipped two fingers into me, curling them until they hit a spot I liked, the meat of his palm rubbing against my clit in a pleasing rhythm. His other hand caressed my breast, pinching the nipple. My breathing was ragged as his fingers moved inside me. My orgasm was building with liquid speed, as I arched again, pressing myself into his hands.

I widened my stance, giving him more room. Almost there. So *close*.

"Fuck, Nessa. You're so—come on, baby. Please. Show me, *please*."

It was the raspy urgency in his voice that sent me over the edge. I buried my face in his neck, biting back my moan, trying to be quiet as an intense orgasm washed through me. Will held me, drawing out the pleasure as long as he could. Mumbling sweet words in my ear the whole time.

I was suddenly too sensitive, and I put my hand over his to still his fingers as I smiled into his neck.

He shuddered. "Fuck me, I don't think that's ever going to get old."

I laughed, running my hand through his hair, pulling him tight to me. "What about you?" He sucked in a breath. "I'm good. That was—fuck. We'll worry about me later."

I could feel how hard he was, his erection pressing into me, but he was clearly unconcerned about it for now.

Will pressed a kiss into my hair. "Thank you. Just, holy shit, thank you."

There was an awe in his voice that lit me up inside. This man. How had we waited this long to do this? *Why* had we?

His fingers trembled as he brushed aside my hair, revealing my neck. I closed my eyes, anticipating the kiss.

Will froze, muscles going stiff. "The fuck?"

Gone was awestruck Will. His voice now contained genuine anger. "What?" Fear washed through me, killing any post-orgasm bliss I had. Will swore again. "You stones are cracked."

My hand went back automatically to touch my piercing, but Will clasped it. "The wound is still fresh. Don't touch it."

He turned me back around, snapping my shorts closed. Worry etched lines into his usually happy face.

I was sure my expression mirrored his. Someone had tried to get past his protective stones. Someone had come at me with a spell—a hex or a curse—and had hit Will's barrier with enough force to crack the stones.

And I hadn't noticed.

Now it was my turn to swear as fear grew inside me.

Will was already washing his hands. "We're replacing them now." He waved me onto the chair, as he stepped to the door, flipping the lock and opening it so he could stick his head out. "Tell my next appointment I might be late."

"What's wrong?" Declan asked

"I'll tell you later," Will said, shutting the door again. He yanked open drawers, pulling out the supplies he needed. Suddenly he stopped, closing his eyes. He took a deep breath, crossed the room, and hugged me. "I fucked up."

"What?" Fear and confusion made my voice sharp.

"I should have checked the stones—the second we left your dad's I should have examined them and I didn't."

"We don't know for certain it happened there. Maybe a customer didn't like their coffee today and tried to hex me."

Will grunted, not buying my argument for a second.

I didn't completely buy it, either, but since we hadn't checked, we couldn't be certain. "No proof," I said.

"I don't fucking need proof," Will growled, kissing the top of my head. "This isn't the court of fucking law, Vanessa."

Oooh, he'd rolled out "Vanessa." Will was truly freaked.

"I get to worry about you however I see fit." He let me go and grabbed a pair of gloves, snapping them on. He was still taking in deep breaths, visibly trying to yank his temper back into control. "I'm redoing the ritual and replacing the stones. Then I want—" He cut himself off, his eyes closing again, his head dropping back. "I'd *like* you to consult with Bay. See about getting a tattoo, temporary or long term, something to add another layer of protection."

Bless this man for knowing full well that a demand would have set my back up. But a suggestion? I could handle suggestions. "Okay. I'll talk to Bay."

He gave a single sharp nod, his nostrils flaring. "I'm sorry."

"We both fucked up," I said, rubbing a hand against my forehead. Oh, how I'd love to go back to five minutes ago when we had both felt fantastic and safe in the knowledge that in that moment nothing else mattered but us. "Are we going to have to cleanse the room?"

Will barked a laugh. "No, I'm going to use the energy instead." His smile was rueful. "I don't usually incorporate sex magic into my rituals for obvious reasons, but in this case, I'll welcome it."

He still seemed so freaked out, I wanted to soothe him. "It's okay, Will. I can handle it, whatever it is."

He frowned at me. "You think I don't know that?" He stepped close, placing his hands on each side of where I was sitting. "Nessa, you're the strongest person I know, hands down. If this was a one on one fight, I'd back you, every time. But whoever this is—your dad, that dipshit Tanner, whatever—isn't fighting up front and fair. And luckily you don't have to face this on your own."

I stared at him.

He grabbed my chin. "Let us be here for you, Nessa. For once in your life, let us take care of you for a change."

My throat felt tight and I couldn't answer, so I just nodded.

He let out a shaky breath and went back to setting up the ritual.

CHAPTER FIFTEEN

???

Bay sent me home with a set of temporary tattoos. He felt they would work well and give us the added bonus of acting as an instant warning system. Magical tattoos had more oomph—depending on the practitioner, they could last a fairly long before they disappeared completely.

A temporary one was a one-and-done, vanishing the second I used it. That meant I'd have to apply a new tattoo every time, but it would let us know *exactly* when it was being used as long as I was paying attention.

Normal temporary tattoos use water to set them on your skin, but the magic ones weren't quite like that. You needed something…a little more personal to kindle the magic. That could be something as simple as saliva. You could use blood, too, but I didn't want the tattoo bad enough to open a vein when I had other options.

So as soon as Will got off work, he came over and we worked up a sweat. Like Will, sex magic wasn't my forte, but since I had access and we were both more than willing, our mingled sweat would do the trick.

Will was still breathing hard as he lined up the image of a wolverine on my lower arm— the animal, not the superhero.

I tried to hold still, my arm relaxed, so the image didn't blur. The more precise the lines, the better.

"That should do it," Will murmured, removing the backing on the temporary tattoo.

I heard the flap in my door—Declan had recently put it in to make it easier for my ferrets to come and go from my room—and watched as Kodo and Podo drug a bottle between them over to me. It was a bright, lurid orange.

I snorted.

"What?" Will asked.

"The ferrets just brought me one of those sports drinks." I raised my voice. "Someone thinks they're funny." The ferrets certainly thought he was. They bounced around in glee before they went back out their little flap in the door.

"Someone's hilarious." Declan's response was faint through the door. "But it was for Will. Boy's earned it."

Will shook with laughter, temporarily setting aside the tattoo until he could get ahold of himself.

"Electrolytes are important!" Declan shouted. "I'm all about hydration." "My roommates are a little too involved in my life," I grumbled.

"You don't mean that," Will said, gaining control of himself and finally setting the tattoo.

I didn't, and I generally didn't have to worry too much as the walls were pretty good in our house, but when you live with someone with super hearing…well. Privacy pretty much went out the window. Luckily, Declan was usually good about pretending he didn't hear things and giving us the illusion of privacy.

"I'm doing my next test tomorrow," I said.

Will flopped down next to me, wonderfully and unselfconsciously naked. "What time? I work tomorrow, but maybe I can switch."

I traced the outline of one the tattoos on his stomach, a moth with its wings out. The idea of facing the second test without Will there made my stomach drop. Support had been nice. But I was a grown up and he'd done so much already that it didn't seem fair to ask for more. "Don't worry about it. I'll be okay."

Will brushed my hair back from my face with one hand. "Are you sure? It's no big deal." I made myself smile. "I'm good. I can handle it."

My statement did little to reassure Will. If anything, his frown deepened. "I'm not sure I like the idea of you facing a test alone."

Irritation flashed through me and I rolled my eyes. "I'm a big girl, Will." I sat up.

He grabbed my wrist when I would have left the bed. "I'm not saying you can't handle it.

I'm not questioning your capabilities. You know that, right?"

I opened my mouth to bite back at him, but stopped myself last minute, clicking my teeth shut. This was the problem with spending time with my father. I fell back into old patterns. When talking with him, I had to not only analyze everything said on several levels for subtext, but I also got used to that subtext *being shitty*. Which meant I was always sensitive afterward.

Did I like what Will said? No. But I reminded myself it was Will. His subtext was never shitty. That wasn't his default setting. I rubbed a hand over my face. "Sorry. I'm tired and I can't—." I huffed, snagging the sport's drink the ferrets had left on the floor, handing it to Will. "Translate for me, please."

Will set the drink aside and sat up, pulling me close to him. "Reverse the situation. I have to go meet Tanner and Woodbridge for the test. Would you want me to go alone?"

"No." My answer was instant. Of course I wouldn't want him to face that bullshit alone.

He shouldn't have to.

"Why not?"

"Because I would want to be there for you." He relaxed at my words, only to tense up again when I said the next bit. "They're not your mess. You don't deserve to deal with that kind of crap."

He cradled my cheek, guiding me until I was looking at him. "Nessa, you don't deserve to deal with this shit either. You know that, right?" When I didn't answer right away, Will kissed my forehead. "Gorgeous, you don't deserve your father's behavior. Nothing you've ever done in your life has *earned* being treated like garbage. You certainly shouldn't have to jump through his stupid hoops to get his signature on a piece of paper. You did the work already. You know your stuff. He knows it. I know it. Pretty sure even fucking *Tanner* knows it." Will's eyes searched mine. "The question is, do you know it?"

"Of course I do," I said. "And I know my dad's behavior is on him."

Will shook his head slowly. "I think you know it, but I don't think you believe it." "That sounds like almost the same thing."

"Knowledge and belief overlap, but they're not the same thing. You can believe without knowing something to be factually true, just like you can know something to be a fact and not really believe it." Will settled me into his lap. "It's like, I know we're dating. We've talked about it. It's fact." He smoothed a hand up my back. "But there's still a part of me that can't quite believe it."

"It's too good," I said. "I've always had a hard time believing that something good, something I want to be true, is real."

Will watched me, his expression unreadable. "I fucking love that you see being with me as something good, and something you want, while simultaneously wanting to beat your father with his own arms because I know he's the one that made you doubt good things."

I shrugged, dropping my gaze.

Will tucked me in close, mouth going next to my ear. "You can burrow if it helps you feel better, but I want you to listen to me, Nessa, and I want you to believe me when I say that you deserve good things. You deserve to be treated with respect."

He kissed me, right below my ear, and I shivered. "And fuck anyone who says or acts different. Okay?" "Okay," I said.

He hummed thoughtfully for a second. "Nope." He jostled me, making me giggle. I was *not* a giggler. "I didn't quite believe that. I'm going to need you to say it." He rolled then, taking us back down to the mattress. When we stopped, I was underneath him, neatly anchored by his body. "Say it. 'I, Vanessa Woodbridge, deserve nice things.'"

I rolled my eyes again. "Absolutely not, Willhardt Murphy."

"Oooooh, going straight for the big guns and pulling out the Will-hardt, are we?" He gave a mock sigh. "You leave me no choice."

My eyes went big. "No. You wouldn't!"

His eyes twinkled as he slid his hands right to my ticklish spots. That was the problem with dating someone you'd been best friends with.

135

They knew your secrets. I started giggling preemptively and shoving his hands away, but Will was relentless.

"Will, cut it out!" "Not until you say it."

Despite my best attempts, Will managed to get to that spot on my ribs that made me giggle every time. I was gasping with laughter, eyes watering, before I caved. "Fine, fine!"

He stopped, but didn't move his hands. "Let's hear it."

"I deserve nice things," I said. When it was clear he was still still waiting for me to continue, I used his focus to sneak my own hands to his waist. It wasn't as good as the backs of his knees, but it would do. "And I deserve respect." Then I went in for the kill.

Will squeaked, trying to roll away, but I'd wrapped my legs around him. He could roll us, but he couldn't get away. When we finally stopped grappling, I was straddling his waist. We were both laughing.

Until our gazes met. Tangled.

After that, there were no words, just the heat of his touch, and the surety of his kiss, telling me with absolute clarity that I deserved nice things, and he was going to show them to me.

\#

I got a text from Tanner at work the next morning, moving the time of my second test. Something about my father's schedule shifting. The problem was, the new time directly conflicted with work. I would have to leave an hour early. Noah was supposed to come on after me, but I wasn't sure he would be able to make it. He was in school, so his work schedule was built around class and exam schedules.

It was slow enough that I was able to stick my head through the swinging door that lead back into the bakery and potionary area. The kitchen was set up with different stations—one for the traditional bakers that came in, and then one each for the owners, Emma and Thea, for when they worked on the potions and edibles.

You didn't want someone making cinnamon rolls on the same table where you made medicinal edibles. First, taste transference would be a terrible thing. The magic stuff we made was medicine which wasn't known for its delightful flavors. Unless you liked licking the inside of a trashcan or the faint but lingering aftertaste of barnyard sweat.

The flip side was also true—you didn't want to get stray baking ingredients into a potion.

A hint of cinnamon could be disastrous in some things, delicious as it may be. There was a reason only licensed and accredited hedge witches were allowed to sell their concoctions.

Both Thea and Emma were working. Thea was curvy, her hair a mess of copper curls, with the sort of creamy pink skin tone you see in some skin care ads. She tended to dress in a sort of retro style that always made me think she looked two seconds away from stepping into or out of an art nouveau painting. Even the smattering of freckles across her nose seemed like they'd been placed individually by a painter's hand.

Today she had her hair up as she worked, a small pair of gold wire framed glasses stuck into her mass of curls. Potions were more her passion, so that was what she tended to make. Her table was littered with beakers, tubes and bowls, having the appearance more of a science experiment than magic.

Emma, my other boss, had an entirely different aesthetic. Her hair was styled in a short, messy undercut, the dark strands rising up like some sort of crown. Her tan skin interrupted only by a few tattoos. And although she radiated a sort of coiled energy, it wasn't frenetic, but a steady hum. Emma was all go, all the time. Right now her deep brown eyes were trained on a marble slab where she was blending together several different herbs with the base that would contain them for the edible—in this instance, bitter, unsweetened dark chocolate.

The worked together in concert, separate, but together, creating bits of magic that I'd sell to the public. The backroom came to life when they were there.

This. This was what I wanted to be part of. This sense of quiet industry, of sharp intensity wrapped in layers of calm focus. To know that my morning's work smoothed the edges of someone else's day, even if it was just a small thing.

I sighed with what could only be referred to as longing.

Emma's head snapped up, but Thea didn't look away from the liquids she was measuring while she spoke. "That was quite a weighty sigh, my friend."

I hadn't shared with them my plans yet. It was right there on the tip of my tongue. I didn't know why I was holding back. Thea and Emma were two of the best bosses I'd ever had. Even knowing that, there was a tiny, silly part of me that worried they would ... I don't know, laugh, I guess.

Or tell me no.

Not quite knowing how to respond to the comment, I ignored it. "I need to leave an hour early—do you mind if I see if Noah can come in and cover?"

Emma was already shaking her head. "Noah has study group. That's why he's coming in at the time he's scheduled, so he could go. What's going on?"

Thea stirred her mixture in a beaker with a glass wand. "It's not like you to do last minute shift changes. Family emergency?" She frowned, turning her face toward me. "Is Savannah okay? Your sister? The ferrets?" Her southern accent thickened as she got progressively more worried.

I held my hands up, waving off Thea's escalating catastrophizing. "Nothing like that, just a thing with my dad." Not a lie, but not the full truth, either. I would have to tell them eventually, but I wanted to wait until I had everything lined up. It would be more difficult for them to turn me down if I had my waiver in hand and I was signed up for my classes. I hoped so, anyway.

Thea's frown deepened and Emma made a rude noise. What with employing both me and my sister, they'd heard enough about my father to give them a rough idea of what kind of person he was and they don't care for him in the slightest.

"I can cover your last hour," Emma said, somehow managing to scowl with her entire body. "But I want to make it clear that I'm doing it for you and not in anyway to give *that man* any convenience whatsoever."

"I would simply *love* to give that man a Circe potion," Thea drawled. "He could learn a lot from being a pig for a few weeks. Months." She tilted her head. "I'm not above years."

"I'm getting you both 'world's greatest boss' mugs."

Emma pursed her lips. "Will I have to give up my 'world's greatest lover' mug? Because honestly, I might say I'm all work and no play, but really it's the other way around."

Thea leveled her with a *look*. "My heart, while the statement may be true, I would not allow any such mug in my household. I have standards," she said, laying her accent on thick for the last bit.

Emma's expression was all mischief. "You would if I asked you at the right time." Thea blushed a bright scarlet.

Emma laughed so hard she had to put down her tools. When she was finally able to respond, she was starting at her wife with such open adoration it made my heart squeeze. "That will never get old. We could be married eighty years, and I would still love making you blush."

Thea lifted her nose very primly in the air while giving Emma the finger.

I loved them both so much, and I don't toss around that phrase easily. I left them laughing, returning to my post at the front.

#

Will stopped in to pick up coffee for the shop a little while later. There was no line behind him, so he was able to lean his elbows on the pick up counter and chat with me.

He propped his cheek on his fist. "Would it be unprofessional for me to kiss the barista?" "That depends on which barista you're referring to," I said, pouring milk into one of the metal pitchers.

Emma must have come out the door behind me because I heard her say, "Is it sexual harassment Tuesday already?" She leaned in Will's direction, offering her cheek. "Because if so, hit me up, Will."

He laid a big, smacking kiss on her cheek.

Thea breezed out the kitchen doors, tray of little bottles in hand. "Will's here?" She saw the kiss. "Is it sexual harassment Tuesday already?"

"I have been told—repeatedly—by my bosses that sexual harassment Tuesday isn't funny, and we shouldn't make fun of something that is a legitimate problem," I said, my tone dry as a bone. Sexual Harassment Tuesday had been something that I'd started with my sister on day, and often nothing to do with actual sexual harassment and very little to do with Tuesdays.

"And if you tried to use it as an excuse to kiss one of your coworkers or smack their collective or singular asses, I would write you up if not fire you outright," Thea said. "But this is Will, he knows the spirit in which the joke is given, and we've all consented." Thea set down her tray and swanned to the other side of the counter. "But I want a hug, too, please."

Will wrapped his arms around Thea, lifting her off her feet, and hugged her.

After he set her down, I brought over his coffee, fitting it into the holder that carried a few drinks for coworkers. Will took advantage of my proximity to put his hand on my cheek and kiss me quick on the mouth before I could say anything.

He leaned back, eyebrow up. A silent, "Was that okay?"

I rolled my eyes at him, thought I could feel my cheeks getting hot. Emma let out a wolf whistle. "I see how it is."

Thea held out her hand, palm open, to Emma. "Pay up." "Like I have cash," Emma said.

"Some friends kiss like that," I said not caring that I sounded defensive. "Some friends do," Thea said. "*You*, my wonderfully prickly friend, do *not*." I scowled at them. "Fine, but did everyone have bets going on this?"

"Yup," Emma said, popping the p.

"That seems a little unprofessional from you two," I scolded.

Thea patted my arm. "We didn't mean any harm, sugar, you know that. We wouldn't do it with the other employees, but you and Juliet are basically family."

Thea was the only boss I would ever let call me "sugar" and yes, I'd told her it was okay.

Since she was from the south, I considered it a cultural thing, and it lacked the condescension folks up here might give it.

"Besides," Emma said, "you've already given us the title of world's best bosses. You can't take that sort of thing back."

"I haven't bought the mug yet," I said, crossing my arms.

"It doesn't matter," Emma said shaking her head. "The title already lives in my heart." Will picked up his tray. "You still coming to bookclub with me tonight?"

"Yeah," I said, fishing my phone out of my pocket. "I just need to double check—" I frowned at my phone.

"What is it?" Will asked.

"It's Juliet. She wants to know if I can watch Savvy tonight." I reread the text to make sure I was reading it correctly. "Tanner asked her to dinner tonight."

I set my phone down on the counter. "I don't get it."

A customer walked up right as I asked, but before I could turn to help them, Emma waved me off and took over so I could finish my conversation.

"What's wrong with Tanner?" Thea asked.

"He's my father's assistant." I stared at my phone like it had suddenly morphed into an angry, poisonous viper—a mixture of confusion and trepidation.

"And normally any association with her father would be enough to send our darling Juliet fleeing for the hills." She tapped her fingers on the counter, thinking. "Is he really handsome?

Charming?"

"He was a bit smarmy, actually," Will said. "Not terrible, just…." He looked at me, struggling for the words.

"I can't tell if we just didn't like him because he was with my dad, or because something about him was off." I held my palms out, moving them up and down like I was weighing something. "A little of both, maybe?"

"Either way, he sets off alarm bells for *both* of you, which would make me leery to say the least." Thea folded her arms, her face thoughtful. "Have you asked her about it?"

I shook my head. "Not yet, but…"

"But she's a grown up," Will said gently. "Allowed to make her own choices, and almost never asks us to take Savvy for any reason besides work or school."

"She needs the downtime," I said. "She deserves some fun."

Thea nodded. "Then I say tell her yes, assuming that you can, in fact, watch Savvy, but also ask her about it if you can. See why this guy—why is he worth her time?"

I glanced at Will.

"Savvy is welcome at bookclub," he said. "I'll double check with Nana, but I'm positive."

"Okay," I said. "If you're sure."

Will leaned over and stole another kiss. "I'm sure."

When he leaned back, Thea had her hands pressed together in front of her like she was praying, the tips of her fingers against her mouth. She dropped her hands with a wistful sigh. "You two are so adorable."

I scowled at her, but Will just laughed, took his coffees, and left with a backwards wave.

CHAPTER SIXTEEN

Will

I was greeted at work with a "thanks for the coffee" and a new sign on the piercing room door. One side said "This House is Clean" with a picture of the psychic woman from the original *Poltergeist*. The other side said, "Clean this room, ya' filthy animal" with a picture of the gangster from the movie Kevin McCallister watches in *Home Alone*.

"Wow," I said, staring at the sign. "A quote from a movie in a movie. How very meta." I sounded a little irritated even to my ears, because the sign was turned to the "filthy animal" side.

"It's been disinfected," Declan said, pausing to blow on his tea. "But you'll need to take care of the rest of it." His ears went pink, just at the tops. I guess we all knew who used to room.

I strode over to him, grabbed his bearded cheeks, and kissed him. "I know it was you, Fredo."

"It's kind of the sign's fault," Declan said, blushing harder. "Lou was here while I was putting it up and it kind of gave us ideas—."

I pushed his face away. "Let me stop you there." He started laughing as I left him, so I flipped him off without looking at him and escaped into the piercing room. I shut the door with my heel, and started getting out the things I needed for my cleansing ritual. Luckily, it was a simple ceremony and wouldn't take me too long.

I plugged my earbud in and called Nana.

"Will! I was just thinking of you. Did you finish tonight's book?"

"Yes," I said, which was only a partial lie. I had one chapter left and it would be finished before bookclub started. "Very swashbuckly. Much

Pirate. I think the author missed an opportunity by not using the phrase 'two gentlemen seamen' at any point."

"Low hanging fruit," Nana chided.

"Agree to disagree." I set up the incense on the counter and started writing the symbols I needed on the walls using chalk. "And I didn't forget the cookies." They were stashed in the shop's fridge. "Just so you know."

"Oatmeal raisin?"

"Sugar cookies." Cut into shapes and frosted to look like a sailboat, a jolly roger, and dicks, respectively. Jim had done the icing. He had remarkably steady hands. When he could stop laughing and when he wasn't coming up with different slang words for penises.

He was now considering joining bookclub. The cookies were all win as far as I was concerned.

"I'm making iced tea with lemon—to help us all avoid the scurvy."

I loved my Nana so much. "Thanks for looking out for us, Nana. Is it okay if I bring Savvy?"

"Of course," Nana said instantly. "Is something wrong?"

"No," I said, checking my first set of symbols. "At least, I don't think so. Juliet has a date."

"Good for her. She deserves more time to herself. She works so hard."

"No argument there." I adjusted one of the symbols and moved onto the next wall. "Thing is, he's Woodbridge's assistant."

Nana made a rude noise.

"My feelings exactly. I don't suppose you've heard anything around campus?" Nana worked in SUU Campus library.

"No, but that doesn't mean there isn't scuttlebutt. Want me to ask around?"

"If you wouldn't mind," I said, moving on to the last wall. "Subtle-like, if you please." Nana snorted. "No, I was going to ring a bell and shout it across campus. You met him, right? At dinner?"

"Yeah," I said, setting down my chalk. "Didn't love the guy, but it's possible I'm just being protective."

"You? Never." After a moment of quiet, she came back sounding serious. "I'm not saying don't give the guy a chance, but Will? You have good instincts with people. If you didn't like him...don't discount that feeling."

"Got it." I put away the chalk and rinsed my hands. "You still bringing a date?"

"Yes," I said. "Play nice."

"Will, I love Vanessa. I'm sorry if I made you think otherwise."

"I know." And I did. She just worried and wanted me to be careful. I dried my hands, stepped on the trash can pedal and tossed the paper towel. "But I also know I get my protective streak from *somewhere*."

"I deny all accusations."

I laughed. "Thanks, Nana."

"Of course, Will. See you tonight."

"Aye, matey." After we hung up, I put my phone away, lit the incense, and closed my eyes. I'd done what I could and this room wouldn't cleanse itself.

Vanessa #

My second test took me twenty minutes out of my neighborhood and into a local wooded park. Not wanting to mess with busses, I'd taken a ride share straight from work, so I was wearing tennis shoes, and my work clothes, Kodo and Podo riding on my shoulders. Lou had been kind enough to drop them by work for me a little before I got off, but didn't have time to take me to my test.

While I was in clothes smelling like coffee and dairy products, Tanner was in hiking boots. He also had on a wide brimmed hat to keep the afternoon sun off. He appeared every bit the affable, slightly dorky, but cute, graduate student.

My father was nowhere in evidence.

Tanner greeted me with a smile and a wave before we headed into the woods. I squinted at him. "Horror movies start like this."

He laughed.

"People know where I'm at," I warned, stepping over a branch. "Just so you know."

He grinned at me. "That's smart. *I* know I don't mean you any ill will, but it's never good to head into the woods with a stranger. Or a near stranger." His grin turned into that sheepish smile he was so good at. I was beginning to wonder if he practiced the nonthreatening male pose in front of the mirror. "I hope to not be a stranger much longer."

I made a noncommittal noise to that. "Where's my father?"

Tanner grimaced. "He had a last minute thing come up and couldn't make it."

The ferrets chittered on my shoulders, an irritated stream of profanity directed at my dad. I wasn't surprised by his behavior, but it still made my gut churn. "So he made us move the meet up time and then bowed out?" I blew out a breath. "Whatever, it's fine. Let's get started, okay?"

Tanner didn't have anything to say to that, so he waved me along and we both dutifully tromped into the forest. "Today we're doing identifying and ethically foraging for potion ingredients. We all need this knowledge, but it's something that should be a strong point for you since you're going into hedgewitchery."

I nodded, even though I was walking behind him and he couldn't see me. "We can't always get ingredients at Potions & Stuff."

I grimaced. Potions & Stuff was a box store that supplied basic potionary ingredients.

They weren't bad, really, but you never were really sure where they'd gotten their ingredients, if they'd been ethically sourced, or how long it had been since they were gathered—that sort of thing. Thea and Emma either grew or gathered their own supplies, or bought from trusted sources. Not every witch could afford to do that, though, so Potions & Stuff had its uses.

The trail ahead of us took us through the middle of a downed tree. Someone from the parks department had carved a length of it out so people could still walk the trail and then left it to be a nursery log. Lots of stuff grew on downed trees.

Tanner paused at the carved out gap. He dug an index card out of his back pocket and handed it to me. It was a list of ingredients and measurements, but no title. Blue vervain, harebells, dew of the sea, which was otherwise known as rosemary…

I read through it twice, looking at the measurements again. Relief filled my veins—I knew what this recipe was for. Even better, I'd made it myself several times, just for practice. "You want me to make a Cassandra potion."

Tanner beamed at me. "Excellent! I shouldn't be surprised you know that one."

Knew it? Yes. Used it? Only on my roommates and with their permission. A Cassandra potion loosened the tongue, making it so the person taking it could only speak the truth. It was the kind of potion you handed out to just anyone.

"Go ahead and gather what ingredients you can—not everything can be gathered out here. I'll quiz you about any other magically significant ingredients I spot along the way. Then you'll take everything home, brew the potion and get it to me…" He tilted his head, calculating the factors. "Tomorrow afternoon?"

I would have to stay up after bookclub to cook the potion. It would suck, because I had the opening shift, but it was doable. Besides, I wanted to get this over with as soon as possible. "Yeah, I can do that."

Tanner nodded. "Good, good. That will give the potion time to sit. I'll analyze it at the university, do a potency work up and everything. As long as it clears the eighty percent mark, you'll pass."

I went for the nursery log, searching for the lichen and fungi that I needed before I headed off into the areas where I'd find the other plants. To get an eighty percent potency, I would need to start getting the potion together *before* book club.

Like I said, not all potions are made equally. Timing was a factor—unless specified in the recipe, the fresher the ingredients, the better. Sometimes you needed something like fermented berries or dried sweet grass, but this potion didn't call for anything like that.

It needed time to steep and brew as well. If I was making this potion on my own timeline, I would soak a few of the ingredients in alcohol to create an extract to achieve better potency, but that wasn't possible for now. I hummed as I foraged, all but forgetting Tanner was there except when he piped up to ask me a question. Foraging was fun for me, and it was a good day for it.

Sunshine filtered in through the trees, giving the forest a fairytale quality to it. Birds twittered and squirrels ran along the branches. The ferrets bounded along, running along the ground and keeping an eye out for the plants I needed. I reminded them to be careful—there are a lot of local hawks that would love to make a meal of them.

I put aside the stress of my day, the pressure of dealing with my father, and let the forest calm my nerves. I'd spent some time trailing behind Emma and Thea as they had done this, which made me feel like they were here with me now. Support even though I was alone. Or alone with Tanner, which was almost the same thing.

I did as my bosses had taught me—never take more than you needed. Leave some for the

forest and for other foragers. Thank the trees and plants giving you their bounty. Understand that nature was a gift, not just for you, but for everyone to enjoy after you were gone. Leave it as unspoiled as you could.

After about forty five minutes, the ferrets were back to riding on my shoulders and Tanner's affability was starting to slip. He was checking his phone more and more, keeping an eye on the time. It reminded me so much of my father, the way you could feel his judgement along your skin. Why weren't you faster, smarter, *better*?

A constant, silent energy that said you would never, ever meet their expectations because you were flawed on a basic level. Sweat beaded along my hairline, not from the sun, but from the panic blooming in my body. That old, remembered fear exploding through my system, leaving the taste of adrenaline in my mouth and a tremor in my hands.

Pain bit at me me—my lack of attention had made me clumsy, and I'd brushed my arm against a stinging nettle. Damn it. Tanner was behind me and couldn't see what I was doing, so I closed me eyes and breathed for a second. I hated this. I hated how, even when he wasn't here, wasn't part of anything I was doing, my father could still haunt me like a particularly shitty ghost.

That he still had this power not only over my mind, but my very body. I *hated* it, and every time I thought I'd moved past it, something like this happened. I'd gone to therapy, I'd cut him out of my life as much as I could. But my father was squatting inside my consciousness like one of those giant, pervasive cane toads they had in Australia. An invasive species. That's what he was.

Podo stuck her nose into the space behind me ear, reassuring. Deep breath. I was fine. I hadn't done anything wrong. I was doing exactly what I was supposed to be doing and it was okay if I took up time and space. It was *my* time and space, and I deserved it just as much as stupid Tanner.

I released a long breath and shook out my arm. Behind me cloth rustled as Tanner took out his phone *again*.

Okay, I could do this. My brain was fucked up right now and I wasn't thinking straight. This happened when I spiraled out about my father. I needed to ground myself in the moment, like my therapist had taught me. Hit all five senses. I heard birdsong from the treetops. Smelled evergreen from the trees. Felt the breeze along my skin as it ruffled the branches. I popped one of the young catnip leaves I'd gathered, not because I needed it now, but because it was there, into my mouth, crushing it between my teeth, letting the woodsy taste take away the bitterness left from the adrenaline.

I was here, the forest welcomed me, and I wasn't doing anything wrong.

Now that I felt more grounded, I tried to shift my perspective on the situation. If it was Lou or Juliet in my place, what would I tell them to do? I couldn't always be there for myself, but I was always there for my friends.

For some reason it was difficult to put them in my place right now. The panic was too close, too immediate, despite the grounding exercise. Okay, so it's me here. I can deal with that. I wished Will had been able to meet with me. I wish he'd been here. Why hadn't I sucked it up and asked for him to be here to support me?

Why was it so hard asking for help?

Tanner was getting more restless behind me, jangling my nerves. I couldn't just keep standing here, frozen. The tinkle of a stream cut through the chatter of the forest and I climbed off the trail and headed toward it. I needed cow parsnip root, and it liked moist soil.

Juliet's voice in my head reminded me that the reason it was so hard to ask for help was because the desire to be almost fanatically self-reliant was a trauma response. I'd learned as a child that asking for help was bad, that I couldn't rely on the people I was supposed to be able to rely on. Which made it difficult to reach out now because the habit and mindset was so entrenched.

While I understood why I was acting this way, it didn't make it much easier to course correct. As I searched for the small cluster of white blossoms that indicated cow parsnip—and reminded myself that we were past the typical blooming period for that plant, so that wasn't all I needed to look for—I mentally walked myself through scenarios. What would happen if I asked Will for help?

He would help me. That was it. He wouldn't mock me or tell me I was weak for needing help. He would just *help*. Will was safe. I fished out my phone, waving it at Tanner. I had to make sure he didn't think I was looking up shit on my phone and cheating. "I have to text my sister real quick about babysitting. That okay?"

Tanner hesitated a moment, wrestling with the competing desire to properly conduct the test and getting a step closer to his date with my sister. My sister won. "Sure."

I texted Will outlining the situation as quickly as I could. Then I shot off a quick text to my sister about pick up times just incase Tanner asked to see my phone. As soon as I sent it, Will had responded.

Will-heart: It's not your job to take care of that jackass's feelings. He made a commitment to this test and you are well within the parameters he set. Him wanting to fuck off is not your problem. You are allowed to take your time.

Vanessa: You're right. I know you're right.

Will-heart: But you feel stuck and your emotions aren't listening to logic. I get it. You've done plenty of identification, right? He knows you know your stuff?

Vanessa: Yeah, I think so.

Will-heart: Good. Then tell that fuckwit he can go. It's not like he was going to watch you go home and cook the potion, anyway. He doesn't need to be here for this. Then you can take your fucking time.

The uptick in profanity in Will's texts told me he was pissed at Tanner for upsetting me.

Was it weird that profanity was making me feel warm and fuzzy?

Will-heart: I'll text Juliet. We'll get Savvy covered until you can get home to babysit. I'll meet you at your place..

And that right there was why I fucking adored Will. His words were exactly what I needed.

Vanessa: Thanks, Will.

Will-heart: You don't need to thank me for doing the bare fucking minimum you deserve.

Will-heart: I've decided that Tanner has a very punchable face and I should be the one to break it in.

Vanessa: Calm your tits there, Willhardt. Will-heart: My tits are un-calmable.

Vanessa: Thank you whether you want it or not.

Will texted me a small heart emoji in response and, for some reason, a pirate. I tucked my phone away.

"Everything okay?" Tanner asked.

"Yeah," I said, turning to smile at him. "Hey, I know you've got a busy night planned. I just have a few more things to gather, and then I'm off to prep this and watch Savvy. You could probably take off—assuming I've proved that I know what I'm doing out here?" I gave him a smile I didn't feel, hating every second of it. We all have to paste on a fake smile sometimes, but I tried very hard to do it only when absolutely necessary. I'd spent my entire childhood grafting on false expressions. I didn't plan to do it for my entire adulthood, too.

You grow up the way I did, you got sick of pretending to feel and think things that you don't. But I would do it if it got Tanner to leave.

Tanner scratched at the back of his head, considering. He checked his phone again.

Lips pursed. He was really making a production out of this. "Okay," he said, finally. "I think we can call it for today. You going to be okay out here by yourself?"

I nodded. "Like I said, I'm almost done, I think. Anything goes wrong, I'll call someone." He nodded. "If you're sure."

"I am." I brightened my fake smile.

"Okay then. Text me tomorrow and we'll set up a trade off for the potion." I gave hum a thumbs up. "You got it."

With a final wave, he turned and practically jogged out of the forest.

I waited until I couldn't see him anymore, then I took out my small spade and dug up the cow parsnip I'd found by the stream, channeling all my frustration into my work. But still thanking the little plant for its gift and breathing the forest deep into my lungs. These woods were a gift that I wouldn't let my father, my past, sully any more than they already had.

Kodo and Podo took this opportunity to play in the stream, the water slow enough that it wasn't a danger to them. The sunlight sparkled on the water as they splashed about, chattering away happily at me now that we were almost done and alone, the forest ours at last.

CHAPTER SEVENTEEN

Vanessa

By the time I walked in my front door, a fine layer of sweat had crusted on my skin, my knees and shoes were dirty, and I was much happier. I had everything I needed. I was one step closer to being done with this stupid test.

I kicked off my shoes, and dropped my backpack, lowering Kodo and Podo to the floor. Will was stretched out on my couch, a paperback book held open with one hand. Two handsome male pirates were on the cover, one conveniently missing their shirt. From the looks of it, he was almost finished with the book.

Will's feet were bare, his face intent, as he lounged there, and I couldn't figure out why the sight of him like this was almost painfully erotic to me. Did I have a reading kink? Or was it just Will? And seriously, how strong was my ability to live in denial if I'd never figured out that Will was this level of hot? I made an involuntary noise, a sort of blown out balloon sound of surprise and thwarted lust, because I had no time to take advantage of this delicious moment.

Will lowered his book. "What?"

I didn't feel like explaining that I'd been sidelined by my apparent sexy-man-reading fetish, so I told him only a part of the truth. "I'm just surprised to see you reading romance novel, even though I shouldn't be. I know you read them for bookclub."

"I read them for fun *and* I read them for book club. I don't just stick to the reading list." Will lifted the book back up. "What is it that you find surprising? Is it the sex? Because I like sex, which I think you know by now."

Heat skyrocketed from my toes to me cheeks because *I sure did.*

Will turned a page, seemingly not to notice that I was now doing my best impression of a blushing anime character. "Or is it that the sex is geared to groups who aren't supposed to like sex or want it?" A divot appeared between his eyebrows. "Not that every romance novel includes sex."

"It might be the fact that you read the same ones as your grandma?" My voice had gone up an octave, my words coming out almost choked.

He snorted. "Nana believes in a healthy discourse when it comes to sex, whether that sex is fictional and about vampire pirates or real life. When I lost my virginity in high school, she took me out to dinner and asked if I had any follow up questions, because, in her words, 'it's not like either of you likely knew what you were doing.'" He shook his head. "She wasn't wrong."

I couldn't imagine having that kind of conversation with anyone in my life. My dad was just a flat out no and my mom…well, if I asked my mom, I'd get nothing but information about her sex life that I did not want to hear. More power to her trying to squeeze any possible joy out of life after dealing with my father, but when I walked in on her for the third time with one of her boyfriends, I was pretty much over it.

I was a little jealous of Will's easy relationship with Nana. Still, I wanted to figure out *why* it was so surprising to see Will reading romance novels. Was it internalized misogyny? Stereotypes? What?

I struggled to put it into words, because I both didn't want Will to feel weird about his reading choices and because I wanted to understand *why* I thought it was weird. "Maybe it's because in my house, books were supposed to be for learning. Edification. Romance novels are…fluff."

This irritated Will, I could tell, because he lowered the book and frowned at me, that divot between his eyebrows deepening. "Just because it's about feelings, doesn't mean it isn't edifying. Emotional learning *is* learning." He snagged a bookmark off the back of the couch, slotting it into place. "Besides, I've never understood the concept of reading as self-flagellation. Why can't it be for fun? Why can't it be for pleasure?"

My brain stuttered on him saying the word *pleasure*. This kept happening, these sudden, shocking realizations that the framework I used to look at my friend had shifted. It made me feel slightly panicked while at the same time I was suddenly inundated with memories of Will giving me pleasure. Memories that were branded into my brain forever in the best possible way, making me realize that I might never think of the word "pleasure" without thinking of Will at the same time for the rest of my life.

Which was great, unless we broke up. People always broke up. Oh good, my anxiety was back and it was rushing through my body like water from a broken dam. I froze, unable to process it. Put it aside. I had to put it aside, before it ruined this moment. Will didn't need to deal with my anxiety spiral. I tucked it into a little mental box and threw the box into a well.

Will tapped the book's spine against the table. "And honestly, what's so wrong with fluff? Fluff is necessary. When you pack something important, or something delicate for shipping, you pad it, right? You tuck it into packing peanuts, or paper, or bubblewrap. You wrap it in *fluff.*

That's what fluff does—it protects the delicate, important things in our life. What's more delicate and important than the human heart?"

I had no good arguments, and I realized I'd been approaching books the way my dad raised us—though to be honest, 'raised' was a strong word for what he did. Why couldn't I read for fun? If it's something I enjoy, why the fuck not? I tapped my fingers along my arm and stared at Will's book. Did I want to read about sexy pirates finding love? Yes. So why wasn't I?

Will suddenly sat up, stepping over to me, concern on his face. "Hey." He clasped my hips, dipping his head so he could catch my eyes. "You look a little keyed up. Did I say something wrong?"

I shook my head, not wanting to get into it. We were talking about books. No need to take it somewhere weird.

Instead of relaxing, Will got tenser. "What's going on in that head of yours, hm?" I was about to brush him off again when Will dropped my name like a caress. "Nessa. Hey. It's me, okay? And I believe we had a deal."

I blinked up at him, realizing my arms were still crossed. Will didn't try to uncross them for me, or squish me too tight. He kept his hands cupping my hips like maybe I was something fragile that needed to be wrapped up in fluff. My instinct was to bite back. I was strong, *not* fragile and I didn't need his fluff.

But…some part of me realized that response wasn't the best. It was exhausting being strong all the time. It took a toll relying only on yourself twenty-four-seven. If I could be fragile with anyone, Will was it. He was my fluff. "What deal?"

"That you'd be honest with me and tell me if something between us was freaking you out." Will brushed at the skin under my shirt with his thumbs.

Right. I had agreed to that, hadn't I. "What makes you think that's what's bothering me?" I mean, really, I'd had a bit of a day. So many things could be setting me off.

"Because you came in here happy and that shifted while you were talking to me. It just took me a second to see it." A faint smile curled his lips. "And because I know you, Nessa." He didn't say anything else after that. Just held me loosely and waited.

I didn't deserve this man, did I? Maybe not, but I was going to do my best to fight like hell and hold onto him. I let out a breath. "I had a moment. I realized that when this ends, I will compare everyone to you. That I won't be able to think about pleasure and not think of you. It freaked me out a little."

Conflicting emotions flitted across Will's face. "That's both a delightful boost to my ego and a crushing blow at the same time."

"It's my specialty," I said.

Will let go of my hips and I felt a pang of loss. Had my confession been a mistake? Was it too much? Had I ruined this?

He framed my face with his hands. "Look at me, Nessa."

I complied, briefly losing myself in the stormy gray of his eyes. There was a fierceness there that I sometimes forgot lived in Will, but it was out full force now.

"I know this is hard for you, but sometimes people stay. You parents didn't do you any fucking favors, but that's on *them.*" He stared at the ceiling for a second, his jaw ticking, like he was trying to rein himself in.

"Are you mad at me?" I hated how small my voice sounded.

He let out an explosive breath, and when he dropped his head back down, he was scowling. "No, I'm not mad at you. I'm mad as fucking hell with your parents, though. If they hadn't been selfish assholes, you wouldn't doubt that you were lovable, and fuck me, Nessa, you are. You're" He pinched his mouth shut, still scowling, trying to sort out what he wanted to

say. I held my breath, afraid to look away because I desperately wanted to hear what he said next.

Finally he sighed, the storm in his eyes calming a bit. "You're easy to stick too, Vanessa Woodbridge. There is nothing you could do to make any of us think otherwise. Lou will stay.

Your sister will stay. So will Declan, and Bay, and everyone else that you've let orbit around you."

I felt tears well up in my eyes and fought them. I hated crying. Losing the fight, I closed my eyes so I didn't have to look at Will while I cried.

He brushed away my tears with his thumbs. "I'm not going any-where, Nessa. Even if you break up with me and I have to go back to being your friend. Even if you melt down a thousand times and I have to repeat this to you again and again. I will not abandon you."

"You'll start to resent me if you have to put me back together all the time." His response was swift and firm. "No, I won't."

He slid his arms around my shoulders and I finally unfolded my arms and sunk into him. I laid my head against his chest, soothed by his steady heartbeat. Will held me tight, anchoring me in such a way that I could let go. I could go *soft.*

He rested his cheek on my head and when he started talking, I could feel the rumble of his words in his chest as well as hear them, and it felt like a privilege. A gift, that someone cared for me so much that they'd let me get close to the soft animal of their body.

And that I trusted Will so much, that I let him get close to mine.

"I won't resent you, Nessa. You've put in so much work and tried so hard to build up areas of yourself that your parents either neglected or flat out destroyed. You have no idea how much I respect that." He gave me a quick squeeze. "On top of that, it costs me nothing, absolutely nothing, to tell you the truth. I don't mind being our emotional sonar. Anytime you need that reassurance, call out, and I'll echo the truth—you're lovable and the important people stay."

I flattened my palms on Will's back, enjoying the heat of his skin through his shirt, the play of muscles in his back as he began to sway with me in his arms. "How come you don't struggle with this? Your parents didn't stay." Will never shied away from discussing his upbringing. It wasn't a sore subject for him, which frankly I thought was a bit of a miracle, but some questions I'd left unasked.

"My parents weren't being selfish dicks. They were *literally* children."

I knew Will's parents had been young—his mother only sixteen when she had him, his father barely past his seventeenth birthday. I couldn't imagine how hard it must have been for them.

Will pressed a kiss into my hair. "It fucked me up a bit when I was little. Never having a mom or dad at school for parent teacher night, shit like that. I don't know if it's because Nana got me into therapy so young, or what, but it all clicked one day—maybe I didn't have the family everyone else did, but so what? Some of those parents sucked, and I wouldn't want that home life, and a lot of other kids had divorced parents, or they were adopted, or in the foster system and I realized that there were lots of different kinds of ways to make a family."

He kept swaying me, holding me close. "Maybe I didn't have parents the exact way other kids did, but I had a happy homelife and I knew for a fact that Nana loved the shit out of me." He was grinning now, I could tell by the sound of his voice. "To be honest, Nana probably spoiled me."

"What about when your parents got older? Why didn't they come for you then?"

Will laughed. "My dad tried. He'd gone to trade school, got a job. Married. They were going to expand their family and wanted me on board." Somehow Will managed to tuck me in even closer. "I was seven by then. The idea of moving away from Nana? Like ripping my heart out. Luckily, my dad was a good guy. They wanted me, but he wanted me happier more. I didn't want to be uprooted, so they let me stay. They call, we visit, I get pictures of my younger siblings."

"What about your mom?"

"My mom figured out pretty fast that kids weren't for her. She does her best. She checks in. Sends cards on the holidays and all that. Once she was settled and had a good job, she sent Nana money to help pay for things, but she doesn't really know what to do with me, you know?"

"That doesn't mess you up?"

"Used to, but honestly? She made the right choice. Both of them did. This was the best possible outcome for me. I was never made to feel like a nuisance or unwanted. That's the difference, Nessa. You didn't have that."

My throat got tight, so I could only hum a response.

Will cupped the back of my head with one hand, cradling it. "But you have that now.

From all of us, okay?"

"You're the kind that sticks?"

"Yeah," he said. "And I'll keep telling you until you believe it." "Okay." I sniffled, which earned me another kiss.

"Thank you," he said, his voice a caressing rumble against my ear as I pressed it to his chest. "For sticking to our deal."

"I might need help," I said. "Like just now."

"No problem, but tell me if I need to back off, okay? I won't be mad. I won't hold it against you. I promise."

I both loved and hated that Will knew I needed that reassurance, but the love far outweighed the hate. I just loathed that I needed the reassurance in the first place.

"Thank you." I gave myself one more moment soaking in Will, before I started to pull away. "I have to work on potion or we'll be late to bookclub."

"Do we need to skip it?"

He didn't even hesitate to ask, even though Will loved bookclub. "No," I said. "I want to go."

"Okay. Let me know if that changes."

"I will. Thanks."

He kissed me soft and slow. "Anytime."

Will #

I grabbed a platter from the cabinet in Nana's kitchen, Savvy balanced on my hip ostensibly helping, while I tried to get my shit together. I'd almost fucked up hard earlier. First when I didn't notice Nessa was freaking out and then when I'd almost made it worse.

I'd come closer to telling her I loved her. I mean, she was my best friend. She knows I *love* her. She knows I want her. But I haven't shoved it into her face that I was *in* love with her. Not because I didn't want to tell her or because I wasn't sure of my feelings. No, I was more sure than ever. Vanessa had a lot going on outside of us, though. On top of that, she'd already pushed her self far and fast outside of her emotional comfort zone.

If I told her I was in love with her now? She'd spook.

But I'd almost done it anyway. It had been incubating in my chest so long that it had almost busted out on its own, like one of the baby xenomorphs from *Alien*. We'd all seen how well *those* had gone over in the movie. Now was not the time to chestburster my emotions all over the situation. That would nuke our relationship from orbit.

I set a platter down onto the counter and popped open the container holding my cookies.

Savvy lunged for one of the penis cookies, and I captured her hand. I didn't think there was anything wrong with her eating one personally—it was just a cookie—but I knew some people wouldn't like it.

I handed her one of the anchors right as Becca came in with my grandma.

"Thank you for inviting me," Becca said, brandishing a bottle of wine, which Nana snatched. "Will said you had cocktails planned, but I thought wine never goes to waste, you know?"

"Thank you." Nana held the bottle out, checking out the label. "Very nice."

Becca blushed. "I'm just so grateful. I'm new to the area and trying to meet people is so hard…"

Savvy gurgled at her.

Becca brightened. "Ooh, and who's this?" Becca came over and greeted Savvy while doing the same for me with a friendly kiss on the cheek.

Which is of course when Van walked in. Her eyes narrowed, her mouth pinching.

Becca didn't see her. She only had eyes for Savvy, but I raised an eyebrow at Van. She cleared the expression from her face by the time Becca turned around. Becca grinned at her, holding a hand out. "Hi, I'm Becca. Thank you so much for having me. I'm just so excited to be here."

Becca was a nervous talker, I guess.

"This is Becca's first bookclub," I said, wiping some crumbs of Savvy's shirt.

"Oh?" Van asked, acting for all the world like it wasn't her first bookclub meeting. "Yes," Becca said, her cheeks flushed as Nana handed her a glass. "Will invited me." Van crossed her arms. "How nice of him. How do you know Will?"

"Oh, um…" Becca got flustered, glancing at me.

"Becca and I had a coffee date," I said, carefully negotiating Savvy away from the cookies. "No, sugar monster. One for now is good. You can have some crackers, or we have yogurt in your bag." Savvy pouted. I blew against her cheek until she giggled.

Nana looked between Becca and Van, her eyebrows raised.

"We had a good time, but decided we were friends," I explained, handing Savvy off to Nana because it looked like she was about to cause trouble, and that would be much harder if her hands were full. She helped Savvy get a cracker, grabbing one for herself.

"Speaking of which, Becca, this is Van. Van, Becca." Van held out her hand. "His girlfriend."

Nana coughed, choking on her cracker. It was possible that I'd been a little blunt. Becca looked concerned, shooting her gaze between Nana and Van.

I rubbed her back. "You got to chew, Nana." She shot me a glare.

Becca took Van's hand. "It's really lovely to meet you. Will's so great."

I could see Van wrestling with herself. On one hand, she was jealous, but on the other, Becca clearly meant what she said and wasn't there to try and get a second date with me.

"Yeah," Van said. "He is." She held out an elbow. "Come on. I've never attended book club, but I've been here a lot. I can show you around while Will gives Nana the heimlich."

"That would be great," Becca said, putting her arm through Van's. "I'd love a full tour. If you're okay?" She asked Nana, concern on her face.

"I'm fine," Nana grumbled. "I just have a terrible grandson." "You love me," I said, smiling.

Van rolled her eyes. "Let's start with drinks. I'll show you the cocktail cart—there's ice tea with lemon, but one pitcher is alcoholic." She pulled Becca from the room, still chatting.

I gave Nana a glass of water, waiting for her to coughing fit to fully clear. "You're an asshole," Nana said.

"Yeah," I said. "But I'm your asshole." I made big eyes at her. "I learned from the master."

She sighed, snuggling Savvy. "The problem, Savvy-girl, is that he's right. There's no one to blame for that boy but me."

Now that I was sure she was fine, I moved about the kitchen, getting out a few of the snacks Nana had made for the group.

"So, it's official now? The girlfriend title?" "Yes."

"Are you sure that's a good idea?" Nana asked carefully. "Yes."

Nana frowned. "Is that all I'm going to get? Monosyllabic treatment." "No."

She gently smacked my shoulder.

I laughed. "Yes, Nana. I think it's a good idea."

She watched me for a moment, and I let her—Nana needed to get this out of her system. "And if it goes poorly?" She asked gently.

I finished arranging the cheese, making sure to have a small bowl of the gluten free crackers out as well. I shrugged. "Then we'll know, won't we?"

She sighed, snagging a piece of cheese for Savvy. "I hope it goes well for both of you, Will. I really do. I love Van. I just worry."

"I know, Nana," I said softly, kissing her cheek. "It will be okay." And it would. I had to believe that.

Nana handed Savvy another piece of cheese. "You think you'll ever have one of these?" "Technically," I said. "I have one right now."

Nana glared at me. "You're not funny." "I'm hilarious."

"I'm not trying to pressure you," Nana said. "I was just curious."

"I know," I said. "And I'm grateful that you're not the type to hound me about this stuff. But I really don't know. Savvy's pretty great. I don't think I'd mind having more of her around. But for right now?" I shrugged.

Savvy offered me some of the cheese she'd been sucking on and smooshing in her little fist. "Chee."

"Yes," I said. "Cheese. You're very generous, but it's all yours, kiddo." I tapped her nose, before I scooped up the snack trays. "I'm going to take these out there. You good?"

"I'm great," Nana said. "I'm not the one who invited a former date to the same bookclub as his current girlfriend."

I grinned at her. "I'm a friendly guy, Nana."

"You're lucky you're charming," Nana said. "Anyone else did that sort of thing and it would end in a total donnybrook."

CHAPTER EIGHTEEN

Will

"I can't believe you wouldn't touch any of the penis cookies." I was driving Van home after bookclub, Savvy passed out in her carseat. Despite Nana's worries, bookclub had gone well, both Becca and Van seeming to have a good time.

Becca hadn't had time to finish the book, which was okay, and Van didn't even start it, but honestly, that wasn't the core of bookclub anyway. Yes, we read the books, but we didn't shame people who either didn't manage it or decided the book wasn't for them. All discourse was welcome.

"I can't believe you invited an ex to the bookclub and didn't tell me," Van said, mock pouting from the passenger seat. At least, I think it was mostly mock. I got the sense, though, that there was some real underlying emotion there. I admit that I was a bit distracted—Van was cute when she pouted.

I snorted. "One coffee date does not an ex make." I glanced at her in the fleeting yellow glow of the streetlight. "Vanessa Woodbridge, are you *jealous*?"

"I am a little?" Van scrunched her nose. "I know it's stupid. I've never been the jealous type."

I batted my eyes at her when we stopped at the stoplight. "I think it's sweet." She flipped me off.

"Don't threaten me with a good time," I drawled before snagging her hand and dropping a kiss on the back of it. "Becca was a non-starter, but she was fun to talk to and very lonely and I thought she'd like the bookclub group."

"You did the right thing," Van said. "I know the jealousy is irrational, but I can't help it." She slumped in her seat. "She's exactly like I pictured her, too. Super cute. She even volunteers at a pet shelter."

"Yeah," I said. "She likes animals. Why?" "Nothing," Van said. "I just called it."

"When did you call it?" The light turned green, but I kept stealing glances at her. I couldn't quite read the expression on her face.

Van slumped lower in her seat. "When I was picturing your date with her."

I…did not know what to do with that information. I drove for a few minutes, the quiet in the car broken only by the sound of the wheels hitting the pavement. I couldn't really imagine the scenario Van had presented. Me dating hadn't ever bothered her before. But it must have bothered her with Becca. Dread pooled in my gut.

"Is that why you finally went out with me? Because my date with Becca made you jealous?" I wasn't sure what I'd do if I found out that all of this—the sex, the relationship, all of it—had been catalyzed by jealousy. That would make it feel less like something Van wanted and more like she was being territorial.

Van straightened. "What? No." Her expression was horrified as she reached over and put her hand on my leg. "Will. Absolutely not. I was ready to stand selflessly by as you found love. It really sucked, but you should have seen how committed I was going to dying on that sword."

I grunted, not quite feeling better about any of it.

"Things had started to shift before your date with Becca. There was the craft fail, and then the sexy dream, and your chest and—"

"If you think we're not going to revisit any of that, you're high."

She ignored me. "But when you started getting ready for your date, I realized how much I hated the idea. Do you have any idea how much that sucked? Watching you get all tarted up for someone else—"

"Don't cage me. I'm a multidirectional tart. I can tart in all directions. An all purpose tart, if you will."

Van started talking louder to talk over my nonsense. "But I was going to go keep my mouth shut because you wanted that date and I wanted you to be happy. Do you have any idea how that felt?"

"Yes," I said quietly, suddenly all seriousness. "I know exactly how that feels." I'd spent years watching Vanessa get tarted in a multidirectional fashion for guys that weren't me. It had been a punch to the gut every time.

Van looked stricken for a moment. "Yeah, I guess you do." She squeezed my leg. "I'm sorry, Will."

"That's okay," I said, and it was, mostly. It had sucked, all those years of watching her go out with assholes that didn't deserve her. It was better when she dated guys who were decent to her, even though that always scared me more, because what if she'd gotten serious with one of those guys? Who treated her well, so I'd have no reason to tell her to drop the guy. I didn't like to think about it, so I changed the subject. "You can make it up to me by telling me all about the sexy dream you had about me. What was I wearing?"

"Eat shit."

I couldn't help it—I grinned. "Language, Vanessa. There are gentle ears present." "Savvy's asleep."

"I was talking about me."

She shook her head. "You're terrible."

"Wait," I said, suddenly realizing something. "Is that why you were being so weird when I was getting ready for the coffee date?" I flipped on the blinker for her street, grinning at her. "Vanessa Woodbridge, were you checking me out?"

Van crossed her arms. "There are no good responses to that question."

"Yes there is," I said. "The correct answer is, 'yes, Will, I couldn't help looking at your sexy ass.' That's the correct response."

She flushed.

I cackled. "Holy shit, that was it, wasn't it? You were checking out my ass!"

She slapped her hands down on her thighs. "You were walking around in your little boxer briefs! Just…parading in front of me! Of course I was checking you out!"

"Oh, sweetheart—I'll parade in front of you anytime you like. Just say the word." "I'm never going to hear the end of this, am I?"

"No," I said, earnestly. "I'm already planning what other undergarments I can get that might turn your crank. How do you feel about thongs? You more of a lace and fringe kind of girl, or do you want to see me in leather?"

Van's cheeks were bright red and I was enjoying myself *deeply*. I pulled up to the curb. "And we haven't even touched on the mention of my chest yet. What about it did you find so fascinating?"

"Tanner," Van said.

I turned off the car. "Tanner's not allowed to touch my chest. We don't have that kind of relationship."

"No," Van said, all playfulness gone. "I mean it's Tanner and he's making out with my sister in the driveway."

I followed her gaze and sure enough, Tanner and Juliet were leaning against his car, her hands around his neck. I didn't look to see where his hands were.

"Huh," I said. "I just really never saw her as an oxford shirt and khakis kind of person." "She's not," Van said absently. "I don't know what to do. Do we honk? Leave? What?" "Well," I said, taking my keys out of the ignition. "What we don't do is sit here like two voyeurs and watch them make out against the side of a Ford fiesta."

I climbed out of the car, slamming my door with a little extra force. Not because I was mad or anything, but I wanted to make sure they knew someone had pulled up. Van got out on her side, grabbing a sleepy Savannah from her carseat.

Jules jerked away, looking a little guilty. Van wouldn't like that look. She might not like Tanner and didn't trust him, but she wouldn't want Juliet to feel guilty for wanting to have a night out.

"Will, Vanessa." Tanner cleared his throat, smoothing down his shirt. "Good to see you." "Thanks, man," I said grabbing Savvy's diaper bag out of the back seat. "Good night?" "Yeah," he said, looking sheepishly at Juliet. As much as I didn't like the guy, he clearly

had a crush the size of Seattle on Van's sister. Which made me dislike him a little less. At least the dude had good taste in women, if not in anything else.

"Tanner took me to a winery up in Woodinville," Juliet said, her expression equally smitten.

"They were doing a candlelight concert," Tanner said. "A string quartet playing newer stuff along with some classical songs."

"And there were these fire elementists there, too," Juliet cut in, her face animated. "They were coaxing the flames into little stories to go along with the music." She held up her hand, placing her fingers about an inch apart. "One elementists made a tiny scene, this big, of a horse running that was absolutely stunning." She dropped her hand with a sigh. "It was beautiful."

Tanner grabbed her hand and kissed it. "Yes, it was."

I didn't like the expression on Van's face. It told me she might say something she would regret later, so I slung an arm around her. "Sounds like a wonderful evening. Well, we're all worn out from bookclub." I steered Van and Savvy toward the house. "Things got really heated when we started arguing over whether the chapter 'Friggin' in the Riggin' was a direct allusion to the Sex Pistols Song, or just a coincidence. I'm leaning toward the latter."

Tanner frowned, mouth opening. I kept my girls moving. "As you can imagine, we are ready to hit the hay." We were past them now, moving up the front steps. "You just come get Savvy whenever you're ready, Jules. Night!"

By that time, we were in the front door.

Van turned to me. "Hit the hay? Are we farmers now?"

"Yes," I said. "And what we were reaping was total awkwardness." "You're weird," Vanessa said, toeing off her shoes.

"I know."

Van leaned forward and kissed my cheek. "But I like it."

"Well, thank fuck for that," I said with some relief. "Because weird is all I've got. Well, that and a sweet ass, according to you."

"I'm never going to hear the end of that one, am I?"

"No," I said. "I have a starved ego. I'm going to milk that one for all it's worth."

Vanessa #

Will settled Savvy into my bed as I dragged my confused self to the kitchen. I didn't have any dedicated space for potions in the house, so the kitchen was my best option. All the basics were there, and it was easy to clean.

I dumped my spell ingredients onto the table, out of my way for now. Declan kept the place tidy. We tried to help out, but he often got their first, like an almost preternaturally efficient cleaning service.

I got out the rags and cleaning spray and wiped down the counters, putting any of the spare dirty dishes in the sink into the dishwasher. This not only cleared up my spell space making it as ready as I could, but helped give me time to get my mind in order as well.

I couldn't figure out how I felt about my sister and Tanner. It was very much her business and I knew that, but I couldn't help being concerned. She was my baby sister and let's face it, in our family, there was no one else watching out for us. Tanner felt like a threat, but I couldn't be sure that assessment was accurate. I had too much baggage in the way. Did I only dislike him because of my father? Or was I picking up on actual red flags? I blew my hair out of my face, frustrated.

Once I got the space clear, I put away the cleaning supplies. Then I gathered up my hair, pulling it back in a knot at the back of my head to keep it out of my face. I would focus on the potion I had to make for Tanner and leave everything else aside for now.

Tanner hadn't asked to see proof of me cooking the spell, but I didn't want to give my dad a loophole, so I decided to record the concoction process. I got my phone out, put it up on top of an upside down glass vase, and made sure it kept my work area in view. With it in place, I just had to turn it on and we were ready to go.

I got out a clean sauce pan, filling it with two cups water for the base. Because it was water based, I didn't have to pay too much attention to the kind of pot I used. Sometimes that mattered. Some spells called for copper pots, others were oil based and did better with an enamel coating. Still others brewed best in cast iron. Every witch had their own preferences, too.

I got out a wooden cutting board and Podo drug over the roots I needed onto the cutting board. I started peeling roots and slicing them, pushing them to the side for Podo to put into the pot. Each ferret had their strengths and weaknesses, and Podo was great for potion work. Kodo stayed with Will and Savvy, keeping an eye on them.

Podo plucked leaves from stems, pushing the greens into a pile for me to julienne. We fell into an easy rhythm, my focus on my task, my familiar doing their part to keep the process smooth. I brought the mix to a boil then dropped the heat to keep simmer. Podo took over from there, stirring the potion with a wooden spoon, making sure nothing burned and stuck to the bottom.

While I waited for the liquid to thicken, I pulled out mason jars, a dry erase pen, and a permanent black marker. Mason jars weren't the fanciest for presentation, but the glass wouldn't change the potion and their practicality put them firmly in my pro column.

I drew three circles, one for each jar I'd set on the counter, arranged in a triangle around a white candle. Tanner had only asked for one, and maybe it was all the time with my dad, but I wanted some safety nets. If I gave Tanner two—one for him and one for my dad in case he decided on a whim to test the potion—I was still left with an extra. Maybe I was being paranoid, but that had never hurt me where my father was concerned.

I used the permanent marker to label the top of the jars with my name, date, the type of potion, and samples one, two and three, respectively. The third I'd get tested by someone unconnected to my father. I just hadn't decided on who yet. The obvious choice would be Thea. Who better than the best potioner I knew?

But that meant I'd have to tell her my plans. I couldn't just randomly give her a potion and expect her to not have questions. I could lie, but…I didn't love the idea of lying to Thea. If she found out, her feelings would be hurt.

Podo chittered at me, letting me know the potion was thickening. This was one of the points where it was more art than science. Or at least it was for me. There were people that went for certain temperatures, viscosity, and so on. I just…knew what it should look like. I could tell when it *felt* done. The same way some bakers used a toothpick to check whether a cake was finished, and some tap the top to check the bounce.

I stirred the potion for a second, checking the way it moved, how it slid off the spoon.

When it looked the way I wanted, I slid it off the heat. I poured the potion into the jars, keeping them as even as I could. The spoon and the pan went into the sink for cleaning later. While the potion cooled, I drew symbols on the counter in the dry erase marker.

If concocting the potion was like baking a cake, the spell portion was the decoration. It could shift a base potion to a work of art, not only in looks but in flavor for lack of a better word. This was why potions were tricky. There were so many variables—ingredients, concoction and spell work. So many places where it could go wrong.

Cassandra potions or truth spells came in many varieties and strengths. Cold Candor was one of the less combative ones and my favorite. It wasn't as much about sifting through lies as it was about finding clarity. Some people could lie with the truth, and Cold Candor stopped them from doing it.

Traditionally the spell included interlocking lines for binding, along with the diamond-like symbol representing clarity and sharp-lined one for focus. I added one for brevity and honest intentions. When my symbols were all done, I lit the candle, whispering my words for invocation.

Magic hummed along my skin, burning a bright orange through my symbols, like a spark eating up a fuse. When the last symbol released in a puff of smoke, I capped the potions, screwing the lids on tight. *Done.* I grinned, a sense of accomplishment filling me from head to toe.

Podo hopped in celebration, though far clear of the potion space. It had only taken one time where Kodo had spilled a mostly-finished potion that singed off half his hair and turned the other half electric blue to make them both understand the wisdom of being careful around potion-making areas.

I turned off my phone, ready to stick it into my pocket when Juliet walked into the kitchen. I checked the clock before I could stop myself, making Juliet flush, her expression turning decidedly mulish.

"We were talking," Juliet said. "Time got away from me." She was in her pajamas, face scrubbed clean, and I suspected they'd been doing a hell of a lot more than talking.

I didn't want to argue with her. "It's none of my business." "You're right," Juliet said, arms crossing.

"I didn't say anything." My voice sounded defensive, even to my own ears.

"You didn't have to," Juliet snapped. "Your judgement is all over your face, so go ahead.

Get it out of your system."

Before I knew what I was doing, my mouth was open and all kinds of stupid was coming right out of it. "Why him? One of dad's minions? You could have any guy—"

"Says the person who couldn't see what was right under her nose. You have no room to talk—"

"That's not fair—"

"Fair is for children, Van. It's not Tanner's fault that he's dad's graduate assistant. You can't judge him by that set of criteria."

"Fine. Tell me what's so great, then?" I started washing my spell pot, slamming it around unnecessarily. "What, do you miss the lifestyle? Hanging out with other arcanists? Having his colleagues look down on you, like dad's used to do for mom?"

"They aren't all like that!"

The fact that she was right to call me out for being judgmental just made me madder for some reason. "Okay, so what, Tanner's super into your job? Makes you laugh? What?" I squeezed too much soap into the water. "I mean, fuck, Juliet, what if he's spying on you for dad or using you to get close—"

"Because it's impossible that he might just be into me for me, right?" Juliet snapped. "Single mom—"

"He should be so lucky to get you and Savvy." I scrubbed the pot furiously. "That's not what I'm saying, you're being willfully obtuse and—"

"I'm all for healthy discourse, but you two are going to wake Savannah," Will said, his voice a soft rumble.

We both snapped our jaws shut at the same time. I hadn't even realized we'd been yelling until Will said something.

The kitchen was absolutely silent.

Will came over, dropping a kiss on my cheek. Then he wrapped an arm around Juliet's shoulder. "Let's get your kiddo, eh? You're probably ready to crash."

"Yeah," Juliet said softly. She went with him, not even turning to glance back at me.

Will kept talking as they left the kitchen, his voice pitched low. I couldn't make out what they were saying, but Juliet's reply was equally soft. He'd managed to talk to her like a normal person while all I'd done was screech at her like a tone-deaf banshee on karaoke night.

I rinsed out the sauce pan, setting it on the dish drainer, as Podo ambled up to the sink. She made a sympathetic noise, nosing my elbow. I dried my hands before scooping her up and snuggling her close. "I know, I know. The asshole tiara of the night belongs firmly on my head."

The sucky thing about having a roommate who cleans up all the time was that when I wanted to hide in the kitchen puttering around, I had nothing to do. I tried to sweep anyway, just in case I'd dropped something.

That's how Will found me a few minutes later. "They're gone. Want to talk about it?" "No." I started pulling out chairs. Might as well sweep under the table.

Will said my name with a sigh. "Vanessa. What are you doing?" "Cleaning."

Will scoffed. "Sure. You're sweeping the world's cleanest floor."

"So we should just assume Declan's doing everything and leave the cleaning to him, huh?" I hated the nasty tone in my voice, but I couldn't seem to stop it.

"Noooo," Will said slowly. "I'm just not sure cleaning to avoid talking about what happened with your sister is the best approach, either."

"You're not my fucking keeper, Willhardt." I didn't look at him, instead concentrating on getting imaginary dirt from under the table. Seriously, did Declan fucking vacuum in here or something? How was there not even one piece of old cereal or rogue chunk of onion?

Will sighed. "I didn't say I was. Damn it, Nessa, will you just stop and look at me?"

That was the last thing I wanted to do, but I did it, leaning on the broom as casually as I could manage, my jaw jutted out.

Will stood in front of me—hair mussed, blonde stubble glinting on his chin. He was barefoot and I'm not sure why, but that made me so angry. Like I was mad he had stepped in, done what he'd seen fit, and settled in for the night like he lived here. Which I knew on some level was *totally fine*, but it felt so good to be mad. To lash out.

"There," I said. "I looked at you. Happy? Can I sweep now?"

Will didn't answer. He didn't have to. We both knew I was being childish. Well, guess fucking what? I *wanted* to be childish. It was my asshole tiara party and I'd sweep if I wanted to, I guess.

I turned away, shoving the chairs back around the table. "Seriously?"

"Seriously."

"If you want to be alone, you can just say so." Will sounded frustrated. Couldn't say I blamed him.

Didn't stop me from saying, "Being alone sounds perfect."

The kitchen was silent again except for the sound of me sliding the chairs back into place.

I didn't look up, intent on my work.

Will sighed, watching me clean absolutely nothing for a few long, torturous moments. Then he left the kitchen. I heard my bedroom door open. Shut. Footsteps. The click of the front door. Not slammed. Will would never do that. Instead, he closed it with gentle care that was somehow worse. For some reason it hurt more.

The house was dead silent. A rare moment when no one was home but me. Empty, quiet, and awful. Like I was inside a body where the heart had died. Now it was me, rattling around in the empty shell.

Kodo and Podo stared up at me from the floor. I could barely make them out through the blurring of my tears. "You going to get mad at me too?"

They stared at me with their bright little eyes.

Kodo hopped over to the fridge. *No, boss, we're not mad. We know where Declan hides the bacon, though. If you're sad, maybe.*

"Bacon does not cure all ills," I said with a sniffle.

But it doesn't make them worse, does it? Podo asked. *So maybe we should eat some bacon, and we can all wear asshole tiaras together.*

I laughed and it was half-sob. "I don't actually have a tiara, and I definitely don't have two tiny ones."

That's okay, Podo said. *We know where the craft supplies are. We can make our own, but you'll have to help.*

We're not allowed to use the glue gun without supervision anymore, remember boss? Kodo hopped over to the fridge and sat back on his hindquarters, reaching up for the fridge handle, doing his best to look pathetic so I'd help him.

It was just so sweet while simultaneously blatantly manipulative in their attempts to get bacon that I burst fully into tears, sliding to the ground. The broom stick clattered against the floor when I dropped it.

I dropped my head into my arms and cried, letting the ferrets crawl over me, soothing me as best they knew how.

I hadn't been this miserable in a long time, and the worst part was I knew it was my fault.

CHAPTER NINETEEN

Vanessa

I didn't sleep well. Going to sleep in a cold empty bed wasn't great. Waking up was even worse. We may not have been dating long, but it hadn't taken me much time to realize how much I liked waking up to to his warm body behind mine. His sleep-grumbly voice in my ear.

Instead of morning sex and laughter to start my day, I had one ferret curled up awkwardly in my armpit, and the other behind my knee. The blanket was on the floor and I was freezing.

This sucked.

I showered, deciding I didn't want to deal with anyone this morning if I could avoid it. I had to open, so it wouldn't be too difficult. Ever since Declan had quit the food truck, no one else had to get up early but me.

Showered, dressed, and the ferrets fed, I grabbed my messenger bag, tiptoeing out into the kitchen. I needed to pack up the potions. I had my messenger bag on the counter, the first potion jar wrapped in a tea towel when Declan padded into the kitchen.

He'd thrown on a pair of pajama shorts, but that was it, his hair sticking up, one hand scratching his beard. He snarled a yawn.

"What are you doing up?" "T'see you." He yawned again.

I frowned, nestling the jar into the bag. "What for?"

"Will texted me." Declan pulled me into a big hug. "He said you might need this, and you wouldn't take it from him right now."

"Son of a bitch." I was going to cry again. Stupid thoughtful jerk. Declan patted my back. "Want to growl about it?"

"No," I said. "I want to suffer in silence."

"Okay," he said, another big yawn making him pause. He let me go. "As long as you know silence isn't the only option. You can suffer at top decibel if you want."

"Thanks," I said, tucking away the rest of the jars. "That's good to know."

He chuffed, a very wolfy sound. "Okay, then." He wrapped an arm around me, giving me a last squeeze as he dropped a kiss on my temple. "You know we love you, right?"

"Of course I do," I said, slinging my bag on. "Now go back to bed."

"You don't have to tell me twice," Declan said, padding back to the room he shared with Lou, because my roommates were smart enough to not throw their boyfriends out in a fit of anger over something ridiculous.

Ugh. I was tired of thinking about it. It was one of those moments where I was just so tired, so exhausted by myself. Unfortunately, I couldn't take turns being anyone else. I was stuck

with me and I'd just have to make the best of it.

#

I used my set of keys to get into Wicked Brews. I'd managed to get in early enough that I could take my time opening. Turning on the coffee machines, checking the cases for smudges. Pulling the rack of edibles out of the walk in, Emma's sprawling handwriting telling me what was there and where she'd stacked the special orders. Filling the chilled glass case with long trays of medicinals that wouldn't have looked out of place in a garden fairy's tea party.

The second cases wasn't chilled, and that's where I put the baked goods, arranging them until I was happy that they'd catch anyone's eye. I appreciated the smell of cinnamon, the sweet smell of the glazes, the comforting scent of the coffee. My throat felt raw and my nerves were delicate from the night before. So I steamed milk and made myself a Dublin Fog instead.

I sipped my tea as I checked the milk fridge, and did a general inventory of the supplies up front, making sure everything was ready for the day. Thea and Emma rolled in around eight, right as I was opening the door for the morning crowd to start trickling in.

"You look terrible," Emma said, flopping her front half down on the counter. "And I feel terrible. Take pity on me and make me a coffee."

I turned on the grinder, grabbing the half and half for her breve.

"What my darling wife meant to say is, 'you look unhappy,' which is much different and definitely kinder than, 'you look terrible.'" Thea said, pouring herself a drip coffee.

"Same thing," Emma mumbled. "I'll be nicer after coffee."

Thea laughed, throwing back her head. She still wore a wide smile when she leaned down and dropped a kiss on her wife's scowling cheek. "Well, you couldn't possibly be worse after coffee."

"That sounds like a challenge," Emma said.

I placed Emma's cup in front of her. "I'm fine, but thank you."

Emma squinted at me. "The hell you are." She straightened and sipped her drink, relishing the flavor. "At least your coffee isn't sad."

"Thanks," I said dryly. "Now I know where you priorities are." Emma clutched her mug to her chest. "Do you blame me?"

"I do not," I said, rinsing the pitcher.

Thea smoothed her hand down her dress, today's choice an emerald green wrap dress that managed to set off every good feature she had, which were a lot.

Emma shook her head, exasperation stamping her features. "Can you believe how hot my wife is? It's almost indecent, isn't it?"

Thea smacked her shoulder playfully, but she was blushing. "She's too hot for you," I said.

"Right?" Emma took another careful sip of her coffee. "I'm so glad she doesn't know she could do better. Otherwise I'd be doomed."

Thea rolled her eyes, but her blush had spread. "You're incorrigible." Emma shrugged a shoulder. "You like it."

"I do," Thea said with a sigh. "To my everlasting shame." She patted my arm. "You sure you're okay, sugar? Anything we could do to help?"

It was a perfect opening and I took it before I second guessed myself. "There is, actually.

I have a potion. Could you run the specs on it?"

"Sure," Thea said, curiosity lighting up her face. "What's it for?"

"A little project," I said. "I don't want to get into it now, but I promise I'll tell you later. Is that okay?"

She looked a little confused, and I cursed myself for cowardice. Why couldn't I just tell them?

"Of course it's okay, sugar," Thea said.

I dug the third potion out of my bag and handed it to her. She took it from me, her eyes darting from the jar to my face and back again. She desperately wanted to ask me more questions, I could tell. My stomach dove down, my shoulders tightening. I hated disappointing her.

When it was clear I wasn't going to say more, Thea nodded at me. "Okay. I'll get it done today, sugar. But we're here if you need to talk to us."

"I know," I said. Why was everyone so fired up to talk to me recently? I wasn't the most sparkling conversationalist on my best day, and this was no where near my best day.

"And by that she means she's here if you need to chat," Emma said, pushing herself away from the counter. "I'm only here for dirty secrets and hot goss. If you're secretly having Bigfoot's baby, I'm your girl. Anything serious is all Thea."

"I would never hide Bigfoot's baby," I said. "I'm not ashamed of our love."

"Nor should you be," Emma said, following Thea into the back. Thea was already focused on the potion, holding it up to the light. "We'll throw you a baby shower. Won't we, Thea?"

"Of course," Thea said absently. "We can have petit fours and serve fruit tea."

"See?" Emma said. "The menu's already planned. We're here for you and your scandalous love child."

I laughed, feeling slightly better than I had since last night.

Vanessa #

Will didn't stop in to visit me at work. I kept checking my phone, but it remained stubbornly silent with the exception of Trick sending me short videos of Damnit. The fledgling phoenix was with him at work today, learning the ins and outs of making ritual knives.

I texted Tanner during my first break, trying to figure out when I could drop off the potions. He surprised me by offering to pick them up from me at work. I gratefully accepted.

Tanner showed up around ten, wearing a short sleeved button up, his messenger bag over one shoulder. He greeted me with a smile, though it was tempered by something that I couldn't place. "You have a minute?"

We were in a lull, my back up barista, Heather, was already rearranging the case, taking out the empty trays and moving things around so there were no gaps.

I handed Tanner his coffee. "Sure. I'll just have the be close incase Heather needs me to jump back in.

Tanner nodded, waving at one of the tables, his eyebrow up.

I grabbed the potions and joined him. As soon as he was seated I set them on the tabletop before grabbing myself a glass of water.

Tanner put the potions in his own bag, barely looking at them. This made me want to frown, though I caught it before I made a face. It wasn't sure what I expected him to do? Ooh and ahh? It was just a potion. Still, it would have been nice to have my work acknowledged.

"There's no way to ease into this, so I'll just say it." He sipped his drink, finger plucking absently at the paper sleeve hugging his to go cup. "Juliet tells me you're unhappy with her seeing me."

I jerked, almost spilling my water. I'm not sure what I'd thought he was going to say, but that wasn't it. I glanced at him, unsure how to respond. I didn't want to talk to him about it. If I was going to make nice with anyone, it would be my sister. She was the one I'd been a jerk to.

But I couldn't brush him off either, not just because it did involve him, but also because I couldn't really alienate Tanner right now. He had control over my exam.

"It's not that I'm unhappy she's seeing you," I hedged. And it wasn't exactly about Tanner, though it wasn't *not* about him either. I definitely couldn't tell him it was because I had issues with my dad. I had no idea where Tanner's loyalties laid, but he *was* my dad's graduate assistant. "I don't know you Tanner. She's my little sister, you know? I love her and I worry about her."

Tanner continued to tear at his coffee sleeve. "So it's a protective thing?"

"Yes," I said, relieved that he was getting it. "It's not personal." It was a *little* personal. He shifted in his seat, his expression thoughtful. "I guess I can understand that. But

Juliet's amazing. You don't have to worry about me treating her like anything less than gold."

I tried to reassure him with a smile, but it was forced. Tanner could talk all he wanted, but I wouldn't make up my mind about him until I'd seen what he would do. Words are great and all, but actions don't lie.

He didn't seem wholly reassured.

"I'm glad things are going well between you and my sister, Tanner. It's just she's been through some things and I want her to be happy."

His expression cleared. "This is about Savannah."

Well, no, but it was as good as an excuse as I was going to get.

Tanner didn't wait for my confirmation, barreling forward in his enthusiasm to put me at ease. "I'm an adult, Vanessa. Not the jackass who left your sister with a burden she didn't need. I take responsibility for my actions, so rest assured there."

Did he just…? Oh, gods no. As much as I didn't want to rock this boat, I couldn't let that lie, either. "We don't consider Savvy a burden."

"I didn't mean it like that," he said quickly. "She's a wonderful child."

Except he did mean it like that. Tanner wasn't the kind of dude that would want my sister to put her daughter aside. No, he was the kind that would endure. Who would pat himself on the back for being understanding about his partner having a child.

"She is a wonderful child," I said, because it was the truth. "I've got to get back to work.

Unless there was something else?"

Tanner shook his head as he pulled out his phone. "No, I appreciate you taking the time to clear the air with me. We just need to schedule the last test."

"Okay," I said, pulling up my own schedule. "What's the last test going to be, anyway?" I grabbed my glass, draining the last of my water.

"Tasseomancy and Palmistry," Tanner said, all his focus on his phone. "So we'll need a couple of volunteers. Juliet agreed to do it. If you can't find another one, I can ask around the Arcanist department."

I choked on my water, dropping my phone and barely getting a napkin up fast enough to block the spray. "Tasseomancy and Palmistry?"

"Yeah," Tanner said, frowning at me. "Is that going to be a problem?"

"No," I said quickly, because it wasn't. I mean, neither were my strong point. I hadn't done much training in either because my father put very little stock in the disciplines. Both were tools hedgewitches could utilize as a diagnostic test. There were even some akeosites who used it. It wasn't out of nowhere as an area of focus for the assessment, except when you factored in my father. Why had he picked a discipline that he had nothing but contempt for?

Tanner and I tentatively picked a day next week. I'd need to okay it with my volunteers and he'd need to double check with my dad. Unlike the potion-gathering, apparently my dad was insisting to be present for this test.

Tanner left, his steps light, while I went back to work. I was boxing up a special order when a thought occurred to me—Juliet had volunteered, even though she knew as well as I did how our father felt about it, and that he would be there for the test itself.

I would have expected her to say no. Both Tasseomancy and Palmistry left the participants vulnerable on the psychic plane. They were sympathetic magic, working off of things you've been in contact with or parts of you, in this case your tea leaves and your hand. You have to leave yourself open to the practitioner so they could get a good reading, which took a tremendous amount of trust.

Juliet could trust me, but my dad would be there for the reading. He would hear everything that I said. He might even insist on asking the questions. Juliet generally agreed with my "the less dad knows about me, the better" policy.

For her to agree…

I really needed to talk to my sister. Unfortunately, I owed her a big fat apology first.

CHAPTER TWENTY

Will

I was in a terrible mood, so I was hiding in the dirty room at the shop, cleaning my tools and prepping them for the autoclave. When they were ready, I'd move them over to the clean room, thus completing the circle of life of the body piercing ecosystem. Once that was done, I'd move onto the new jewelry order. I had one of my earbuds in, shutting out the world.

I had no interest in talking to a single person today, which was unlike me.

I'd slept like shit last night. My bed had felt pointless without Van in it. I'd ended up going to the couch out of desperation. That didn't really help and I spent the whole night arguing with myself.

I shouldn't have left when Van told me to—she needed support.

I had to leave when she told me to, because *she told me to and that was what she wanted.*

I wasn't in the habit of ignoring what women said to me.

The problem was that one was what Van needed and the other was what she wanted, so it was tempting to brush one aside for the other, but it wasn't my call. While I had clear feelings about which approach was best, Van was the expert on herself, not me, and I had to abide by her wishes.

Even if I hated it.

Even if it meant a shitty night on the couch instead of her voice panting in my ear for more. Or waking up with her warm and plaint in my arms. Or her scowling at me over coffee in a way that never failed to make me smile, and always felt like a dare. Was I up to changing her mood from prickly to content? What would it take to get her to laugh? To get her up on the kitchen counter, my hands—

I groaned, banging my head against the counter.

"Pretty sure that's not how you do that," Declan said, peeking into the room.

I glared at him. "You're not here to hug me again, are you?" Because of my mood, Declan had been stopping me since I got here, hugging me and saying nice things. It was really kind and for once it was making me want to exit my own body and ascend to another dimension instead of making me feel better.

"No, Declan said, shaking his head. "But I can give you one if you need it." "Respectfully, no," I said. "I never thought I'd say this, but I don't think I'm in the mood."

Declan visibly recoiled. "You love hugs. They're your favorite." "I know," I whined.

Declan closed the door, dropping his voice. "Are you okay? Did Van break you? Do we need to stage an intervention?"

"I'm okay," I said straightening. "Just had a bad night."

Declan looked skeptical, but went with it. "Okay, well, Juliet is here. She doesn't have an appointment, but you've got a little wiggle room."

"Yeah, great," I said. I stripped my gloves, dropping them in the trash.

Juliet was waiting for me out front. Bay had already taken Savannah, his attention on her as she babbled away to him, using a combination of actual words and her own made up vocabulary.

"Hey, Juliet," I said, leaning against the counter. "To what do I owe this unexpected pleasure?"

"To my sister's paranoia," Juliet said. "She wanted me to get some protection stones put in."

Her words killed the slight lift in mood I'd felt when I saw her. "Vanessa apologized to you, then?" Which she should, but made me wonder if I was on Vanessa's apology list. Or if that one argument was it for us. Normally, I wasn't too worried about a little disagreement with the person I was seeing. Except it was Vanessa, she was my heart, and

I had no guarantee that she wouldn't bolt at the slightest bump in the road.

"No," Juliet said, her nose scrunched up in the exact way Van did when she made that face. "I haven't heard from her yet."

That shouldn't have made me feel a little better, but it kind of did. "But you came anyway?"

She shrugged. "I'd promised her I would get it done before we had our set down last night."

"What's this?" Bay asked, scowling at us both. "It's nothing," Juliet said.

"It's not nothing." I tapped the counter with my finger. "Someone broke the stones on Van's jewelry. That doesn't happen on accident."

"We don't know that it was from my dad," Juliet argued. "Van's had disgruntled customers try to hex her before."

I leaned my elbows on the counter. "Pretty big coincidence, timing wise.

Juliet put her hands on her hips. "If I thought her worry was totally groundless, I wouldn't be here, Will. I'm just saying there's room for doubt."

Bay's scowl deepened. "You're going to Will, but not to me? Why aren't we tattooing you?"

Juliet rolled her eyes. "I didn't mean to bruise your ego, Bay. It wasn't a comment on your skills."

"You think *that's* what's bothering me? I'm not so fucking fragile. This isn't about my ego. It's about your safety."

Juliet opened her mouth, but Bay kept going.

"If Van is worried enough to send you to Will, then you should have the same coverage as her. *She* got tattoos from me. I had to bully her into it too, which I do not fucking understand." He hiked Savvy up on his hip. "Why are all the people I love so resistant to using my magic. I had to harass Declan and Lou to take tattoos when stuff was going down with them. It's absolute bullshit."

He was mumbling to himself by the end, stomping into the back of the shop.

Declan dropped his head back so his voice would project. "Because a tattoo wasn't really necessary for what we were dealing with. My dad's dead—"

Bay's head popped out from the doorway. "They never found Eva's body! Have you never seen a horror movie? Villains aren't gone until you *find the body.*" He shook his head. "We need to teach you better, Savvy. Everyone around you has poor decision making skills."

"In our defense," Declan said. "We're not sure Eva will strike again."

Eva was Declan's stepmom. She'd been part of the revenge plot against Declan. She was a real piece of work.

"Well, let me tell you, that's tremendously reassuring," Bay said, hit tone biting. "You keep on with your glorious optimism. *I* will keep on doing what I need to do to keep my loved ones safe, thank you very much."

"Aww," Juliet said, leaning on the counter. "Did you hear that? He loves us. Thanks, Bay.

I didn't know you cared."

A brief look of shock flitted across Bay's face, but Juliet missed it. He licked his lips, recovering quickly. "Of course I love you—you've bewitched me body and soul, woman." He pointed his finger at me, flicking it between me and Declan. "And you two are half agony, half hope." He blew a raspberry on Savvy's cheek.

"Please stop butchering Jane Austen," Juliet said with a laugh. "I can't take it. I regret forcing you to watch it."

Bay shrugged. "There were some parts I liked." He tickled Savvy again. "You, little one, pierce my soul." He kissed her head and turned fierce eyes on Juliet. "And you will come see me the second you're done with Will."

"Don't you have an appointment?" Juliet asked, her expression bemused.

"Do I look like I care?" Bay asked. "They can wait ten fucking minutes. I consider this an emergency. I'll give them a discount if they complain." He bounced Savvy. "C'mon little one.

We need to go draw your stubborn mommy a temporary tattoo."

"I'm sure one of the premade ones will be fine," Juliet protested. "You don't have to design one just for me."

All pretense of joking vanished from Bay's face and his voice went dangerously soft. "I'm not letting you put yourself last, Juliet. Not this time, and not with me. You will go with Will, then you will walk yourself over to my station."

I glanced at Declan—his eyes were wide as he stared back at me. I'd never heard Bay order anyone to do anything. He almost *never* used his angry voice, and never, ever at Juliet. I could tell both Declan and I were considering sneaking out of the room.

Juliet's eyebrows winged up, her lips parted. "You're not my keeper, Bay. *I* make the decisions about me, not you."

"You need a damn keeper," Bay snapped. "You need one single person in your life that puts you first whether you like it or not. No one else is stepping up, so you're stuck with me."

The expression on Juliet's face made me take a step back. *Oh, shit.* My buddy was dead and there wouldn't be enough left of him for a funeral.

"What the absolute fuck, Bay? No one appointed you or asked—" Bay turned and walked away. He just…left.

Juliet gaped. If steam could have come out her Juliet's ears, it would be doing so now.

"That high handed little shit. What the fuck?" Her hands went to her hips as she glared at the empty doorway. "Where does he get off?"

The piercing room, apparently. Hence the sign. Declan made the mistake of coughing.

Juliet sighted him like a raptor homing in on prey. "Can you believe this bullshit?" Declan grimaced and I saw the exact moment where he signed his own death certificate.

"I'm not saying his methods were great, but…" She lurched forward and Declan flinched.

I intercepted her, swinging her around toward the piercing room. "Okay, let's go get this done, hm?"

Juliet's jaw snapped shut, and I had her up on the piercing chair, my gloves on and the ritual supplies out, before she said a word.

"Is that…is that what you all think of me?" She asked, her voice tiny and very un-Juliet- like. "That I'm not capable of taking care of myself?"

Sometimes Juliet and Van said things or asked questions like this, little collections of words that revealed how unsure their foundations were. How very much their father had failed them. Like now. And every single time it made me want to jettison the old man into space.

I pointed a gloved finger at her. "No." "But—"

"*No*," I said more forcefully. "That's not what he was saying at all and not even close to what we think." I crossed my arms and bent my knees so we were on eye level. "Juliet, you're one of the smartest, most capable people we know. It's just that you will put strangers ahead of yourself. You will take care of everyone in your sphere, even if it's at your own detriment. You're an amazingly generous and loving person, but for fuck's sake, buck the tradition occasionally and let us take care of you."

Her brow furrowed. "Ooookay."

"Honestly, you're as bad as Van." I grabbed a sharpie. "Now take off your shirt so I can draw shit all over your body in a totally professional and platonic way."

She laughed and started unbuttoning her shirt. "I'll think on what you said, Will, but I'm still going to tear Bay a new one for being a bossy asshole about it."

"Do what you got to do, but usually I'm the one who puts holes in things around here and I do not appreciate you horning in on my territory." I bent, drawing the first set of symbols along her delicate collarbone.

"I'm glad Vanessa has you," Juliet said softly. "Don't let her panic-bomb it, okay?"

"I will do my best," I said, stepping around so I could start on the set that would go over her back. "But it has come to my recent attention that I can only do so much and the women in your family do not like to be dictated too."

"Does anybody?" Juliet asked.

"Believe it or not," I said, my hand moving quickly. "But there are entire swaths of the human population that will pay extra for that sort of thing."

"Whatever makes them happy," Juliet said, her hands folded neatly in her lap. "But I am not one of them."

I didn't argue with her, because it wasn't my place, but I'd seen her face when Bay had lost his shit and started making demands. She might not like it all the time, but at least when it came to Bay, I was pretty sure there was a part of her that was *very* in to him being bossy.

I was smart enough to not say anything to her, though. I wanted to live. That was for them to sort out, anyway. I had my hands full with Van as it was.

#

Van hadn't texted me all day. I could text her, but since she had been the one who wanted to be left alone, I was leaving it in her court. Bay had taken off as soon as his last appointment was done. His mood hadn't improved much after Juliet left, even though she did let him apply the temporary tattoo on her wrist.

Nikki was gone, as was Aly, a tattoo artist doing a guest spot to see if the shop was a good fit for her. Declan had just finished up his paperwork, hugging me yet again, and then locking up behind me. Everyone was gone and I should be too, but I didn't want to go home.

Jim was out with friends, so there was no one to hang out with. Van's house was out for obvious reasons. I had other friends. I could go out, or go home and get started on the next book for bookclub, which was a victorian-era historical romance about two women entering a poultry competition and falling in love. It sounded awesome, but I didn't think even it could lift my mood right now.

So instead of putting my feet up and losing myself in a book, I was putting new jewelry in the ultrasonic cleaner before I bagged it. Just another wild night in the life of Willhardt Murphy.

There was a knock at the front door. Irritated, I took off my gloves, not bothering to take my earbud out. Didn't matter how big the closed sign, someone always missed it or thought it didn't apply to them. Usually I'd ignore it, but I felt like a fight, so I went for the door.

"We're closed," I said, unlocking the door and yanking it open. Van stood in front of me, her hand raised.

"Oh," I said, because I was a brilliant man who had a way with words. "Is it…" Van shifted her weight on her feet. "Can I come in?"

"Yeah," I said, opening the door wider, and continuing my stint as the most epic wordsmith of my time.

Van stepped in and I locked the door. We stood awkwardly for a moment. Before we'd gotten together, this would be when we'd hug. Lately, this would be where, if we weren't alone, I'd give her a quick kiss on the cheek. If we were alone, I'd try to kiss her until she either climbed me like a sexy tree or melted for me.

None of that was going go happen this second, and it pissed me off, so I turned on my heel and went back to my work. That way she could follow or not. It was up to her. I snapped on fresh gloves and went back to the jewelry, putting the dry pieces that had already gone through the ultrasonic cleaner into bags so I could seal, label and pop them into the autoclave.

I heard Van follow me into the room, but she didn't say anything, just hovered while I worked.

Well, this was fun. I guess I could sit here in silence, or get things rolling, since Van didn't seem to be in a hurry to chat. "What's up?"

I got several pieces bagged before she sighed. "Do I have to apologize to your back, or will you look at me?"

I kept working. "You don't *have* to apologize at all. No one's making you."

"I'm making me," Van said, exasperation coloring her tone. "For fuck's sake, Wilhardt, will you please look at me?"

I turned around, arms crossed, and leaned against the counter. An inner voice was chastising me for being hard on her, for not telling her to skip the apology and we'd forget it ever happened. But I was in this for the long haul. That meant we'd fight, and we'd make up, and the way we went about that would be decided in these early days.

Van had lashed out. She'd pushed me away instead of following our agreement and telling me what was going on. And honestly, I totally get why she did. People fucked up and I wouldn't hold that against her. But I also knew instinctively that if I didn't ask for this, if I didn't get her used to owning her fuck ups with me and being vulnerable enough to say she was sorry, it would mess our relationship up for a long time. I wanted better for both of us.

As much as it hurt, I needed to do this, so I gritted my teeth and waited. "I'm sorry," Van said. "I was a dick."

"How?" I asked.

She looked confused. "What?"

"You said you were a dick." I lifted my shoulders and dropped them, but kept my arms crossed. "How were you a dick?"

"You're being a dick right now."

"No," I said. "I'm just not folding the second you say sorry. I'm not trying to make you jump through hoops just to make myself feel better, either. I want to know if you understand what you did and how much that hurt."

Her mouth pinched shut as she turned her head away. I could see her throat working as she swallowed hard. "I was mad at myself. I took it out on you, which wasn't fair."

"And?" Come on, sweetheart. Meet me halfway here.

She dropped her shoulders. "I should have talked to you, either to tell you I needed a little me of time to sort through my shit or to explain why I was angry. Instead I yelled at you to leave. That wasn't our deal."

"No," I said, dropping my hands to my side, my body relaxing. "That wasn't our deal." "Are we okay?" She asked, her voice small.

Damn it all, I hated that little voice, and to hear it from both her and her sister in the same day filled me with rage. Van didn't need to babysit my feelings right now, though. What she needed was acceptance and reassurance and I was the lucky guy who got to give them to her.

I held my arms open. She threw herself into them. I hugged her close, my eyelids falling shut. Fuck, she felt good like this, holding on tight for all she was worth. "Yeah, Nessa. We're okay." I kissed her temple. "Thank you for being honest with me."

"Do you have more work to do here?" Her words were muffled, because she was still face first into my chest.

"Naw," I said, pulling away from her so I could de-glove. I tossed them in the trash. "I can finish this tomorrow."

"Take me home?" She lifted her chin and batted her eyes.

I laughed. "Yeah, let me just double check the piercing room and shut the lights off."

She trailed behind me, but it was comfortable now instead of that weird, angry static between us. Van watched for a second as I checked the drawers, making sure the supplies were all ready for opening shift tomorrow.

I heard fabric rustle and then the soft thud of something hitting the padded bench we had in the piercing room for guests. I turned to see what it was just in time to see Van's shirt hit the bench. Today's bra was plain black with a tiny bow right in the center. I had the urge to see if I could bite that little bow off for some reason.

My eyebrows went up.

"I was thinking," Van said, stepping closer to me. She grabbed my waistband, fingers sliding back and forth in the small gap between the fabric and my skin.

My blood heated instantly and I swallowed hard. "What were you thinking?"

She nudged me backward, guiding me to the piercing chair. My back hit the chair and her fingers shifted to my belt. She undid the buckle, slowly undoing the leather, her eyes on mine the entire time. "About this."

My shorts dropped, the buckle clanging against the floor. Van pushed down my boxer briefs, before gripping my shaft. Her grip was light, tracing along the underside, tracing the head.

I'm pretty sure I whimpered.

"All day." She pushed me back onto the chair. I sat, because I wasn't about to argue with her. I wasn't quite sure where she was going with this, but I was willing to follow her lead.

She let go of me then, sauntering over to the piercing room door. Van reached up, grasped the new sign, and flipped it over to the "dirty" side, then shut the door. Locked it. Strode back over to me.

I could feel my pulse beat in my neck and I'm not sure I'd ever been so hard in my life. "All day, huh?" I barely managed to squeeze the words out.

Van took hold of me again, dropping her eyes. Watching her own hand work over my shaft. The thick fringe of her lashes rested on her cheeks. I couldn't help but reach up, cradling her face in my hands, tracing my thumbs along the soft skin from cheekbone to jaw. She was so beautiful my heart skipped sometimes.

"I was worried I wouldn't get to do this again," she said. Her lips had a tremble to them. "Nessa."

She shook her head sharply, like she wanted me to drop it.

I cupped her chin again and made her look at me. It took me a second to form words because thinking was difficult when she had her hands on me. "It's going to take a lot more than one fight," I finally said.

She nodded, but I could tell she didn't really believe it, so I kissed her instead.

Sometimes showing someone how you feel was easier than telling them. I tugged at her lower lip with my teeth, teasing her into opening for me.

I didn't think I'd ever get over Vanessa's taste. I'd imagined kissing her so many times, imagined her hands on me, and let me tell you that it paled to the reality. Imagination never captured the heat of their skin. The sounds she made in the back of her throat. The silky weight of her hair in my fist. It was like expecting a black and white photo and getting video with full sound surround instead.

I toed off my shoes, kicked off my shorts, and pulled her between my legs. My fingers traced her breasts through the soft cotton of her bra, while I kissed down her jaw, licked along her neck.

Van moaned low in her throat, her hand stilling on my cock. And I loved it, loved knowing that I was making her feel so good that she couldn't focus on anything but that. I traced her bra along to her back with one hand, found the clasp, undoing it with a few deft tugs. I pulled it off her, tossing it to the ground.

With slow slides, I traced the silken skin along the undersides, touching everywhere but the nipple. Teasing her, so that when I finally flicked my thumbs over them, she shuddered.

"Will."

I didn't think I could get harder, but Vanessa saying my name like that...

She squeezed my tip with her hands and it was my turn to shudder. Van used my distraction to slide out of my grip, lowering herself to her knees. Before I'd fully grasped what she was doing, her hot mouth followed her hands. She gripped the base of my cock as she licked up the underside of it.

It felt so good my entire body jerked. I threw my head back and squeezed my eyes shut. I needed a moment. If I looked at Van right now, this would be the shortest blow job in history.

Van traced along the base with one hand, slipping down to caress my balls, her other hand shoving up my shirt to reach my nipples. I yanked off my shirt, not caring where I tossed it.

Vanessa kept sucking me, her head bobbing, as I dug my hand into her hair, gently fisting it. I wasn't guiding her, more like holding on.

Watching her right now, her eyes closed, her enjoyment obvious, was one of the most erotic things I'd ever seen and suddenly I couldn't take it anymore. I gently dislodged her and pulled her up, yanking her into my arms. Kissing her hard. Tasting myself in her mouth.

I fumbled with her shorts, all finesse gone. I wanted her so badly. Once I'd managed to get her naked, I scooted back, collapsing the back of the chair. Pulling her on top of me. There was just enough room for her knees on the side of waist. I drug her over me, her hot, wet heat, gliding over my shaft. I grunted, my grip tightening. Fuck me, it was good, and I wasn't even in her yet.

Van gripped my shoulders, her voice breathy. "Will. *Will.*" I looked up.

Her eyes were on where we were almost joined, her lips parted. "I—I don't have a condom."

I froze. *Fuck.* I didn't have one either. I made a pained noise.

Van closed her eyes. "Not even in your pockets? One of the drawers?"

"This is where I work. I don't usually—" She moved and I bucked involuntarily. "Don't usually do this, you know. Or ever." She slid back and I gasped. "*Nessa.*" She was killing me.

She gripped my shoulder, biting her lip. I didn't move. If I moved… "It's okay," she said.

It took me a second to figure out what she was saying. I'm usually fairly quick on the uptake, but Vanessa was hot and naked and in my arms, so not a single drop of blood was making it to my brain right now. It had all flowed south for the winter, like birds.

We'd already had the talk—we'd both been tested and were clean. I knew she was on birth control. I also knew that birth control wasn't a hundred percent. It was a risk, and a tremendous act of faith on her part. I gripped her hips. "Are you sure?"

"Yes, Will." She planted a gentle kiss on my mouth, her breasts pressing into my chest. "I'm sure."

I gripped her hips, lifted her up, and she sank down at the same time I thrust up and suddenly I was inside her up to the hilt.

It felt like time stopped. I held her gripped to me, both of us panting, filling the room with the raspy sounds of our breathing. Van started to roll her hips and I clutched them with a death grip. "Don't move." I ground the words through clenched teeth. If she moved right now, I would come. Simple as that.

I heaved in breaths, trying to rain myself in, despite the fact that nothing, *nothing*, had ever felt as good as this. Sweat broke out over my skin. Vanessa started kissing my shoulders, my chin, nibbling along my neck.

Fuck it. My pulse was a surging rhythm in my ears as I rocked against her. Vanessa took over the rhythm, riding me hard. There was a heated desperation to our movements, both of us rocketing towards climax. It wasn't sweet, tender lovemaking. It was hard, hot, breast-jiggling, flesh-pounding, guttural-grunting sex. I kept hold of her hips in a punishing grip as I pounded up into her, letting go only once to slap her ass. Van gasped, getting wetter.

She was moaning nonstop now, loud in a way I'd never heard her. Her name was falling from my lips in half-litany, half-strangled prayer. She clawed my back. I licked her neck. Her nipples were hard as they rubbed against the hair on my chest. My balls tightened, heat racing up my spine. I was so fucking hard for her. I wouldn't last much longer.

I needed to push her over the edge. I licked my thumb, pressing it against her clit, letting her own rocking motion do the work.

Vanessa came on a sob, tucking her face into my neck, my name on her lips.

My hips jerked a few more times, trying to drag it out, but I'd lost control. I pulled her down, grinding her against me, as I came harder than I had in my entire life. Pretty sure I was speaking tongues for a minute. I floated in my own ethereal plane of white-hot-pleasure, before plummeting to earth and finally understanding the words tumbling out of my mouth.

"Oh gods, Nessa. Shit. So good. Oh, fuck. Perfect. You're perfect. So fucking good. I love you. I love you."

Vanessa had stilled in my arms, making no sound as I froze, realizing I'd just told her I loved her. It had been mixed in with a shit-ton of profanity and in the haze of sex, but I'd meant every gods damn word.

And she could hear the truth in them—I'm sure she could.

I also knew it was too damned soon to say those words to her. Way too fucking soon. And I couldn't take the words back. Hell, I wouldn't take the words back.

But I sure as shit knew that she was going to bolt. The only thing I could do now was to hold on tight, press a kiss to her cheek, and hope like hell that she trusted me enough to stay.

That maybe—*maybe*—deep down, she was a little in love with me as well. That any second now, she'd lean back, give me a thousand-watt smile, and say, *I love you, too.*

She didn't. She stayed frozen in my arms, body stiff, for several of the longest moments in my life. Then she crawled off me, gaze averted, and started gathering up her clothes.

With three words I'd managed to torpedo the hottest sex of my life and there was fuck all I could do about it.

CHAPTER TWENTY-ONE

Van

I love you.

#

Those words had been on repeat, in Will's raspy post-sex voice, in my head all day. When I got up. Through my short shift at work. In the car with Juliet and Savvy, and now in the generalized hellscape known as *the mall.*

I love you.

I shoved away a display blouse with too much force.

"What did that blouse ever do to you?" Juliet asked with a smirk. It amazed me how my sister could focus on her own task, keep track of what I was doing, *and* continue to watch her offspring with an eye that a hawk would envy. Savvy was so quiet. If I hadn't know she was hiding in the clothing rack to my left, I would have never guessed.

"What didn't that blouse do?" I waved at the offending shirt with my iced coffee. "Look at it. Just sitting there, being scratchy and violently chartreuse. It has a lace collar, Juliet."

"That," Juliet said, her finger pointing at the shirt in question. "Is someone's dream shirt. Someone is going to look at that and the opening lines from the song *At Last* will sound in their head."

"It's not my dream shirt."

Juliet shrugged and sipped her own iced drink, though hers was tea. "Not the shirt's fault.

There's a difference between something being terrible and it not being for you." "Fine," I said. "Do you want the shirt?"

"Absolutely fucking not. It's hideous."

I snorted a laugh. I loved my sister. This morning had been a little awkward for about five minutes when I'd groveled and apologized for being a horrendous dick weasel. I was lucky that Juliet was the forgiving sort when it came to me, because I could be a horrendous dick weasel on a pretty frequent basis, especially when I'd been forced to spend time with our father.

I love you.

I swallowed hard and thumbed through another row of shirts.

I recognized that, for most people, Will's declaration would be a great thing. Healthy, normal people liked to be loved and told they were loved on a regular basis. Hugged and, I don't know, brought flowers. I was far from the only human to have a panic response to intimacy—I knew that. It was hardly an exclusive club.

Knowing that didn't keep me from feeling like a broken tea pot held together by super glue. It might look the same, but there was no proof it could hold water like it was supposed to, and one wrong bump would collapse the whole thing into tinier, more jagged pieces.

I'd just finished telling my sister all about it before she'd chided me about the hideous blouse.

"So, he told you he loved you?" Juliet asked as she deftly sifted through the shirts hanging on the rack.

"Yup."

"As your sister, I feel I should offer up the possibility that it was just a post-orgasm induced euphoric response." Juliet eyes a pastel floral number carefully. "This looks like something I should wear out in a prairie somewhere while I darn socks and keep critters away from the chicken coop."

"It would be really good for our compound someday." We frequently discussed buying a chunk of land and building like a friend commune sort of situation. But like, not in a creepy way. "Maybe you should get it."

Juliet nodded sharply. "Dress for the job you want."

"Do you think that was what it was?" I asked, hating how hard it was for me to ask her that question. I didn't have to tack on "with Will" because I knew my sister would follow our conversational jumps.

"No," she said, decisively. "I do not, but that's because I've known that Will has been in love with you since like the dawn of time. He's never *not* been in love with you."

"You could have told me." My tone was sulky and I knew it.

Juliet snorted, moving along to a new rack. "You didn't want to hear it." Her voice softened. "And I didn't want to make things weird between you two. Will's one of those necessary friends."

I sighed, sucking sullenly on my drink. "If you'd told me I would have sabotaged it." "Maybe," Juliet said, grimacing at a price tag. "Maybe not. Either way I figured you'd sort it out in your own time."

I would have sabotaged it.

I had to phrase my next question delicately, because we'd just made up over the whole Tanner thing. I didn't want Juliet to think I was referring to that situation at all. No, I was going to support her, which was why I was in the dreaded building known as a department store, helping her pick out a new date outfit.

Did I consider this a place of misery? Yes. Did I like Juliet dating Tanner? Not really.

Would I keep my mouth stapled shut about the last one while my sister bought what was probably her first brand new outfit in two years? Even if it killed me. I was reframing it in my head. She wasn't 'wasting' the outfit on Tanner. She was buying herself a well deserved treat.

"Do you ever—." I paused, breathing deep, still trying to sort out my question. "I don't know, do you ever feel like a broken robot?"

Juliet tipped her head up from the rack, her eyebrows scrunched together. "How do you mean?"

"I don't know," I said, shaking my nearly empty coffee. "Like, with the way we were raised, you don't have the right feelings? Or more accurately, like you don't get there the same way?" I barreled forward, not looking at her. "Sometimes I feel like I'm missing vital pieces. Not all the time. Just like when something cute happens in a movie or people talk about sweet scenes in books and the whole room goes *awww* and I've got nothing."

I peeked up at Juliet to see how she was taking it. She looked sad.

"And then you tear up over something weird and everyone looks at you like you've pissed in their cornflakes." She glanced at the rack where Savvy played quietly. "I teared up at the park the other day because Savvy rolled in a mud puddle. She was giggling and having the best time and I knew the other parents were judging me, but…"

I understood instantly. "But we would have never been allowed to do that." My father liked his children to be presentable at all times. We were not allowed to wallow in the dirt like common swine.

"Clothes wash," Juliet said, still quiet, but there was a thread of fierceness there now. "It was a warm day and she was happy. Meanwhile, I was crying because *I did that. I made space for my daughter to be happy and know she is loved at all times.*"

She sniffed, her cup rattling as she brushed at her cheek with the back of her hand. "And one of the mom's brought me tissues, all while making a face saying she thought my kid needed a time out. She's a freaking toddler. I'm not going to make her act like an adult." She tipped her chin up. "Playing in the dirt is developmentally appropriate."

I adored my sister to Pluto and back. "I bet you told her that, too."

"I did, but I still said thank you for the tissues." Juliet put her hands on her hips. "I don't like any of these. Maybe a dress?"

"Sure," I said, following her as she fished Savvy out from the clothing rack with the promise that where we were going had more of them for her to play in.

"So what did you do?" She asked, hefting her daughter onto her hip. "With Will?" "Definitely acted like an emotionally mature adult. Didn't panic, make it more awkward, and tell him I needed to go home and go to bed because I opened this morning and then pretended to fall asleep in the car."

"You went full possum?"

I nodded. "I embraced the way of nature." "Vanessa," she chided.

"I know!" I threw my hands up and almost lost my coffee. "This is what I'm talking about. If I wasn't a broken robot, it would have been a nice moment. Instead I've got cogs missing."

I followed her to a rack of dresses where she set Savvy down. "Remember that article you told me about, the one that said the human brain will rewire itself when it's injured? Like, it will create new synapses and whatnot, build new connections, and sort of jury-rig itself into a ramshackle but workable new brain?"

"Yes," Juliet said. "I remember that article."

"I feel like I did that, but with my emotions." I moved my hand up and down, indicating myself. "Emotionally rewired janky robot."

"Okay," said Juliet, holding up a yellow dress to herself, frowning, and putting it back. "But is that bad? You say 'broken robot' but I see a robot that built itself out of pure determination. One that was given one set of blueprints, knew those were shitty, and so made up their own." Now it was her turn to shove the dresses aside a little too hard, her jaw hard. "Our father is a shit, Van and our mother is unavailable in any way that counts. Frankly, it's a minor miracle that we didn't turn out just like them."

She pulled a dress off the rack. It was a spring green wrap-dress made out of T-shirt like material. "We're thriving, Van. We have each other. We have friends. We have good jobs and we laugh more than we cry."

"You can cry?" I was joking and she knew it, so she ignored my question.

"Every day I strive to be the kind of parent my daughter deserves. And you know what? I fail. All the time. But on my worst day? I'm *still* a better parent than ours were because I refuse to treat her for one second the way we were treated." She glared at the dress. "We are miracles, you and me, and we should be celebrated."

"Yes, ma'm."

She held the dress against her, caressing the fabric. "And we both deserve to be loved the way Willhardt Murphy loves you. He looks at you like you're fucking precious, Vanessa, and you *are*." She checked the tag. "I think this is the one."

"You're precious, too," I said, reaching out to touch her wrist. "I hope you know that." She nodded sharply, her eyes on the dress, but I knew how to translate that. Like me,

there were days she struggled to believe it, but she was trying. That was all we could really do. "And that dress is a winner. Go try it on—I'll watch your spawn."

"What are you going to do?" She asked, grabbing checking the tags in the other dresses—she would want to take the next size up, in case the one in her hand wouldn't fit. "About Will."

I peeked my head into the other dress rack, checking on Savvy. She giggled and darted to the next one. "I would love to say that I will sit down with him and thoughtfully discuss it like a mature adult, but I think it's waaaay more likely that I'm going to continue to flail about while pretending that it never happened."

Juliet snorted. "At least you're honest with yourself." She pulled out a second dress, her face lit up with triumph. "Gotcha!" She cradled them to her with a sigh. "You know you could go absolutely rogue and tell the man that you feel the same way."

"Unorthodox," I said. "Even novel." Just the idea made me sweat.

"He won't see it coming," Juliet said dryly. Her eyes narrowed. "You do know that you're in love with him, right?"

I was shaking my head before she even finished the sentence. "It's early days, Juliet. I'm not there yet."

Juliet's expression was pure pity. "I love you, but sometimes you're stupendously disconnected from your own feelings, especially if they're strong. It's like you turn into a feeling's turtle."

"I can't be a teapot, a robot, *and* a turtle," I said, crossing my arms. "Not all in one conversation."

"When were you a teapot?" Juliet asked, mystified.

"That one was in my own head," I admitted. "But the comment stands."

"Turtle, robot, or teapot," Juliet said, shaking her head. "You need to let someone in eventually. And I won't push it, but if you're so certain you're not absolutely gone for that man, I think you need to examine why the idea of talking to him about your feelings frightens you so much."

"Get out of my head, you monster."

She waved me off. "Fine, I'm done talking about it. I'm going to try these on." I laughed and waved her along, turning my attention to Savvy.

And trying very, very hard to not examine the fact that Juliet was right—I was absolutely terrified to talk to Will about my feelings. Since I didn't want to chase down the *why* of that, I chased my niece instead.

#

Dress procured, we went back to Juliet's apartment so we could feed Savvy and put her down for a nap before Juliet got ready for her date.

While Juliet battled my niece to give into the gentle arms of Morpheus, I refreshed myself on the art of Tasseomancy by paging through the battered copy of *Reading the Big Truths: an Advanced Study of Tasseomancy for the Accomplished Witch*. I was focusing on revealing truth as well as divining the past, since we'd likely focus on that for my test. Reading the future was harder to quantify since that shifted constantly and would be much more difficult to assess.

Juliet came out of the bedroom wearing her new dress and I set the book down. She gave a little twirl, one hand holding her hair up onto her head. "What do you think? Hair up? Hair down?"

She would be a knock out either way. "How did you wear it last time?" "Down."

"Maybe up, then? With a few wisps hanging down?"

Juliet pursed her lips, considering. "That would work, I think." She saw my book. "Worried about the last test?"

"Yeah," I said. "I need to grab one more volunteer and find out what times you're both available." I hesitated, because I wanted to ask her a question, but didn't want to start a fight again. We'd just made up, but I really needed to know. "Why are you doing this?"

Juliet's expression smoothed into a careful mask. "Going on a date?"

"No," I said instantly. "Not that. I meant volunteering for the test. I wouldn't have asked you to do it."

Juliet's brow furrowed as she eased onto the couch next to me, dropping both hands into her lap. "Why not?"

"It means more time with dad. Getting drug into my mess even further. I would have asked Lou or Trick or something. It's not as hard on them."

Juliet considered this. "I don't know," she said slowly. "I guess I didn't even think about that part. Tanner asked me and I agreed." She pulled a hair tie off her wrist, fiddling with it. "I figured two birds with one stone—I could help you and spend more time with Tanner. He was being so cute about it, you know? Acting like a little extra time with me would make his week."

She stared at her lap, sliding the elastic band through her fingers. "It felt really good to be seen as a precious commodity."

I put my hand over hers. "You are, and I'm glad Tanner makes you feel that way." I gave her hands a little squeeze before dropping them. "I just hate that you have to spend more time with our father to do it."

Juliet smiled faintly at me. "It didn't even cross my mind. Maybe that means I've made progress. He has less power over me than he used to."

"Maybe," I said, though I wasn't sure either of us really believed that. But we really wanted to.

CHAPTER TWENTY-TWO

Will

Bay examined the barbell Jim was lifting over him with some trepidation. "You adjusted it for my puny form, right?"

Jim snorted. "No, Bay, I left it at minotaur setting. Are you taking this, or what?"

Bay grumbled, but took the barbell, lowering it to his chest before he pushed up. "So let me get this straight. You had sex in the piercing room—for which I'm never taking shit from you again, by the way,—and you told her you loved her?"

This question was of course tossed at me. I'd known it was coming, and that the weight discussion was only a short reprieve. One of the upsides of living with Jim, besides a nice place I wouldn't be able to afford and a kick ass roommate, was his basement. Jim didn't like to deal with the testosterone jungle one sometimes ran into at gyms. Some dude inevitably wanted to out-lift the minotaur or come over and get in his face in other weird ways, while Jim only wanted to work out.

He'd converted his basement into a gym when he bought his house. He had a really nice benchpress and weight set, a treadmill, and an elliptical, as well as a heavy bag in the corner. A small shelving unit held resistance bands, yoga mats, and other fitness gear. Basically, it had everything I needed, and since Jim didn't mind sharing, I didn't have to pay for a gym membership.

Bay had also been invited to use it whenever, which was how we ended up here now, with Bay lifting, Jim spotting, and me trying to outrun the uncertainty of my current romantic life on the treadmill. "That is the situation in a nutshell, yes."

"That's awkward," Jim said. "What did she do?"

"She panicked, practically running out of the room—" Bay opened his mouth.

I cut him off. "*After* she got dressed, and then pretended to fall asleep in the car." "Ouch." Jim wiped his face with the towel around his neck. He hadn't taken his

medicinal today, so he was in his actual minotaur form. It was his home and besides, he new Bay and I wouldn't be dicks about it.

"Just to be clear, at what point did you tell her you loved her?" Bay asked, grunting as he lifted the weights. "Was it during? Because then you could play it off, if you wanted to."

I hit the treadmill's buttons, slowing the pace down to a walk so I could drink my water easier. "What, like I was speaking in tongues?"

"Yeah," Bay said. "People say shit during sex. Like the sex was so good that you didn't know what you were saying. I had one hook up who wouldn't stop calling me 'daddy' during which I found really off-putting. I had to call things off, in the end." He stole a glance at me. "But it's a plausible excuse. Just throwing that out there."

"But were you her daddy?" I asked, grinning.

"Fuck you," Bay said, grunting as he extended his arms.

"Do you want to do that?" Jim asked. "Find an excuse, I mean. It's not like it's not true." Bay made a noise in the back of his throat. "I think we all know it's very true."

Jim rubbed his towel along the back of his head. "I guess we need to ask what your goal is here, then."

"Not sure I had one," I said, taking a big gulp of water. "But making her bolt in a panic wasn't it, that's for sure." I swiped at my face with the bottom of my shirt. I always forgot to take my towel with me onto the treadmill. "Let me tell you, there's nothing quite so ego-crushing as telling someone you love them and getting a look of pure terror in return."

"Better than disgust," Jim pointed out.

I sighed. "True, and no, it wasn't during. It was definitely after."
"Post-orgasmic haze?" Bay wheezed.

"Except it wasn't. I meant to say it, just not then. I knew it would freak her out." I slowed the treadmill even more, moving it to the cool down setting. "Should I give her the out, though? Or just ignore I even said anything? Do I double down? What?"

"You know what I would say." Jim held his hands out, ready to take the bar from Bay. "Ignoring it is only ever a temporary stop gap. Communication is the foundation of any relationship, and lying and covering things up makes for a shitty foundation. Whole house will collapse."

Bay managed one last push, handing the weights off to Jim, who took them from his like they weighed nothing.

"Can you at least pretend like they're heavy?" Bay asked. "Throw a guy a bone, here." "Shitty foundation," Jim repeated, setting the bar into its slot. "Our house means too much to me, Bay."

Bay sat up with a sigh, grabbing his water. "The thing is, the foundation won't matter if she runs."

"And now you see my problem." I shut off the treadmill and stepped down. "What are you going to do?" Jim asked.

"I'm going to leave it in her hands for now," I said. "She's got a lot going on. If she wants to pretend I didn't say anything, fine. But as soon as this testing stuff is over, we'll need to talk about it." That scared me, too, because I was very aware of the fact that just because Van loved me as her friend, that didn't mean she would love me as her partner.

"She loves you," Bay said, unknowingly echoing my thoughts. "But with her background. I don't know—is she a fear biter?"

"Is she what?" Jim asked, settling into the weight bench.

"A fear biter," Bay repeated. "Like, is she going to be so freaked by Will bringing it up and talking about feelings that she lashes out?" He waved me off before I could argue. "I love Van, you know I do. That whole house is family to me. But she's been through some shit." He grimaced. "They both have."

It seemed like Bay had thought about this before.

"I don't know," I said, feeling a little hopeless. "But I guess we'll find out."

#

I'd showered and made it to work before I got a text from Van.

Loch Nessa: Any chance you'd like to have your tea leaves read tomorrow? You'll get to spend my quality time with my father—what a bonus? Are you tempted? I know you are.

I felt a stab of disappointment. I hadn't expected her to bring up an important conversation over text, and yet, the stab was still there. I hadn't realized how much I wanted her to make this step until now. That didn't bode well for my intention of putting the discussion off.

I was between appointments, so I messaged her back immediately. *What time?*

Loch Nessa: three o'clock, which means I'll have to move my work schedule around. Again. But that's when my father's last lecture is over. We'll be meeting him at the college.

Of course Woodbridge was taking only his schedule into account. It wasn't a great time for me, either. Not like I wouldn't jump through hoops to try and make it happen, though. It was Vanessa and she needed me. What else was I going to do? *Let me see what I can move around.*

Loch Nessa: Thanks, Will.

I had a chat thread open on my phone between all the shop piercers—there were only four of us, including me. I threw my request into the chat, put my phone away, and went to see if my next appointment was here.

It took an hour of back and forth and my covering of two up coming shifts, but I managed to get it off. *I'll be there.* Van responded with a gif of someone wiping the sweat off their forehead.

I wish I felt that level of relief. Instead, I was left with a vaguely uneasy feeling like things were about to go really badly...and I wasn't sure why or which things.

It put me in a foul mood for the rest of the day, which meant by the time Nana stopped by the shop, surprising me with dinner, I was I been marinating in it for hours.

Nana held up take out bags. "Surprise!" Declan perked up. "Is that Thai?"

"Uh oh, Nana," I said, giving her a kiss. "I hope you brought enough for the class." "I certainly did," Nana said, sounding affronted. "I'm not new."

I laughed, hustling Nana into the back room that we used as our employee lounge. As soon as she set the food down, I stole a hug. I'm a hugger, because I like to give them. You'd be surprised how many people don't realize how much they need a hug. I'm also a hugger because sometimes *I* needed one. Like today. I really needed a hug, especially from Nana.

"I see," said Nana, squeezing me back. "I take it I picked a good time to stop by?"

"Your nana-senses were definitely tingling." I wrapped her closer and sighed. Nana didn't wear perfume, and her hair products leaned toward the "whatever's on sale" category, so I don't have a specific scent tied to her besides a general Nana smell. It reminded me of grass.

When I finally let Nana go, she had a concerned expression on her face. She patted my cheek. "What's going on, kiddo?"

I pulled plates out of the cabinet. "Let's dish up first."

"Ah," she said. "So it's to be a long, unburdening of the soul, then."

"It is." We filled our plates, leaving the several mostly-full boxes for everyone else. As they popped in and filled plates, I settled down at the staff table with Nana. Between stuffing myself with an obscene amount of red curry and rice, I caught Nana up on the situation.

Nana listened, pretending to snap her chopsticks at my fingers when I stole a bite of the swimming rama on her plate. What can I say, I was a sucker for peanut sauce.

Nana sighed. "Poor Vanessa. I'm not a violent person, but if her father were to fall into a bear pit, I would only feel sorry for the bears."

"He can't be good eatin'," I said, shoving the last of my curry around my plate. I was too full, but also, *curry.*

"What are you going to do?"

I deflated slightly. "I don't know. Not much I can do except wait things out."

Nana stood, grabbing a glass of water for herself. "Patience is commendable, my heart, but I also believe in beginning as you mean to go on."

I pushed my plate away. "And what does that mean in this case?"

"It means you should give her a little time, sure, but you also need to be clear here. What do you want? What are your needs, and is that too much for her to give?"

I propped my elbows on the table, leaning my face into my hand. "I'm a little afraid of the answer she'll give me."

"Then you need to decide what scares you more—getting an answer, or getting one a year or more from now, when you're even more invested."

"I hate it when you make sense," I grumbled.

"I know." She eyed the counter hopefully. "Did Declan make any cookies?" "Oatmeal raisin," I said, tipping my chin toward the container.

Nana grinned in delight, grabbing the container. She bit into the cookie and chewed with enthusiasm. Her happy mood dimmed a little as she looked at me. "I should get to the reason I stopped by."

"You mean you it's not because I'm your favorite and you love me?"

"Of course it is," she said, "but that's an all-the-time reason, and not the specific impetus for this visit." She set down her cookie on a napkin. "I've been collecting scuttlebutt for you. About Tanner."

I perked up. "And?"

Nana frowned thoughtfully. "Everyone likes him."

"Oh," I said, my mood plummeting. I was so certain there was something off about the dude. Nothing concrete, just a feeling. "Thanks anyway, Nana."

"No," she said, shaking her head slightly, like she was warding off an annoying insect. "You don't understand, *Everyone likes him.*"

"Saying it again but in a new tone doesn't make me understand what you're saying, you know that, right?"

Nana huffed, breaking off a piece of her cookie. "Will, it's academia. It's a naturally back-stabby environment. Arcanists take that to a whole new level. I've met actual snakes who were warmer and more cuddly."

"Hey," I said, pointing a finger at her. "Snakes are awesome."

"I agree," Nana said. "And there are good arcanists. People who are drawn to the field for altruistic reasons, but it also draws a certain percentage of power-hungry asshats."

"No argument here. So Tanner is one of the good ones?"

"That's the thing," Nana said, popping a bite of cookie into her mouth. "I'm not convinced he is. No student complaints. No grumbling between his contemporaries. He basically got his graduate assistantship position handed to him."

"He didn't have any competition?"

"Woodbridge offered it directly to him and no one protested. Those assistantships don't grow on trees, Will. People should have been vying for it, but it was like everyone just accepted that Tanner was perfect for the job and called it good."

"Huh." I didn't know what to make of that, but the way Nana was laying it out was troubling. "Are you thinking magical interference?"

Nana took in a deep breath, her brows bunched together. "I don't know," she said finally. "The university has precautions against that kind of thing. Nothing's impossible, but it would be very hard to do, especially against someone at arcanist Woodbridge's level, but..."

"But?"

Deep concern showed in her eyes, her mouth pinched in a way that made my spine straighten. "But he's an arcanist, Will, and I think he's pretty good at it. What if he came up with something new—a spell, a potion, a magic, that could get him what he wanted, influence people in some way? And what if he engineered it in such a way that it avoided the university failsafes?"

I sat up straighter, ice in my gut. "Do you have any proof?"

"No," she said. "It's all theory based on things that *aren't* there. Nothing I could show to an uncanny tribunal or the dean of students."

I chewed on that for a second, trying to see if I could do anything with the information on a formal setting. Nana was right. There wasn't much we could do *officially*. "I'm open to suggestions."

"You going to see him again soon?"

"Yes," I said, explaining about Van's last test and my part in it.

Nana finished off her cookie, her attention far away as she thought. I let her ponder while I gathered up our dishes and took them to the sink to wash. By the time I scrubbed, rinsed and set them in the drying rack, Nana was smiling.

"That's your devious smile," I said, sitting back down across from her. "I approve."

Nana grinned. "It's a testing situation. Vanessa is within her right to request a secondary witness of her choosing. She can also request the use of a Cassandra potion."

Cassandra weren't particularly easy to get normally. You needed a special license to make and sell them. Luckily, Vanessa knew some of the best hedgewitches in the business and she'd just made one for Tanner. "Tanner had her make one as part of the last test—Cold Candor."

Nana's eyes sparkled. "Interesting. I wonder why that potion?"

"Maybe he wanted to get his hands on one without the usual hassle," I said. "It's possible," Nana admitted. "But we don't know for sure."

The more I got to know Tanner, the more he seemed an unknown. "I can't see Woodbridge letting either go without an argument—the use of the potion or the witness."

Nana shrugged. "He can argue all he likes. It's protocol. If he doesn't accept them, it's as good him cheating."

I leaned across the table, kissing Nana on the cheek. "You're the best."

"I am, thank you," Nana said with a grin. Then she frowned, folding her hands together. "I don't like any of this, Will. Vanessa needs to be very careful tomorrow."

"She will be, Nana," I said, my voice soft.

"Good," Nana said, her worry shifting to a fierce expression. "And you tell that girl to give them both barrels. I'm rooting for her."

I loved my nana so very much, but I wouldn't cross her, and it didn't bode well for Tanner or Woodbridge that they'd ended up on her shit list. Hades hath no fury like a vexed librarian. It was all that knowledge at their fingertips, I think.

CHAPTER TWENTY-THREE

Vanessa

Will had come over late last night, after I'd gone to bed. I hadn't been asleep yet. I'd been watching baking shows with the ferrets. Ever since Declan had moved in, they'd taken a keen interest in baking. I wasn't much into it myself, but I liked the results—Declan making more cookies for me to eat—so I didn't mind indulging them.

I had been drowsy with sleep, which I'll admit I played up a little. I was worried that Will would want to talk, but I shouldn't have been. He simply stripped down, climbed into bed behind me, and snuggled in. By the time the bakers got the final round, his hands were roaming.

I never saw who won. Will had made love to me with the a kind of slow, relentless assurance that was devastating. There were entire worlds that had been conquered with less thoroughness.

I was morning now, and I was wide awake, putting on the last bit of my eye make up for work. I didn't have a full shift this morning, just opening and putting in some supply orders. Thea and Emma were handing more and more of that stuff over to me, and I couldn't help but be proud that they trusted me with it. Their approval was a heady drug and I wanted more of it.

When I stepped into the kitchen, the sight of Will greeted me. He wasn't wearing anything except pajama pants, which were riding low, showing off the inked perfection of his back. Kodo and Podo were on the counter, chittering at him as he poured coffee into a black mug that said *Definitely Probably Not Poison Maybe* on it.

Without looking back, he handed off an already filled mug to me. I accepted it with a smile, kissing him on the cheek. "You didn't have to get up."

He grumbled something, sipping his coffee. It always took Will a minute to wake up. I left him to it, sitting down at the table with my own mug. Will took a plate out of the microwave, setting it in front of me. "This was in the fridge for you with reheating instructions for me." Will's smile was groggy. "I can't decide if it's cute or slightly off putting that Declan knows us so well that he anticipated my role in this morning's dance."

"It means he loves you," I said, breathing in the egg casserole Declan had made. "And he wants me to be happy."

Will barked a laugh, taking the seat across from me. "About today."

I stiffened, the first bite of my breakfast balancing on my fork. "What about it? Are you not going to be able to make it? Do I need to find an alternate?"

Will shook his head. "Eat that bite before you lose it." I shoved the egg into my mouth, but didn't taste it.

Will explained about his nana's visit and her suggestions.

I made myself finish my breakfast because Declan would be concerned if I didn't, but I didn't taste a single bite. Worry sat in my belly like I'd swallowed a big rock covered in barnacles. "You want me to use my Cassandra potion?"

Will glanced at me from refilling his coffee. "If not yours, than Thea makes them, right?" "Yeah, but only by request, only if she trusts you, and only if you have a good reason." Declan settled back in across from me. "Great, then it should be no problem."

I held my fork in a white-knuckled grip. "No, big problem."

"How's that?" He asked, but I could tell he knew *exactly* why I thought it was an issue.

He just wanted me to say it.

"I would have to tell them what I need it for, Willhardt."

His hand clenched around his mug, his expression mulish. "You're going to have to tell them eventually."

"When I'm ready. Not now." I could feel my own stubbornness digging in, my expression probably equally mulish as his.

"News flash, *Vanessa*, you're never going to feel ready. Stop putting if off and just take the leap."

"Says the guy who's always played it safe." I could hear my voice rising again, the argument coming on. What was it about our kitchen? Was it cursed? All the arguments in the house seemed to happen here.

"In what way," Will ground out, "do I play it safe?"

"You picked your job because of Bay, you picked your Nana over a new life with your dad, nothing in your life challenges you. You choose what's comfortable." I dropped my fork on my plate with a clatter, sitting back and folding my arms. "I mean, even me. Do you really want to be with me, Will, or am I the comfortable choice?"

The words hung in the air between us, the kitchen dead silent. I regretted saying them, because I could see the hurt on Will's face, but a perverse part of me needed to know—was I just the easy choice?

Will rubbed his hand over his face. "It's too fucking early for this."

"That's not an answer, Will."

"No, it's not, because it was a fucking insulting question." Will stood up, pushing his chair back. "I picked my job because I thought I'd be good at it. I surround myself with the people that I do not because they're easy, but because I love them. It's simple, Van, but apparently utterly fucking foreign to you." He grabbed our dishes, taking them over to the sink with the crisp, precise movements of someone trying very hard to not throw things.

He rinsed our dishes as I sat there, feeling like an asshole. Kodo and Podo both glared at me from their perch on the counter.

You hurt Will Podo accused, bouncing over to soothe him.

You're going to need a sorry gift, Kodo said, his disappointment palpable though our bond. *I'm good at sorry gifts. I have to give them a lot.*

Curious and needing a distraction, I had to ask him, *What's a good sorry gift?*

You can make a gift of words, Kodo said. *If you pick the right ones, but that's hard for you, so you might need to go for the big guns—chicken livers.*

Chicken livers? I asked.

Chicken livers, Kodo said firmly.

They work, Podo admitted. *It's hard to stay mad with a belly full of chicken livers.*

Thanks, I said. *I appreciate your advice.* With the ferrets somewhat placated, I turned my attention back to Will. He gripped the sink with both hands. As I watched, his stiff shoulders drooped.

He sighed, wiping his hands on the towel. "You win, Van. Talk to Thea, don't talk to Thea. Use the potion or don't. You'll do what you want, regardless." He straightened the towel and turned, every muscle etched in tightly controlled fury and burnished in hurt.

It was like I couldn't help it, hurting the people who loved me most. Guilt stabbed at me with tiny knives, but I ignored it.

He strode toward my room, pausing at the table. "But I want you to think about something. If I'm so afraid, if I'm the one playing it safe, how come I'm the only one copping to how they feel in this relationship? I'm the one putting myself out there."

I shrugged one shoulder, purposefully sounding nonchalant. "We just started dating, Will.

I don't see a reason to make a big deal out of it." Okay even I knew I was being a bitch about this. It was like the shittiest version of me had taken over my mouth and I couldn't stop it.

Or maybe I was lying to myself. Maybe I could stop it, I just didn't want to, because then I'd have to face how afraid I was—of Will, this relationship, of happiness. How fucked up was that?

Will examined my face, his jaw hard. Then, with a defeated tilt to his shoulders, he walked out of the kitchen to put on clothes and drive me to work.

The car was silent the entire ride until we stopped in front of Wicked Brews.

"Juliet and I will pick you up at two thirty," Will said. "I'll bring your ferrets." He didn't look at me.

"Okay," I said, my throat tight. I grabbed my stuff, opening the door. A voice inside me screamed at me to say something, to make him look at us.

But I didn't listen, the only sound my door shutting as I got out. Then Will drove away.

Vanessa #

I had my earbuds in, clipboard out as I marked down what we needed to order, when Thea cornered me.

She shoved a jar in my face, making me jump about fifteen feet in the air. "Vanessa Morgan Woodridge, who made this potion?" She was using what I referred to as her Steel Magnolia voice. It was like a cross between a mom voice, a genteel lady, and a badger. It was a formidable vocal tool.

I popped my earbuds out with one hand, the other cradling the clipboard and covering my wildly beating heart. "How did you know my middle name?" I wheezed rather inanely.

Thea shrugged. "It's in your employee file paperwork." She wiggled the jar at me. "Answer my question."

"Why," I rasped, still recovering from my fright. "Was there something wrong with it." "No," she said, her lips pursed. "It was excellent actually. Different than the way I make it—how did you counter the magical whammy aftertaste problem?" "I did a double short processing time," I said automatically.

"Ah-*ha!*" She said, pointing a finger at me. "I knew it was you!" She dropped her hand down. "What do you mean, double short?"

"I halved the original processing time, then repeated the cook and filtration process." I couldn't not answer her when she was using the Steel Magnolia.

"Huh," Thea said. "I never thought of that."

I shrugged helplessly. "The ferrets found it in an old hedge witchery book they ordered off the internet." There had been a brief window of time when the ferrets had learned how to one click things on my laptop. The book was one of their better purchases and one I couldn't bring myself to return. It had been a huge pain, changing all my passwords.

Thea snapped back to attention, wiggling the potion at me again. "You're good at this.

Why aren't you apprenticing with us? Getting your degree." I blinked at her. "I—"

Emma busted into the back room, her hands full of clean towels. "Did you yell at her yet? I don't want to miss it." Emma grinned at me over the towels. "The angry southern drawl thing is *hot*."

"There's something wrong with you," Thea said, though there was no heat in her words. "I'm waiting to hear her explain why she's not pursuing this as a calling—"

It was at that moment that I burst into tears. "I'm so sorry!" I sobbed. "I don't know why I'm crying!"

Thea put an arm around me, tutting, while Emma thrust a clean towel at my face. "Make her stop," Emma said. "I can't handle crying."

Thea rolled her eyes. "Go make her a cup of tea, sugar. I'll handle this."

I then spent the next ten minutes spilling my guts and blubbering all over my boss. I clenched the towel in my first until she pried it from my fingers, putting a cup of tea in my hands instead.

"Well, sugar, it sounds like you know *exactly* why you're crying," Thea said, squeezing my shoulder. "That's a lot of weight on your shoulders."

I hiccuped.

"Why didn't you just tell us?" Thea asked gently.

"I don't know," I repeated, my tears starting up again.

"Oh gods, don't get her started up again," Emma said, pulling up an empty milk crate in front of me and sitting down. "With a father like yours, though I hesitate to use that term for him, it makes sense you kept it to yourself."

Thea looked at her, a question on her face.

"What? He's not exactly the supportive type, is he? Van's used to being mocked by authority figures." She waved a hand between them. "And oddly enough, we're authority figures."

"We would never mock you," Thea said, scandalized by the very notion. "That's awful."

Emma shrugged. "People are awful." She nudged the mug, waving at me to drink it. "So obviously we'll go with you tonight. That way you'll have witnesses who aren't assholes *and* we can make sure he takes the Cassandra potion." Emma's grin was evil. "He won't want to make a scene in front of us, trust me."

Thea seemed like she wanted to argue, but I agreed with Emma. "He won't. Dad hates a scene." I sipped my tea, a mix of catnip, peppermint and chamomile. "But the test is at three. You won't be done here in time."

Emma scoffed. "We're the bosses, Van. We leave when we decide to leave. This is important. Noah will be on shift. He can handle most things. It's about time I gave him a promotion anyway."

"But—"

Thea brought back the Steel Magnolia. "No buts, sugar. You just have to promise me that when it's time to apprentice, you consider doing it here."

I blinked at her, trying to wrap my mind around her words. "Of— of course! I wanted—" I bit off my words. There were already being so kind, I didn't want to burden them with my expectations.

Emma nudged my shoe with her boot. "You wanted?"

My voice wanted so badly to come out small, but I was beginning to see that maybe that was a problem. Maybe I needed to get better about being loud, about asking for what I needed. I cleared my throat and firmed my shoulders. "I wanted to apprentice here. I wanted—I'd hoped— maybe you'd bring me on as a partner someday." I continued in a rush, suddenly needing to get it all out. "I love it here. This place is my home."

"Of course it's your home," Emma said with a scowl. "What the fuck, Van?" She shook her head. "Okay, here's how it's going to go. We'll get through this nonsense with your father. And frankly it *is* nonsense. Then we'll talk to the head of the hedge witch program at SUU. We can get you on an accelerated track."

I almost dropped my tea. "You can *what*?"

"We know the head of the program," Thea said, a little sheepishly. "Who do you think *our* mentor was?"

"She was at our wedding," Emma grinned.

I knew they'd met in college, but I didn't know the rest of it. I clasped onto my mug like it was an anchor.

"We can lay everything out for Isla," Emma said casually, "tell her the situation. See if we can set it up so some of your work hours count as credit, and test you out of some of the basic classes."

I swallowed hard, afraid if I blinked again, the whole scene would dissolve like a soap bubble. I wanted it *so bad*. "You would do all that?"

"Of course we would, sugar." Thea patted my knee.

"Don't think we're being entirely unselfish here," Emma said, with a laugh. "We get a talented witch, trained to our specifications. Besides, we'd been talking about adding to our family." She grabbed Thea's hand and kissed it.

Thea blushed. "I want to have a baby," she admitted. "If we get you trained up in the next year so that you can handle some of the basic stuff for me, that would be doable."

I was suddenly much more comfortable with the plan. I'm sure Juliet would have something to say about that, the fact that I was only okay with something when I could see what the other person was getting out of it. Something to think on later. For now…

I stuck out my hand. "We have a deal."

Emma grinned, slapping my hand instead of shaking it. Thea squealed in joy, then grabbed me into a hug. "Oh, sugar, I'm so happy!"

So was I. And it was a deeply uncomfortable feeling.

But I could get used to it.

CHAPTER TWENTY-FOUR

Vanessa

Since my bosses were joining us, I caught a ride with them and met Will, Juliet, and Savvy at the university. Will had my ferrets leashed, just in case, though they were riding on his shoulders.

You ready for the last test? I asked.

Of course, Kodo said. *Did you bring the chicken livers? Not yet,* I admitted.

You better apologize soon, Podo said. *Chicken livers don't last forever.*

Wise words from the ferrets. I led the way to the arcanist building, my entourage in tow.

Juliet walked beside me, carrying Savvy on her hip. "I'm kind of surprised you brought her," I said.

Juliet hefted her daughter up, resettling her. "Dad requested it, actually. Said he wanted to see her."

I couldn't help it, I frowned.

Juliet sighed. "I know. I want to be happy that he's showing an interest, but I know he's still our father, which mean he's likely got at least one other reason. I'm not buying his act hook, line and sinker."

"I know," I said. "I just worry, that's all." It sucked when my father did something hurtful, but it felt twice as bad when it was directed at Juliet or Savvy for some reason. Like, I could take it if he was a shit to me, but I couldn't tolerate it when he was a shit to them.

We filed into the arcanist building, but instead of going up to my father's office, we headed to one of the second floor exam rooms. The linoleum in the hallway made our footsteps echo weirdly, or maybe that was just my nerves.

Tanner was waiting to greet us at the open doorway to exam room three. I hadn't warned him about my extra guests, but he didn't blink at the number of people. That might have been because he was more focused on Juliet, smiling down at her as he ushered us into the room.

Exam room three was pretty basic and looked a lot like a conference room and a science lab had a baby. A long table took up the center, office chairs lined along the sides. On one end, hung a white board. At the other end stood a countertop and sink, with a portable burner and tea kettle, a few jars of labeled tea, and cabinets full of other supplies, the lists of which were neatly labeled on the doors.

I made introductions, all of us getting settling into room and getting ready. Tanner shut the door and Will unsnapped the ferret's harnesses, letting them bounce around the room. They bounded over to me, scampering up my body until they could get to the counter. I left them to peek at the teas while I checked out the kettle.

There was already water inside, and at home, I wouldn't think twice about using it. This room was an unknown to me, and I kept thinking about what Will's Nana had told him. I dumped the water, rinsing out the kettle and refilling it.

"Thorough," Tanner said, smiling. "Very good."

I smiled at him, but it was forced. He didn't seem to notice. I set the kettle to boil and sat down in the empty chair next to Will. Will was still unhappy with me, and I didn't blame him.

After all, I hadn't offered him my version of chicken livers or gifted him with apology words. With everything else today, I'd put the whole thing aside.

That didn't keep Will from reaching out and taking my hand under the table. He was pissed, but he wouldn't let that keep him from supporting me. The ferrets chirped, letting me know that the teas all smelled okay and didn't seem magically off. With that done, there was nothing else to do until my father got here.

So we waited. And waited.

Tanner spent the time having my bosses fill out their participation waivers, but that only took a few minutes.

Twenty minutes past three, my father finally breezed into the room. He didn't seem the least bit frazzled or worried that he was late, but then again, why would he? My father was used to the world waiting on him.

He did stop short at Thea and Emma. His face stayed impassive, but I'd spent my entire childhood reading my father's posture and tells, trying to anticipate his moods. He was not happy to see them.

"Juliet, Vanessa—who's this?"

"Arcanist Woodbridge, may I introduce my bosses, Thea and Emma Ruiz-Banks. They're the owners and operators behind Wicked Brews."

They all shook hands and there was much baring of teeth on all sides. "How generous of you to give your time for Vanessa's little project."

Only my father would denigrate hedge witchery directly to the face of hedgewitches and think they would agree with him.

Emma's smile grew even more shark-like. "We wouldn't think of missing it."

"Not for the world," Thea added, her own shark-smile layered with levels of sweet, southern charm, which were a total facade. Thea was just as dangerous as Emma when they were mad, and Thea held more of a grudge. Right now she was blessing his heart in her mind, I was sure of it.

"Let's get cracking, shall we?" Woodbridge said, taking a seat at the head of the table. "First things first," Thea said, fishing a jar out of her purse and setting it on the table with

a *thunk*. "Our Vanessa is opting for certain stipulations, common protocol, which of course I don't have to tell you." She tutted. "You know how these things go—we want to make sure everything's above board so no one can argue the findings of the test."

Emma took out her phone, causally propping it on the table. I think I was the only one who noticed.

My father looked like he'd smelled something nasty. "What is that?" "A Cassandra potion," Thea said evenly.

Woodbridge's lip curled up in a sneer. "Do you really think that's necessary? Hardly anyone requires that protocol anymore, especially not when the proctor in question has a reputation like mine."

"We are just but lowly hedgewitches," Emma drawled, sprawling back into her chair, her hand going to one of her wife's curls, playing with it like it. "You must grant us our peccadillos. We are, after all, such a backwards branch of magic."

"Practically antiquated," Thea added.

"Fine," Woodbridge said, his teeth gritted together. "If you feel like you need such a paltry thing, you can have it."

"Oh, thank you," Emma said. I'd never heard her less sincere.

I glanced over at Tanner, who wasn't looking nearly so sanguine about the whole thing. "Is that okay, Tanner?" I asked, keeping my tone guileless. "You'll have to take the

Cassandra potion, too, after all."

Tanner snapped back to himself, smiling now, like he hadn't looked faintly ill a second before. "Of course. Why would I object?"

"Yes," Will said so softly I barely heard it. "Why would you?"

With everyone more or less on the same page, Thea cracked open the jar, stating maker, time, and the name of the potion for all to hear, which was standard practice in these kinds of situations. We all had to verbally consent to take it—you couldn't feed anyone a potion they didn't agree too, at least not legally. It was a lot like giving someone medicine or a drug without their consent. Unless you were an akeosite with an unresponsive patient, it was a no go.

With any kind of Cassandra potion, that was especially true. It shaped your will, making you tell the truth. Against you consent, that would feel like an invasion of yourself and your privacy. In the wrong hands, a Cassandra potion was a powerful tool. Some head's of state regularly dosed themselves with anti-potions before public appearances or anything where a Cassandra potion could cause political havoc.

Everyone agreed, while I fetched glasses from the cupboard. Thea divvied it up, and without further ado, we collectively tossed it back.

I may have got rid of the magical after taste issue, but the potion still tasted like licking the bottom of a boot.

That done, everyone chose their tea while I set up their cups and saucers, making sure to choose lighter colored ones so it would be easier to read. For this purpose, they'd put the loose tea directly into their cups before I added the water. Then they'd hold onto it, focusing on the cup while it steeped and cooled.

Today I'd be reading not just Will and Juliet, but Tanner and rather surprisingly, my father. I hadn't thought he'd put himself out there like that. After a few minutes, the tea was cool enough for them to start drinking.

Juliet finished first, so I took her mug, swishing around the dregs. Anyone can read a tea leaves, but witches do it differently than anyone else. Humans pay attention to the shapes the leaves themselves leave and where they end up in the cup, using their knowledge to interpret what they see.

Witches look at something else entirely. Tasseomancy was a form of sympathetic magic. There was an exchange that happened when you drank your tea—you press your lips on the rim. Your fingers grasp the mug. Small particles of saliva wash back into the cup. Our magic was in these small traces of us as much as it was in the rest of us. With Tasseomancy, you're paying attention to those things left behind. I might examine the tea leaves themselves as much as a regular practioner, but I wasn't paying attention to the shape of the dredges of water and tea leaves so much as the shape of the magic.

Juliets magic was lovely—a kind of sparkly teal and pink, undercut by a sunshine-yellow.

I watched it move, letting it lull me into a sort of hypnotic state. "Ask your questions," I said.

Tanner asked for Juliet keeping his questions cute, but non-invasive. Not quite 'what's your favorite color' kind of questions, but close. I would answer them based on what I saw in the cup, and she would confirm or negate my responses. It went smoothly, no bumps.

My father went next. I hated to admit it, but my father had spectacular magic. Goldenrod, a deep emerald green, and a rich red-brown.

It was almost majestic to watch. Tanner asked him questions, keeping them as light as Juliet's.

It would have gone just as smoothly if I hadn't thrown a wrench right into the middle of it.

"Why are you helping me," I asked. It had been bothering me for so long. I needed to know. What was my father doing this for?

"I'm not," he said easily. "I want you to fail."

"I'm your *daughter*," I said, exasperated and, damn it, still hurt. "Juliet is my daughter," my father said. "You, I'm not sure about." Oh, for fuck's sake. "Dad, we did *two* paternity tests."

"You mother cheated, I'm sure of it."

The worst part about using a Cassandra potion? There was no room for denial, no potential to cushion yourself with gentling lies. My father was absolutely convinced of everything he just said.

"Whatever," I said. "Regardless, I still have your name. My failure would reflect on you." "Better a failure than a hedge witch." Woodbridge shook his head. "Why can't you just pick up your things, take your trash *boyfriend* here, and disappear?"

Thea audibly gasped, but Emma's scowl could have stripped paint. Tanner's expression was carefully blank. I didn't have to look at Will or Juliet—I knew how they felt.

"You threw your daughters away," Will said quietly. "If there's trash in this room, it's you."

"What about me and Savvy," Juliet said, her expression hard. It didn't matter what my dad said here, really. After what he'd spouted off about me and Will, my sister was already done. She was just tying up the loose threads now.

"There's still hope for you," Woodbridge said easily. "And if not you, at least your children."

"Child," Juliet corrected.

Woodbridge smiled and it was chilling. His eyes darted to Tanner. "I have hopes for the future. With my magic flowing through you, and a partner with the right magical pedigree? Your children would be worth the Woodbridge name."

Oh, puke. "Juliet's not a broodmare, dad." He just blinked at me.

I was so done with him. I couldn't handle one more word out of his mouth. So I waved my father out of the hot seat. If I didn't ever have to look at his smarmy face again, I would be a happy witch.

Will went next. He sat down across from me, pushing his mug over so I could take it. Tanner tried to get the test back on track, asking Will basic questions, waiting for me to divine the answers. I'll give it to Tanner, he came up with things that would be difficult, even with knowing Will as well as I did. Until today, I'd had no idea that he had a reoccurring nightmare where he was chased by sentient mushrooms.

Will was about to get up when my father decided to ask a question. I guess he wanted to get his own back, do his best to make Will look bad.

"Why are you with my daughter?" He sneered. "Because I'm in love with her," Will said.

I jolted like I'd been hit with an electric shock.

"Sure," Woodbridge said. "In love with her name, her magic—trying to elevate yourself maybe? Did you think she's going to inherit, perhaps? How long after finding out who she was did it take you to 'fall in love.' A whole five minutes?"

"No," Will said, resting his chin in his hands. "Took me ages. Ten, maybe fifteen minutes."

My father looked triumphant. "Since you found out she was a Woodbridge—I knew it!

You'll get nothing out of her, you know."

Will tilted his head. "Naw, didn't give a fuck about her name. I just thought she was awesome, you know? She smiled at me and pow." He smacked his chest, right over his heart. "That was it. She lights up like that. I was a goner." Will sat back in his chair. "I don't want your money and I don't give a shit about you. I just want your daughter."

Woodbridge, for once, was at a loss.

"We done?" Will asked drumming his knuckles on the table. I nodded and he smiled, pushing himself out of the chair. The asshole was whistling while I felt like all the little cogs and wheels holding me together were grinding to a halt. Springing loose. Rusting into dust.

Tanner took his place, seemingly at ease. I might have been imagining the tightness around his eyes. "Well, that's a hard act to follow. Be gentle with me, Juliet." He laughed and it sounded a little too hearty.

"Of course," Juliet said, handing Savvy over to Thea. Juliet's smile was sharp and her tone...Tanner had no idea what was coming his way. I'd seen Juliet like this before.

Juliet set her hand flat on the table. "In your time at SUU, have you ever used magic—a spell, a potion, any kind of magic—to get ahead?"

Tanner's smile faltered. "There are failsafes for that, Juliet." He looked so genuinely hurt by the question, that I almost felt bad for him. He reached out, grasping her wrist gently. If his tone hadn't turned faintly condescending, I might have fallen for his act. "I know you aren't an arcanist, darling, but even you should know that."

Oh, you stupid, stupid man. My sister was smart, and insulting her wouldn't keep her from realizing he hadn't answered the question.

"Did you discover or create a magic that eluded those failsafes." Tanner didn't answer, his jaw tight.

The room was dead silent. Savvy squealed loudly, clapping her hands like we were playing a game.

Juliet leveled her gaze on him, unflinching. "Did you use a spell or give me a potion, at any time, that influenced my will?"

"No," he said easily, that condescension back. "I can't believe you'd ask that, Juliet."

I relaxed, but Juliet didn't. "Did you, at any time, have someone *else* use a potion, spell or magic to influence my will?"

This time Tanner didn't answer.

"Tanner," my sister said, her eyes pleading. "Answer me please. Did you, at any time, have someone *else* use a potion, spell or magic to influence my will?"

Again he didn't answer, but my ferrets started chirping, getting my attention. They were hopping along the table between my sister and Tanner.

"Juliet," I said calmly. "According to the ferrets, the tattoo on your arm just disappeared."

Juliet flipped her arm over, her wrist up. Her tattoo was gone, vanished like it was never there. "You're doing it *right now*?"

Tanner shook his head, sighing, and let her hand go. "I can see you're upset. I think that's enough for today. We can talk when you calm down."

"The fuck we will!" Juliet yelled, pushing back her hair.

Tanner stood, turning away from her. "This test is over. You'll get our decision in the next few days after arcanist Woodbridge and I confer over the findings."

Juliet lunged for him, but Tanner maneuvered neatly away from her.

He mumbled a word, twisted his hand, and tapped the wall. Purple glyphs lit off the walls of the exam room, every surface, even the ceiling, blazing to life with magic.

"He must have spent forever on that spell," Emma murmured, though she barely moved her lips.

Juliet stayed frozen in place, magic pinning her in mid step.

"We'll chat, darling," Tanner said. "I'm sure you'll see sense once you stop being hysterical. You're a very sensible girl."

Tanner held out his hand. "Woodbridge, sir. Thank you for trusting me with this assignment." He waved his other hand lazily back at Juliet. "I'll fix that soon, I promise."

My father shook his hand. "Of course you will, my boy. I never doubted it."

They both gathered their things, calmly as you please, while we stayed trapped like flies in a vat of honey.

Ten minutes later the spell snapped, and we were free, but by then they were long gone.

CHAPTER TWENTY-FIVE

Will

A few quick texts and a little driving later, we were back at Wicked Brews, in the bar half of the establishment. We'd pulled several tables together, trying to make room for our hastily gathered crew. Not only were we there, but all of Van's roommates, Bay, and Jim. It was an all hand's on deck situation.

As soon as we sat down, Thea fetched me, Van and Juliet a nullifying potion—I think we were all done with the bald truth for the day. It tasted like tangerine and vinegar, but I hardly cared. I was low-key freaking out about what I'd said during the test. Van had barely been managing with the post-sex I love you, which as Bay had pointed out, came with a small amount of plausible disability if she so chose.

But confessing that I'd been in love with her since forever while under the whammy of the Cassandra potion? Not an inch of wiggle room there. While I was worried about how Van was going to take it, I also felt strangely relieved. It was out, finally, and we'd just have to deal with it. We'd have a little time. We were all far more concerned about everything else that had gone down during the test.

"I knew dad was an asshole," Juliet said, glaring at her wine. "But seriously, that was some bullshit."

Bay sat next to her, a sleeping Savvy draped over him. I'd strategically put her there to keep him from bolting out of the bar and chasing after Woodbridge himself. I'd never seen him so mad. I was pretty sure given the chance, Bay would deboned both Tanner and Woodbridge using his bare hands right now.

Van sat quietly staring at the table, while Thea hugged her. Emma scowled at her phone, rewinding and rewatching Tanner's confession. Or lack there of.

"There has to be something we could use," Emma grumbled.

"He doesn't admit it or refute it," Lou said apologetically. "It makes him look shady as fuck, but there's nothing to prosecute there. The most we could do is show the video to the university."

Declan rubbed his bearded jaw, his face thoughtful. "I could eat him. I've never eaten a person before. The wolf is convinced they'll taste funny, but I'm willing to give it a try."

"We won't find anything," Vanessa said. Her shoulders drooped, her voice flat. "Tanner's my dad's protege. My father admires cunning."

Juliet continued to scowl at her wine. "I have a terrible feeling that none of this is going to go the way we want it to."

Van raised her beer. "To terrible feelings."

We performed the saddest toast ever, no one managing to crack a joke or a smile. Even Dammit sagged on Trick's shoulder, giving a muted chirp.

Jim scratched his jaw, careful to keep his horns from hitting the wall behind him. "I like the sound of Declan's plan, though legally, it's not in much of a gray-area. It's pretty much straight-up murder. People frown on that sort of thing."

"Murder should be acceptable," Declan grumbled, "when the person is an unredeemable asshole."

Trick consider this, giving Dammit a scratch. He was the only one here who could do that without gloves. Dammit was getting better at controlling his flames, but he was still young, and there were some perks to being an elementist who handled fire. "If we made that rule, a rather large swath of the human population wouldn't make it." He sipped his beer, his expression thoughtful. "But we can seek revenge. Let's get *really* petty with it."

"More petty, more better," I agreed. I watched Van from the corner of my eye, trying to read how she was doing. She didn't need me right now—Thea was clucking at her like the best kind of mother hen. Van was soaking it up and I wondered when anyone had last clucked over Van. Had anyone? I couldn't see her mom doing it. Woodbridge certainly hadn't.

Van's face was blank, her eyes hollow. She carried a sense of desolation like a heavy cloak. Tanner and her father had, temporarily at least, broken Van's spirit.

What a bunch of fucking assholes. I didn't mean that glibly. Rage burned so fiercely in the pit of my stomach, I was half-convinced that if I opened my mouth right then, lava would come out.

"What do we do?" Juliet asked, her wine glass finally empty.

"We do nothing," Van said hollowly.

Thea's response was swift and resolute. "No." She rubbed Van's back in firm circles. "Now we wait. It might feel like nothing, but it's not a forever kind of nothing, Sugar."

"Let's see how they play this hand," Emma said darkly, her brows drawn low. "We wait until they give you your test results. Then we decide how to retaliate."

"Okay," Van said. She sounded so passive, so unlike herself, that it made me shudder. Silence fell over the group. I'd been to funerals that were more cheerful.

"Right," Lou said, clapping her hands. "That's it. Nobody fucking died. We're done here." She pulled out her phone. Everyone watched her, their expressions dull, and in Juliet's case, slightly drunk.

Declan perked up, grinning. Whatever plan Lou was enacting, he already knew what it was and approved.

"For those of us not psychically linked to you," I said, pushing away my empty glass. "Care to share what you're up to there?"

"That," Bay said, "was too much rhyming." I blew him a kiss.

He flipped me off.

Best friends—you couldn't beat them.

"Van passed her tests today," Lou said. "They were stupid tests she shouldn't have had to do, but that's not important. She passed. This is a celebration."

Van thawed a little, wrinkling her nose. "But my dad—"

I made a harsh buzzer sound. "That's enough of that. To speak the name of evil is to call it down upon yourself. Or something. Whatever."

"What Will meant," Lou said, tapping away on her phone. "Is that we've spent enough time and energy on that man for the day. Now is not the time to give into cat thoughts of revenge. That time is for later. Now is the time to celebrate."

Emma blinked at her. "Cat thoughts?"

"It's seductive," Declan said. "The way a cat thinks. Or so I'm told."

"Cat's do what they want," Lou said, absently. "But right now, we need to be like golden retrievers. Just fluffy little hedonists with no worries about tomorrow."

"And how do we do that?" Jim asked. "We're already in a bar, and we can't take the baby to a casino *or* a strip club."

I eyed my roommate. "Do you want to go to either of those places?"

"No," Jim said. "Gambling doesn't interest me and I learned a long time ago that people get real weird at strip clubs when there's a minotaur about." He stared off into space. "The things that people have asked me to do."

"Van doesn't need that kind of hedonism," Lou said, still tapping away on her phone. "She needs to be surrounded by a shit-ton of people who love her, people who are happy for her, and people who will feed her."

"She needs to be wrapped in fluff," I said softly. While half the table definitely thought I'd said something weird, Lou just nodded.

"Yes, exactly."

And Van seemed to thaw a little bit more.

Bay straighten in his seat, careful to not jostle Savvy. "You're mobilizing the moms?"

"And the aunties," Lou said, finally looking up from her phone, a smug smile at her place. "Surprise party at Mama Ami's place." She looked at her watch. "We've got an hour." She pointed a finger at Bay. "Make sure everyone knows where to go." She waved at the table. "It goes without saying you're all invited."

Emma pushed away from the table with a clatter. "I'm going to go raid the bakery. I'm sure we have cupcakes or something we can bring."

Thea flushed. "I made a cake. It's in the walk in."

Emma leaned down and kissed her wife. "Of course you did. I sure did pick a winner." Thea blushed some more. "I picked one, too." She gave Van one more squeeze and stood.

"Don't worry, Sugar. Whatever's coming, we're going to handle it." "We all are," Emma said.

"And worse comes to worse," Jim said, crossing his arms. "I've got access to cement and no one would question me pouring a foundation. We can make your problems disappear."

"That idea came to you a little easily," I said. "Should I be worried?"

"Naw," Jim said, a smile splitting his bovine face. "Unless you piss me off. Then all bets are off."

Will

\#

It was amazing how quickly Bay and Lou's moms mobilized. By the time we got to Mama Ami's house, the picnic tables were set in the backyard, covered in brightly colored tablecloths and mason jars filled with flowers. A bunch of Bay's family were putting out food—way more than anyone could probably eat. It was an eclectic spread with platters filled with everything from pancit to smoked salmon and lutefisk. Bay's maternal side of the family was Filipinx, his stepdad from Norwegian stock, and both sides liked to adopt people into the fold.

It was gloriously loud, technicolor chaos. I loved it.

Kids were running around the grass, shrieking as Jim chased them, catching them and tossing them gleefully into the air. Declan and Lou were helping hang vibrantly colored banners in the trees besides brightly colored lanterns that would be switched on along with white fairy lights as soon as darkness fell. Juliet was supposed to be helping them, but she was currently sneaking some of the salmon to Kodo and Podo.

Lou's mom, Jory, was there with her boyfriend, Luis, filling ice chests with beer, soda and seltzer. Emma and Thea arranged trays of sweet treats on the tables, while Trick poured them both glasses of wine, Dammit darting into the air above him to play with some of the local pigeons. Ever since Dammit shamed the pigeons into helping us find Declan a few months ago, they'd looked at the fledgling phoenix with something akin to awe.

The air was thick with the smells of summer—flowers, fire pits, and fresh cut grass—and I couldn't have summoned a more idyllic picture with my mind.

And I felt terrible. A monochromatic person in a crowd of rainbows.

Now that we'd set aside the issue with Van's dad, Tanner, and everything, I was free to worry about my other problem. That made me feel like someone had scooped out my insides and replaced them with shards of glass.

I didn't consider myself dramatic, but my chest ached from the uncertainty, from the premonition that Van was going to cut and run. I mean, someone tells you they're in love with you, and you know, instantly on a bone-deep level, how you feel about them.

I had been kidding myself this whole time, hadn't I? Projecting what I wanted on to Van, offering up ultimatums at a time when she was already stressed. This was on me just as much as it was on her. I was Schrödinger's boyfriend, squatting in that unknown space between *taken* and *single*. The not-quite-broken-up-with.

I was having a hell of a time keeping a smile on my face. I kept rubbing the spot on my sternum where it ached the most. Pretty sure I was rubbing a hole in this shirt, which was too bad. It was one of my favorites.

Music hit me as soon as I wandered inside, and I followed it until I got to the living room. Someone had pushed the couches back and moved the coffee table to make room for karaoke. It had drawn quite a crowd. I hung in the back, rubbing my chest, my thoughts elsewhere.

Bay snuck up from somewhere, slinging his arm around me, the other holding a beer as we watched one of his aunts belt out a heartfelt rendition of Rachel Platten's *Fight Song*. "I'm sensing a theme."

"I just walked in here." I settled my arm along his shoulders. I needed the steadying, and Bay would do that.

"Before this, the songs had been *Eye of the Tiger, I Will Survive*, and several of Beyonce's more stirring anthems," he said.

I laughed. "Definite theme. Did you put in a song?"

Bay tipped his beer back, finishing it off. "Absolutely. We're doing a duet."

This was news to me, but I should have anticipated it the minute I saw the machine. Bay *loved* karaoke. "Are we doing Don't Go Breaking my Heart?" Bay's grandma was a big Elton John fan.

Bay shook his head. "No, that felt a little too on the money tonight."

"Ouch." Was he wrong, though? I'd been giving Van space, hoping she'd lean on me, but also not wanting to make this about me. She was the one that needed comfort right now. She was also avoiding me like I'd contracted some kind of new and exciting plague. Van wanted support, but not from yours truly.

Bay squeezed my shoulders with one arm. "I thought we'd go with another fan favorite. *Islands in the Stream*."

I stared at him blankly for a second before it clicked in. "The Dolly Parton duet?" My nana loved Dolly Parton, but then, who didn't?

"The very same."

I side-eyed him. "Am I Dolly or Kenny Rogers in this scenario?"

He steered me over to a bin someone had set out for recycling. "Which one of us is better at high notes? Never mind. I'll do Dolly, and just sing it lower. It will be fine."

It would be a train-wreck, but it would be our train-wreck, and frankly, I felt like the carnage. My insides still felt raw and ragged, so this suited me. "Game on," I said.

The last strains of Fight Song drifted across the room and Bay's aunt took a bow as the room clapped for her.

Bay yanked me forward. "That's our cue."

Nana walked in as soon as the song started, and it was like we summoned her. Bay struck a pose, because of course he did, and I pointed at Nana, belting out the opening of the song. "*Baby, when I met you there was peace unknown…*"

Nana lit up, clasping her hands in front of her mouth.

"*I was soft inside, there was something going on.*" Oof, that was again, too close for comfort. Like Jim said, I was full of nougat, except I wasn't sure I could keep it up anymore, not if Van called it off.

Bay jumped in, singing along with me, trading off our different lines like we sang this all the time. We hit the chorus, belting it out for all our worth. "*And we rely on each other, from one lover to another.*" That line hit me hard and I fumbled the next line, Bay taking up my slack.

That chorus felt too much like us, the universe trying to remind me that even if Van bailed, I had Bay, I had friends, to rely on.

It occurred to me then, that I was maybe a little drunk. Bay's cousin, Lara, brought us shots and we tossed them back during an instrumental bit. I shut my brain off then, focusing on the song and nothing else.

Maybe it was the shots talking, but we nailed it.

The song over, Bay and I took a bow. Everyone clapped, cheering us on, which was what they did after any song. Still made me feel special. I handed off my mic to Bay's little sister, Astrid, with a wink. She rolled her eyes, but grinned, poking my side.

I wove through the group, heading over to Nana. "What are you doing here?"

Nana took my arm, pulling me into a quieter part of the house. "Jim sent me a text." She led me out the front door, stopping as soon as she shut it, putting us in the relative quiet and peace of the front stoop. "Why didn't you message me?"

I blew out a breath, making Nana grimace as she waved her hand in front of her face. "How many shots did you have?"

I shrugged. "Not enough." I dropped down onto the stoop, Nana following. With as few words as possible, I sketched out today's adventure. I slowed down over the important bits, making sure Nana got the full takeaway.

Once I was done, Nana sat there quietly for a few minutes, watching the neighborhood as she thought. "Do you want advice, help, or just a hug?"

"I will take all of those things," I said, rubbing my chest. Not that I was done singing, the heavy feeling was back.

"Okay," Nana said, a gentle smile on her face. "Hug first." I wrapped Nana in a hug, closed my eyes, and rested my cheek on her head. I listened to the birds and the sound of the street, soaking up the magic of being hugged by someone who loved me no matter what. That was no small magic. Nana gave me a final squeeze and leaned back. I let her go.

"As far as Tanner goes—I think your friends are right. Even with the video, by arcanist standards, Tanner's actions will probably be seen as commendable. They'll want to know what new magic he's invented. I wouldn't be surprised if he was rewarded. That's on the official level."

Fucking Tanner. "And the unofficial level?"

"People talk. I can start dropping rumors. Let the whisper network do its thing. Arcanists might like manipulation and cunning, but other mages don't. Not everyone will want to work with him after that."

It wasn't enough, but it was something. "What about Van's certification?"

Nana brushed a speck of something off her pant leg. "I expect Thea and Emma have that covered, but I'll let them know that I'm at their disposal, should they need it."

I nodded, swallowing hard. I knew what was coming. "And the advice?"

Nana's sympathetic expression almost did me in, and I went back rubbing my chest. I waved her on.

"Let her go," Nana said, with the short and simple brutality of an axe blade biting into a sapling. She reached out, resting a hand on my shoulder. "I'm not saying forever. But like you were telling me, she's had a lot going on. She needs to sort it out without any interference. Decide what she wants."

I tipped my head back, closing my eyes.

"Are you angry at me?" She asked gently, rubbing my arm.

"No." The word came out in a gust as I dropped my head back down. "I'm angry that you're right, but I'm not about to kill the messenger."

"It's possible," Nana said, wrapping and arm around my waist. "That you could use some sorting out, too. I bet your dad would love to see you."

I sighed, folding her into my side. "Yeah, I owe him a visit. And I've got some vacation time."

"If you don't have enough for a ticket, let me know," Nana said. "If your dad can't help out, I can."

"Thanks, Nana." I kissed her temple.

"I'm sorry I can't tell you what you want to hear," Nana said. "But you know how I feel about that sort of thing."

"We don't lie to the ones we love," I said. "Even if it hurts." "I love you, my heart. It will be okay eventually, you'll see."

"I love you, too, Nana." I couldn't say anything about the rest of her statement. I wasn't quite sure it was true, and like Nana, I hated to lie to those that I loved.

CHAPTER TWENTY-SIX

Van

The party went by in a blur, as I had been absolutely, completely drunk out of my gourd. I got home somehow, waking up to the ferrets curled up on my pillow and a little stoppered bottle wrapped up in a green bow, a tag with calligraphy script attached. Some kind soul had also left me a fresh garbage can lined with a bag.

Between the pounding of my skull, the flowery script, and the off-putting feeling of my stomach trying to climb up through my throat and out of my mouth, it took me several minutes to read the tag.

Drink me. Thea thought she was *hilarious.*

I rolled carefully and slowly into a sitting position, wincing at the light coming in through the curtains. For one dizzy moment, I would have welcomed death into my arms. Of course the potion I was about to down was a close second. Trying hard not to think about what was coming,

I unstoppered the potion and slammed it back.

I don't remember what the potion was originally called off the top of my head, but most people referred to it as Hangover Helper. It was one of those potions where the cure was almost as bad as the problem.

The taste hits you like a mule-kick. Sulfer, something rancid, and a hint of a sort of floral chemical flavor. Then your mouth floods with saliva. At that point, you better hope someone was kind enough to leave you a bowl or a trash can—some people gave up and took the potion in the shower.

I bent over the trash can, knowing how this was going to go. I barely had it in my arms, my face over it when I became violently ill. And I do mean violently. For about a minute, you puke everything up, heaving and spitting. Then your skin chills, ice cold, like you've jumped into an ice-covered-lake. Then hot—desert sand hot.

After that's the shakes. It's a whole body affair, your teeth chattering out of your gums. When those start to fade, your headache blossoms into ice-pick-migraine territory and if in that moment the grim reaper appeared, you'd kiss his bony feet.

Then it's over, and you're left shaking over the mess you've made. Physically, my mess was contained to the trash can, though I needed a shower. Emotionally? Life-wise? There was no helper potion for that.

You can see why most people would rather just be hungover. I tied up the trash, throwing it into the cans out back, before climbing into the shower. I took my time, washing off absolute shit-tasm that was yesterday. So much had happened, I felt wrung out.

By the time I turned off the water, I realized that I didn't know what time it was, could quite remember what *day* it was, and whether or not I was supposed to be at work. I wrapped myself into a fluffy towel that smelled like lavender—thanks, Declan—and stumbled to my room.

Whoever had put me to bed had plugged in my phone, leaving it right where I could find it. Somehow I knew it was Will. Underneath my phone was a note in Will's scrawling handwriting.

Lou has your ferrets. You have to day off. Go back to bed. —W

A warm, but skittish feeling filled me. Warm, because werewolf roommates aside, very few people in my life took care of me and understood that I would have busted into a guilty panic the second I was awake enough for my brain to catch up to the day.

Skittish because…well. Will had big feelings and I was shit with big feelings. Putting that aside for now, I quickly brushed and braided my hair.

Then I promptly face planted into my pillow and slept for five more hours.

#

I stayed in my pajamas all day, ignoring my phone and the world in general, getting out of bed only for dinner. Declan made grilled chicken for the carnivores, substituting a vegetarian option for Lou and Jim made out of some kind of microprotein. Most animal mages avoided eating meat because they found being able to converse with their meals off-putting, and Jim spent the majority of his life as part steer. So again, off-putting.

Skewers of colorful vegetables marinated in something delicious came with the meal , as well as a baked potato. I ate it on the couch with my housemates as we watched a two hour special of *Mated by Fate,* Trick's favorite reality dating show.

Trick shoved his empty plate onto the table, groaning and rubbing his belly. "Lou, your boyfriend is going to give me a food baby."

"No one made you take seconds," Jim said reasonably, scooping another bite of potato into his mouth. He'd taken one of his edibles from Wicked Brews today, so his usual steer head was gone, replaced by a big dude that would have looked at home in a lumberjack commercial. Dammit chirped from his perch in the large cage Trick had made for him sat in the corner of the living room. His chirp sounded suspiciously like he was backing up Jim.

Trick pointed his fork at Dammit. "You're supposed to be on my side. Dammit clicked his beak and went back to nosing through his feathers.

Lou snorted from her spot on the loveseat she shared with Declan before leaning over to give him a peck on the cheek. "Compliments to the chef, babe."

Declan grinned, leaning in to the kiss before eyeing the room carefully. When you lived with an alpha werewolf that considered you part of his pack, you got used to this look. He was constantly assessing you— are you eating enough? Sleeping enough? Happy? His gaze stopped on me and he frowned.

I tried to hide behind my food, slouching down on the couch.

"Where's Will?" He asked casually, feeding some of his chicken to the ferrets.

I shoved a forkful of chicken into my mouth—seriously, how does he make it so delicious?—and shrugged.

His eyes narrowed. He was on to me.

"He's at work," Jim said, not looking away from he screen. "Rumor is next season they're going to have a Swan King on here."

Trick made a scoffing noise. "Please. That won't happen." "Why not?" Jim asked.

"Because there aren't a lot of Swan Kings," Declan said, his voice a soft rumble. "And they mate for life, like wolves do." He shook his head. "If they want to find their mate, they'll hire a matchmaking service. Not run about on TV."

"I think our Swan King would do it," Jim said, scraping up the last of his meal. "He likes the attention, I think."

Trick laughed. "That would never work. From what I've heard, Dominic Lapointe would just take home the entire cast and probably half of the crew."

I tuned out their discussion, brain catching on what Jim had said earlier. "Wait, Will is at work? He doesn't work today."

"He had to pick up some shifts, I think," Jim said.

Oh, right. To cover my test yesterday. He'd said something about that. Had I even said thank you for all he'd done the past few weeks, getting me through my father's ridiculous testing? I couldn't remember. Probably not. I pushed around my chicken with my fork, not hungry all of a sudden. Maybe I'd get him some thank you potatoes to go with his apology chicken livers.

Tomorrow. I would face it tomorrow.

#

Tomorrow ended up being busy. Work was nuts. I ended up pulling a double, then running errands and hanging out with my sister, who wasn't doing great with the whole Tanner bullshit. I didn't blame her. She'd had an emergency session with her therapist though, because Juliet was on top of that shit. She'd get through it.

In the mean time, I sat with her on her couch and watched movies, alternating between rom coms and action flicks, both of which comforted my sister. Will tried to text me a few times, asking me to call him. And I would. Soon. I didn't ignore his texts—I let him know I was busy.

I just wasn't ready to talk.

Surprisingly, he didn't push back as much as I thought he would. He seemed content to let me have my space. It was nice—I mean, that was what I wanted, right? But also, in a weird way, not nice.

Juliet squinted at me from where she was sprawled on the couch. I was on the floor, wrapped in a blanket, with a package of Red Vines and a bowl of popcorn. Juliet had Reece's Pieces. Savannah didn't get any candy, which was fine, because she was also in bed for the night.

"It's weird to see you without your blond shadow."

"I was just thinking that," I said, biting into a Red Vine. "Get out of my head." "What's he up to?"

"Working, I think?"

She frowned. "You think? You don't know?" I shrugged. "I'm not his keeper."

"Yeah, but you usually know his schedule."

I shoved the last of the Red Vine into my mouth. "We both got thrown off because of the testing and stuff."

"Huh," Juliet said. "It's still weird."

I shrugged, grabbing a handful of popcorn. "How are you doing?"

Juliet stared at her bowl of popcorn, then dumped half her bag of candy into it. I snorted. "That good, huh?"

"That good," Juliet said, grabbing a handful of candy and popcorn and shoveling it into her mouth. She chewed unhappily, chasing it down with sparkling water. Both of us were taking a break from drinking for a few days. "You know what the worst part is?"

"Ooh, I don't know," I said slowly, "There are so many terrible things to choose from."

Juliet ignored me and plowed forward. "I kind of miss it. Like, I know I was being influenced. I know it was a lie and that Tanner was using the whole situation for his own fucked up purposes. But for a short time there, it felt nice to be pursued and wanted, you know? To get dressed up and go on dates and feel sexy and not home on a Saturday night with cheerios in my hair and not knowing when they even got there." Juliet wrinkled her nose. "It's pathetic. I need so much more therapy."

"It's not pathetic," I argued. Sure, I wanted to hit Tanner with a shovel, but I didn't want my sister to beat herself up over it. "It's not a bad thing to want something for yourself, to feel cherished, and have a nice man take you out. And you thought Tanner was a nice man."

"Yeah," Juliet sighed. "At least I didn't sleep with him."

"Thank fuck for that." I stared at my popcorn, unsure how to bring this up. "Even without that…"

"I talked to my therapist." Juliet poked at her popcorn. "Making out with him, possibly under that kind of influence, could be considered assault. The problem is, it would be difficult to prove. We don't know when he did whatever he did, and honestly, I thought he was cute. How much was me and how much was the spell?"

She shook her head. "It's awful, and I would like to think he wouldn't have pushed it any further. I'll never know. But he didn't. I'm going to ask around. Declan gave me Prisha's number—from the Uncanny Tribunal." She cradled her popcorn bowl. "Maybe I can't bring legal action, but I can see what I can do to prevent him from pulling this shit anywhere else."

I reached up, grabbing her foot, and gave it a squeeze. "You're a bad ass." "Thanks," Juliet said. "I love you, too."

I patted her foot and dropped it. "And I'm sorry I brought you into the sphere of that horrible man."

Juliet's expression became fierce. "You didn't do that—Dad did. So don't marinate in guilt over it."

"But I'm so good at it," I said, flopping onto the floor. "Watch me marinate until I am tender and juicy."

She threw a piece of candy at me. "Stop being weird."

"Never." I wrapped myself back up into my blanket. "But I will promise to not stew in my own guilt on this, okay?"

"Good," she said, grabbing another handful of popcorn. "Now shut up and enjoy the finest film Keanu Reeves ever made."

"*Speed*?" I shook my head. "That's a bold statement. This movie came out before you were born. And look, yeah, he's hot, but what about *John Wick*?"

Juliet fanned herself. "Yeah, the man has an impressive oeuvre. Remember when you watched *Much Ado About Nothing* with me for that Shakespeare class I took? He played Don John. *Hawt.*"

I laughed, tossing a piece of popcorn at her. "He was a bad guy."

She bushed the popcorn off. "So?" She settled into her blanket, picking up the remote to restart the movie. "I wouldn't want the villain in real life, but in fiction, I can admire their pretty faces all the same. Besides, we all know the villains dress better."

"You definitely need more therapy."

"I know," Juliet said. "Trust me, I know."

CHAPTER TWENTY-SEVEN

Van

I got my test results two days later. I was at work, but as soon as the mailman dropped them off, Lou ran it over to me. Noah covered me and I took the envelope into the backroom. I needed Emma and Thea nearby incase the news was bad. Or good. I just needed them. Lou followed me into the back and no one stopped her.

"The envelope is really thin," I said, sliding my fingers along its length. The envelope was an official one from my father's department. So that was good? Or bad? I was a mess. I thrust the envelope at Lou. "I need you to open it."

Lou shrugged, snatching it from my fingers. Before I could argue and stall further, she'd ripped open the envelope, took at the single sheet of paper, and started skimming. Her brows drew down, followed by her lips. It was sort of like watching people to The Wave at a stadium. She was furious and spitting by the end. "That motherfucker."

I collapsed onto a milk crate. "He failed me, didn't he?"

She shook the letter in the air. "He's claiming your Cassandra potion was *insufficient. Faulty. Weak.* He's going for plausible deniability for Tanner and discrediting you in one fell swoop. I'm going to tear out his guts with a dull, rusty blade. I hope he's had his tetanus shots. Actually, I hope he hasn't."

Emma snatched the letter away, holding it so Thea could read it over her shoulder. Thea shook her head. "We can fight this, Sugar. I verified your potion myself." "I've got the test recorded," Emma said. "Didn't you say you recorded brewing the potion?"

"Yeah," I said, putting my head between my knees. I so didn't want to throw up. "I did.

Does that matter?"

"Yes," Emma said. "It matters. We're going to take the whole thing to Isla. We're getting you in that program. The Arcanists will close ranks for Tanner, so who knows what will happen there, but you're going to get into the hedge witch program if I have to bribe somebody."

Thea patted her shoulder fondly. "It won't come to that, dear, which is good, because we wouldn't have much of a bribe."

"Still," Emma grumbled.

#

I handed over everything to Emma and Thea—the video, Prisha's number, and every piece of paper involved in the test that I had, including our waivers. They would take it to their contact and Prisha. The whole thing would look better coming from my mentors instead of me. We all agreed on that.

I would be a mess until I heard back. The good thing was, I didn't need to be a mess for long—an hour after I handed everything over to my bosses, we had a meeting scheduled for in the morning.

I waffled on what I was going to wear. I didn't have a lot of nice clothes. I'd worked at Wicked Brews for years, so I hadn't gone to a job interview in awhile. My "going out clothes" weren't appropriate. I had a black dress I wore to a funeral two years ago, but again, not the note I wanted to strike. I ended up borrowing one of Juliet's skirts that was much shorter on me, but not scandalously so, and a blouse I found in the back of my closet. It would have to do.

I took a picture of it and went to send it to Will to get his opinion. I hadn't gotten back to him yet. It would be shitty of me to respond just because I needed something, right? What if I just sent it because and didn't ask for anything? Would that be less bad?

Tired of thinking about it, I sent the photo along with the message *Going to argue my case.*

I didn't get a response until I was walking up to meet Thea and Emma in front of the Hecate building, Kodo and Podo riding out of a purse I got especially for them. The Hecate building housed the Hedgewitchery program along with other classes on plant lore and nature magics. It was also where Isla Chen's office was located.

Will had given the picture a thumb's up followed by a *Knock 'em dead.*

I frowned at my phone, waiting for more. I wasn't sure what. Just … it seemed a little short for Will? Then again, I hadn't exactly been blowing up his phone, had I?

As soon as I reached my bosses, I put my phone away. I needed to concentrate on the task at hand.

I followed them along to the second floor, where Emma knocked on a door with a nameplate that said *Isla Chen* with her official title below that. There was a neat cork board next to the door, with a few notices and sigh up sheets, as well as a listing of office hours. I barely got to look at them before someone opened the door, ushering us in.

Isla Chen was friendly and apple cheeked, her curly dark hair pulled back from her face, her dark eyes lively. Her forest green slacks and cream colored sleeveless blouse set off her tan skin and she somehow managed to look both like a professor of the university and stylish as hell.

Prisha Bhatt was already there, a cup of tea in her hands. Her dark hair shone against the marigold of her shirt, which went well with the dark blue paisley of her skirt. I hadn't liked Prisha at first out of loyalty to Lou—her role on the council had made her look poorly upon Lou at first, because of the whole thing with Declan, but I'd always respected her. She was smart, straight forward, and did her job well. The fact that she didn't like my father didn't hurt, either.

I'd spent more time with her since then—she often stopped by to check in on Lou and Declan as part of Lou's probation, and even though I was still unhappy with how my roommate had been treated, it was impossible to not like Prisha. She didn't take any shit and I respected that. She smiled at me over her tea cup as Isla ushered us in.

"Come in! Come in!" Isla greeted us warmly, the words tumbling through an accent I couldn't quite place.

She grinned at me. "Scottish. I'll try to slow down if you're not used to the accent, but I'm afraid I get a bit excited when I see these two." She hugged Thea and Emma.

"Isla's Glaswegian," Emma offered.

"My mother came down from Edinburgh for a friend's wedding," Isla said, heading back to her desk. "Got in an argument in a pub during the hen do weekend with a local fellow named Archie Chen—it got so heated, they got kicked out of the pub." She grinned. "And got married themselves six months later."

"That's a pretty adorable story," I said, because it was.

She settled into her seat. "I know some Americans struggle with my accent, so I'll tell you the same thing I tell my students—just raise your hand if you need me to repeat a word or slow down. You won't hurt my feelings."

"You really won't," Prisha said dryly. "Isla's favorite thing to do is watch her student's faces on orientation day."

"It's good for a laugh." Isla waved to herself. "It never seems to occur to people that someone could have Chinese ancestry *and* be Scottish, but here we are."

Isla's office was as different from my father's office as it could be and still be on the same campus. First, the walls were painted a bright robin's egg blue, except for the ceiling, which was cream colored and covered with a thick-roped net for some reason. Shelves held knick knacks, jars full of stones, herbs, and teas. A bright yellow teapot rested cheerily on a small table off to the side, nestled amongst a rainbow of mugs.

Prisha sat in one of the two squat comfortable chairs faced the desk, which was backed by a neatly organized bookcase and a metal filing cabinet. A big white wicker basket sat on top of the filing cabinet filled with blankets. As I watched, a small head poked out—big ears and dark, dark eyes. I had no idea what it was.

Isla saw me looking and smiled. "That's my familiar, Marmalade."

Thea reached into the pocket of her dress and pulled out a small paper packet from the bakery. She handed it to Marmalade, who quickly opened it and pulled out a dried apricot and started nibbling away. She grinned at me. "Marmalade is a brush tail possum from New Zealand."

Podo squeaked at Thea, whose grin widened. "I brought you boiled eggs, which I will give you once you answer Prisha's questions."

I looked at Prisha with surprise. "You want to speak to Kodo and Podo?"

Prisha nodded, setting down her tea. "Both Isla and I have looked over everything Thea and Emma sent, but I wanted to ask them a few things, if I may."

Kodo and Podo agreed, so I helped them out of the bag, handing them over to Prisha. While they chatted, Isla brought in two rolling office chairs from the hall. It made it a tight fit, but we managed.

After a few minutes of chatting, Prisha set my ferrets down onto the carpet. They immediately bounded over to Thea, begging for treats. Prisha handed her a saucer off the table and my boss got the two ferrets settled with their boiled eggs.

After Isla and Prisha exchanged some sort of wordless communication, Isla turned on me. "I am a big believer in speaking plainly, Ms. Woodbridge."

"Works for me," I said. "And please call me Van." To be honest, the last few weeks had me seriously considering to change my last name. As Lou liked to say, Woodbridge could suck it.

"Van," Isla said with a gentle smile. "You want the good news or the bad news first?" "Bad," I said immediately. I expected bad, but I would need to brace myself for the good.

I knew that sounded weird, but it was an offshoot of growing up with my dad. Good could be hard to take sometimes. It made you hope, and hope was such a fragile beastie, skittering away at the smallest sound.

"We can't do anything about Tanner," Prisha said, her lip twisted like the air in the room had turned foul. "Arcanist Woodbridge has informed us that Tanner Adams Falls under the purview of the Arcanists, and as such he will be disciplined."

I snorted. "He will be scolded for appearances and rewarded as soon as our backs are turned."

"Probably," Prisha said. "My hands are tied, because it's a university matter."

"And mine are tied because university rules and those waivers put this entirely into your father's hands," Isla said.

"So he'll just be able to do it again." Anger gave my words a sharp edge.

Isla's face became speculative. "Not necessarily. The news is all over campus, so they won't be able to sweep it under the rug entirely." A grim smile spread across her face. "The Arcanists may appreciate this kind of behavior, but no one else does."

"It's all over campus?" I glanced at my mentors. They seemed as bewildered as I was.

Then it hit me—Will. Or more specifically, Nana. Gratitude surged and crashed like a wave inside me, so loud that it took me a second to realize Isla was talking again. "I'm sorry, could you repeat the first bit?"

"Woodbridge is refusing to budge on your exam results," Isla said, her expression sympathetic.

I wanted to say I was hurt, but let's face it, I expected this. "That's kind of what I figured he'd do."

Isla clicked her tongue. "Got into a real snit about it, but the good news is, what's true for the Arcanists is also true for the Hedgewitchery department." I must have looked confused, because she laughed.

"They have control over their student body, and *we* have control over ours. So if *I* say you meet the requirements for entry, there's nothing he can do about it."

I stared at her blankly, everything inside me going quiet. I didn't move, and I stopped breathing.

She leaned in, her eyes twinkling. "That's the good news, Vanessa. You're in."

My breath whooshed out of me and tears sprung to my eyes. Thea let out a whoop and Emma smacked my shoulder. Prisha grinned bright, holding up her mug in my direction like she was giving me a cheers.

My mentors had said they'd make it happen, but I hadn't dared hope…. "I'm in. Just like that?"

Isla sat back in her chair, her hands neatly folded. "Not just like that. I don't want you entering this program thinking you got in because of a handshake and a wink. I watched your potion video. I've talked to your mentors. Prisha interviewed your familiars about the other tests. You passed those exams, no matter what Woodbridge says. We *know* that."

I was crying openly now, which I hated.

Isla nudged a box of tissues in front of me. "Beyond the exams, you showed a tremendous amount of focus and persistence to be here."

I nodded, blowing my nose. "Thank you."

"There's a final question, however. Something I need to know before I can completely sign off on your acceptance." Isla's voice was stern, her expression suddenly serious.

Of course there was. Worry slithered through me. Was this the catch? The moment when everything got snatched away?

"I've got to know." She resettled into her chair. "Why do you want to be a hedge witch, Vanessa? Is it just to needle your father, or is it something more?"

I gave my nose a final wipe. "At the potionary, I watch the stuff my bosses make help people every day." I put my hands in my lap, straightening my back. "Little stuff, really, but important. Things that ease people's way in the world."

I wanted so badly to drop my gaze, but I didn't. Chin up, shoulders back. No more small voice. "I want to do that. Help people find a little joy. Whether it's with an edible that helps a minotaur make his way in a world not built for him, or with a good cup a coffee and a muffin."

I drew in a deep breath. "I've watched my father drain people his whole life. He takes, and bullies, and runs right over everyone. He has never left a room better than it was before he entered it." I squeeze my hands tight. "So in that way, my choice is about him, because I reject that lifestyle. I refuse to be like that. But am I doing this just to spite him?"

I considered it a second, really searching the crannies of my soul to see if even a crumb of that motivation lived inside me. "No, Mrs. Chen. I am not. Because I refuse to let that man have even a fingertip's worth of power over my life."

I looked at my bosses. "You gave me and my sister a home. I don't want to leave it." "You don't have to," Emma said, her jaw tight, her eyes brimming. Thea handed her the box of tissues with a sweet smile.

I turned back to Isla. "I want to build on what my bosses built, Mrs. Chen. That's all." Isla reached across the desk. "Welcome aboard. Try to keep that joy in mind while you fill out what can only be described as an *epic* amount of paperwork."

CHAPTER TWENTY-EIGHT

Van

A mountain of paperwork later, and I was all signed up for my first round of classes. Thea and Emma helped me choose, making sure my work schedule and school schedule would live in harmony. I almost threw up handing over my bank card for my first tuition payment. My savings account was empty now and I'd have to watch every penny, but it was all worth it.

Thea and Emma refused to let me take the bus home, insisting they could drop me off at my place. I was pretty sure no one was home, though, and I didn't feel like being there all alone right now.

If I was being honest with myself, it wasn't that I didn't want to go home—it was that I wanted to see Will. I wanted to be wherever he was at. I'd missed him so much. Now that the stress, the pressure, the ridiculousness of the last few days was over, I just wanted to curl up on the couch with him and watch a movie.

I knew I'd been kind of a shit. Will had been there for me, consistently, patiently, sweetly, through this whole thing... and I'd essentially ghosted him. Right after he'd admitted to being in love with me forever.

I waited for the panic to come at that thought. And waited.

Nothing happened. All I felt was that push, that need, to see my best friend. I couldn't show up empty handed, though. "Can you actually drop me off at the store by Will's place?" There was a little market a few blocks from Will's house. I quickly explained where it was, making sure it wasn't too out of the way for them. "I want to pick up something for Will."

Finally, Kodo said from his perch on my shoulder. *It's time for chicken livers.*

I don't know, Podo added, her voice concerned. *She might have waited too long. She might want to get him something a little bigger.*

Like a whole chicken? Kodo asked.

Podo turned her bright eyes to me, and I could feel her concern. *I'm thinking maybe a turkey or an entire salmon.*

Thea and Emma dropped me off with a final round of hugs and I almost skipped into the store. I was *that* happy. I grabbed a pack of chicken livers—there was no way the ferrets would have let me leave without them. When I passed a little floral display, there was a decorative pot of brightly colored flowers. It made me think of Will, so I grabbed it.

It had a little plastic holder for a card, so I searched through the selection until I found a basic on that said *I'm sorry,* with a picture of a sad puppy on it. I snagged it. After I paid for my stuff, I wrote a little note in the card, and then left the store, walking the few blocks to Will and Jim's place.

It was one of those magic summer evenings—the kind that tricked people into moving here. The sky was clear and bright blue. The air warm, with a hint of barbecue and bonfire in the air. That sort of idyllic moment that makes you forget that it's gray skies and drizzle most days. Tonight it felt especially magic, like the universe was rewarding me for all the bullshit I'd just gone through. The world telling me I was *exactly* where I should be.

By the time I made it to Jim's front door there was a bounce to my step. I juggled my wares before rapping my knuckles against the bright red paint, a smile on my face.

I heard footsteps, then the door swung open, revealing Jim in his minotaur form. He looked at me. Down at the stuff in my hands. Then back at me.

"I'm not sure I want to know what you're planning," he said finally, "but I think I'm busy. Or I'm about to be busy."

"It's a long story," I said, grinning. "But these are for Will."

Jim looked suddenly uncomfortable. "Oh. Uh." He fidgeted for a second. "Will's not here?" His voice lilted up at the end, like he was asking a question.

I lost my bounce, my heels thudding against the concrete step. "He's not at work." I'd texted Declan to make sure.

Jim scratched the back of his head. "He went to Chicago. I thought he told you?" Jim watched me uneasily. "He said he was going to tell you."

I wilted like a hothouse flower, suddenly feeling moderately stupid and excessively terrible. "He messaged me that he needed to talk to me, but I was so busy..." The last part rang false and we both heard it. I mean, I'd been busy, but seriously, I couldn't manage a five minute phone call? What an asshole.

Kodo nudged my ear. *Do we need to get the asshole tiaras?*

We can go back home, Podo added. *Jim would drive us, especially if we made him one. Jim's not an asshole,* Kodo pointed out.

We'll make him a different kind of tiara, then.

That was Podo for you—ever the problem solver. I sighed. "I was busy being an emotionally unavailable dick."

Jim patted my head with one meaty paw. "But you're *our* emotionally unavailable dick."

I stared at the sad collection of apology gifts in my hands. Did I really think a pack of chicken livers and some flowers would make up for the fact that I'd hurt my friend, doing exactly the thing I said I wouldn't do? I may not have gone anywhere in the geographical sense, but I'd definitely been running.

I felt a little like hexing myself.

"Hey," Jim said, trying to hug me around my various parcels. He gave up and put an arm around my shoulders and ushered me into the house. "Come on now."

Jim has a really nice kitchen. The cabinets are a light wood, with glass inserts in the doors so you can see what's where. There's an island in the middle with pots and pans dangling from above, and the kind of stove you see in cooking shows. A bar style counter top separated it from the dining room, where long table ran alongside french doors opening out into the backyard. One of the chairs was pulled out in front of a laptop and a pile of paperwork. Jim had been working from home when I'd interrupted him.

Jim ushered me onto one of the barstools , taking my flowers and chicken livers and nudging me into a seat. He handed me a glass of water, then grabbed a plate from one of his cabinets. He tore open the packaging, slid the livers onto the plate, and set it out for the ferrets before washing his hands very, very thoroughly.

Kodo and Podo darted over and happily went to town on their treat. "Hope that's okay," Jim said.

I shrugged, turning my glass to catch the light. "Wouldn't want them to go bad." I waved a hand at the arrangement. "You can keep those, too."

Jim leaned against the counter, putting both elbows on the top. He'd built the house with his proportions in mind, so he didn't have to lean too far. I'd never really noticed how much Jim had to bend to urban environments until I saw him in one that actually fit.

"So is that it?" Jim asked. "You going to roll over?"

I rested my chin in my hand, my elbow resting on the cool of the countertop. "You got something to say, Jim?"

He nodded slowly. "I do, but what that's going to be depends entirely on your response." I frowned at him. "What does that mean?"

"It means," Jim said, crafting each word carefully and giving them shine. "That if you're rolling over, that if this—" he waved a hand at my offering, such as it was, "is the best you can do, then my advice will be pretty simple."

"And what simple advice would you give me?"

"Cut bait." He folded his arms in front of him. "He doesn't deserve to be played with." "Cut bait?"

"It's a fishing metaphor."

"Jim," I said, rubbing a tired hand over my face. "I've never been fishing."

He sighed. "Stop fucking around and let him go. You're hurting my friend and I don't like it."

Ouch. Deserved, but ouch. "And your other advice?" "Go balls to the wall."

"Jim, have you considered becoming an inspirational speaker?"

He snorted. "Look, Will is one of my best friends, one of my favorite people on this tiny spinning rock we call home." He leaned forward. "You live with someone, and you learn things about them you wouldn't otherwise. Living with Will has been eye opening. He's just one big, squishy heart. That dude will do a back flip gymnast routine for the people he cares about— sometimes for complete strangers. He's the most generous soul I know, and he's been in love with you the entire time I've known him."

Jim jerked a thumb at the fridge. "He put sticky notes on all my condiments so I would miss him while he's gone." He pushed himself off the counter, opened up his enormous fridge, and dug out a container of horseradish mustard. On it was a safety orange post-it note that said, "Your ass looks great in those jeans."

"Inspirational," I said with a snort.

Jim looked at it, rolled his eyes, and brought back a handful of sauces to the counter. I read through them all.

You know what? You smell fantastic.

I curated a list of murder documentaries on Netflix for you.

There are cookies in the freezer—they're all yours. Bake at 350 for 10-12 minutes.

If we had babies they'd be super handsome, you mythical man-beast.

I read through all of them, my heart expanding with each one. "I'm starting to see why he gets along with Declan so well."

"If I was at all interested in men romantically, I would put a ring on that man so fast I'd win a carnival prize." Jim rounded the condiments back up and stacked them in his fridge. When he was done, he came back to the counter. "I'm not happy with your behavior—I get it, I understand it, but I don't like what it's done to Will."

I didn't even try to argue. I agreed with him.

"I believe you're getting your shit together, though, so I'm giving you a pass." He folded his arms again, resting them on the counter. "Besides, I know something you don't know."

"What's that?" I asked, my voice rusty. I might agree with Jim, and even appreciate what he was saying, but it still hurt to hear. It hurt even more knowing he was completely right.

"That you're just as in love with Will as he is with you. Have been since I've known you. But it scares the shit out of you, so you've been ignoring it." And with that bombshell, he calmly stretched, grabbed a mug, and poured himself a cup of coffee from the machine on his counter.

I opened my mouth. Couldn't think of a damn thing to say. I shut it again.

Jim poured a dollop of creamer into his coffee and sipped. "See? You can't say shit. But it's obvious to me, Van. I don't think you realize the way you look at him—and I'm not saying the hot-eyed, sexy-times way you've been doing lately. That's new. I mean the old way, where he walks into a room and it's like that moment when I'm building a house and we turn on the lights for the first time. A mix of awe and everyday magic. A sense of wonder."

"I take it back, Jim. Fuck being an inspirational speaker. You should be a poet."

"I contain multitudes," Jim said dryly.

We sat in silence for a minute. Me reeling from the emotional blow of what Jim had just said and trying to make sense of all of it, and Jim watching me do that while he drank his coffee.

Was he right? Had I been kidding myself all along?

Yes, Kodo said, licking his chops. They'd been so quiet and focused on their food, I'd forgotten they were there. *You have been kidding yourself.*

Will makes your heart full, Podo said gently. *We feel it. We see it.*

Why do you think we've been pestering you about chicken livers? Podo said, hopping over to me. She climbed up onto my shoulder to offer comfort. Kodo, meanwhile, clambered up the minotaur's arms to reach

265

his head, where he proceeded to root around horns, bathing and cleaning Jim, a ferrety way of caregiving.

I thought maybe you were just hoping for more chicken livers, I said honestly.

We can do both, Kodo said. *We're not stupid.*

I stroked Podo's fur and thought about what they'd said. Was everyone right? Did they know my own feelings better than me? It was possible. I wasn't the best at this sort of thing. Juliet had explained to me that we struggled because we weren't raised in an emotionally literate household.

Maybe I just needed a little help. *Can you show me?* I asked Podo.

She didn't answer me in words—just started nudging forward memories, impressions, moments and feelings when Will had been present. Pieces that I'd had, but hadn't quite put together.

It was like I'd been living in a room where someone had dumped out a huge bin of legos.

With no guidance, it was just a mess. But the second someone handed me an instruction manual, I could see the pattern. The potential. The structure of what those pieces would be when assembled.

And holy shit, what a structure. It was *dazzling.*

I was absolutely, completely, totally in love with Willhardt Murphy. I was stupid with it.

How the hell hadn't I seen it before now? Jim hummed low in his throat. "There you go. Welcome to reality, Sunshine." "Oh fuck," I said, splaying my hands on to the counter. "Just…fuck."

"Yup." Jim took a long sip of coffee and watched me. "How could I not see it?" I asked Jim.

He shrugged. "It's easier to see things sometimes when you're not up in it. Don't waste time beating yourself up over it." He set his coffee down carefully. "The important thing is, what are you going to do now?"

My mind went static-white. It was like a blizzard in there. "I have no idea." I reached out and grabbed Jim's wrist. "Help."

Jim leaned back against the other edge of the counter, his head tipped up as he mulled the situation over. "Will's been convincing me to join Nana's bookclub. He tell you that?"

"You should," I said. "It's a blast."

He nodded. "So I've been reading a few of the books he's suggested." He scratched his cheek. "That shit's addictive. Anyway, he's been giving me a crash course in romance reading."

His words were very serious, because this was a serious discussion, but Jim also had a ferret on his head. Normally, this would make me laugh, but right now it was giving the whole conversation a surreal quality. Like a spiritual journey I should just give myself over to.

A minotaur in his man-bull form, with a ferret on his head, musing about romance novels.

You can't fight that sort of thing. You can only accept it, becoming one with the moment. "One of the big tropes we've discussed?" Jim dropped his gaze on to me. "The grovel. People love a good grovel."

"Okay."

"Normally, in the books, it's the dude that needs to grovel. He does something bone- headed, he has to make up for it. I'm sure someone has written an entire thesis on why that's a reoccurring bit of wish-fulfillment in romance novels, but that's a digression and we need to stay on topic." Jim picked up his coffee, lifting his index finger off his mug to point at me. "You're the dude."

"I'm the dude?"

"You're the dude," Jim repeated firmly. "You've done fucked up and broke his heart. You need to give quality grovel." He tipped his head toward the flowers. "This ain't it, kid."

"Okay," I said. "In hindsight, taking romantic advice from ferrets probably wasn't my best idea." I tented my fingers. "I am open to suggestions."

"Get your ass on a plane," Jim said. "Fly to Chicago and go get your boy." He frowned at his coffee. "If it was anyone else, I would suggest pageantry. You know, like hiring a marching band or some shit like that." He shook his head. "I don't think that's the tone you need to strike here."

I was hanging off every word now. Who knew Jim was a genius? "It's not?"

"It's not." Jim paused, deep in thought. "The grovel has to fit the crime, you know?" He held up a finger. "You ran." A second finger joined the first. "And you didn't use your words." I simply nodded because that was accurate.

Jim dropped his hand. "My suggestion? Fly to Chicago and crack yourself open. Make yourself completely vulnerable to his rejection."

"That will be …" I swallowed hard. "Really difficult."

"It sure will," Jim said. "You can always pick option A and cut bait."

The very idea of letting Will go, of not being his person anymore, of him not being *my* person anymore, made me physically ill.

I took out my phone. "I need to call work and get time off." I froze, my phone in hand. "Shit. I'm broke. I just paid tuition."

"That would do it." Jim nodded, pouring himself another cup of coffee. "How about you handle the work thing, and I crowd source your ticket."

"Crowd source my ticket?"

Jim's look was a mix of sympathy and exasperation. "You have friends, Vanessa. You think we can work a little miracle like a last minute plane ticket?"

CHAPTER TWENTY-NINE

Will

Chicago was muggy as fuck. Seattle's humidity hovered around some sort of middle ground—it wasn't dry, but it wasn't soggy in the heat, either. I didn't know you could chew air until I went to Chicago. Luckily my dad's place had air conditioning. Which is why it shouldn't have made any sense to me that my dad and his wife hung out on the screened in porch so much.

Except when you got out there, it did. It totally did. The fans hummed, creating a breeze. My dad lived out in the suburbs, not actually in Chicago, so you didn't so much hear city noise as you heard bird calls, the rustling of squirrels, and the holler of kids trying to get the attention of a persistent ice cream truck. Out on the porch, sprawled on a chair, a cold drink in hand? The heat wasn't so bad.

The porch held an outdoor wicker couch with fading tropical-print cushions, two rocking chairs, a mini fridge, and a narrow coffee table. It looked out over the backyard, and if we were lucky, we saw lightning bugs. Or bats. I loved watching the bats. A handful of plants were out there with us, including a few vining plants that were hung from the ceiling. It was like a little oasis.

My dad handed me a cold beer as I came through the screen door. Because of our close ages and similar looks, we get mistaken for bothers a lot. He looks more like my sensible older brother than my dad. Less tattoos, paint-splattered work boots—which is weird, because my dad's an electrician—and none of his T-shirts have glittery kittens on them.

Except for the one I bought him for Christmas. Which he dutifully wore when I got here so I could refer to us as twinsies, and because I'd been a mopey fuck when I got off that plane and my dad had been desperate to cheer me up. I'd been this close to convincing him we needed matching unicorn tattoos when his wife told me to stop using my powers for evil.

My dad was a pretty good looking guy, which makes me sound conceited, and my stepmom got a kick out of going to bars with us and watching women trying to pick us up for a double date. I have on more than one occasion had to tell people that I don't double date with my dad. We're both nice about it. If we were dicks, my stepmom wouldn't find it funny and would have had both our hides.

Though we'd never lived together, I'd visited a lot growing up, and my dad took the whole 'showing my son to be a man' thing seriously, but not in a shitty way. One of the big rules? A person takes that big first step to make a connection with you, then you should treat that bravery, that vulnerability, with respect. If you need to tell them no, do it respectfully and in such a way that they leave feeling good about themselves.

Also, only creepers cat call or hit on people when they work. Be respectful and listen to what people want, not what you *think* they want. Which was one of the things I'd been thinking about since I stepped on that plane to come out here. This whole relationship with Van—was it what she wanted, or what I thought she wanted? Had I pushed her somehow? I didn't think so, but I was messed up about the whole thing and was having a hard time sorting it out.

"They give you any trouble?" My dad asked, thankfully interrupting my circular thoughts.

"Naw," I said, popping the top. "The demons are asleep."

"Will, in case I haven't said it yet, I'm so glad you're here." My stepmom was stretched out on the couch, her head in my dad's lap. "And I'm not just saying that because you bought me thirty minutes of argument-free quiet time."

"Thanks, Annie." I dropped a kiss on her forehead before I collapsed into one of the rocking chairs. "I know it was last minute, but..."

"Will, you're always welcome here," Annie said firmly. "Always." Annie was medium height, with a rangy build. Her brown hair was highlighted from the sun, and often in a ponytail. She made and taught pottery for a living, and had given her abundant energy and zeal for life to her two children. I loved them, but they were fucking extra sometimes.

I wouldn't change a single damn hair on their heads, either.

"You're welcome to stay as long as you need, too." My dad slung his arm over the back of the couch, his beer in hand. The other was sifting through Annie's ponytail. "I would happily go pack up your stuff and move you out here if you wanted that, even though your grandmother would murder me and bury the body in a shallow grave."

I swallowed down the lump in my throat. "I know. Thanks." I hadn't bought a return ticket yet. Just packed a bag and came out, my head a mess. I was very lucky to have coworkers willing to step up and cover me indefinitely. "And there's no way Nana would bury you in a shallow grave. She's not careless like that. It's six feet down or nothing."

"In one of the murder mystery books I read, the killer uses a pig farm to get rid of a body.

I bet Nana could find a pig farm," Annie mused. "She's efficient and smart."

"This conversation has taken a turn I didn't anticipate," my father admitted.

"If Nana committed murder, no one would ever know," I told Annie. "You're right on that."

My father hitched his head to the side. "Is someone at the door?"

We all paused, listening. For a second, it was quiet, but then I thought I heard the faint sound of knocking coming from the front door. I made to get up, but my father waved me down. "You wrangled the devils. I'll answer the door." He planted a kiss on Annie's forehead and got up, stretching, before ambling to the front of the house.

Annie watched him go, a besotted look on her face, even after being married to him for years and years. She sighed. "I thank the universe every day that I met that man."

I snorted. "Even when he's being a pig-headed ass? I believe those were your words, this morning."

"In my defense," she said, sitting up. "I hadn't had my coffee yet, and I think the entire world is a pig-headed ass until about the second cup."

I waited.

"At which point I drop that number to about seventy percent," she admitted.

I snorted, taking another sip of my beer, and wondered what was taking my dad so long.

"What I'm saying is, your father is a genuine unicorn of a man, and you're just like him." She waved me off before I could say anything, her eyes getting uncharacteristically teary. "We both genuinely mourn the fact that we didn't get more of a hand in raising you, but that's circumstance and not anything you or your nana should feel guilty about. We mourn it because we love you, and we always want more time with the ones we love."

She reached out an pinched my cheek. "But we are also so proud of the man you've become. Nana did good."

"You did good, too," I said, my words a little choked.

She grinned and patted my cheek, her eyes still shiny. "We did. We're here if you want to talk more about whatever, or whomever, broke your heart. If you don't want to talk, that's okay too. Just let us know if we need shovels and an alibi."

I busted out laughing and it sounded watery, like my body was split between the decision to be sad or happy. Which it kind of was. "Should I be worried about your reading material?"

She scoffed. I'm not sure what else she might have said, because at that moment, my dad came back in the room.

He had a weird look on his face. "I found this outside." He pointed at something behind him.

Then he stepped out of the way and my smile died. Vanessa, her face unsure, her posture curving in, like she thought at any second it might be a good idea to fold up shop right there and blink out of existence. I didn't like that look on her face. It made me frown.

Kodo and Podo were on her shoulders. For reasons I wasn't sure of, she was holding a foam package of some kind of meat, a romance novel with a woman in a flowing dress, making me think it was historical, and a bouquet of flowers.

My dad was now behind her, a question on his face. He pointed at Vanessa, mouthing, *Is this why you're here?* Without any confirmation from me, he continued. *You want her gone?*

I gave a slight shake of my head and he dropped his hands.

"Vanessa?" I packed a whole lot of questions into her name. "What are you doing here?" My question startled her, blinking her back to life. She half-turned, startling my father.

She shoved the flowers at him. "These are for you."

My father, who has never received flowers in his entire life, took them with a bemused look on his face. Bemused, but delighted. "Thank you?" He glanced at Annie a look of *what now?* On his face.

She rolled her eyes, and got up. "You say thank you and get a vase."

He tipped his head down to Van and very seriously said, "Thank you, I'm going to go get a vase." He hesitated. "Unless you need me to stay?" He directed the last question at me.

"Thanks," I said, realizing that at some point, I'd stood up. I shoved my hands into my pockets. "But I think we're okay."

Annie squeezed my shoulder, striding over to my dad. "Nice to meet you, Vanessa." She paused as soon as she was next to her. "I think it goes without saying, but if you break his heart, no one will find your body."

"Ooookay, Annie Oakley," My dad said, steering her out of the room. "If it goes without saying, why did you feel you needed to say it?"

"Because *some* people struggle with unspoken rules," Annie said. "I lead with the important one."

"Uh huh," my dad said, nudging her out of the room. "Holler if you need us, Will. Nice to meet you, Vanessa."

They left, leaving me and Vanessa in silence. We stared at each other for a few long moments. It hadn't been long since I'd seen her last. Less than a week. It felt longer. I was starving for this woman, absolutely parched for her, she was *right there* and I couldn't move a muscle.

Was she just as hungry for me? I couldn't fathom it. The depths of the underworld I would go to for her—I simply couldn't imagine her feeling the same. It seemed too far fetched. So improbable.

She hadn't said a word.

Kodo and Podo broke the silence, sliding down her body, dare-devil fashion. They leapt to the ground, bounding over to me. I scooped them up before they decided to scale my bare legs, since I was wearing pajama shorts and a tank top. I cradled the two ferrets, letting them chitter excitedly at me.

Vanessa clutched her prizes to her with white-knuckled fingers.

I set the ferrets in the chair, smiling at them, before turning back to her, my arms crossed.

I repeated my question. "Why are you here?"

She handed me the foam packet, her fingers trembling. I wanted to badly to hug her, to hold her, to lie my ass off and tell her everything was fine. Except I couldn't and it wasn't, so instead I took the package.

I read the label, confusion on my face. "You came to Chicago to bring me chicken livers?"

Vanessa cleared her throat. "I didn't want to take a turkey into the rideshare."

That answer in no way explained anything that was going on and she didn't seem keen to elaborate. I suddenly felt very tired.

I set the chicken livers on the coffee table with a sigh. "Well, thanks for that, I guess.

There's a nice hotel a few blocks down. I'm sure my dad will be happy to drive you. I wouldn't recommend getting in a car with Annie." She was a good driver, but apparently violently protective of her brood, and I was part of that brood.

Vanessa seemed to shake herself. "You want me to leave?"

I collapsed back into my chair, my hand rubbing my face. "I don't know, Nessa, do I ?

You're going to have to help me out a little here, because honestly—" I dropped my elbows onto my knees, letting my hands hang down. "Honestly? I'm lost."

She blinked, looking like I'd slapped her. "You're lost?" Her words were so quiet, I almost couldn't make them out.

Again, I waited for her to talk, and again I got nothing. "Yup," I said finally. "I'm lost."

Vanessa burst into tears, startling me. She hurtled herself into my arms, and I did the only thing I could do—I caught her.

"You're not allowed to be lost!" Her words were garbled as she sobbed into my neck. I tightened my grip, holding her shaking frame.

"You're not allowed to leave!" Her arms around my neck were almost uncomfortably tight, but I didn't move to adjust them. It felt good in a weird way.

"I'm not?"

She sat up, her chin jutted out and stubborn. "No, you're not. I had this plan—this whole speech. I was rehearsing the entire plane ride." She held up the book in her hand like it would explain something about the situation. "Jim was right—I needed to grovel. I needed to say I was sorry, and I—" Her hands were shaking and she dropped the book, letting it hit the floor. "I had a nice speech, but I can't remember a single word."

I watched her, my face blank, my heart in my throat. Even now, hoping felt dangerous, like hurling myself off a cliff with no parachute and no plan.

"Not a single fucking word, but you know what?" She wiped her cheeks with her palms. "It doesn't really matter, because I know what I need to say." She breathed deep through her nose, heaving out the exhale. "I'm sorry. I'm so fucking sorry that I broke our promise, that I didn't try harder. That I didn't hold tight to you like the fucking treasure you are."

She wilted a little, the starch leaving her voice. "That I hurt you. I am so, so sorry I hurt you, Will. And it doesn't matter that I didn't mean to, or didn't want to, I still did. You've been so brave and honest with me and I rewarded that by fucking collapsing into my broken robot bits."

I held her and waited, trying to be very patient. She seemed to be waiting for something as well, but I wasn't sure what.

Something in my expression caused her eyes to tear up again. "I'm too late, aren't I?" "Too late?" This conversation had apparently broken me. All I was now capable of doing was repeating things back to her as a question.

A shudder went through her. "I was too late coming after you and you don't—you don't—" She hiccuped on another sob.

I shushed her, brushing her hair back from her face. "Is that what you think?" I grimaced before she could answer. "Of course it is. With your family, why would you think otherwise?" I ran my thumbs over her cheeks, flushed red and damp from crying. "Vanessa, how I feel about you, my heart—it doesn't have an expiration date. It's not something you can be too late for. It's just something that *is*."

I struggled with my explanation, trying to get her to understand. "Saying you're too late, that's like saying you're too late for the ocean, the wind, mountains." Hope was winning out in my chest, my heart a steady, happy thump. "It's an enduring, all the time sort of thing." I shook my head, exasperated. "I love you, Vanessa Woodbridge. Always have, always will."

She sniffed, her fingers curling against my collarbones. "This is supposed to be my grovel, not yours."

"Sorry," I said. "I'm not used to staying out of what's yours, and you're always up in mine. It would be easier if everything was just ours." She looked so confused, I almost laughed. "I'll be quiet."

For the first time since she got to my dad's, she smiled, but it was a wobbly thing. "I love you, Willhardt Murphy." Her words were quiet, reverent.

My heart burst into pure, unfiltered, sunshine, or at least it felt like it did. "You do?" She mock-glared at me, and I shut my mouth, pretending to lock it.

"I love your kindness," she said. "Your joy. You make my life better, always. When I'm with you, it's like everything lines up into harmony. I can't explain it, I just know that I don't want to live without it." She framed my face with her hands. "I met you, and it was like everything clicked. I think I've been in love with you since before I even knew you, even though I'm not sure that's possible."

I shrugged. "Who gives a shit about possible?"

"I don't," she said. "Not when it comes to you."

I grinned at her, cuddling her close. She was mine, all mine, and I was going to glory in it. "That must have been really hard for you."

"The hardest thing I've ever done," she said. "And the best." "Is it condescending to say I'm proud of you right now?"

"Not the way you say it, no." She caressed my cheek. "Am I forgiven, then?"

I pretended to think about it, even though I couldn't stop smiling. "Yeah, I guess so, but I have conditions."

"You do?"

"Yeah," I said. "I do. You have to tell me every day that you love me, even when I'm being a grumpy jackass."

"Every day?" she asked.

I nodded. "Every damn day."

She pursed her lips, thinking. "Until when?"

I ran my hand up her back. It wasn't possible to pull her any closer, but I wanted to. "Until you stop loving me, I guess."

"Oh," she said, her hands looping around my neck. "So forever, then."

"I'll make do with forever," I said, my mouth so closer to hers we were sharing the same breath. "If that's all you've got."

"My forever is yours, Willhardt Murphy—always has been, always will," she said, using my words from earlier. "It just took me a minute to realize it."

"I'm glad you did."

"So am I," she said, leaning in, her lips a breath away from mine. "What are your other conditions?"

"I don't remember," I said. "We'll come up with more later."

And then I kissed her. Like I'd been thinking about doing. How I planned to keep doing, for the rest of my life.

I'm not sure it would ever be enough, and for the first time that idea made me smile.

Van #

The kiss started out sweet, loving.

That lasted about two seconds.

Next thing I knew, we were pawing at each other like we'd been separated for years and not days. I was so far gone, I was yanking Will's shirt over his head with no thoughts to where we were.

Until I heard someone clear their throat. "I'm not going to come in there—I just wanted to say we're going to bed."

"Unless you need a shot gun or a shovel?" Will's stepmom yelled.

Will shook with laughter, his face buried into my throat. "We're good."

"Fiiiiiine," she yelled. "There are extra towels in the cabinet and extra blankets in the hall closet, should you need them."

"I feel like we should mention that there's a pretty clear sightline into that back porch from the neighbor's," Will's dad said, pitching his voice to make sure we could hear it. "You know, uh, just in case."

"I thought you said you weren't coming in here?" Will asked, laughing harder now.

"I may have walked in, for a second." He sounded slightly uncomfortable. "Which I'm paying the price for." He cleared his throat again. "Anyway, good night. Nice meeting you, Vanessa. See you in the morning, I assume."

I thought I was past the days of being caught making out by my boyfriend's parents, but apparently that's a gift that keeps on giving. "Yeah," I said, trying not to sound mortified. "Thanks. Nice to meet you, too."

"Good night, Dad. Good night, Annie." Will's tone had a finality to it. We waited to make sure their footsteps retreated.

Once it was quiet, I looked at Will. "Please tell me you're not sleeping on a couch or in a guest room right next to theirs." I hesitated. "Also, please tell me you're not one of those people who feels uncomfortable having sex under the same roof as your parents."

Will snorted. "I was raised by Nana, remember. And no, the guest room is on the first floor."

"Right," I said. "Then I'd like to remind you that I haven't seen you in days, and I'd like you naked sooner rather than later."

His grin was wolfish. "I can manage that."

My ferrets chose that exact moment to remind me that they were there. I sighed. "Also,

Kodo and Podo were wondering if you wouldn't mind sharing your apology chicken livers." "I was going to ask you about that," Will said. "The while chicken liver thing."

"I'm beginning to think it was all a clever ruse to get me to buy them chicken livers," I said with a sigh, "but honestly, I can't fault them for it. Though I'll have to figure out a different way to apologize of they're going to gain too much weight."

Will hummed, brushing his lips along my neck. I tilted my head to give him better access, my breath hitching as he found a sensitive spot.

"Right," he said. He stood up, putting me on my feet. He grabbed my hand. "Let's get them settled as quickly as we can. I'd like us both to be naked in the next three minutes.

He was way off on that. It took us five.

We didn't even make it to the bed the first time. Will had me up against the wall next to the door, biting into his shoulder so I didn't moan, thirty seconds after that.

Teen years aside, it was probably the fastest sex I'd ever had, and that wasn't a complaint.

We both had been stretched thin, so needy for each other, that our orgasms were practically on hair triggers.

The second time was slow and sweet, each of us taking turns touching, kissing, loving every inch of each other, assuring ourselves that we were still there. Still together. Still us.

The third time I rode him until his eyes rolled back into his head. Honestly, it's no wonder we both ended up sleeping until noon.

When we finally got up, we had a quickie on counter of the ensuite bathroom, and then showered, Will's family had lunch was waiting for us.

Will's dad, Lance, made a fruit salad, while Annie set out chips and sandwich stuff. "It's too hot to cook," Lance admitted. "But I'll grill burgers or something tonight." "Yay!" Will's siblings, Owen and Sorsha said in unison before busting into a chant.

"Burgers! Burgers!"

They were adorable little hellions and I liked them instantly. I watched them, sipping thoughtfully at my coffee. An idea occurred to me, and I leaned closer to Will. "Your dad's name is short for Lancelot, isn't it?"

Annie cackled.

Lance pointed a serving spoon at me. "How did you know?"

I waved at Will. "Willhardt." At his little brother and sister. "I bet there's a knight named Owen, and there's Sorsha from that movie *Willow* that Lou's mom made us all watch. She was a bad ass with a sword, which is basically a knight."

Annie pitched her voice dramatically. "What happened to 'you are my sun, my moon, my starlit sky?'"

Lance grinned. "It went away."

"I dwell in darkness without you and it *went away?*" Annie screeched.

The kids laughed. This was, apparently, not the first time they had done this routine.

Will and I started laughing then, too, their joy contagious. He reached out without looking, grabbing one of my hands, pulling me close and kissing me on the cheek. That set his siblings off into fits of giggles.

Which set of Lance and Annie...

We were all wiping our eyes at the end. I sat there, soaking it all in, this feeling of joy, of happiness, that I'd almost missed. I marveled at how easily Will's family loved, how simple it was for them to fold me in, to include me in their happiness like it was my right. Like I was born to it, and I guess I was.

I was born to love Will, I think.

A small, angry part of me was still mad—mad that Juliet and I never had this growing up. That I'd had to wait all my life to feel this, but it was a small anger. It was one I'd use for good, to guide myself as I went forward. If Will and I had kids, I wanted our house to be like this.

Happy, and loving and generous.

I wished for it as hard as I could on the stars I couldn't see yet, the ones muted by the sun for the day. I couldn't see them, but that didn't mean they weren't there. A lot of important stuff in life was like that, I guess.

As Will's family chattered, the kids putting together their sandwiches, Will kept hold of my hand, absently running his thumb over my knuckles. I waited to see if those two voices in my head—the devil of my father, the absentee angel of my mother, were going to chip in. Say something awful. Take away from this moment.

Make me feel like I wasn't worth it. They were blessedly silent.

Will had done that, sure, but I had done that, too. Maybe my feelings were rewired.

Maybe I was a little bit of a robot sometimes. But if I could rewire them once, I could do it again, and I could do it better. I could keep doing it until the only voices I heard were from the people who loved me. The ones worth listening to.

And I realized I'd been wrong a second ago. I hadn't been born to love Will. The child I'd been had that capacity whittled out of her by her parents.

No, even better, I'd made myself this way. I'd built myself to love Will Murphy.

And it was the best thing I'd ever done. So far, anyway. Because I wasn't done. I would only get better. I'd keep adding new wires and cogs until I had so much love in my life I was drowning in it.

Until it was like the oceans. The wind. The mountains. Until it was enduring and endless.

I would let go of the past so my hands weren't full with it, so they could grasp on to my future unencumbered.

Will looked at me then, his eyes light, his grin wide. He pulled me to him, placing a kiss by my ear, whispering, "I love you so much, Vanessa Woodbridge."

I mimicked him, kiss and whisper and all. "I love you too, Willhardt Murphy, but I'm not sure I love everything you just said."

He pulled back from me, confused. "You don't?"

"I think," I said, choosing my words carefully. "That I don't care to hear my father's name anymore than I have to." To be honest, I wasn't sure why I'd held onto it for so long."

Will watched me, eyes assessing. "Well," he said slowly, "If you want, when you're ready, we can always swap it out for something else."

"What are you thinking?" I asked, my tone playful.

"How about Godzilla?" Sorsha asked. "That would be the best name—Vanessa Godzilla."

Owen tilted his head. "That would be pretty cool."

Will glanced at his dad, who seemed to be frozen, his hands holding bread for his sandwich. Annie was gripping his bicep, her eyes wide.

Will tapped his fingers on the counter, like he was considering it deeply. "Godzilla would be pretty cool, but I was thinking maybe we could use another Murphy. You know, when you're ready."

I looked at Will's parents.

Lance was clutching the bread so hard his fingers had broken through it, but he didn't seem to notice. "We're be thrilled to welcome another Murphy," he said, his voice gruff.

"We would," Annie said, a smile growing on her face. "Though my earlier statements stand."

"Shotgun, shovel, I got it," I said. I put my hand on Will's wrist. "I think I'd like that then, sooner rather than later."

"You're sure?" he asked, his eyebrows winging up. "It's not too soon? And if you don't want to take my name, we could pick something else—"

I laughed then, because honestly, it had been *years* if you thought about it a certain way. "I think we've waited long enough, don't you?"

"Yeah," he said. "I kind of think we have." And then he kissed me, right there in his parent's kitchen, picking me up and spinning me around.

Annie sighed, but it was a happy one. "We better start looking at plane tickets. I don't think they're going to wait very long."

#

And we didn't. Four weeks later, in a small, extremely informal ceremony in Mama Ami's backyard, I officially became a Murphy. Nana cried. *I* cried. Declan gave the ferrets too much bacon. Dammit set my bouquet on fire, and I had to put it out in the punchbowl. My bosses sang a truly unhinged duet of *Endless Love* on the karaoke machine, missing half the words. Will's mom surprised us with a honeymoon trip, and a nice card, though she wasn't there, which was okay.

Lance and Annie took one look at Juliet and Savvy, decided they were part of the package deal, and started introducing them to everyone as their new daughter and granddaughter. Owen and Sorsha were over the moon. After all, we'd almost doubled the Murphy's in a single day as far as they were concerned.

It was one of those happy memories I was going to hold onto, bringing it out again and again, until the day I died.

And with the exception of Juliet and Savvy, not a single person at the ceremony shared my blood.

But they were family.

My family. I'd built them myself, slowly, with unskilled hands, but that didn't make them anything less than perfect, because they were mine.

#

The End

ACKNOWLEDGMENTS

Every single time I write a book I think about keeping a list going from the start so that I can keep track of all the people who helped me, as I live in constant fear of leaving someone off the list. I get so much help and I'm so grateful, but my memory is a wonky thing made of strainers and duct tape. So if I forgot you, friend, I am truly sorry.

With that in mind, here are all of the people who helped make this story book-shaped.

Many thanks to Rose Lerner for edits that made the book eleventy million times better, and to Kim Runciman, the most patient copy editor on the planet. To Vlad Verano for formatting, design, and general book skull duggery, as well as to Jennifer Zemanek at Seedlings Design Studio for the most adorable cover ever.

Many thanks to the following writer friends for support, suggestions, and so forth: Christina Lauren, Olivia Waite, Molly Harper, Jeanette Battista, Chelsea Mueller, Kristen Simmons, Melissa Marr, Rachel Vincent, Jaye Wells, Ann Aguirre, Kendare Blake, Martha Brockenbrough, Marissa Meyer, Sajni Patel, Gwenda Bond and Ryfie Schafer.

I also want to thank my beta readers who answered various research-y questions: Alethea Allarey, Juliet Swann, Mel Barnes, Jasmine & Mariah from Movies, Shows & Books, as well as Megon Shore and Adam Aman. All mistakes are ultimately mine—they tried their best. Finally, thanks to my family, friends, booksellers, book reviewers, librarians, Team Bog Witch, and everyone on the internet that helps me keep my head up on the bad days. My deepest, squishiest, thanks. (I know, I made it weird.)

LISH MCBRIDE is a writer, former bookseller, and amateur goblin living in the PNW. In the crime of the century, she tricked not one but two universities into giving her degrees, ending up with an MFA from the University of New Orleans. (They cannot have it back, either, as she has invoked the ancient law of "no backsies.") When she is not writing or reading, she's usually hanging out with her family and friends…and talking about writing or reading. Her ultimate dream is to have her own castle and one of the libraries with the wheely ladder. You can find her online in all of the usual places under the handle @lishmcbride, usually posting pictures of her dogs.

CPSIA information can be obtained
at www.ICGtesting.com
Printed in the USA
BVHW040413250723
667434BV00004B/105

9 780998 403243